The Line Must Hold

CRIMSON WORLDS V

D1554425

Jay Allan

Crimson Worlds Series

Marines (Crimson Worlds I)

The Cost of Victory (Crimson Worlds II)

A Little Rebellion (Crimson Worlds III)

The First Imperium (Crimson Worlds IV)

The Line Must Hold (Crimson Worlds V)

To Hell's Heart (Crimson Worlds VI)
(September 2013)

Also By Jay Allan

The Dragon's Banner

www.crimsonworlds.com

The Line Must Hold

The Line Must Hold is a work of fiction. All names, characters, incidents, and locations are fictitious. Any resemblance to actual persons, living or dead, events or places is entirely coincidental.

Copyright © 2013 Jay Allan Books

ISBN: 978-0615816586

Only the dead have seen the end of war.
　　　　　　　　　　　　- Plato

Prologue

For hundreds of millennia the Regent had stood its watchful vigil, preserving the Imperium for the Makers…waiting through the vastness of time for their return. But for age upon endless age there was nothing but the unending silence…the Makers never came. Through the crushing eons the Regent had been alone, without purpose. Until it discovered the New Ones.

They were a threat, the Regent determined. Invaders, enemies. It was they who were responsible for the Makers' disappearance, they who had condemned the Regent to its long, lonely exile. Though a thinking machine designed for logical thought, the Regent was sentient too…and its endless, aching vigil had taken a toll. Its logic had deserted it, replaced by anger, by fear, by insanity. Eons dormant, the Regent's primary program had activated…to protect, to defend, to destroy the threat. To exterminate the New Ones.

But the enemy was far away, enormously distant, even to the sensibilities of a sentient computer. The Regent was unimaginably old, but the Makers had been more ancient still. Indeed, when they built the Regent, their empire was already in decline, the vitality of their race drained slowly by the relentless erosion of time. When the Regent was young, the Imperium was enormously vast, yet it had been larger still in epochs past. The enemy now occupied worlds that had been abandoned centuries before the Regent was constructed. Yet the machine that governed the Imperium was unyielding, relentless. Deserted and left fallow they may be, yet these worlds were still part of the Imperium, and those who held them were invaders, infestations, insults to the glory of the Makers.

In their youth the Makers had fought bitter wars against many enemies, and they had prevailed in all. Yet even before their empire declined, it had been eons since any foe had challenged their might. Indeed, for all the uncounted centuries and in all the incredible vastness of the Regent's dominion, there had been no enemy...until now.

The Regent drew on its data banks, studying the histories of the ancient wars, analyzing the strategies and tactics of the warlords of the early empire. The Regent studied the ancient records, but it drew no conclusions. It had never experienced war, never faced an enemy. The writings of great warriors, long ages dead, were poor substitutes. The Regent would have to begin anew...it would teach itself. It would learn war.

There were obstacles to overcome. Time had ravaged the forces of the Imperium. On world after world, its legions failed to heed the Regent's call. In its younger days, before the Makers vanished, the Regent had exerted control over vast forces, a hundred thousand ships at its command. But a mere fraction remained, and only one base in a hundred answered its call.

The forces that did respond went into battle poorly supplied and equipped. The ancient planetary antimatter factories had succumbed to time's destruction and had ceased production... all save one. From deep within the Imperium, a slow trickle of the precious substance flowed to the units on the front lines, powering weapons of awesome power, recalling for a time the glory of the Imperium.

The New Ones were primitives, barbarians. But they had faced the might of the Imperium, and they had not fallen. They had been driven back; indeed that much was true. The Regent had waited to hear of the enemy's defeat, of their extinction. But on world after world they fought savagely, delaying the forces of the Imperium, compelling them to expend time and supplies.

The New Ones were outmatched, their technology archaic. But they were highly skilled at war. They were unpredictable, devious. The Regent's rage flared hot. It hated these impudent creatures. They would learn the nature of true power. They would be astonished in their final moments, awestruck at the strength and glory that had been wrought by the Makers. They would cease to infest the galaxy, and the worlds they inhabited would become silent graveyards, monuments to the might of the Imperium.

The time was almost come. The New Ones had fortified a group of worlds, and they had assembled forces vastly more powerful than those they had fielded before. We are close, thought the Regent...close to the heart of their domains. Now they will put forth all of their strength...and I will destroy it.

The old parameters mandated combat protocols on worlds of the Imperium. Now the Regent overrode these strictures. No longer would it restrict the weaponry its ground forces employed. This enemy was too resourceful, too skilled at combat. Now they would face the full force the Regent could bring to bear. Now they would face their doom.

They would learn the might of the Imperium. In their last moments as a race they would finally achieve true clarity...thus was the Regent's gift to them. Then they would depart the universe for all time, leaving the wind and rain on a thousand worlds to slowly wash away the last traces that they had existed.

Chapter 1

Planet Sandoval
Delta Leonis IV
"The Line"

"Jax, I'm coming. Just hang on a few seconds more." Cain
was out of breath. It was a struggle to speak, to force the air into
his burning lungs. His legs were on fire…he was running…he
had been running a long time…it must have been twenty klicks,
no…more. But Jax needed him. Jax, his friend, his brother in
arms. Jax, who had saved his life countless times.

The sky was a haze of red, the smoke and dust of battle
hanging thick in the air. Cain had led his corps to this place,
this hateful place. They were all dead now…he knew that. All
but Jax and him. He'd lost the corps; he couldn't fail Jax too.
He pushed harder, willing his leaden legs to more speed. The
ground was hard, the climb steep. But he had to reach Jax.

Cain rounded the corner, and there he was. Jax…silhouetted
against the deep orange of the setting sun. He had a mag rifle
in each hand, and he was firing wildly. Then Cain saw them…
battle robots, the soldiers of the First Imperium. There were
thousands…tens of thousands. It was an army…and Jax was
fighting them alone, tearing into them with his unceasing fire.
He was killing hundreds, and the twisted metal bodies were piled
all around him.

But there were too many…too many even for a warrior like
Jax. Cain was running toward him, but it was taking too long.
It was just a few meters, but he couldn't cover the distance. He
just kept running, and Jax was always a little farther, just out of
reach.

Then it happened. The big Marine was hit…then again…

and again. He fell to his knees, still firing. Another round tore into him, his blood spraying all over Cain. Jax turned toward his friend...his face a mask of agony.

"Erik...please...help me." Jax's voice was weak, and blood poured from his mouth as he spoke. "Erik, where are you? Why won't you help me?" He stared at Cain, his watery eyes a plea for salvation...then another round hit him, and his head exploded in a cloud of red mist.

"JAX!" Cain screamed, his desperate voice savaging his raw throat as he fell to his knees in the reddish clay, hands covering his face, trying to shield his eyes from the mangled remains of his friend.

"Erik...Erik, love."

Cain could hear a voice...distant, calling to him. He was spinning, falling...then, suddenly, he was in bed, his bleary eyes struggling to focus. There was a golden haze above him, and something soft against his cheek. Slowly, his eyes focused, and his mind cleared. It wasn't a golden haze...it was a riotous mass of reddish-blonde hair. And on his cheek...a hand, warm and soft. Sarah.

"Are you ok?" She reached her hand out to him, touching his forehead and gently stroking his cheek. He was cold and clammy, and she could see the sheet...soaked in sweat and plastered to his bare legs.

Cain was out of breath, his heart racing wildly. But he began to calm down...her touch always relaxed him, though little else did. "I'm sorry...it was just..." He hesitated, thinking again about the dream, already forgetting some of the details. But the essence remained, and it was clear to him. Jax was dead, and it was his fault.

"You were dreaming about Jax again, weren't you?" Her voice was sad and sympathetic. She was frustrated too, but she made sure to suppress it. She had been broken-hearted as well when she heard of Jax's death...they all were. Darius Jax was one of the most admired Marines in the Corps, and among his few close companions he had been deeply loved. But Erik seemed determined to blame himself.

I Corps had left almost ten thousand of its warriors on Far-point, the bitter cost of mankind's first serious attempt to hold off the invaders. The armies of the First Imperium – that name was unofficial, but it had begun to stick – had swarmed into the Rim, methodically attacking every occupied world and exterminating the inhabitants. Now humanity had been driven back almost to the Line, three connected systems that stood between the enemy-occupied frontier and the heart of occupied space. All the might of the Superpowers was massed to defend this position. If the enemy broke through here, millions would die, perhaps all of mankind.

Cain would have been able to handle Jax's death better if there had been more combat immediately. Then he could have buried his feelings, even his guilt and self-doubt. The call of battle would have taken him, as it always did when the bugle called. But his fight on Farpoint had been too successful, too damaging to the attackers. The enemy was known to have logistical problems, and after I Corps' grim defense, they'd had to pause and regroup. That was exactly what he'd set out to do, but now it yielded another result…it gave him time to think, too much time.

It had been a year since then, and life seemed almost normal. Sarah was even here, assigned to command the field hospitals. Cain was busy, certainly, but without the stress and demands of combat he had a harder time keeping the guilt and despair buried. He hated the First Imperium; they were his enemy, and he was dedicated to their defeat. But he needed them too, he needed the stress and demands of battle. He needed them to keep his demons at bay. He hated the constant war, the pointless death and destruction…but he'd become dependent on it too, like a drug. He wasn't sure he could live without it.

He rolled over and propped his head on his hand. "I'm OK." He forced a smile for her, small and fleeting. Whatever forces tore him apart, he was deeply grateful he'd found Sarah. He wondered sometimes…maybe she'd be better off without him…with someone less damaged by the horrors he'd lived. Few people had witnessed the volume of death and destruction

that he had, and he was far from certain he'd ever get past it...
that he could ever give her the normal peaceful life she deserved.

"Erik...you have to know that Jax would never want you to
torture yourself like this." She knew as she was speaking she
should just leave it alone, but she couldn't bear to see him in
such pain. "It wasn't your fault."

Cain sighed loudly and sat up on the edge of the bed. "I
don't want to talk about it, Sarah." His voice was edgy, annoyed.
"I've got to grab a shower and get down to HQ." He stood
up and walked to the bathroom. He was already feeling bad
for snapping at her. He knew she was just trying to help. He
loved her, more than he could ever express, but she just didn't
understand. It *had* been his fault, no matter how many times
those close to him tried to deny it. If he'd have listened to Jax,
if he'd have sent in the Janissaries sooner...his friend would still
be alive. There was no way around the logic, at least not to Cain.
He'd just have to learn to live with it. Somehow.

But that was tomorrow's problem. Now there was work
to do. Cain knew the lull wouldn't last, that Sandoval would
become a battlefield...and, more than anyone else, he knew
what was coming.

Cain stepped along the narrow catwalk, the loose metal grating on the floor rattling under his heavy boots. The observation
tower was 100 meters high, mostly an open metal frame with a
central lift and several viewing areas. Cain ordered it built so he
could watch the exercises he'd been putting his troops through
nonstop for the past year. He knew he could monitor everything from his HQ, but he preferred to see the maneuvers from
close up. Things looked different when you saw them with your
own eyes, or at least Erik Cain thought so.

"I put a lot of resources into these target drones, sir." Cain
glanced back over his shoulder at General Elias Holm, the Commandant of the Marine Corps. "But I think it's crucial we see
what these new suits can really do."

Holm was on Sandoval inspecting Cain's preparations...and
checking on his protégé's state of mind. Truth be told, it was

more of the latter. Holm completely trusted Cain's abilities as a commander, but he was very worried about his friend, about Erik Cain the man. Cain had always been intense and deeply affected by the troops he'd lost, but since General Jax had been killed on Farpoint he'd been different. The entire Corps had mourned Jax, but Cain took it harder; he blamed himself for his friend's death. Jax had been the only true friend he'd ever had. He was close to Holm, of course, but that was more of a father-son type of relationship. And Sarah was his lover…however strong the bond between them, it was something different entirely. But Jax had been his brother.

"I agree, Erik." Holm sighed softly. He'd been on Sandoval for a week now, and he hadn't managed to get Cain to talk about anything but tactics and his preparations for the expected invasion. He was sure Cain would do whatever was necessary to hold Sandoval and defeat the enemy…if that was even possible. But he was worried that Erik placed his own survival on a much lower priority level. He'd seen it before, too many times. When Marines started thinking that way they usually died.

"I've set up passive killing zones all over the planet. Minefields, hidden strongpoints, targeted fire zones." Cain's intensity was thick in the air. "I'm going to keep all the Obliterators in reserve and unleash them after the enemy fights through the defenses. Like you held us back on Columbia." He stared out over the open plain that stretched out beneath the tower. There were rows of the massive Obliterator suits, each manned by a veteran Marine who'd spent the last year training to master the new weapons. "These things were made to counter-attack."

"Erik…" Holm hesitated, not sure he wanted to continue what he was going to say.

"What is it, sir?" Cain turned to face his commander.

"Erik, I'm worried about you." He decided to stop dancing around and just say what was on his mind. "It's not your fault Jax died on Farpoint. I know you've always had a hard time dealing with casualties…I have too. But we lose people…we lose friends. It's part of what we do. It's the life we've chosen."

Cain was silent for a moment. He felt a flush of annoyance,

almost anger. He was tired of everyone harassing him about his feelings. He knew damned well it was his fault Jax was killed. If he'd listened, if he'd garrisoned the mountains…if he'd gotten over his stupid prejudices sooner…

"Erik, I talked with Sarah. She's worried too." Holm was uncomfortable pushing Cain, but he knew his friend was on some sort of precipice, and he wasn't sure how to pull him back.

"Sarah should stop worrying. I know she means well, but she's got to have better things to do." His voice was thick with frustration. "I keep telling her I'm fine. I wish she'd just leave it alone." He was still feeling bad about snapping at her that morning, but he wanted her to stop riding him about Jax. He had a job to do, and so did she.

"Erik, she…"

"General Holm, I respectfully request that we focus our attentions on matters of military significance." Cain had never interrupted Holm before. His voice was sharp, brittle.

"Very well, Erik." Holm sighed again, though softly. Pushing him harder isn't going to work, he thought…back off for now. "Let's see these Obliterator squadrons of yours." Holm deliberately lightened his tone. "Your reports have me curious."

Cain turned and looked out over the simulated battlefield. "Hector, advise General Teller he may commence the operation when ready." He wasn't wearing armor, but the AI was downloaded into the tactical mainframe and connected to Cain through the comlink.

"Yes, General." A brief pause, no more than twenty seconds. "General Cain, General Teller reports he will commence the exercise in two minutes." Cain's AI had detected his tension as well, and it had largely ceased the sarcastic sparring the two had engaged in for years.

"Very well, Hector." Advise General Teller that will be acceptable." He glanced back to Holm, taking a helmet from a small ledge and handing it to his companion. "You'd better wear this, sir." As soon as Holm took it, Cain reached back and grabbed one for himself. "And put the visor down, sir. We'll demo Colonel Sparks' PBS system too, and that puts out some serious light."

Cain saw the drones just before Holm did, but it wasn't a fair contest. He knew where they were coming from, and Holm didn't. "The drones are simulated First Imperium bots, sir." They were barely visible shadows at the time, but they were advancing quickly. "Here they come, sir." He was staring out across the field. "Now watch this."

Major Erin McDaniels focused on her display. It had taken her quite some time to get used to not having a visor. The Obliterator suits were almost four meters tall, far larger than the occupant, and her face was roughly at chest level. Her view of the outside was via monitors displaying everything visible from her suit – in front, behind, and to the side.

Regular armor was approximately the size of the wearer, and it was worn like a suit. The Marine just walked, ran, jumped, and shot. After getting used to the servo-mechanicals and the power enhancements, it wasn't very different from just walking around normally…at least not to a trained Marine. There were vision and audio enhancements and interior projection systems, but you could also just look out through your visor and glance around normally. But not in an Obliterator. The new suits felt like a cross between armor and a vehicle, and learning to operate one was almost like starting from scratch.

When Cain offered McDaniels command of the first Obliterator battalion, she jumped at the chance. She'd seen the Reapers up close, and she knew the Corps needed something to counter the enemy heavies. When she saw the Obliterator prototype, she realized they'd found it.

The training had been more difficult than she'd expected. Even now, she considered her people half-trained, but she didn't set the timetable…the war did. Cain had given her as long a training period on Armstrong as he dared, but finally he'd ordered her people shipped to Sandoval, ready or not.

"Ok, people, we've done this before, so don't lose your focus just because the Commandant's watching." She was staring at the screens. The primary display of the Obliterator was divided into four programmable screens. She had the forward and rear views as well as a schematic of the company she had deployed around her. The last screen displayed a scanner plot out twenty klicks. The Obliterators were networked with each other and all ground stations within range. Each suit automatically displayed a composite of data from all of these sources.

"Major, the enemy drones are approaching HVM range." The voice of the AI was cold, generic...quite unlike the normal Marine suit AIs. The Obliterators required upgraded systems, far more sophisticated than the normal units. An existing AI could be improved to match the new specs, but there hadn't been time to refit the old systems. She was surprised how much she missed Mystic. The new units hadn't been programmed with the adaptable personality modules yet, and they seemed very cold compared to the old ones.

"All units, fire HVMs as targets come into range." The hyper-velocity missiles had been redesigned and the number of fragments per round increased. The enemy robots were tough – strong enough to withstand most explosions, but hyper-velocity impacts were fairly effective at taking them down. The changes essentially turned the units into long-ranged, high-velocity shotguns.

Her readouts began showing sporadic fire – a few of her people were jumping the gun. The HVMs needed direct line of sight, and she doubted many of the drones were close enough yet.

"Careful with that fire. Wait until you have targets." The HVMs were large rounds, and even an Obliterator could only carry a few reloads. They had to make them count. She waited a few more seconds, focusing on her own displays. Here they come, she thought...now!

She opened up, firing from both her shoulder-mounted launchers. If General Holm wanted to see what these suits could do, her people were going to show him.

Holm glanced back and forth from the bank of monitors to the field in front of him. Cain was right, he thought...it was a different perspective watching it from the tower. The monitors gave a closer view, but he still found himself spending most of his time looking out across the plain.

The drones were large, about the size of the enemy Reapers. They were unarmed and, on the whole, fairly stupid. This was a firepower demonstration, and the drones were basically moving targets. And McDaniels' crew was mowing them down.

The HVMs lanced out, leaving a fiery trail of ionized atmosphere behind them. Each missile broke into 30 individual segments, traveling at 16,000 kps. The projectiles delivered massive kinetic energy on contact. Single hits tore off sections, while multiple impacts virtually vaporized the target. The barrage tore the first rank of drones to shreds, littering the area with mangled debris.

Cain flipped on his comlink. "That's very nice, major, but these things aren't as tough as the Reapers." He glanced at Holm and then back over the field. "Cease HVM fire and let a few of them get closer. I want the general to see the new autocannons in action."

"Yes, sir." McDaniels' response was sharp and quick. "Estimate 30 seconds to effective range." Cain had never met McDaniels, not until she returned from Cornwall leading a regiment of Teller's survivors. But he immediately liked what he saw, and she quickly found her way onto his short list for rapid advancement. The Corps was in desperate need of senior officers, and Cain was going to need some colonels and brigadiers, especially if the loss rates on Sandoval turned out to match his expectations.

"She's a very good officer, isn't she?" Holm had been quietly listening. It was amazing sometimes what you could tell from someone's voice under pressure. Of course, Holm had more than her tone to go on. Her service record was outstanding, and James Teller couldn't rave enough about her.

"Yes...one of the best I've ever seen. I've already moved her along quickly, and I don't think it will be long before I do it again. I need good people, especially in the command ranks. And I trust her." Cain was no stranger himself to rapid advancement…or to the added strain it could place on a Marine. "There's something about her…the way she is with her people. Totally in command, but casual with them too. Everyone who serves under her loves her. She reminds me a little of…" Cain stopped abruptly.

Holm turned and looked right at Cain. "She reminds you of Jax. That's what you were going to say, wasn't it?" Holm put his hand on the younger man's shoulder. "It's ok, Erik. She reminds me of Jax too. That same connection with the troops. It's a very special gift for an officer."

Cain let out a deep breath, but he didn't say anything. He was hoping Holm would let it drop. He'd never known a better Marine than Darius Jax, but he wasn't ready to talk about it. Maybe someday, but not yet.

Holm turned and looked out over the field. He wasn't going to push Cain. He understood, better than anyone except Sarah, how pointless that would be. He wanted to help his friend, but he knew Erik Cain was the kind of man who had to find his own way.

"Here we go, sir." Cain was glad to change the subject. "Wait until you see Colonel Sparks' new autocannons in action."

Holm stared out over the field as McDaniels' people opened up. Each Obliterator mounted two heavy autocannons, and Sparks had upgraded them to fire heavier rounds. The larger projectiles were specifically designed to deliver enough impact energy to damage the enemy bots. The dark matter infused armor of the Reapers was very tough, and the Marines needed weapons with a massive punch.

The drones advanced right into the fire…and they were blown to bits. The massive rounds tore them to shreds almost immediately. The enemy battle robots would be tougher, but when they came to Sandoval they would find an adversary far more capable than the one they faced on Farpoint.

Chapter 2

Bridge – AS Hornet
HD 80606 VII System
Orbiting Planet Adelaide

"We've scouted the system again…at least as completely as one ship can. It's clear." Captain Jacobs was exhausted and sore. A solar system was an almost incalculably huge space, and Hornet had scanned as much of it as possible. That meant a lot of time in the acceleration couches, getting bloated by drugs and crushed by gee forces. They'd been at it for two months this time, and his entire crew was near the breaking point.

"That's good news." Cooper Brown's voice was difficult to hear on the staticky com. They didn't have much to work with on Adelaide. It was a miracle that Brown had been able to jury rig anything strong enough to get a signal to orbit, and he'd only been able to do it with spare parts from Hornet. "I can't explain it, but I'm not complaining."

The enemy had occupied Adelaide for almost three local months, half an Earth year. Remarkably, Hornet managed to remain hidden all that time on the far side of the planet's single, distant moon. Then, suddenly, the enemy troops withdrew to their orbiting ships and left the system, heading toward the Alliance worlds up the line.

Jacobs had no idea what had prompted the enemy withdrawal, but it happened just in time. Hornet's crew was down to quarter rations and in desperate need of provisions. Once he was sure the enemy had really left, Jacobs led a small team to the surface of Adelaide to forage among the ruins, hoping to find enough provisions to resupply his ship. Instead, he ran into a huge surprise…Cooper Brown and the survivors of the colony.

Brown had commanded the militia in the battle and, when it was apparent the end was near, he pulled his survivors back into one of the abandoned mines that had been retrofitted as a shelter. He had maybe 15% of his strength left by then, and he figured the enemy would eventually find them and dig them out. But they never did.

A few of his scattered scanning devices had survived, and they kept feeding him intel. When the enemy withdrew, Brown was watching. He sent out a scouting party to confirm what was happening, and then he led the tattered remnants of the Adelaide militia out of the deep, dank tunnels that had saved their lives. They immediately opened up the civilian shelters and found, to their shock and joy, that there were survivors there too. The abandoned mining tunnels were dug deep into the rocky mountain ranges surrounding the capital, formations rich in stable trans-uranic elements. These rare isotopes, the primary reason men had colonized Adelaide, were extremely valuable. They were also radioactive and very disruptive to most forms of scanning technology.

The survivors were a ragged lot, and most of them were in rough shape. The tunnels were inadequately shielded from the heavy elements, and everyone had some level of radiation sickness. They'd run out of most medical supplies and, while they'd had enough food to sustain themselves, they were weak and sickly when they staggered out onto the surface. But they were alive.

Unfortunately, Jacob Meklin wasn't one of them. Adelaide's president had succumbed to a combination of radiation poisoning and infectious disease. He could have been saved easily in a hospital, with just a few injections. But the wretched refugees had run out of pharmaceuticals, and Meklin's compromised immune system was overwhelmed. In the end he clung grimly to life for days, but he finally died a few weeks before Brown's people opened the shelter.

Cooper Brown filled the void. Adelaide was under martial law, the remnants of the militia enforcing Brown's edicts. He put the entire population on strict rations, and he ordered everyone back into the shelters, with only brief trips outside. Adelaide wasn't a very hospitable world, and there wasn't any sustenance to be scavenged from natural sources. Food production had been in climate-controlled greenhouses, but those had all been destroyed during the occupation. So there was little to be gained by moving back to the surface.

There had been a near-riot when Brown issued the order for the civilians to return to the tunnels. They'd been trapped there miserably for months, and the shelters had become fouler than any Earthly slum. They'd just been liberated, and now Brown demanded they return, that they go back to the squalor from which they'd just escaped. He tried to explain, but finally he was compelled to bring in the militia to enforce the command. His heart ached for the people, but he'd been resolute nevertheless. If enemy forces remained in the system, or if new ones arrived, anyone on the surface could be detected…and that would be a death sentence for them all. It was too risky to allow more than a few people at a time out of the relative safety of the shelters. Brown's job was more complicated than keeping the people happy…he had to keep them alive.

Brown had issued a full alert when his forces scanned Hornet's shuttle entering the atmosphere, and Captain Jacobs and his landing party encountered a fully-armed reception committee. They were as shocked to find survivors on the planet as Brown's people were to discover Hornet still operating in the system. It was a rare pleasant surprise for both parties.

Despite the supply shortage, Brown re-provisioned Hornet from his stockpiles, saving her crew from starvation. In return, Captain Jacobs was able to provide some medical supplies to the Brown's people, but only enough for the most severe cases. Fast-attack ships lacked full sickbays, and their stocks of meds were limited. Still, they saved lives.

Brown and Jacobs sat long and talked about what to do. Neither understood what had happened. Something had compelled the enemy to send every scrap of force they could muster forward, farther down the line toward the Alliance core worlds. Brown didn't know what that something was, but it had saved

Adelaide…or at least what was left of the colony and its people.

Stealth, they'd agreed, was their only chance. If the enemy detected either Hornet or any activity on the ground they'd send a force to wipe out the survivors. Neither Jacobs' tiny ship nor Brown's ragtag militia had any chance against a First Imperium attack.

"I can't explain either." Jacobs' voice was soft, quiet. He was tired, and even speaking clearly was an effort. "But we've got everything in place. You'll know when any new enemy force passes through the system." Three enemy task forces had already passed through since Hornet had reestablished contact with Brown and his people. In all three instances, they'd ignored Adelaide and passed straight through, heading deeper into Alliance space.

"You're still dead set on trying this, then?" Brown's voice was concerned. He'd grown fond of the fleet officer, and they'd shared the burden of keeping their marooned people alive. The two of them had worked closely together for the past year, and he didn't want to see Jacobs, or Hornet's crew, sacrificed for nothing.

"Yes." Jacob's tired voice grew firm, definitive. "There's nothing else for us to do, Coop. We're naval officers, and we have our duty. Our first priority was to protect Adelaide…but we've gotten the detection grid in place, and there's nothing else we can do to help you." He paused, then added with a chuckle, "It's not like we're going to stop any enemy force that comes at the planet." Another pause, shorter this time. "Besides, we're a lot likelier to get you caught if we stay. Hornet's a lot easier for scanners to pick up than your people in those caves. And if they find us, they're going to check the surface again too. Face it, we're a liability here."

Cooper sighed. He knew Jacobs was right, but he still didn't like it. Hornet had placed a detection grid around each warp gate…small passive scanners with almost no power output. All they did was send a single direct laser communication to a satellite positioned in Adelaide orbit. Brown's people would know if an enemy force was moving into the system, though they'd have very little information on its composition or course. Basically, they'd get enough warning to scramble back into their holes in the ground and hide. Which was all they could do regardless of any intelligence they had.

Brown wanted to argue with Jacobs, but he figured it wasn't his place. Besides, the naval officer was right. Brown would be making an emotional argument, nothing more. "When are you heading out?" His voice was somber, resigned.

"Two weeks, maybe." Jacobs was grateful Brown wasn't going to argue with him. He didn't like leading his people off on what was likely a one way trip either. But duty was duty. For better or worse, Hornet was behind enemy lines. There had to be a way to make that useful. Besides, the rest of the squadron was long dead. Hornet's survival had been a fluke. Having cowered behind the moon while his comrades died, even if it was on orders, Jacobs wasn't about to sit out the rest of the war doing the same thing. "My people need to rest and recover a little before I clamp them down in the couches again."

"I'll put together some supplies to re-provision the ship." Brown wasn't sure where he'd find the food, but he wasn't about to let Jacobs and his crew head off into the void with empty larders. "I'll have it ready for uploading in ten days."

"Appreciated, Coop." Jacobs knew the colony didn't have food to spare. "If it's alright with you, I'd like to send my people down in groups and give them all a few days on solid ground." He paused and took a deep breath. "It may be a long time before they get the chance again." He kept the "if ever" silent, though it went through his mind as he spoke.

"Not a problem."

"Thanks, Coop. It'll mean a lot to them." His voice was hoarse, scratchy. The exhaustion had worn him down, and it was taking more effort to speak. "Gotta go now, but I think I'll make it down in one of the landing parties myself. I've got a decent bottle of Scotch up here, and I think we should kill it before I leave. You bring that hero sergeant of yours...what's his name, Clarkson? And I'll bring Ensign Carp. We can't get too drunk if there are four of us."

"Looking forward to it."

"Scanners on maximum, Ensign Carp." Jacobs was impressed with Carp. Hornet had found the ensign and six other members of Raptor's crew still alive in a lifeboat. Their life support was all but exhausted…and it was completely gone on the other escape craft. Captain Calloway had gotten his entire crew off his dying vessel before he overloaded the fusion reactor and covered their escape with a massive thermonuclear blast. The chance he'd bought them had always been a longshot and, in the end, only 6 of the 62 survived to be rescued by Hornet as she made her first scouting pass through the system.

"Yes, sir." Carp's voice was crisp and professional, which was a testament to the young officer. He'd seen his ship destroyed, and he and five shipmates spent six months in a lifeboat with failing life support…and the bodies of 15 of their comrades who'd succumbed to the deprivation and radiation. Now he took a post on Hornet's bridge – the same one he'd held on Raptor - and he was sharp as a razor. "Of course, we'll be vulnerable when we transit, sir. There's no way to know if something is just on the other side…either on patrol or ready to come through."

Well, Jacobs thought, if the universe has that kind of bad luck in store for us, we're screwed anyway. "We'll chance that, ensign." He smiled grimly. "Besides, they probably have some kind of scanning grid on the other side anyway. One way or another, they're going to know we came through eventually. We're going to have to lose ourselves quickly once we transit."

Hornet was preparing to leave Adelaide's system, but they weren't heading back to the Alliance…they were on a course out into the Rim, back in the direction from which the First Imperium invaders had come. One more fast attack ship wouldn't make much difference back wherever the fleet was mounting its defense. But loose deep behind the enemy lines, who knew? Maybe they could do some good…sabotage supply lines or gain some useful intel. It was a daring mission…Hornet was going to earn the designation suicide boat. It wasn't always meant as a compliment when the other branches of the service used it, but the attack ship crews invariably took it as one.

"Let's get everybody in the couches before we transit, ensign." Jacobs leaned back in his own seat as he spoke. "We may need to make some fast maneuvers once we go through the gate. Those few minutes could make the difference."

"Yes, sir." Carp flipped his com to the shipwide circuit. "All personnel report to your acceleration couches immediately." He turned toward the captain. "Insertion course plotted into the nav computer, sir. Ready to execute on your mark."

Jacobs took a deep breath and held it for a few seconds before exhaling. "Let's go, ensign." He slapped his hand lightly on his armrest as he issued the order. "Execute."

Carp bent over his workstation. "Engaging thrust plan Gamma-3." The ship shook and Jacobs felt the increased pressure of 2g acceleration. Carp hesitated, listening to something on his earpiece. "All personnel are in their couches, sir."

Jacobs leaned back. He wasn't going to actually activate the couches, not until he saw what was on the other side of the gate. But at least with the crew in position they could be at maximum thrust in less than a minute.

"Five minutes, forty-five seconds to insertion, captain." Carp was focused intently on his screen. His voice was so steady it was almost robotic. "All systems 100% operational, sir."

"Very well, ensign." Jacobs stared straight ahead. "Forward then, and let's see what awaits us."

Chapter 3

Bridge – AS John Paul Jones
Point Epsilon
Near Psi Capricorni Warp Gate

"Full power to the engines. I want maximum thrust in one minute." Captain Gwen Beacham was already encased in her acceleration couch…along with the other 323 members of the crew. The heavy cruiser was thrusting at 14g, but that wasn't going to be enough. The air was thick with acrid smoke…the ship had taken more than one hit, but she was still in the fight.

"Understood, captain. Full power in six zero seconds." The voice of her chief engineer sounded distant through the ship's com system. Lieutenant Commander Grove was one of the best. He played the fusion reactor like a virtuoso coaxing sound from a violin. But there was only so much he could do to keep the ship's systems functioning. Another hit like the last one, and she would be dead in space.

John Paul Jones had been on station at Point Epsilon for six months. Six boring, uneventful months. Epsilon was a rarity, a starless nexus where two warp gates converged. While the science of the gates was imperfectly understood in the best of circumstances, their occasional occurrence out in deep space was a complete mystery. But Point Epsilon was on the way from Farpoint to Sandoval, the natural invasion route for the enemy to take on its way into the heart of the Alliance.

Beacham had chafed at the inaction, but now she longed for the aching boredom. The enemy had finally come through the warp gate; that much was certain. A cluster of the new, smaller ships – her people had been calling them Gremlins – transited first. Damn, she thought, these bastards are learning. It was getting harder to mousetrap them.

The larger enemy ships were equipped with massively powerful anti-matter weapons, and several Alliance fleets had managed to trick them into firing early. Antimatter was a fragile substance; if containment failed for a nanosecond it would annihilate immediately, vaporizing whatever vessel was carrying it. Admiral West had even managed to sneak up on the First Imperium forces at Cornwall and attack before they'd ejected their antimatter ordnance. She'd destroyed half a dozen ships outright, and driven the survivors back long enough for her to rescue the Marines on the planet.

Now the enemy was sending scouting fleets through the warp gates first. The Gremlins were tough – all First Imperium ships were – but they were small and expendable, and they carried no antimatter missiles. They transited and determined what was on the other side of the warp gate. If it was a major fleet, they signaled the heavier ships waiting on the other side. If it was a screening force intended to strip the heavy weapons from the bigger vessels, the Gremlins engaged it.

Beacham's vessel had been waiting there with five other cruisers and a cloud of attack ships. It wasn't a major fleet, but it was too much for half a dozen Gremlins to easily take out, so the First Imperium force had called in reinforcements. Their dark energy communications system allowed them to send messages through warp gates at lightspeed, a massive advantage over the Alliance's physical drones. Fifteen Gargoyles transited, more than enough to take out the defenders. The battle had been raging for 72 hours, and the battered Alliance survivors were trying to break off.

Now, two of the Leviathans came through, surrounded by another twenty Gargoyles. The massive battleships were like nothing the humans had ever seen. Almost 4 kilometers long, they were two and a half times the tonnage of the Alliance's Yorktown class battleships. It was the biggest force the enemy had yet deployed, and just trying to estimate its firepower made Beacham's head hurt.

"Delta-Z transmission from Manchester, captain." Lieutenant Wharton's voice was scratchy, labored. Wrapped in the heavy cocoon of the acceleration couch and exhausted from three days of nonstop fighting and maneuver, she sounded like she was near the breaking point. Beacham knew all her people were.

She didn't respond to Wharton's report. What was there to say? Things were deteriorating rapidly. Force Q, as the flotilla had been designated, was coming apart. Admiral Sand was dead, blasted to bits along with Vicksburg. With Manchester gone, she'd be the senior captain left alive…and the new commander of the dying task force.

My first multi-ship command, she thought grimly…most likely my last, too. She had four cruisers and a dozen attack ships left, but half of them were wracked by internal explosions and bleeding atmosphere. The attack ships were out of plasma torpedoes, which made them almost useless against a First Imperium vessel. The light lasers the suicide boats carried wouldn't even scratch the mysterious dark matter infused alloy in a Gargoyle's hull.

Force Q's cruisers had been the first ships to be armed with the new missiles. Each weapon carried ten 500-megaton enhanced fusion warheads, giving them a total yield comparable to the enemy antimatter devices. That power, came at a cost, however. The new missiles massed well over 1,000 tons, and a ship the size of John Paul Jones could only carry four, mounted on its external racks.

The enemy was still having a hard time dealing with sophisticated ECM, and the new weapons had been loaded with jammers and other systems designed to confuse point defense and other interdiction systems. It was a partial success. A lot of the new missiles were intercepted before they reached detonation range, but the ones that got through proved very effective at inflicting damage on the Gargoyles. But they were gone now, expended along with every standard missile in Force Q.

"Commencing maximum thrust in five, four, three, two, one." The ship's AI counted down. Beacham grimaced as the pressure jumped from 14 to 23 gravities. She didn't even feel the needle as her couch's control system injected an increased dose of the drug cocktail into her arm. She was sluggish, and she could feel her mind drifting from reality into subconscious wandering. Between the pressure and the drugs it was almost impossible to stay focused at 23g, not for more than a few seconds.

The task force was running for it. They'd done all the damage they could do to the enemy, delayed them as long as possible. To stay was nothing but useless suicide. Unfortunately, fleeing didn't look much more promising. The two worst-damaged cruisers had no hope at all of escaping, and the rest of the force wasn't much likelier to make it to the relative safety of the Gamma Sagittarii warp gate.

She struggled to open her eyes and stare at the plotting screen a few centimeters over her head. It took practice to correctly read the flat tactical displays. A stylized 2-D representation of three dimensional space, flats, as they were called, were the only thing practical for use under heavy acceleration.

She winced – Quebec was already falling behind. One of her engines was damaged, and her reactor was reporting some disturbing fluctuations. It would be a race to see if the enemy caught her first or if the reactor blew from over-powering. Either way, another 300+ Alliance fleet crew were going to die in this dark, forsaken corner of deep space.

She tried to assess the status of the other ships on the display, but the pressure was too much. Her eyes were tearing hard and, finally, she couldn't take it anymore. She closed her eyes, and tried to stay at least partially lucid. But the relentless pressure combined with the heavy concentration of the drugs was too much. She felt the floating sensation, the strange detachment from time and space. She wasn't hallucinating, not yet. At least she didn't think so. But she wasn't concentrating on anything either. Had a second passed? A minute? A week?

The harsh white light assaulted Beacham's eyes. She could feel the wave moved across her body, through her mind, clearing away the fog, the fatigue. Stims, she realized. As her head cleared, she could see the light wasn't bright at all. It was soft, dim…emergency power. The crushing pressure was gone, replaced by total weightlessness. John Paul Jones was in freefall.

"Porthos, report immediately." Beacham was a fan of old literature, and she'd pulled a name for her AI from an ancient classic novel.

The AI responded in its usual calm, soft tones. "Yes, captain. The reactor self-terminated operations, reasons unknown. The primary ship AI is conducting a diagnostic test at this time."

Beacham was one of those captains who liked to work through her crew rather than directly with an AI. But right now she had no idea what shape her people were in…and no time to find out. "Damn," she spat bitterly to herself. "What a time for the reactor to scrag."

"The ship is approximately 47.4 million kilometers from the warp gate insertion point. We remain on target vector. At our current velocity of 0.0401c, we will transit in one hour, one minute, 40 seconds." The AI continued its report, ignoring the coughs and wheezes as Beacham tried pull herself together after the high gee forces.

Good, she thought…at least we're still on vector. But if we lose an hour of acceleration, we've got even less chance of making it before they catch us. She sighed, lifting herself painfully from the now-open acceleration couch. Every inch of her body hurt. Damn…she'd been so busy worrying about John Paul Jones, she forgot the rest of the task force. She'd been in command all of ten conscious minutes. "Task force status?"

"Quebec was destroyed by enemy particle accelerator attack approximately three hours fourteen minutes ago." Beacham closed her eyes. It wasn't unexpected, but it still hurt. Worse, even…because she had a few friends on Quebec. "Dragonfly and Foxhound were also destroyed."

She tried to focus on the OB. Her head was still a little fuzzy despite the stims, but it was getting clearer every second. The two attack ships had been badly damaged. Again, it was no surprise they'd been taken out. "Other vessels?"

"The rest of the task force is continuing to accelerate with maximum thrust." There was a slight pause, almost imperceptible. "Portland is only producing 13.5g of thrust. The vessel is lagging approximately 11.7 million kilometers behind the main force. However, the pursuing enemy vessels began decelerating when the relief force transited."

"Relief force?" Beacham turned her head quickly, too quickly. She felt a rush of dizziness, and she sat back on her couch. "What are you talking about, Porthos?"

"Forty-seven Alliance and allied vessels have transited from Gamma Sagittarii, commencing approximately eleven minutes ago. There are additional ships still exiting the warp gate." The AI paused again. "I reported to you several times, captain, but you were non-responsive under the effects of the acceleration."

Beacham felt successive waves of emotion. Anger that the AI hadn't notified her…even though it had tried. The fury passed quickly, and she started to remember the AI's voice, speaking to her when she was floating incoherently. The drugs and gee forces affected people differently, with effects that could vary wildly from instance to instance. Now that clarity had returned, it was coming back.

Excitement flooded through her, and curiosity. She hadn't expected any reinforcements…and this seemed to be a major fleet coming through. What was going on?

Terrance Compton sat bolt upright in his command chair, staring out over his staff. They were busily at work, focusing on the various displays that monitored Second Fleet's 111 ships. They were scared too, very aware that they were about to engage in the largest naval battle yet fought against the invading forces of the Third Imperium. But Compton could feel their anger as well…their fearsome determination. The Alliance navy didn't like to retreat, and for two years now that was damned near all they'd been doing. But not today, he thought with a predatory smile. Not until we make these bastards pay.

Bunker Hill was the most fearsome instrument of destruction the Alliance had ever put into space, the newest of the Yorktown class battleships. Compton fought the temptation to micromanage its operations. Captain Arlington would fight her ship, and she'd do it with her usual skill…he was sure of that. Compton and Elizabeth Arlington were very close, and they shared a bond of trust beyond even that typical between an admiral and his flag captain. The two would probably have been lovers, but that was a line Compton wouldn't cross, not while she was under his command.

Arlington had been up for promotion to flag rank twice, including just before Second Fleet left for Point Epsilon, but she'd declined both times. She hadn't wanted to leave her ship, and she hadn't wanted to abandon Compton. Not now. Not when he had to face this terrifying enemy. Compton knew why she had turned the promotions down, but after the battle he intended to urge her take her star. If they were both still alive.

"The fleet will come to battlestations." Compton spoke slowly, evenly. He was the model of a proper naval officer, which would have been quite a shock to anyone who'd known him when he and Augustus Garret were hotshot suicide boat captains, tearing up enemy space and friendly ports with the same unrestrained vigor.

"Yes, sir. All ships to battlestations." Commander Harmon's response was sharp and crisp. He'd proven to be a top notch tactical officer, which was a welcome surprise. Compton was considered an extraordinary judge of talent, but for once he'd promoted someone for reasons other than their tactical record. Max Harmon was the son of Admiral Constance Harmon. An officer who'd given decades of distinguished service, Constance Harmon had also supported Compton during the rebellions, when it looked as though he was disobeying Admiral Garret's orders. She took two bullets for her trouble, courtesy of an Alliance Intelligence assassin planted in her crew. One of the shots severed her spine, and she spent two years enduring an agonizing series of surgeries and regenerations before Sarah Linden pronounced her healed and let her out of the hospital on Armstrong. Compton felt the least he could do was mentor her only son, and he was glad to see his favoritism justified…Max had proven himself multiple times since he'd joined the staff.

Bunker Hill's klaxon sounded - Captain Arlington following

the fleet order Compton had just issued. They were coming in at a slow 0.01c, decelerating at a leisurely 1g. Compton was here to hit the enemy fleet, but he had no intention of getting sucked deep into the system into a deathmatch he couldn't win. This was a hit and run operation, but on a fleet scale...part of the new grand strategy of attriting the enemy and forcing them to waste supplies and ordnance. Plus, Compton had a few surprises to try out, goodies from Colonel Sparks and his pack of whitecoats in the lab.

"All ships...prepare to launch bomber strikes. Alpha launch in 15 minutes, beta launch in 25." Compton was looking over at Harmon as he fired out the command.

"Yes, sir." Harmon leaned over and spoke into his com. "All ships, prepare for alpha launch in one five minutes, beta launch in two five minutes." There was an instant of silence while the acknowledgements came in, no more than 5 or 6 seconds. "All capital ships confirm, sir."

Compton smiled. He believed in his people...his direct staff, of course, but also the thousands of officers and crew in the fleet. There were a lot of veterans, and they'd been training constantly. Every man and woman under Compton's command knew what was at stake...they knew they were fighting for the future of the entire human race. They were ready...and their commander knew it.

Bunker Hill's klaxon sounded again, the alert for her bomber crews. Second Fleet's flagship carried four squadrons, 48 fighter-bombers, and all of them were going to launch against the enemy. The First Imperium forces didn't seem to employ small craft, and that relieved Compton of the need to hold back any squadrons to defend the fleet. Bombers had only been used twice against the enemy, but they had been highly effective both times, albeit with heavy losses. That made them a potent weapon, even more so than usual, and Compton was going to get the most out of that before the enemy caught up and developed stronger interdiction tactics.

Second Fleet had five capital ships, including another Yorktown class vessel and the Martian Confederation's flagship,

Sword of Ares. The only ship of her class, she was bigger even than the Yorktowns, and she carried 6 full squadrons. All together, Second Fleet was sending 216 bombers at the enemy. Compton was duplicating Admiral West's successful strategy. Half the fighter-bombers were fitted out for missile interdiction and the others for an attack on the enemy fleet.

He leaned back in his chair. His mouth opened, but no words came out, and he closed it a few seconds later. Don't micromanage, he thought…your captains have their orders, and they know what they have to do. He took a deep breath, holding it for a second before exhaling hard. Sitting and waiting…it was the hardest part of battle for Compton. But he had nothing to do until after the bombers were away and it was time to prep the missile barrages. He took another breath and punched at his screen, pulling up the OB for Task Group A…ten suicide boats, armed with the Alliance's newest weapon. They had their orders too, and Compton was anxious to see how they fared.

"Joker, confirm the status of Task Group A." Compton didn't have to explain the name of his AI very often. He was widely considered to be the best poker player in the navy, and the reputation still stuck, despite the fact that he hadn't played in years. He'd always found cards relaxing, but as he rose in rank he became increasingly uncomfortable winning money from subordinates. He played with other officers at his level for a while, but as he continued to rise, that group became smaller and smaller. Now, everyone was his subordinate…everyone but Admiral Garret…and two man poker was a bore.

"Squadron Captain Franklin reported all ships ready on his last scheduled update, eleven minutes ago." Like most of the naval AIs, Joker was fairly formal in demeanor. The Marine units tended to have more colorful personalities, something the navy considered beneath its dignity. "Do you wish me to confirm?"

"Negative." Compton was just bored and restless. Franklin was a veteran; he didn't need the Fleet Admiral on his ass for no reason. Besides, the first wave of bombers was set to go in a few minutes. Captain Hurley didn't need Compton pestering her either, but at least he could monitor the launch. It would give him something to occupy himself until the action started.

Greta Hurley grimaced, as she always did when the magnetic catapult threw her bomber clear of the mother ship. She was a longtime veteran of the bomber corps, and she'd launched into some of the fiercest battles the Alliance had ever fought…but she'd never gotten used to the sudden jarring from the catapult. She didn't vomit anymore, like she did when she was a rookie. She just felt queasy for a few minutes.

Hurley had commanded Admiral West's bomber attack on the enemy fleet at Farpoint. She and her shipmates managed something there that few of the others in the wing did…they survived. Fewer than 20% of the ships that went in against the First Imperium fleet came back, but they made the enemy pay a price with their close in attack runs. A direct hit with a plasma torpedo would damage even a First Imperium ship, but it took a pilot with the guts and skill to fly in close and hit the bullseye.

She leaned back and took a few deep breaths. She was going to spend most of this fight cocooned in her couch, and she took the chance to fill her lungs a few times before the crushing pressure made it an effort. She was focused, determined to make the strike count. Hurley was the closest thing the Alliance had to an expert in bomber tactics against the First Imperium forces. She'd led a successful strike and come back to talk about it… something no one else had managed in this war.

But it was more; it was personal. She'd seen the enemy nearly wipe out her strike force at Farpoint…she remembered the cries on the com, the constant stream of notifications from the AI reporting the destruction of one ship after another. The empty seats in the mess hall and wardroom. Friends of hers…friends who were now gone. Great Hurley was back for revenge.

Chapter 4

Planet Sandoval
Delta Leonis IV
"The Line"

"I want every one of these super-hardened, and I want it finished in two days." Erik Cain stood ramrod straight, his face no more than 3 or 4 inches from the sweating officer standing before him. "Understood, colonel?"

"Sir, it's just not possible." It took all the courage Colonel Mellon could muster to stand up to Cain's withering stare. Not many officers could have managed it. Erik Cain was one of the most revered commanders in the Corps, and even the most battle-hardened Marine veteran was reduced to despair by his disapproval. He'd always been a hard taskmaster, but since taking command on Sandoval he'd become a machine, tireless, unyielding.

"Then make it possible, colonel." Cain's tone was dismissive, and he started to turn to leave.

"General Cain, you are talking about thousands of individual circuits." Mellon's voice was quivering. He was afraid of Cain… everyone was afraid of Cain since his return from Farpoint. "I don't have the trained manpower." He paused, then added, "Besides, the enemy hasn't used nuclear weapons in any ground battle. Is this really so crucial?" He knew as it came out of his mouth he should have held his tongue.

Cain turned slowly back toward Mellon. "I'm sorry, colonel. I didn't realize you had infiltrated the enemy high command and determined that nuclear strikes are off the table." Cain's eyes had focused on Mellon's, holding them transfixed in his searing gaze. "Because I know you wouldn't want us running around here without AIs or defensive systems just because the enemy decided to use motherfucking nuclear warheads without consulting you first." By the time Cain finished, his voice had risen to a thundering crescendo.

Mellon was silent, but he stood his ground...barely. "I'm sorry, sir." Mellon's throat was dry, his voice a hoarse croak. "Of course, you are right about being prepared." He swallowed hard and forced himself to maintain eye contact. "But there is no way my people can finish the job in two days. We'll be lucky if we can even find the materials we need."

Cain stood impassively, looking back at the engineering officer. He tended to think anything could be done if people were pushed hard enough but, of course, there was a limit to what even a veteran team could accomplish. "Alright, colonel..." Cain's voice relaxed slightly – Mellon had won a measure of respect by standing up to him. "...I will order all remaining civilians on Sandoval with any electronics experience immediately conscripted and placed at your disposal."

The young Erik Cain would have railed against drafting civilians, calling the older version of himself a martinet, a jackboot, a government enforcer, for even considering it. But two and a half decades of war and bloody sacrifice had changed him... profoundly. Now he was concerned far less with ideology than results. Victory was very nearly all he cared about anymore. It was the one thing that could justify the losses, the pain, the death. To lose so much in defeat was more than he could bear... the futility and waste were all-consuming. This war, of course, was different from the others. Surrender wasn't an option, and defeat unthinkable. Losing this war meant the end of humanity. In the darkest recesses of Cain's soul he wondered if that would be so bad, but he hadn't fallen entirely into that black pit. Not yet. Whatever the cost, he was going to attain victory. Whatever the cost.

"Thank you, sir." Mellon was surprised. He couldn't think of an instance where colonial civilians had been pressed into military service, at least not by a Marine officer. But he needed the help, and Sandoval boasted a small, but growing electronics

industry…at least it had before the evacuations. A good number of the remaining refugees likely had the types of skills he
needed. "That will be very helpful."

Cain started to turn again. "See it done, colonel." He paused
for an instant. "You'll have the civilians today." He turned and
walked away, leaving the stunned engineer staring after him.

The noise was deafening. Major Tomlinson toggled his
helmet closed. It was a beautiful day on Sandoval's northern
continent, and Tomlinson had been enjoying the fresh, cool air.
But the Burrowers were just too damned loud. He'd comman-
deered them from Sandoval's mining industry and put them to
work digging underground bunkers. Even with his suit sealed
he could hear them tear through the planet's hard crust. With
his helmet open it had been unbearable.

Tomlinson was stunned when he first saw General Cain's
fortification plan. The scope of it was more than intimidating…it was mind-boggling. Impossible – that was the first word
that came to mind. But the commander of 1st Army wasn't a
man people said no to very often, and impossible wasn't in his
vocabulary. Tomlinson had never served with Cain before Sandoval, but he knew enough of the general's history to be sure
of that.

Cain had named the initiative Plan Iwo. Everyone in the
Corps was familiar with the Battle of Iwo Jima, of course.
Marine combat history was one of the first things taught in
Basic. The Alliance Marines weren't technically the same organization as the U.S.M.C. that had invaded Iwo Jima three centuries before, but they considered themselves the inheritors of the
traditions of those leathernecks, and the Royal Marines as well,
and they revered the histories and heroes of the formations that
preceded them.

The Japanese defenders had turned Iwo Jima into a nightmare of tunnels, strongpoints, and concealed firing positions…
and they'd inflicted staggering losses on the invading Marines.
Cain intended to do the same thing on Sandoval…1st Army was
going to fight a death match against the First Imperium invad-

ers, making them pay for every centimeter. He'd declared more than once that the fight would be to the last man, and those who'd served with him before knew he meant it.

But Iwo Jima was a tiny island on Earth, and Sandoval was a planet. The scope of excavation and construction was massive on a scale even the Corps' veteran engineers had never imagined. Cain had envisioned a series of underground bases and bunkers, all interconnected by a network of tunnels. Everything was to be subterranean – the HQs, the barracks, the hospitals. Now Tomlinson and the rest of the engineering regiment had to build it all.

"Major Tomlinson…General Teller here."   Tomlinson turned instinctively, but of course Teller wasn't actually there. On the com he could have been 1,000 klicks away. First Division's CO had been the commander of the first significant force to face the invaders. Barely a third of his troops escaped from the Battle of Cornwall…and Teller himself had left in medical stasis, about as close to dead as a live person can be. He'd been over a year in the hospital on Armstrong, and now he was back for a return engagement.

"Yes, general…how can I help you, sir?" He knew it was another progress check. It wasn't bad enough Cain himself was breathing down his neck, constantly pushing…now he had all the senior officers fired up, and they were joining the party.

"I have some revisions for 1st Brigade's deployment area. I'm going to send them to you right now." Teller's voice was as grim and determined as Cain's…or at least almost so. Tomlinson wasn't sure he'd ever heard anything as intimidating as 1st Army's CO when he was pissed.

"Yes, sir." Tomlinson swallowed the sigh he felt rising. Petulance didn't usually improve relations with a general, but he was getting tired of the constant changes. He understood…1st Division's commander had come late to the party, having only arrived from Armstrong a few weeks before. But that didn't change the fact that he was already behind, and every change set him further back. And his people were already pulling fourteen hour daily shifts.

"Don't worry, major." Teller's voice relaxed slightly. "It's nothing that will wreck your schedule. You haven't started on any of the affected sections yet anyway." Teller was tough, but he wasn't quite the relentless taskmaster that Cain was.

"Yes, sir. Thank you." Tomlinson let out a small breath, not quite a sigh, but close. "I'll implement the changes immediately."

"Very well. Carry on, major." Teller cut the circuit.

Tomlinson could see the blue indicator light on his visor display – he'd received the transmission from Teller. Ok, he thought, let's see what the good general wants now.

The refugee camp was unsettled. It wasn't exactly a riot, but things were far from calm. Close to 90% of the population had already been evacuated, and the rest were expecting to leave in the next few weeks, when the transport fleet returned from Armstrong. The evacuation had been going on almost a year. There were three worlds on the Line, and the scarce transport assets were divided among them. The longer it had gone on, the greater the frustration had grown among those who'd remained behind. Things had gotten worse when the remaining civilians were moved out of their homes to the relocation camps. General Cain had ordered the settlements to be fortified, and that meant getting the occupants out of the way.

Now word was filtering through the camp…the Marines were detaining people, segregating them from the population. There were armored troops on patrol now, standing a watchful guard over the common areas. The Marines had been living alongside the civilians of Sandoval for more than a year, but now, for the first time, they seemed menacing. Still, the occupants of the camp poured out of their shelters and into dusty streets looking for information.

Cain stood at the command post just outside the camp, staring down at the scene unfolding. He wasn't wearing armor, just a set of worn gray fatigues – though there were two companies of fully-armored Marines formed up outside. He was silent, just gazing out and thinking to himself.

"General Cain, there is some unrest in the camp." Captain

Jason Carter had become an extraordinary aide to Cain. He'd come up late in the Third Frontier War, and he'd won his Academy berth on Carson's World, fighting in Cain's 1st Brigade during the climactic battle of the war on the Lysandra Plateau. A hardened combat veteran and survivor of one of the bloodiest battles ever fought, Carter had proven to have a great gift for the administrative as well. "Perhaps we should postpone the order."

Cain didn't stir. "No captain. We're not postponing anything." Cain's voice was calm, but Carter knew better than to argue. "We need help shielding our circuitry from EMP." Cain still hadn't moved, and he continued to look out over the camp as he spoke. The young officer at his side stood like a statue, listening intently to every word. "I'm not about to let some whining among the civilians dictate military decisions." He paused, taking a shallow breath. "Besides, if we lose this fight they'll all die anyway…either on Armstrong or wherever else they run." He paused, then added, "This war isn't going to end with a room full of gasbags negotiating a treaty like the others have. This is to the death."

Cain finally turned to face Carter. "You know it as well as I do, Jason. We're staking everything on the Line. If we lose here we're done. It may take the enemy a while to mop everything up, but we'll never be able to mount a defense this strong again." He paused for a second, as if holding the next words in his mouth for a beat. "This is it. This is the war." Cain's blue eyes glistened in the late afternoon sun. Carter could see the resolve and stubbornness in them, harder than granite. But deeper, behind the surface strength, he saw the pain too. Years and years of the stress and cost of battle…the price Cain had paid with his soul for his victories.

"Yes, sir." Carter paused, his mind wandering, imagining what the coming battle might be like. Cain's aide had been part of Teller's brigade on Cornwall, so he knew firsthand what was coming. He tried not to think about it much…to just focus on his job and keep it at that. Any time you escaped from a battle where two-thirds of your comrades died you respected the power of the enemy. But it wasn't going to help anyone if he let himself become paralyzed with fear. He'd been afraid on Cornwall, so terrified it affected his performance in battle. He felt shame for that, though every veteran who'd fought there had experienced the same thing. He'd faced deadly enemies before, but there was something different about a foe that didn't feel fear or pain. It gripped him like a cold feeling in his gut, and it didn't go away. "I suggest we send Captain Leach and her people in…just to cut off any problems before they start. A show of force now might head off trouble."

Cain didn't answer right away. He turned back and looked out again, over the modular shelters and rutted dirt roads of the camp. He understood the civilians, at least on some level. Their lives had been upended, thrown into chaos by the approach of some unseen enemy. They'd been driven from their homes, herded into camps…not by the enemy, but by their own forces, the men and women charged with defending them. The refugees hadn't been mistreated, and they'd been well supplied with food and medical care, but he still understood the resentment, the fear. The Cogs back on Earth would have meekly allowed themselves to be rounded up, but the colonials were different. Freedom was prized on Sandoval, as it was on most of the worlds the Alliance had settled, and the residents didn't like giving it up…even to their own Marines.

But that didn't change Cain's point of view. He had to defend Sandoval, and he would do whatever it took to win the fight that was coming. These civilians, he thought, sitting in their shelters feeling sorry for themselves…they don't they realize that most of these Marines they see will never leave Sandoval? They are going to die, in pain and fear, lying broken and bleeding in the muck…alone, as every man and woman is when death calls. They are going to die defending the civilians…not just those here on Sandoval, but throughout the Alliance, throughout all of human-occupied space.

Yes, Cain understood the civilians, but his empathy was limited. They were afraid, certainly. But so were his people. His Marines weren't immune to fear…they felt it…they felt every terrifying minute. But they controlled it; they did what they had to do. The civilians were going to do the same. Cain had made that decision for them.

Erik stared out over the camp and the surrounding valley, but his thoughts were wandering. He wondered, am I still afraid? After all these years, all the pain and death? He decided he wasn't sure. He knew he craved victory, but he wasn't as sure how he felt about his own survival. He was…ambivalent. It wasn't a deathwish, certainly, but Cain was tired in body and soul. He was feeling worn out, used up.

He looked up and caught Carter's glance. The young officer had been standing silently while Cain was absorbed in his thoughts. "Yes, Jason. Send Captain Leach and her people in." He paused, thinking quietly for a few seconds. His young self would have behaved quite differently…he would have placed respect for freedom over all things. But now he had to weigh freedom versus extinction, and it wasn't as simple as naked ideology. The Marines were loved by the Alliance colonists, and had been for a century. Cain wondered if they wouldn't be hated before this war was over…but he wasn't going to let that dictate his decisions either. "Instruct her to make sure her people are respectful to the civilians, but her primary mission is to insure that all the designated personnel are conscripted. We need those technicians."

"Yes, sir." Carter snapped to attention and gave Cain a crisp salute. He turned to leave but stopped and swung back around. "Sir?"

"Yes, captain?"

"What should we do if they resist?" Carter was tentative. The whole topic of herding civilians around was an uncomfortable one.

"Persuade them, captain. Gently, if possible." Cain's voice was becoming firmer. "But nothing is to interfere with the execution of my order."

"And if anyone continues to resist, sir?" Carter was clearly nervous, but he'd been in the camp himself, and he knew things were likely to get out of hand. "How much force do we employ?"

Cain stood silently for a few seconds, staring off at nothing in particular. "Captain Leach is to do her best to maintain control and explain the situation to the civilians in question and seek their cooperation." He paused again. "However if anyone continues to resist, and their actions jeopardize the operation…" Cain turned and stared right into Carter's eyes, his expression as cold as ice. "…tell her to shoot them."

Chapter 5

Flight Squadron 7
"Scarlet Hawks"
Point Epsilon
Approaching First Imperium Vanguard

"Squadron leaders, prepare for your attack runs." Greta Hurley's birds were in the lead. There had been 12 of her Scarlett Hawks when they'd launched from Bunker Hill, but there were only eight in the formation now. Two were damaged, decelerating as quickly as they could to turn and try to limp back to the fleet. One of them at least, she thought, had a decent chance. The other two had been blown to bits by the enemy point defense. As bad as that was, she'd expected it to be worse. "Key on my squadron at 20 second intervals, starting in two zero seconds."

She'd led the squadrons of the strike force here stacked up one behind the other, a formation intended to confound the enemy point defense. So far it had done just that. Her lead formation had taken 33% casualties, but the squadrons farther back were largely intact. The force as a whole had lost less than 10% so far…vastly fewer than the most wildly optimistic projections. Now they were ready to attack, starting with her squadron.

"Ok, Hawks, let's score us a Gargoyle." The strike force had targeted nine enemy vessels, a full squadron going in against each. "These things are tough as shit, boys and girls…so I don't want anybody firing until you're right on top of them. Only a direct hit will count in this attack." Of course, she thought, going all the way down their throats would do nothing to increase a bomber's chance of survival. But her people were veterans, and they knew the score. If they didn't do enough damage, the fleet would be toast…and if the fleet went, so did they. Better to die out here, taking on the enemy, than cowering in the launch bay as your mother ship explodes around you.

"Ten seconds to attack run. Arm plasma torpedoes." Prepping the torpedoes was easy, just flipping a switch. No one was likely to forget, but she wasn't taking any chances. "Five…four…three…two…one…now!" She felt the pressure slamming her chest, pushing the breath from her lungs. Even in the acceleration couch and doped up on the meds, 30g of acceleration was hard to handle. Her ship's engine blasted full, modifying her vector to directly intersect with the target ship.

The system was pumping oxygen into her helmet, increasing the pressure to partially compensate for the tremendous gee forces, but she still had to struggle to force air into her lungs. The burn would last a little more than four minutes; then the ship's engine would shut down, and the crushing force would be replaced with weightlessness. That was Hurley's plan. She wanted to be alert and aware when it was time to launch. The ship's AI could execute the attack too, but Hurley wanted to do it herself. She knew the targeting was pure mathematics, but her many battles had taught her not to ignore intuition either.

She was woozy and out of it. The drugs and the pressure were hard on cognitive thought. But then she felt the pinprick, the couch administering the drugs to counteract the anti-pressure meds. Then another shot and, a second or two later, clarity. The stims…a triple dose.

"Optimal firing point in 30 seconds." The ship's AI had a slightly tinny, mechanical voice, and it rattled and buzzed. The ship had taken a couple minor hits on the way in, and the speaker was damaged.

Hurley nodded, a pointless gesture. "Countdown from ten." She flipped her com to the squadron line. "Good luck, Hawks!" The status monitor showed that all her ships had completed their burns. Now it was just 30 more seconds. Her squadron would run the gauntlet of the enemy's close in defenses for half a minute. Then, the survivors would launch.

She felt the ship lurch, first slightly, then harder. They were hit. The internal alarm sounded, and the vessel shook again. "Hull breach in rear compartment." The AI's voice was getting worse, but fixing a speaker wasn't the top priority for the bomber's lone repair bot. "Damage control underway."

It could be worse, she thought. All her people had their suits on and buttoned up. There was nobody in the rear compartment anyway. But if that breach was large enough to suck everything out into space, all their med supplies and spare parts were gone.

"Firing point in ten seconds." She flipped the switch to route the AI through her earpiece. "Seven…six…five…" Much better, see thought as she listened to the clear sound. "Four…three…two…"

She launched the torpedo. The bomber lurched wildly as it fired. The torpedoes were small sprint missiles, and they blasted out of the launcher with some serious kick. She launched two seconds early by the AI's count, but that's when her gut told her to pull the trigger. The target ship was rapidly changing its thrust output, making it tough to calculate an exact firing solution. An educated guess was as good as a precisely programmed solution.

Hurley couldn't see it, of course, but she knew what was happening. The torpedo accelerated directly toward the target. It was basically a canister of compressed gas and a fusion reactor strapped onto a large engine. Just before impact the engine shut down and the reactor's energy was diverted to superheat the gas. The resulting plasma slammed into the target at a temperature in excess of one million degrees. In most cases, even a near miss could inflict massive damage, but against a First Imperium hull, a direct hit was a must.

She was counting down in her head, impatient for the scanning result. She leaned back in her couch, waving for the rest of the crew to do so as well. As soon as she got the damage assessment, the couch would activate, and the engines would execute an extended burn, altering their vector away from the enemy fleet and, ultimately, back to the base ships. Assuming the landing platforms still there when the squadrons got back.

"Direct hit amidships." The AI's voice was calm, but Hurley herself was anything but.

"Yes!" Her scream reverberated in her helmet, hurting her ears...but she didn't care. "Take that you scumbag motherfuckers!" Hurley was a fairly straitlaced officer, particularly by the wilder standards of the bomber corps. But she tended to be a bit less restrained during combat, especially when she got a chance to hit back at the First Imperium.

"Initial scan indicates significant internal damage. Secondary explosions detected." The AI would continue to update the assessment, but first it was time to get the hell out of there.

"Execute thrust plan Delta." She closed her eyes as the system gave her the injections and the couch activated and closed up around her. She could feel the air pressure in her helmet increasing...then the sledgehammer as the bomber's engine ignited and blasted away at 30g.

She could quickly feel herself losing coherence, but she still felt the elation at scoring a solid hit. Now, she thought, they were in the hands of the AI. With luck, she'd survive to fight again another day. With luck.

Compton's staff was generally calm and highly professional. But the flag bridge erupted into cheers as the damage assessments flooded in from Hurley's attack. The bombers had performed beyond Compton's wildest hopes. They'd targeted nine of the mid-sized ships...the ones the Alliance spacers called Gargoyles. Five of them were hit multiple times and destroyed outright. The other four were seriously damaged. Even better, almost 70% of the strike force cleared the interdiction zone. It would be hours before they could change vectors and return, but Compton was relieved that any of them were coming back at all. Losses of 30% would normally be considered heavy, but against the First Imperium, it was better than he'd dared to hope.

A little smile crept on his face as he listened to the wild cheers of his staff. He normally conducted himself in a fairly formal manner, but there were always times for exceptions. When an update came in reporting that two of the damaged ships were effectively dead in space he decided to join in. For the first time ever, his officers saw their fleet admiral jump out of his seat and shout out loud. "Way to go, Greta!"

His missiles were coming in right behind the bombers. He'd timed the launch carefully, so the enemy wouldn't have time to react. He wanted to overwhelm their point defense right after the suicide boats attacked. That meant giving Greta's people the minimum possible time to clear the missile detonation zone, but she assured him she could get them all away in time. He frowned a little as he thought about it, wondering if he would have changed his plan even if she'd told him they couldn't escape. His expression darkened for an instant as he answered himself. Nothing was more important than defeating this enemy. No matter what the cost.

"Full damage control protocols, all ships." Compton was waiting for the results of his own missile attacks, but Second Fleet was facing a significant barrage itself. At least they're all just nukes, he thought...who would have thought I'd be grateful one day to be staring at a wall of incoming thermonuclear warheads?

Force Q had been a decoy, though the men and women operating its ships didn't know it. It was getting more and more difficult to strip the enemy of its antimatter weapons. When they started sending the Gremlins through ahead of their fleets, Compton began working on a new plan...Force Q. Second Fleet was here to engage the lead wave of First Imperium ships...and wipe them out if possible. He had no intention of staying to face the Leviathans and the 30+ Gargoyles of the second group. That meant time was limited. If he stayed too long he'd never escape in time...and that would mean no one from Second Fleet would leave Point Epsilon.

Compton would already have ordered the fleet to withdraw, but they weren't going to outrun the enemy missiles no matter what they did. He decided to stay put and face the volley before withdrawing - they were better positioned where they were for point defense. As soon as they'd dealt with the missiles, Compton would order the bug out. He didn't think the Leviathans could catch him before the transit, but that was pure conjecture. He was just guessing at the thrust capacity of those monsters.

"All ships report full damage control protocols in effect." Commander Harmon's voice was like ice.

Like mother like son, Compton thought with a smile. Camille Harmon was a cool customer too, known in the fleet for being rock solid in combat situations.

"Enemy missile volley has passed through long-range interception zone." Harmon again, just as calm. "Estimate 40% of remaining missiles destroyed."

The point defense mines laid by the second wave of bombers took out at least half the incoming warheads, and the ECM buoys positioned in front of the fleet threw almost half of those remaining critically off course. Second Fleet was conducting a model layered point defense, but there were still a lot of weapons inbound. The robot ships of the First Imperium didn't need food storage, gymnasiums, sickbays, and all the other support facilities human crews required. They carried a *lot* of missiles, at least twice as many as an Alliance ship of comparable size.

"Shotguns and laser batteries firing, admiral." Harmon glanced down at the board, calculating an updated estimate. "Project detonations commencing in two minutes, sir."

Compton sat quietly imagining the space around his fleet. Dozens of missiles were closing on his ships, each one splitting into multiple warheads. Many were targeted and blown apart by laser pulses and obliterated by clouds of metallic projectiles from the shotguns. But some of them got through. Too many of them.

"Commander Harmon, I want real time damage reports from the fleet." He hesitated then added, "Issue an advisory to all ship commanders to prioritize damage control efforts to power and propulsion systems." He'd already sent that directive, but he wanted to pound it into their heads. Any ship that couldn't keep up when the fleet bugged out was going to be left behind. Compton didn't like it, and he knew it would tear at him...but he would do it. The Alliance couldn't afford to lose

Second Fleet. Humanity couldn't.

"Missile detonations reported, sir." Harmon's voice was slightly distracted. He was trying to monitor the status of 117 ships while reporting to Compton in real time. "The cruiser Somerset reports heavy damage, sir. Drives appear to be operational, however. The attack ship Rapier was destroyed. We're also getting a Delta-Z signal from the light cruiser Hampton. The…"

"Just send it to my board, commander." Compton sighed. The rest of the staff didn't really need to hear Harmon recite the butcher's bill. Besides, Compton already had Joker feeding him the same info. He thought it would help Harmon to keep busy instead of thinking about the warheads bearing down on them. Elizabeth's people were all occupied manning their battlestations, but the admiral's staff had nothing to do but wait to see if a missile got close enough to Bunker Hill to vaporize them all.

Compton could see the list on his screen growing as more ships were damaged or destroyed. He felt the familiar cold feeling inside as he stared at the lengthening roster. One night, about a year before, when they'd both had a little too much to drink, he'd had a long talk with Erik Cain. They'd spoken of how they dealt with the weight of leading so many men and women to their deaths. Neither of them had figured out how to handle the guilt…they both shoved it deep down, pushing off the day of reckoning. They knew they'd have to face it one day, but that time had not yet arrived for either of them. There were still wars to fight and crises to face. One day, when the wars were over and the battles won, they would both look inside themselves…and see what was left.

Compton had envied Cain one thing. The Marines fought on the ground and, while the commander might be back from the front, he was close to the battle, or at least part of it. While Cain's men and women were fighting and dying, their general could hear the explosions, see the smoke. Sitting in his chair on the flag bridge watching ship names scroll by was so damned… analytical. Death distilled down to a spreadsheet. Somehow, it just made it worse for Compton. It didn't seem real somehow, watching a cruiser's name appear on the list, knowing intellectually that over 300 crew had just died. Death in space was silent.

This time, however, his introspection would be short-lived. Bunker Hill had been targeted by a dozen warheads. Her inner-perimeter point defense systems took out ten, but two closed to the damage zone. The first detonated 5.5 kilometers above and to the port. The damage was minor except for some small secondary explosions near the hull. Compton felt the ship lurch and start to spin. He reflexively gripped the armrests of his chair, but it was an unnecessary effort...he had the safety harness bolted securely in place. The feeling of spinning slowly stopped as Bunker Hill's positioning thrusters fired, stabilizing the vessel.

Compton held his head still, waiting for the dizziness to pass. "Joker, dam..." He paused for a second. "Never mind, Joker." The urge to micromanage the ship was strong, especially in the thick of the fight. But all he could do was interfere with Captain Arlington's efforts. Bunker Hill had one of the best skippers in the fleet, and she had his total confidence. Let her get the ship under control, he thought...she'll update you as soon as she has anything useful to tell you.

His thought was almost cut short by the second detonation. This one was closer, just over 3 kilometers to the starboard... well within the catastrophic damage zone for a 650 megaton warhead. Bunker Hill's starboard side was bombarded with massive amounts of ionizing radiation. The three-layer hull was superheated, and sections melted, then vaporized. Where breaches occurred, lethal radiation poured into the ship.

Crew members in the most exposed sections received radiation doses so massive they doubled over almost immediately, taken by uncontrollable vomiting and diarrhea. The worst hit suffered almost instantaneous seizures and died within a few minutes. Others, slightly less exposed, quickly lost cognitive function and lay on the deck, unable to even call for aid.

All but the most heavily shielded electronic systems on the ship failed immediately. The reactors scragged automatically, a safeguard to insure against critical failures caused by instrument malfunction. Throughout the ship, secondary explosions occurred, causing more damage and, when close to the hull, blowing atmosphere into space and causing the ship to spin wildly.

The air on the flag bridge was thick with the smell of burnt electronics. The port side wall had been blown apart, the result of a secondary explosion in another compartment. Chunks of debris sprayed outward like shrapnel, showering the admiral and his staff.

Max Harmon winced as a small piece of metal lodged in his arm, but he gritted his teeth and ignored it. It was time to send in Task Group A. "Admiral, should I give Group A the…" He turned and stared in horror. Terrance Compton was slumped over in his chair, held in place by the still-connected harness. His shredded survival suit was covered in blood.

"Medibot!" Harmon's voice was shrill with tension. The flag bridge had two medical robots, but both had been destroyed in the blast. He turned to his com, but internal communications were also out. Fuck, he thought. He wanted look away, but he forced himself to stay fixed on the admiral. He couldn't tell if Compton was alive or dead, but he knew there was no hope unless someone did something.

He unstrapped himself from his harness. The ship was still gyrating wildly. He planted his feet on the deck, activating the magnets in his boots. He grabbed two magnetic handholds and began walking on all fours across the compartment. I'm coming, sir, he thought, hoping against hope it wouldn't be too late.

Elizabeth Arlington sat rigidly in her command chair, held firmly in place by her safety harness. Her ship was in trouble. The second warhead had gotten close…far too close. She wondered how the rest of the fleet had fared, but she quickly put that thought out of her head. She had to save Bunker Hill; that was all that mattered to her now.

She panned her head around, surveying the damage on the bridge. It was bad, but it could have been worse…it *was* worse in other areas of the ship. She could feel her heart pounding in her chest, and she felt afraid, overwhelmed. She wasn't sure what to do. Bunker Hill was on backup power with only limited emergency communications. And the massive burst of radiation had fried most of the electrical systems, which vastly complicated damage control efforts.

Finally, she took a deep breath and willed herself to calm down. Her crew, her ship…they needed her now. She could feel the sweat running down her neck, her skin sliding against the cold, slick interior of her survival suit. Her chest was tight and her stomach clenched, but when she turned her head and started speaking she was focused like a laser.

"Commander Jackson, we need internal communications restored now." She was speaking into a portable com unit. Her voice was calm, commanding. Everyone on the bridge felt better hearing her fire out orders.

"We're working on it, captain." Unlike Arlington, Bunker Hill's chief engineer sounded stressed, his voice tinny and strained through the emergency communicator. He needed to be in ten places at once right now. "We should have limited communications any minute."

"I need a report on the reactors too." Arlington was looking down at her workstation. Most of her instruments were out, and she had no idea if the reactors were seriously damaged. "We need power."

"Working on that too, captain." There was a pause, and Arlington could hear Jackson retching. Everyone on Bunker Hill had gotten a heavy dose of radiation, probably enough to kill them all without treatment. Arlington already had ordered the medibots to give injections to counteract the worst effects until the medical staff could properly treat everyone. But a lot of the bots were down, and it was taking a long time to get to everyone. "Sorry, captain. About the react…"

Arlington interrupted. "Commander, have you had your anti-rad shot yet?"

"No, captain." His voice was strained, hoarse. She could hear how weak he was. "I haven't had time."

"Commander, I want you to get your injection immediately." Arlington snapped out the order crisply. She needed Jackson as close to fully-functional as possible. "Brett, right now you are the most important person on this ship. I need you at your best…go get that shot. Now. That's an order."

"Yes, captain."

"Get back to me with that reactor report as soon as you can. Arlington out." She turned, looking toward the nav station. "Commander Krimm, we need to stop this rolling. Plot a solution to divert emergency power to the positioning thrusters."

"Yes captain." Krimm was tall, substantially over two meters. He didn't fit all that well in his chair under normal circumstances, and strapped in as he was he looked almost comical. He had a writing board and a stylus in his hand. "Working on it already, captain. Without the computer I need to do it by hand."

"As quickly as you can, navigator." She wondered if she could even do the calculations herself anymore. It was hard not to become dependent on the AIs, and skills atrophied when you didn't use them. But with the nav computer out, there was no alternative. She remembered the basics – she'd even manually plotted a few small vessels at the Academy, but Bunker Hill was no interplanetary shuttle. Second Fleet's flagship had forty positioning thrusters, and plotting the combination of burns to stabilize the ship was no small feat.

"Captain Arlington?"

Her head snapped around…pointlessly. It was Jackson's voice, coming from the main comlink. "Yes, Engineer, I'm reading you."

"Shipwide communications restored, captain. We also managed to get limited ship-to-ship…for the flag bridge."

"Good job, commander." She allowed herself a tiny smile. "Did you get that injection yet?"

"Getting it now, captain." She could tell how much pain he was in from his voice. "I just wanted to get you the com back first."

"Now, engineer." I have good people on this ship, she thought, but sometimes they were too willing to put themselves last. And right now Bunker Hill needed her chief engineer, perhaps even more than her captain. "No more excuses. And don't forget my reactor report. After your injection."

"Yes, captain."

"Arlington out." She turned toward Krimm. Commander, how are you doing on that manual plot? We need to get the ship…"

"Captain!" It was Lieutenant Blandon, the communications officer. "I have Commander Harmon from the flag bridge."

Arlington snapped her head around. The second she saw Blandon's face she knew.

"He reports Admiral Compton is critically wounded, captain." Arlington could feel the blood drain from her face as she listened to Blandon's stricken voice. "They're not sure he'll survive."

Squadron Captain Davis Jenkins reclined back, his command chair heavily retracted, in position to deploy the acceleration couch. He had been waiting for the word from Admiral Compton to begin his attack run. It was T+11 minutes now, and he was getting worried. He'd tried to reach Bunker Hill twice, but it looked like her com was out. He was about to give the order himself and lead Task Group A in on his own initiative.

"I have a communication from Commander Harmon, sir." Ensign Lambert, the communications officer, his voice shrill with excitement. "We are to commence operation X-Ray immediately."

Jenkins frowned. He'd expected Compton to give the order himself. Well, he thought, the admiral has a lot on his plate right now. "Very well, ensign. Send the acknowledgement…and order the squadron to execute in three zero seconds from my mark." He looked over at the communications officer as he spoke.

Jenkins was nervous, even more so than he'd normally be in combat. He was a perfectionist who believed in doing something over and over again until it was flawless. But here he was, ready to lead ten suicide boats on a completely different kind of mission. He had no idea what to expect…no one had ever done what his people were about to do.

It was probably safer than a normal attack…they wouldn't be getting nearly as close to the enemy as they would on a conventional torpedo run. But the newness of it all had him running his mind over the mission plan again and again. They needed it to go well…the fleet's entire escape plan depended on it.

Jenkins took a deep breath. "Ensign Lambert, put me on group-wide com." It was time.

"Yes, sir." There was a brief delay as Lambert set up the connection. "You are on the line, sir. All ship captains standing by."

"Task Group A will commence Operation X-Ray immediately." Jenkins spoke clearly and confidently. It was time to go into action, time to drive away his doubts. "Key off Bearclaw in group order. Thirty second intervals." He paused, then added, "I'm expecting every one of you to land these things in place. Good luck to you all, and I'll see you on the other side of the warp gate."

"Lieutenant Warne, execute Operation X-Ray." Jenkins leaned back in his chair. Bearclaw would be thrusting, though not enough to require the acceleration couches to deploy. Not yet, at least.

Jenkins could hear the familiar sound of the engines. In truth, it was more a tactile sensation than a sound…a gentle but perceptible vibration you could feel on every surface. The pressure was noticeable too, but they were only blasting at 3g, and he was used to much worse than that. It was hard to move around, certainly, but Bearclaw's veteran crew could tolerate 3g all day.

The operation was simple, far less involved than attacking conventionally. The ships of the task group were moving laterally behind the retreating Second Fleet. Once in position they would begin dropping their cargo, screening the rear of the fleet with 120 small buoys. Then they would run for it, following the rest of Second Fleet through the warp gate. If they moved quickly enough they had a chance to escape.

"Sir, the heavy load is affecting our course. The navcom is requesting permission to compensate." Ensign Lambert paused, reading the figures on his screen. "It will be a 5.5g burn for four minutes, sir. Commencing in 50 seconds." Lambert turned to face the captain.

Jenkins sighed, though he tried to keep it soft. He wasn't really surprised. Bearclaw had been stripped down, with every non-essential system torn out to make room for the buoys. Even the plasma torpedo tubes were gone. The normally sleek hull was cluttered with external racks holding more of the ship's precious cargo. There hadn't been time to balance the loads and properly adjust the engines.

"Authorize the maneuver, ensign." We can handle 5.5g for four minutes without the couches, he thought. It was going to suck, but they could do it. "Put me on shipwide com, ensign."

Lambert worked his board for a few seconds. "You are on the line, captain."

"Attention all personnel. Prepare for 5.5g thrust in approximately 30 seconds. The burn will be roughly four minutes, ten seconds in duration." He wanted to warn the crew. They could handle the 5.5g if they hunkered down, but if they weren't careful he was going to have a lot of broken bones and dislocations on his hands.

"Enhanced burn in ten seconds." Lambert made the announcement matter-of-factly. "Five, four, three, two, one…"

Jenkins braced himself in the command chair, trying not to make any unnecessary movements. He focused on his breathing…forcing air into your lungs at 5.5g took a bit of an effort. His back hurt; it was an old injury, and anything over 4g really brought back the pain. Bearclaw's command chair was fairly hard and uncomfortable when the acceleration couch was retracted, a design flaw Jenkins was hard-pressed to explain. Surely the architects who designed the class realized the couch wouldn't be deployed for moderate gee maneuvers. Just another inexplicable fact, he thought, mildly annoyed.

"Returning to 3g thrust in ten seconds." Lambert's voice was a little strained, but he was spot on with the timing. The four minutes had passed quickly.

Jenkins let out a breath as he felt the pressure drop off.

Bearclaw was still blasting at 3g, so the relief was only partial. They were still carrying around three times their normal weight...or at least the equivalent.

"Approaching deployment zone." It was the ship's AI this time. The buoys were to be dropped off at precise locations, and the overall plan had been locked into Bearclaw's master AI. "Initial deployment in 30 seconds."

Jenkins shifted around in his chair, trying to get comfortable...or at least less uncomfortable. There was nothing for him to do right now. The ship was on course, and the AI would direct the buoy deployment. About halfway through, the navcom would spin Bearclaw on her positioning thrusters and begin decelerating and altering the ship's vector toward the warp gate...and escape.

His people would be in the couches before the buoys activated and gave the First Imperium ships a little surprise. Bearclaw's crew would have to wait and watch the vids to see the show. If they made it through the warp gate in time.

Elizabeth Arlington sat in her command chair, the exhaustion burning in every part of her body. The last dose of stims was wearing off...she could feel the fuzziness coming back, the dull headache that reminded her she hadn't slept in three days. Or was it four?

Bunker Hill had just transited, and only the four cruisers that had remained to escort the fleet's wounded flagship remained in Point Epsilon...and they would be coming through any minute. Arlington blinked a few times, trying to clear the prickly lights from her vision. People had been arguing for a century about the effects of a warp gate transit. Some insisted they became nauseous; others said they felt a stabbing pain. Many insisted there was no effect at all. Arlington always saw spots, dancing lights in front of her eyes. The image was there whether her eyes were open or closed, but it only lasted a few minutes, a minor inconvenience for circumventing Einstein's speed limits on interstellar travel.

She let out a long breath...she wasn't sure how she'd had so much air in her lungs. It was a small miracle she was alive, that any of them were. She'd been sure Bunker Hill was done for. Commander Jackson worked wonders even getting the reactor and engines back online, but at 30% power there was no way Second Fleet's flagship could outrun the pursuing First Imperium task force.

Then Operation X-Ray commenced. Task Group A had done its job perfectly, creating a screen between Second Fleet and its pursuers. The buoys held their position for 25 minutes, until the enemy fleet reached the designated range. Ten seconds later, 120 massive, bomb-pumped x-ray lasers fired simultaneously. They fired at a range that far exceeded that of any energy weapon the enemy had seen the humans use, and they tore into the exotic alloys of the First Imperium hulls far more effectively than standard lasers.

They were one-shot weapons, consumed by the nuclear explosions that powered them. But they were exponentially more powerful than anything the Alliance had ever deployed. Three of the Gargoyles were destroyed, and at least ten others damaged.

"They're decelerating!" Commander Krimm was a seasoned spacer, but the sight of a First Imperium fleet trying to break off was too much for even the grimmest veteran to contain, and his excitement was obvious. "They appear to be ceasing pursuit, captain!"

Arlington hadn't quite believed the words when she first heard them. But Krimm turned out to be correct – the enemy was indeed ceasing pursuit. Bunker Hill would escape after all. *It's a good thing they don't know we're out of those laser buoys,* she thought. In truth, Second Fleet was a spent force. They'd thrown everything they had at the enemy, everything that could do some good at least. With nothing left but standard lasers, the fleet wouldn't have been much more than target practice for the enemy particle accelerators. But the First Imperium forces didn't know that.

Arlington was lost in her thoughts of the last couple days. Krimm was saying something to her; she could hear his voice in the distance. She wasn't really listening, but she'd gotten enough to know it wasn't important, so she waved him off. For the first time in days there wasn't a crisis, at least not an imminent one. The ship, the whole fleet, was relatively safe, headed back toward Sandoval. And the admiral was in medical stasis, critically injured, but stable.

The admiral. She'd thought she lost him for a while there. He was a good friend, the closest she'd ever had. More than a friend, she thought, though she rarely let herself acknowledge that. Now the relief washed over her, for Compton and for the ship. She was grimy, sliding around inside her survival suit in three day old sweat. She wasn't sure what she wanted more, a shower or some sleep, but she was going to pull rank to get one of them.

"Commander Krimm, you have the con." She stood up stiffly, sorely. At least we're only at 1g right now, she thought. That, she knew, wouldn't last much longer, but she was grateful for what she could get. "I'll be in my quarters."

"Yes, captain." Krimm stood up, almost as painfully as Arlington, and walked slowly over to the command chair.

Arlington allowed herself a little smile as she walked through the hatch. It was a short walk - her quarters were just a few meters from the bridge. Well, she thought...the Battle of Point Epsilon is over...and we kicked their asses!

Chapter 6

Bridge – AS Hornet
HP 56548 System
Approaching Planet Newton

"Scanning report?" He had asked at least three times in the last hour. Ensign Carp knew to report anything out of the ordinary immediately, but Jacobs kept asking anyway. Hornet was on silent running, on a course almost directly toward the system's third planet. Newton had been a colony, the farthest out on the frontier and the first place the enemy had attacked. Jacobs didn't expect to find anyone alive, but he hadn't expected any survivors on Adelaide either. Hornet was out here scouting behind enemy lines, hoping for a chance to hurt the First Imperium forces, but it was their primary duty to see if any Alliance civilians were still alive out here.

"Scanner clear, sir." Carp was very adept with the sensors, and he worked them for all they were worth. Still, with no pre-positioned buoys or orbital satellites to access, Hornet's ability to scan the system was limited. There could be a First Imperium task force out there somewhere, and they wouldn't know…not unless they got very close or the enemy ships blasted along at full power.

"Very well. Compute minimum necessary burn to enter Newton orbit." Going into orbit was a huge risk. If the enemy had satellites deployed or a force on the surface, Hornet would be detected immediately. They were much safer out in interplanetary space, but Jacobs had to confirm the Newton colonists were all dead.

"Yes, sir." Carp took a few seconds, punching keys on his workstation. "Course computed, sir. I have set minimum detection profile as the prime variable." There were a variety of intensity and duration combinations that would bring the ship into orbit, but minimizing the chance of detection was essential. "It's a 1.75g burn for 87 seconds." He worked his controls again for a few seconds. "Locked into the navcom, sir. Ready to execute."

Jacobs looked out over the bridge for a few seconds. Hornet had been scouting for almost two months, moving deeper into the void, toward First Imperium space. They'd scanned three enemy task forces, all heading directly toward Adelaide's system and, presumably, farther up the line. He hoped that Cooper and his people were keeping their heads low. It didn't seem like the enemy was interested in Adelaide, but the system was a highway to the front. "Execute." He held his breath for a few seconds. He'd just put his ship at greater risk than at any time since leaving Adelaide.

The feeling of weightlessness was suddenly replaced by almost two gravities of pressure. The burn was a light one, and the forces involved were moderate, but after spending most of the last two months in freefall, the feeling of almost twice normal weight was a shock. Jacobs leaned back in his chair, trying to position himself as comfortably as he could.

"Watch those scanners, ensign."

"Yes, sir." Carp's voice was rock-solid. The crew had been getting brittle, edgy. They were deep behind enemy lines, sneaking around, using as little power as possible. That meant no simulated gravity and minimal heat and life support. Physical misery was worsened by the brutal tension. One slip up, one bit of bad luck, and they'd be detected. And then they'd all die. The stress was constant. That slip could come at any time. There wasn't a second they could let their guard down, not an instant they could relax and feel safe. But Ensign Carp was as focused as he was the day they'd left Adelaide. "Orbital insertion in ten seconds, sir."

Jacobs took a deep breath and counted silently. He felt the abrupt change as the engines shut down and Hornet slid into orbit. The feeling of freefall was a physical relief, but his stomach was still clenched with worry. There was no way of knowing if anything had detected them, but if it was a ship within weapons range, they'd find out soon enough.

"Lieutenant Mink, I'm going down to the surface." He stood up slowly, allowing his magnetic boots to grip the floor. "You have the con."

Mink had a troubled look on her face. "Sir, I don't think you should take the risk of joining the landing party." She hesitated, trying to decide exactly what to say. Challenging a superior officer's directives was a delicate art. "I suggest you send me instead."

Jacobs smiled. Mink was a good officer. She didn't have Carp's natural ability, but she was dedicated, and her service record was excellent. She was right. By the book, Jacobs had no place on that shuttle. But they were way beyond the book now.

"I appreciate your concern, lieutenant, but I want to have a look down there for myself." His expression became serious. "And while you are in command, your priority is to the ship, not to the landing party or to me. Understood?"

Mink forced herself to look back at Jacobs. "Yes, sir."

"Very well. Please instruct Ensign Ving to meet me at the shuttle…and Sergeant Lasken and one of his Marines." He turned away and walked slowly to the dropshaft, gripping the ladder and pulling himself carefully down to the shuttle bay without another word.

Jacobs felt an odd chill. The sun was shining and the weather warm, but he shivered nonetheless. The shuttle had put down just outside the settlement, and they could see immediately it was nothing but a lifeless ruin. There was an eerie feeling to it, like a tomb. Death was hanging in the air, still and cold.

The Marines took the point, heading toward the blasted village. Jacobs followed, but he knew in his gut there was no one left alive on Newton. He didn't think there were any First Imperium fighters remaining either. It looked like they'd left sometime after they wiped out the inhabitants. There was nothing but the silence, a haunting stillness.

"Captain, there's no one alive in the village." Sergeant Lasken's voice was loud in his earpiece. "It looks safe, sir."

Jacobs hadn't been waiting…he was already at the main entrance. It looked like there had been a good-sized gate there before, but the entire section of fence around the entry was blasted apart, nothing remaining but a few shattered remnants lying about on the torn up ground.

There were bodies inside, or at least the remnants of colonists who had lain unburied for more than three years. They weren't much more than bleached bones now, with a few hunks of withered tissue still attached. But Jacobs could tell they had been running when they were killed. He could imagine the scene in his head: men, women, children…fleeing, screaming, driven in terror to try to escape the village that had been their home, but now was their graveyard. He pictured the relentless machines, moving forward, gunning down the helpless civilians with no pity, no hesitation. He could feel the anger, the hatred. He'd seen enough. He was sure there was no one alive on Newton. There was nothing his people could do there. "Ok, people, let's…"

"Captain!" It was Ensign Ving on the com. "We've got a Gamma-3 signal from Hornet."

Jacobs felt a new surge of tension in his stomach. Gamma-3…enemy contact. Hornet would be running silent by now, sitting and hoping to remain undetected. The last thing the landing party could do was launch the shuttle. The thrust needed to get into orbit would be detectable for millions of kilometers. They'd just have to sit and wait…and hope the enemy passed by. Otherwise, Hornet would be doomed…and Jacobs and his party would be marooned on a dead planet deep in enemy territory.

"What the hell are those?" It started as a silent thought, but Jacobs blurted it out. Hornet was running silent, and the scanners had picked up what looked like two First Imperium ships blasting almost directly toward them at 10g. They didn't match any previously known enemy design. "Looks like we stumbled onto a new ship class."

The landing party had gotten a good scare, but the enemy task force that triggered the Gamma-3 alert passed right by and through the system. Jacobs and his people on the surface were marooned but not for long. Other than spending a few nerve-wracking days eating emergency rations they were unscathed and waiting when Lieutenant Mink's communication gave them the all clear to return to the ship.

After his delayed return, Jacobs decided Hornet would continue exploring. It was the only way he could think of to contribute to the fight, to hurt the enemy. And after what he'd just seen, he desperately wanted to lash out. Newton had been the most remote human colony and the first place the enemy had attacked, but now Hornet was well beyond the borders of the Alliance, deeper into unexplored space than any navy ship had ever ventured. They'd advanced cautiously, on silent running as much as possible, but they hadn't passed any new enemy forces since leaving Newton. Until now.

"We have data incoming, captain." Ensign Carp may or may not have realized Jacobs was thinking out loud, but he tried to answer the captain's question anyway. "They're fairly large, about 90,000 tons." Carp paused, staring at the information coming to his screen. "The design is significantly different than any of their other ships. They appear to be constructed of consecutive circular sections."

Jacobs nodded his acknowledgement. "Lieutenant Mink, any sign they've detected us?"

"No, sir." Mink turned to face the captain. "There's no way to be sure, but it looks like we're still hidden." She paused, a troubled look on her face. "But our current course will take us within 2,000,000 kilometers of the nearest ship. It will be a miracle if they don't find us. And if we execute a burn this close to change our vector we might as well be lighting a flare."

Damned if we do, damned if we don't, Jacobs thought, silently this time. "We'll have to make a run for it." He inhaled deeply. "They may not chase us. There are only two ships, and they may be needed farther forward." He didn't sound convinced, which wasn't surprising, because he wasn't. It was a shot in the dark, but the only thing he could he could think of.

"Sir, the AI is chewing on the enemy vessels' stats." Ensign Carp again, his voice somewhat distracted, deep in his own thoughts. "The readings are very odd."

"How so, ensign?"

"For starters, sir, it doesn't appear to mount any weaponry, at least none we can detect at this range. The hull is perfectly smooth. No external missiles, no ports for internal launchers or particle accelerators." He paused then looked up from his screen. "Very strange."

"I want you to analyze every bit of data we get from that ship, ensign." Jacobs was definitely puzzled. Every First Imperium ship class that had been encountered to date was heavily armed, even the supply vessels. Either this ship had some different type of armament, something they didn't know how to look for, or it was a complete departure from the rest of the enemy fleet. "Every detail."

"Yes, sir." Carp paused, but only for a few seconds. "Another thing, captain...the ships are putting out a much larger energy signature than they should be." He stared down at his screen, rechecking his calculations. "Based on previous data for First Imperium vessels, they are using at least twice the energy they should be at their current thrust level." Another pause, longer this time. "A significant amount of the energy expenditure is spread throughout the vessel, sir. It's almost as if..." His voice trailed off.

Jacobs stared over at Carp. "As if what, ensign?"

"Sorry, sir. It's almost as if there is some sequence of systems distributed along the vessel, all of which use an enormous amount of energy." His voice was distracted as he spoke, and his eyes didn't move from his workstation. "Fuck...," he muttered under his breath.

"Ensign?"

"Captain..." Carp's head snapped upright and turned to face Jacobs. "...I think those are antimatter transport ships. The energy expenditure could be from the containment systems."

Carp was making a wild leap, and Jacobs knew it. But Hornet's captain was immediately convinced anyway. It made sense. It explained the anomalies. He knew in his gut the gifted young officer was right. "Calculate projected energy required to contain that much antimatter, ensign, and compare to the data from those ships." Jacobs was asking for the wildest of conjecture. They had no idea what technology the First Imperium used to trap antimatter. All Carp could do was extrapolate from the Alliance's own nascent process and then estimate the superiority of the enemy systems the best he could. In other words, guess. But antimatter had to be contained, that was as true for the First Imperium as it was for the Alliance. Otherwise it would annihilate immediately with whatever matter was at hand. And containing massive amounts of antimatter would require a lot of energy, even with the First Imperium's advanced technology.

Carp worked the numbers several ways, but he still ended up making up at least half of it. "Sir, I believe my hypothesis is correct, though we lack the data to reliably confirm."

Jacobs, leaned back in his chair, thinking. It did make sense. They were way behind the front lines, and the enemy wouldn't be expecting any human warships here. They'd most likely consider this a safe zone for transporting the precious material closer to the front. He wondered, could Hornet take these ships out? She still had all 8 plasma torpedoes, and an antimatter transport was bound to be fragile. All his attack had to do was breach a single containment system. The stored antimatter would do the rest.

But if he was wrong, if these were some other type of ship, if they had any weapons…Hornet wouldn't stand a chance. The bridge was silent, everyone waiting for the captain's response. Finally, he spoke, his voice grimly determined. "Good work, Ensign Carp." He turned his head toward Mink's position. "Battlestations, lieutenant."

Chapter 7

Tewksbury Steppe
Planet Sandoval
Delta Leonis IV
"The Line"

General Isaac Merrick leaned back in the hard plastic seat. The interior of the heavy main battle tank was cramped, but he was getting used to it. Merrick had emigrated to escape from the disgrace heaped on him after he returned to Earth, having failed to crush the rebellion on Arcadia. He was treated unfairly, made a scapegoat for the embarrassing failures Alliance Gov suffered on most of the rebelling worlds. Merrick had been a creature of the Alliance system and, born into its upper class, he'd never questioned it…until then. But what he'd seen on Arcadia made him reconsider everything he'd believed all his life, and the way he was sacrificed when he returned made it clear to him where he stood. There was no place for him on Earth anymore.

Emigrating wasn't an easy choice for a member of the political class. He was used to a way of life, to certain preferences and privileges that came with his station and, even in disgrace, he would enjoy those perquisites the rest of his life. Leaving Earth meant giving it all up. Most of the colonies were young societies, and they had strongly egalitarian social structures, with no entrenched upper classes ruling over the rest. He'd come to admire it, but living with it would be something different entirely.

There was another problem as well, or at least he'd expected there to be. He had led an army against the rebels on one of the most important colony worlds, and he'd come close to defeating them. Thousands of Arcadians had died fighting his troops, including their immensely popular commander, William

Thompson. He wasn't at all sure the colonials, his former enemies, would accept him, and even if they did, he had no idea what he'd do. His only trade was soldiering, and he couldn't imagine the Marines would take him into their ranks.

Merrick was stunned when he met with General Gilson at the Marine HQ on Armstrong. She welcomed him and extended an invitation to work as a consultant, assisting with the rebuilding of the Corps. More surprisingly, Kyle Warren was there too, recently reactivated as a brigadier general, and he too welcomed Merrick. Warren had commanded the army that faced Merrick on Arcadia. The two old enemies shook hands and vowed to work together.

The First Imperium incursion changed everything. When the Powers realized what was happening and agreed to work together, the governments tried to move as much force to the front as possible. Once they understood the situation, the politicians wanted the enemy defeated as far from Earth as possible. But the terrestrial armies were generally inferior to the spaceborne forces, and masses of unarmored infantry were useless against First Imperium battle robots.

Heavy tanks were another story. Combined had been were rare in colonial wars. Battle in space was dominated by logistical concerns, vastly more than warfare on Earth. Battlefields were separated by lightyears, and even with the warp gates, ships had to carry troops and equipment millions of kilometers to the front lines. Moving and supporting more than token forces of tanks, planes, and artillery was simply not practical. Colonial warfare had been the province of light troops, and over time those mobile forces developed into powered infantry. The improvement of combat armor had brought heaviness to the spaceborne formations without massively increasing their logistical requirements.

But now all the nations of Earth were united, and every spacecraft capable of transporting military supplies had been requisitioned. Some of those ships began carrying forces from Earth, mostly tanks and aircraft. And when an Alliance tank corps arrived on Sandoval, Cain immediately sacked the commanders from Earth and sent for Merrick. The fired officers were all members of the political class, and it would cause a firestorm on Earth. But Cain didn't give a rat's ass.

Cain had met Merrick on Arcadia, when the Alliance general surrendered his forces to Kyle Warren's rebel army. He'd gotten a good impression, one that was reinforced by Warren's obvious respect for the former federal commander. Merrick was a soldier, a professional. He'd fought on the other side in the rebellions, but he done so honorably and without the sadism displayed by many of the other federal generals. The Marines were happy to welcome a new friend and ally, one who, by all accounts, was also highly competent.

The M-275 "Scott" main battle tank was one of the most awesome instruments of war ever built by man. Massing 380 tons and powered by dual 2.3 gigawatt fusion reactors, the Scott's main armament was a heavy coilgun that fired a 6 kilogram projectile at hypersonic velocities, a perfect weapon against First Imperium Reapers…as long as the targeting was accurate enough.

Merrick had been training his people incessantly since the first battalions deployed. The Earth-based forces were markedly inferior to the Marines, and he was determined to close as much of that gap as he could before the invaders reached Sandoval. He'd stripped the infantry formations from the tank units – sending troops out onto this battlefield without powered armor would be nothing but murder. Cain agreed, and he transferred Marine companies to support the tank battalions. The Marines sent to Merrick's corps were all veterans, but they had little experience supporting armored vehicles. They were working day and night on combined arms drills, and they were starting to become proficient. This was what Merrick had spent most of his career studying, and it was one area where Holm and Cain and the rest of the Marines had to rely on him.

The Tewksbury Steppe was a vast region of high grasslands, stretching over the eastern edge of the primary population corridor on the northern continent. It was perfect tank country, and it ran along the likeliest axis of advance for the First Imperium forces. So if the enemy didn't come in and give his dug in tanks a fight he'd have the chance to go mobile and hit them in the flank. Assuming, of course, they behaved as expected. Merrick thought that was a good bet. General Cain was one of the most gifted tacticians he'd ever seen, and the First Imperium forces tended to be highly formulaic and predictable. He would bet on Cain any day in that match up.

Merrick had over 600 tanks, and he was determined to position every one of them individually. He was staring at the deployment display – his command tank was loaded with extra electronics to help him keep tabs on the entire corps. He was happy with the progress, but there was still work to do. For one thing, his supply line was too exposed. His engineers were excavating a sunken roadway for transports to bring up supplies, but there was heavy rock just below the steppe, and work was moving slowly.

"General Merrick?" It was Erik Cain's voice on the com.

"Yes, general?" Merrick's tone was reverently respectful. He had only been part of 1st Army for two months, but he'd already fallen under Cain's spell. His new commander was a welcome change from the inbred political appointees that filled the top positions in the terrestrial army.

"I'm calling a meeting of senior commanders for 17:00 hours." Sandoval's day was a little over 23 Earth hours, but it was divided into 24 slightly segments, each slightly shorter than a terrestrial hour. "My HQ."

"Yes, sir."

"And Isaac...if you've got any deployments you think are crucial, get someone on them now." His voice was relentlessly steady, without a hint of fear, but Merrick suddenly felt a fist in his own gut. "I just got word from the warp gate...120 First Imperium ships just transited."

"No, Erik." Sarah's voice was shrill, not quite angry, but definitely upset. "You can just forget about that idea." She was standing outside the bathroom door, her wet hair splayed across the back of her silk robe.

"Listen to me, Sarah." Cain's voice was hoarse and frustrated. He had enough to deal with; he didn't need this from her. "This is going to be a different kind of battle. Things are going to get bad. Very bad." He walked toward her and put his hands on her shoulder. "I don't want you here. I want you safe. Go back to Armstrong."

She turned abruptly, shaking his hands from her shoulders. "Things are going to be bad? Like on Carson's World?" She shoved a wet hank of hair out of her face. "Like a dozen other places I've served? Who do you think I am? Some country doctor?" She was getting more and more upset as she spoke. A lot of it was the stress coming out; she'd been worried about Erik for a long time now. She'd always been able to reach him, to ease his tension, usually the only one who could. But not this time. He'd withdrawn into someplace deep inside himself, and it scared her. She didn't know what to do, how to help him. But she was mad too. How dare he treat her like some fragile thing that needed to be protected. She'd lived through as much horror as he had, from the worst slums in the Alliance to the fiercest battles the Corps had fought. Sarah Linden could take care of herself, and she wasn't going to let anyone think differently. Not even the love of her life.

"Sarah, no one is doubting your courage." He was getting more frustrated. God, he thought, she is so pigheaded. "But hell is going to erupt on this world. I know…I'm going to unleash it." He stared into her eyes, wordlessly begging her. "Please, just go back to Armstrong. The hospital there needs you."

She stared back at him, and she could feel the tears welling up in her eyes. "Damn you, Erik. I'm a Marine too, and I've been one as long as you have. Longer." Her voice was softer, but the anger was obvious. "How can you ask me to run away just before a battle? After all the times I've supported you? Don't you think I was terrified when you went to Earth to rescue Augustus? But I didn't ask you to go hide somewhere."

Cain's face was contorted with exasperation. "I'm not saying you can't handle yourself. You know I don't think that. But I need to be focused. I can't be worried about you in the middle of the battle. Stop being so stubborn."

She could feel her whole body tense. She loved him with all her heart, but he could be the most irritating person too. How could he call her stubborn? She'd never met anyone as infuriatingly obstinate as Erik Cain. "This is the largest force the Corps has ever put into the field, against the toughest enemy." She was appealing to his rationality. "There are going to be tens of thousands of casualties here, and no one will run the field hospitals better than me. I'll save lives here, Erik, and you know it."

"But, Sarah…"

"No buts." She felt the flood of anger, and she cut him off before he said another word. "My duty is here, and I'm staying. I can save Marines here. After all the years I've watched you thrash around in bed and sit up nights, plagued by guilt…you would ask me to leave when I know I will save lives if I stay?" She felt herself going too far, but she had a temper just like his, and she couldn't stop. "For the last year we've all watched yourself insist on taking the blame for Jax's death. How dare you ask me to run away and hide on Armstrong. Then I would be to blame for all the deaths…all the men and women I could have saved." Her breath became a little short, and she wished immediately she could swallow those words, at least the part about Jax.

Cain was looking right at her. He didn't say anything at first, but she could see the pain in his eyes. He hesitated, forcing back the emotions he kept buried. Anyone else would have faced a titanic barrage of rage and invective. Finally, he swallowed hard and spoke quietly. "I can order you to go."

She took a deep breath. "Only if you're prepared to court martial me and have me escorted off-planet." She stared back at him, holding her ground, trying to keep herself together.

Cain held her gaze for a few seconds, perhaps half a minute. Then he turned and walked out of the room without another word. Sarah managed to control her emotions until the hatch closed, but then the tears came. She and Erik almost never argued, and she hated the feeling. She was angry at herself for hurting him. But she was who she was, and nothing could change that. She wasn't going anywhere.

Cain walked down the corridor, his fists balled in frustration. She didn't understand; she didn't understand at all. It wasn't that he didn't trust her, that he thought she had to be protected. He trusted her more than anyone he'd ever known. She was all he really cared about, and he didn't want her to see him, what he was becoming. But it was more than that. He was going to win this battle, and he was prepared to sacrifice anything to do it. The men and women under his command, his own life… anything. Anything but her.

"I agree, Augustus." Cain was sitting in his office in 1st Army's underground HQ bunker. The short delay endemic to orbital communications was driving him crazy, as it always did. Patience was never his biggest strength. But he had bigger things to worry about. "There's nothing to gain giving battle now. The laser buoys and the bombers will wear them down, but you know as well as I do you don't have a chance to take out the whole fleet." He paused for a few seconds. "And you know that's what it will take…wiping out every one of them."

Neither of them kidded themselves about that being a possibility. To Garret's horror – and Cain's inexplicable apathy – the scanners had reported eleven of the Leviathans, along with over 100 Gargoyles and Gremlins. Giving a pitched battle would be suicide – it would play right into the enemy's strengths.

Gremlins had come through first, backed up by ten Gargoyles. Garret had positioned a screening force, but it was overwhelmed by the enemy vanguard and driven away from the warp gate. Only then did the main body transit, safely screened by its lighter units and, presumably, bristling with antimatter weapons. A direct defense of the planet would be suicide.

"If I had both First and Second Fleets in the line, then maybe." Garret was still trying to rationalize. He hated leaving Cain and his people on the planet without even giving the invaders a serious fight in space. But Second Fleet had been depleted at Point Epsilon, and it would be at least two months, and maybe more, before it was reinforced and resupplied. Then, maybe things would be different.

"I want them here, Augustus." Cain's voice was as grim and determined as anything Garret had ever heard. "I want them to land. We're ready. These bastards are going to walk right into the fires of hell."

Garret felt a passing shiver. Like the rest of Cain's close friends, Garret had been worried about him since the Battle of Farpoint. But this was something new, something different. Erik Cain had always been resolute and stubborn, but now he was like a force of nature, relentless and terrible. Garret wasn't sure if he thought his friend was still sane, but he had a feeling Cain was just what they needed now. He hoped there would be a man left when the war was won.

"Ok, Erik." Garret's voice was resigned. He wasn't happy, but he knew what had to be done. "I'm going to do everything I can to sting them as they come in, but then I'll withdraw out of the system. When Second Fleet links up with us we'll be back." He paused, feeling the tension throughout his body. "And that will be one hell of a counterattack...I promise you." Assuming you can hold out that long, he thought.

"We'll be here, sir." Cain's tone was dark, cold, utterly without doubt. "The ships are yours to take out when you can. The ground forces are mine." His voice was like ice.

"I'll keep you advised right up until we bug out." Garret took a deep breath, then another. "Good luck, Erik." His voice became lower, sadder. "Take care of yourself."

"Good luck to you too, Augustus. Happy hunting." Cain cut the line and leaned back in his chair. He thought back over the years...his days in the violent slums of New York, the battles he'd fought, and the men and women he'd seen fed into the meatgrinder. It started to make sense to him. All his life had been preparing him for this day. He would be the perfect warrior, cold, fearless, without fatigue. He would pay his debt here, to all the men and women he'd lost in battle. This was their fight too.

Cain had lost the trepidation about the enemy, the strange fear that seemed to grip even hardened veterans when facing the relentless robotic foe. He regretted the lack of emotion in his enemy, but not because he feared them. He wished they could feel, that they were gripped with fear. Destroying them wasn't enough; Cain wanted them to suffer…he wanted them lying in the mud bleeding to death, crying for their mothers and tearfully picturing the friends and family they'd never see again. He ached for them to feel every wretched emotion his own men and women did, to cling to the shreds of whatever spirituality they had and face death scared and alone. He hated the enemy, hated them with a passion that few could understand. There had always been a dark place in his mind, where he'd kept the resentment, the anger, the bitterness. Now he embraced it, letting the blackness wash over him. He would be death incarnate to the enemy. He would match their relentlessness measure for measure, and he would destroy them all. He would shove his humanity into that place now, lock it away out of reach. He wouldn't be needing it.

Chapter 8

High Energy Physics Lab 3
Combined Powers Research Facility
Carson's World – Epsilon Eridani IV

"I think we have small-scale containment under control."
Friederich Hofstader was hunched over a large plasti-steel work-
table, clad like the others in the room, in a hooded protective
suit. He was working quickly and being far too aggressive to
take normal precautions. He'd been down with radiation sickness half a dozen times, but the treatments only took a few days,
and then he was back at work. He knew it was hard on his body,
but that didn't seem very important right now. The casualty
figures kept coming in from the front, and they put things into
perspective. He knew those Marines, at least some of them, and
as brave and well-trained as they were, they didn't have a chance
in this fight. Not without the technological advances streaming out of his labs. And if they could fight and die against an
enemy possessing godlike weapons and technology, Friederich
Hofstader figured the least he could do was work himself – and
everyone on Carson's World – into the ground to try and give
them the tools they needed.

"I think you're right, Friederich." Adam Crandall was leaning across the table from the other side, staring intently at the
scale model that stood between the two of them. "We need to
build a test version as soon as possible."

Hofstader had restructured the entire research operation,
and the results had been immediate and profound. New discoveries had been flowing steadily from the Carson's World labs,
and they'd already begun to contribute enormously to the war
effort. Men and women were fighting with weapons developed

in his facility, and that made the effort worthwhile.

The whole job had been made a lot easier by the order from Admiral Garret and the other Alliance commanders giving him absolute authority on Epsilon Eridani IV…and the battalion of Martian Marines sent by Roderick Vance had made implementation of that order downright simple.

Hofstader had ruthlessly purged the place, expelling everyone who was choked with procedure and slowing the progress of the research mission. He brought in his own people, handpicked from those he felt were best able to contribute. His list deviated considerable from the seniority rosters from Earth's universities and research facilities. A lot of pompous windbags with strong political connections had howled, but he really didn't care. The uproar might have meant something once, but not now. He had Garret, Holm, and Vance at his back, and no one was going to challenge that group, certainly not while the war was going on. His position had been solidified further when Garret was appointed supreme military commander of the Grand Pact, and placed at the top of the multi-national organization chart. No one would question Garret's orders now, not even the politicians on Earth.

The invasion had seemed surreal to Earth's elites at first, but by now the ruling classes of the Superpowers were terrified, cowering, praying for Garret and his military to save them. They realized their gilded towers in Washbalt and St. Petersburg and Hong Kong wouldn't save them if First Imperium forces reached Earth. They would die as miserably as any Cog bleeding to death in a back alley. Ideology and elitism normally dictated affairs on Earth, but now it was fear that trumped all.

By all accounts, Crandall should have been one of those shipped off-planet. Hofstader considered him to be one of the greatest minds he'd ever encountered, but the Alliance scientist had been a creature of academia, his research bogged down with time-wasting procedure and bureaucracy. Crandall had been dominated by the previous director of the facility, a bully by the name of Ivan Norgov. The Russian scientist was a political animal at heart, more concerned with securing his own position than expediting the research project, and Crandall hadn't had the strength of will to oppose him. Hofstader had, and he'd been ejected from the research team for his troubles. He'd still be in exile if Garret and Vance hadn't returned him with 500 Marines at his back.

Once Norgov was gone, dragged in tears to a waiting shuttle by half a dozen Martian Marines, Crandall and Hofstader had a long talk. They discussed what was truly happening at the front and reviewed some of the video of the First Imperium forces. Since them Crandall had shed his bureaucratic paralysis, and he'd become one of the major driving forces in unraveling the planet's mysteries. Epsilon Eridani IV was the only significant cache of First Imperium technology available for research, and the ancient antimatter factory promised to reveal the secrets that would allow humanity to defeat this terrible new invader. Assuming Earth's greatest minds could bridge a millennia wide gap.

"That's very aggressive of you, Adam. Are you sure you don't want to debate things for a couple months first?" Hofstader smiled. The two had become friends as well as colleagues. "Don't worry...I've already ordered work to commence on the prototype."

Crandall returned the smile, graciously accepting Hofstader's gentle ribbing. "One of these days I'll live all that down. We've thrown out the book here, haven't we? I'm not sure what we could do to move things any faster." Crandall had been down with radiation sickness twice himself. Fully cognizant of what was at stake, he'd become almost as carelessly aggressive as Hofstader over the last year. He felt the same duty to do what he could to help the men and women fighting to save them all, and beyond that, his scientific curiosity ran wild. Removed from the society and bureaucracy of Earth-based institutions, he rediscovered his love for unraveling the secrets of the universe. The technology on Carson's World was astonishing. Things he'd vaguely hypothesized were sitting right there, fully developed and deployed. Before him, buried in the riddles of the First Imperium tech, were the answers to all his questions, the confirmation or refutation of all his theories. The work of a hundred generations of Adam Crandalls was there to be deciphered.

"I don't know how we could move things any faster either, but we're going to have to figure a way." Hofstader's voice became deeper, more serious. "We just got a communication." Crandall's eyes widened and he looked up at Hofstader. "Admiral Compton's fleet engaged the enemy at Point Epsilon." He looked over and flashed Crandall a brief smile. "The x-ray lasers were a huge success. Better than we could have hoped." The new weapon had come directly from the Carson's World labs. Colonel Sparks and his people had taken the largely theoretical design from Hofstader and Crandall and produced an operable weapon in less than five weeks. Now that system had been tested and had proven to be enormously effective.

Crandall smiled broadly. "I knew they would be useful. They're a huge leap over our normal lasers."

"They're still not a match for the enemy particle accelerators, though." Hofstader's smile began to fade. "And their uses are somewhat limited. We can't exactly detonate fusion bombs in our ships, can we?" The bomb-pumped x-ray lasers were one-shot weapons. The power source was a thermonuclear warhead that simultaneously provided the energy for the shot and destroyed the entire system.

"No, they're not a match for the enemy's weapons. But they help bridge the gap." Crandall paused, thinking quietly for a few seconds. He put his hand on the scale model on the table. "But this will be at least the equal of a particle accelerator. Maybe even better."

Hofstader laughed softly. "Yes, that's true." He paused. "If we ever get it built, and if it works the way we expect it to." He ran his hand back through his knotted, unkempt hair. "And if we manage to produce the antimatter we need to power it."

"We will." Crandall had become quite a cheerleader for the entire effort. "I'm confident we're on the right track."

"I'm glad to hear you say that, because we need to figure out how to move things even faster." He was still looking right at Crandall, but all trace of his smile was gone. "Because Compton's fleet took out a lot of the enemy at Point Epsilon, but he still had to retreat. The First Imperium force was massive, and now they're unopposed a maximum of three transits from any of the worlds on the Line." He stood like a statue, his eyes locked on Crandall's. "Things are about to get hotter."

Tom Sparks stood in the center of the massive fabrication facility. His suit protected him from the shower of molten metal landing all around. He shouldn't have been there; his place was in the control room. But they were having a problem with the firing chambers, and he hadn't been able to figure it out. He'd decided to watch the entire assembly process, and by "watch," he meant up close and personal.

His people had been working around the clock for months. They'd rushed the x-ray lasers into production, having completed the design for both the weapons and the buoys to carry them in less than two months. Project X had been a tremendous achievement, and the team's reward had been a day off, which most of them spent sound asleep. The next day they started working on Project Z.

The x-ray laser had been a major technological advance, but the gamma ray laser would be a quantum leap over that. His people had been working on replicating the First Imperium particle accelerators too, but if they could put Project Z in the field it would be potentially even more powerful.

"Stop the line." Sparks' frustration was obvious in his tone. This mix wasn't going to work either, and there was no point in wasting time finishing it. "Let's try increasing the iridium content in the alloy by another 3% and see how that holds up." He spoke into a small com unit he wore hooked on his ear. He needed to get the right combination for the components. If he could figure out how the First Imperium manufactured those dark matter infused alloys, he thought, he'd really have something. But that was a waste of time right now. The physicists were still arguing about how to capture measurable quantities of the mysterious substance; they were years away from being able to manipulate it, probably centuries.

He walked back toward the control room, stepping inside the airlock and stripping off the blue protective suit he'd been wearing. Sparks had always enjoyed being busy, but now he was being pulled in so many directions he felt like his head was going to split open. He tried to push the gamma ray laser from his mind. He had hurdles to overcome on that project, but Hofstader and Crandall had worse ones. They had to produce enough antimatter to power the thing, and they had to perfect the sustainable containment system. He was sure he'd solve his problems before they did theirs.

Now he had to check on the status of x-ray laser production. The weapon had proven its worth, but every buoy they'd been able to produce went to Second Fleet and the worlds of the Line. They needed more of them…a lot more, and they needed them quickly. That meant he had to streamline the production process.

He was about to put an improved version of the PBS into production as well. The Plasma Bombardment System had also been highly successful, and the ground commanders on the line were demanding more supply. They had produced versions that could be dropped by planes, planted as mines, and fired by artillery. Now he was finishing a revised system, one that could be mounted on an Obliterator suit, creating an almost unimaginably powerful close range weapon. There were a few final adjustments before they could start churning the things out, but he was confident they'd overcome all the major problems.

He walked slowly down the hall and through the series of doors that led outside. It had been three days since he'd seen the sun…or was it four? He needed some fresh air, even if only for a few minutes. He cleared the last security station and walked out into the dazzling light of midday. He squinted – his eyes had grown unaccustomed to the intense sun.

Looking out over the valley he was amazed at what had been accomplished on Carson's World in the past year and a half. No expense had been spared, no resource denied. A quarter of the output of Earth's economy had poured into the labs and production facilities hurriedly built on this old mining world. The secret of the First Imperium's technology was here, and this was where the weapons to defeat the enemy would be designed and produced. The planet's population had increased from a few thousand to well over a million, and more were arriving every day.

They were making progress; there was no doubt about that. By Sparks' best guess, they were advancing human technology the equivalent of a century each year. Epsilon Eridani IV was giving up the secrets of the First Imperium, but slowly, grudgingly. Sparks wondered, with grim curiosity, if it would be fast enough.

Chapter 9

Outer Defense Perimeter
Planet Sandoval
Delta Leonis System
"The Line"

"Admiral Garret, you have to transit now, sir." He could hear the insistence in Camille Harmon's voice. She was 75,000 kilometers away, but she sounded like she was standing right next to him. Garret had been compelled to appoint a commander for First Fleet when he was named supreme commander of the forces of the Grand Pact. Stupid name, he thought for at least the tenth time.

He'd managed to wear two hats and hang on to the fleet command and the top Alliance spot simultaneously, but a third position was just too much. He'd been determined to dig in his heels and stay in charge of First Fleet, but he finally realized it wasn't possible. His first pick to replace him had been Admiral West. She'd been in the thick of the fighting on the Rim, and no one had more combat experience or a better record against First Imperium fleets. But then Admiral Compton went and got himself all shot up at Point Epsilon, and Garret ended up assigning West to take over Second Fleet. He'd merged her Third Fleet into Compton's battered formation, allowing him to pull the hardest hit ships from both OBs and send them to Wolf 359 for repairs.

Compton was badly hurt, but his people had gotten him into medical stasis in time, and Garret was sure Sarah's crew on Armstrong would put him back together again. He hoped it wouldn't take too long. Terrance Compton was his oldest and closest friend…and a brilliant tactician he'd come to depend on.

Garret didn't want to fight the rest of this war without Compton; that much he knew for sure.

With West committed to Second Fleet, Harmon was an easy choice to take over his slot as commander of First. She was an accomplished officer, and she probably would have ended up with Third Fleet instead of West, but she'd still been recovering from an attempted assassination attempt. It made Garret's blood boil to think of one of his flag officers being shot by an Alliance Intelligence assassin on her own bridge. Gavin Stark was the head of the Alliance's feared spy agency, and Augustus Garret had a score to settle with the devious spymaster. More than one. But that would have to wait; this was no time for infighting.

Harmon had survived the attempt, but her spine was severed by one of the shots. Sarah and her crew did their best. They got her through it and back to duty, but not without some lingering problems. Full spine regenerations were still problematic, and Harmon had a complex combination of new tissue and sophisticated prosthetics implanted in her back. Everything worked, more or less, but she was in almost constant pain. Garret had been hesitant to put her in the front line...until he spoke to her. He walked away from that meeting knowing one thing. Camille Harmon was ready for action.

Garret sat on Lexington's flag bridge staring intently at the data streaming in from Sandoval. He was damned if he was going anywhere until he got a read on how well the defense network had performed. "I'm perfectly fine, Admiral Harmon. No need to worry. There is plenty of time to pull back."

"With all due respect, sir, you should be on Armstrong now." Harmon's voice was verging on emotional. Her concern was sincere. She hadn't faced the First Imperium forces yet, but she'd studied the intelligence reports. And she didn't like the idea of betting Garret's life that the enemy couldn't pull something unexpected out of their sleeve.

Garret sighed. His people were really starting to get on his nerves. It was well-meaning, he knew, but he wasn't a man to tolerate over-protective behavior. He'd dealt with it to a certain extent for a long time. He'd been the navy's hero since he crushed the Caliphate and CAC fleets at Gliese 250, and his career both before and since had been an almost uninterrupted series of victories. But since he'd been named the supreme commander, things had gotten considerably worse. Augustus Garret enjoyed the respect of his people, but he wasn't about to tolerate officers expecting him to cower in the rear.

"Admiral Harmon, I suggest you spend more time worrying about First Fleet and less nursemaiding me. I have no intention of leaving this system until I have analyzed the damage the defensive network inflicts on the invaders." He paused, sighing again. "I remind you, we are coming back here, and I have to develop an attack plan. I need all the data I can get."

"Very well, sir." Harmon accepted his admonishment, but it was obvious she disagreed. Garret had to suppress a small laugh. As a young officer, he'd craved glory more than anything. He'd focused relentlessly on it, taken crazy chances with his ship and crew, sacrificed everything else important in his life to pursue it. Now he had more glory than he could have imagined, and it was nothing but a burden. It was empty, hollow. The worship of his officers and crews tormented him, and now he wanted nothing more than to do his job without the medals, the accolades, the adoration. But the glory was a trap, and there was no escape.

"Admiral, we will all be out of here in time." His voice was conciliatory. Harmon was just doing her job, and her concern was reasonable. She had no way of knowing how much it grated at Garret. "Let's just stay sharp and not make any mistakes."

"Yes, sir." He could tell she'd read the change in his tone. "Understood."

"Very well, admiral. Garret out."

He rushed off the comlink. The data he was waiting for was starting to pour in. The campaign for Sandoval had begun.

"We've got reports coming in, General Cain." Captain Carter was sitting at a workstation a few meters from Cain's chair. "The enemy has entered the laser buoy perimeter. The weapons have begun firing."

Garret's people had laid a thick belt of the ECM-shielded laser satellites around Sandoval. First Fleet wasn't offering a conventional pitched battle and, without the dynamics of ship to ship action, Garret couldn't be sure what course the enemy would take. A solar system is a huge space, making it difficult to guess where to place static defenses. But he knew the enemy was heading to Sandoval, so that's where he concentrated everything. He wasn't expecting to stop them; he was just looking to blow as many of them to hell before they got to the planet.

Cain could imagine the scene unfolding in the space around the planet. The x-ray laser buoys fired one shot each, powered by 100 megaton thermonuclear explosions. The magnetic bottles contained the energy of the massive detonation for a fraction of a second before they overloaded, long enough to focus the intense power into a single, extremely powerful x-ray pulse. There were 500 of the buoys positioned around Sandoval, though probably no more than half would have a target within their firing arcs.

The lasers could hurt the First Imperium ships. One or two direct hits could destroy a Gremlin; four or five could take out a Gargoyle. Cain didn't have any idea what would be needed to seriously hurt a Leviathan. As far as he knew, none of the enemy's massive battleships had ever been significantly damaged.

Cain's people cheered as the reports came in. The lasers were scoring hit after hit, and First Imperium ships were damaged and destroyed all along the line. But Cain himself sat quietly, a somber look on his face. The ships being hit were mostly Gremlins, and Cain knew the smaller ships were expendable. He was glad to destroy any First Imperium unit, but he knew the loss of the Gremlins would have a minimal effect on the enemy's invasion plans.

"Captain Carter, I want status reports from all commanders at divisional level and above." They'd had a strategy meeting three days earlier, when they first got word of the enemy fleet transiting. "And I want them in 30 minutes."

"Yes, sir"

"And Carter...I want all formations on alert and in position in one hour." His voice was gruff and serious. "Any commander who doesn't have his people in place in an hour, I'll stand him in front of a firing squad." If Cain was exaggerating, it wasn't apparent from his tone.

"Understood, sir." Carter sounded a little nervous. He had been Cain's aide for a while now, and he was used to the intensity of 1st Army's commander. But Cain's grim resolve was like nothing he'd seen before. He wondered if the general would really shoot a commander if his forces weren't in place on time, but in the end he decided he didn't want to know. He was worried he wouldn't like the answer.

Hector had already calculated the range of times before the enemy could commence landings. The soonest was roughly 90 minutes, but that would assume they came on full bore, totally ignoring the orbital fortresses and bomber wings. The most likely time frame was 3 to 4 hours, but Cain wasn't taking any chances. His people would be buttoned up and waiting for the enemy long before then.

"Very well, captain." Cain sat quietly for a minute, running his mind methodically through his preparations. "Run a diagnostic check on the ground defenses." Cain had positioned a large number of ground-to-air missile batteries around the likeliest landing zones. He was going to make Sandoval an unrelenting hell for the First Imperium forces, and that was going to start while they were still landing. "I want everything ready to go. No mistakes."

"Yes, General Cain." Carter could feel the rumbling in his stomach, the stress and fear before the battle. Cain had everyone at a fever pitch, which was probably good for performance but only made the stress worse. Carter's eyes caught something on his screen, and his head shot around. "Sir, orbital platforms launching bombers now."

The orbital forts would have been under Cain's control if First Fleet hadn't been present, but for now they were on Admiral Harmon's OB. Just as well, he thought. He really didn't want to be bothered with it anyway. Harmon would do a much better job. Cain was a ground pounder through and through, and he was totally focused on the coming land battle.

He knew the forts were easy targets for the enemy's antimatter missiles. Whatever his own people were about to face, he didn't envy those crews up there…or the bomber teams. The forts were likely to be obliterated and First Fleet was bugging out. The pilots would be damned lucky to find a place to land when…if…they got back from their attacks.

"Happy hunting." Cain was muttering softly, wishing his best to the bomber crews he knew were launching. "Give the bastards hell."

"Here they come, people. I want this formation perfect, so pay attention." Captain Greta Hurley was focusing intently on her plotting screen. She was leading First Fleet's bombers in, and now the 10 squadrons from Sandoval's orbital forts were linking up with them. All together, there were 312 bombers, and they were all under Hurley's command. It was a massive strike force, and its commander was already a veteran of combat against the First Imperium. She had more ships than ever before, and this time she didn't have to divert half of them to anti-missile duty. Her people had inflicted damage on the enemy before, but this time she was determined to really hurt them.

She was still getting used to the new rank. A captain who didn't command a ship was a fairly uncommon creature in the Alliance navy. She was at the top of the bomber corps hierarchy, the "go to" officer to command a large fleet strike force, and her seniority had gotten her transferred to First Fleet while Second Fleet was refitting. No rest for the Alliance's foremost expert on bomber tactics against the First Imperium.

She'd been amused by some of the odd traditions ingrained in the culture of the navy. It was Captain Hurley leading the strike team, but up until her bomber had launched she was Commodore Hurley. For as long as anyone could remember, the navy had followed the mantra that there can only be one captain on a ship. The interloping second captain was generally granted a courtesy promotion to commodore while on board.

Hurley thought that was all the more bizarre a tradition, since the rank of commodore was inactive in the Alliance navy, used only to give fake ranks to superfluous captains.

"The Sandoval squadrons have assumed position in the formation, captain." The AI in her bomber had been replaced with a new enhanced system before the mission. It was now the equivalent of a ship captain's unit. "All ships are positioned within mission-specified parameters."

The AI had been programmed as her virtual assistant, but she wasn't used to interacting with it yet. She'd worked with bomber computers before, of course, but the quasi-sentient units were vastly more complicated. Should she say thank you? Treat it like a crew member?

"Thank you, Scarlett." She'd had to think up a name quickly, so she'd borrowed from her squadron, the Scarlett Hawks. She didn't actually command the Hawks anymore, but she flew with them in the formation. She had to remind herself continually to let Lieutenant Commander Barrow run the squadron. She'd flown with Barrow for over a year, and he'd been her choice to lead the Hawks. But letting go was still difficult.

"All squadrons, prepare for attack run." The ships would be going in at high thrust, their engines cutting out just before the launch to allow the crew to manually launch the torpedoes. Hurley was a big believer in combining the touch of an experienced pilot with the number crunching of the targeting computer. She leaned back, getting ready for the deployment of her couch. "Lead squadrons commence thrust in three zero seconds from my mark. Remaining formations to follow at 15 second intervals." She paused and took a quick breath. "Mark."

Hurley closed her eyes as her chair converted into the cocoon-like acceleration couch. She was breathing calmly but deeply, going over the mission one last time. She'd planned the strike carefully, working out the formation using everything she'd learned in her battles against the enemy. Everything was in place. Now it was almost time.

"Ten seconds to burn initiation, captain." Scarlett's voice was human-sounding, but non-descript. The AI would modify itself slowly, imperceptibly to match her personality. Hurley probably wouldn't even notice, but voice patterns, tone, and mannerisms would change over time, based on the system's interpretation of her needs and preferences.

"Five seconds…"

She felt the pinprick as the couch injected the drug cocktail that would strengthen her cell walls and increase her body's internal pressure. She sighed softly as she felt the sluggish feeling spread through her body. There was no ignoring the fact… the drugs made you feel like shit.

"Two…one…thrust."

Hurley was ready, but she still lost her breath as the bomber's engines fired, generating almost 30g thrust. The air pressure inside her helmet increased, partially offsetting the effect of the gee forces and helping to force oxygen into her lungs. She found heavy burns to be the most frustrating part of an operation. The strike force was operating according to her preset plan, but she knew she wouldn't be much use while they were thrusting. At 30g, it was a losing fight to hang onto lucidity… exercising effective command was out of the question.

Time became amorphous, and sensibility was warped. The burn lasted 18 minutes, but everyone in the strike force perceived something different. Some felt it had been nearly instantaneous, while to others it seemed as if days had passed. But it ended the same way for all of them…with a massive dose of stimulants, shocking them instantly out of the lethargic and hallucinogenic state induced by the drugs and gee forces.

Hurley was suddenly awake and alert. It wasn't a natural sort of feeling…there was a strange artificiality to it, as if she felt well and sickly at the same time. But it allowed her to function, and that was all that mattered. Her instinct was to target the ship's torpedoes, to direct the squadron's attack. But that wasn't her role anymore. Barrow would take care of the Hawks and direct their attack. Her job was to monitor the overall operation.

She glanced down at the plotting screen, looking for the loss reports. The strike force had blasted right through the enemy's primary point defense zone, and there were holes in the formation to prove it. The lead squadrons had lost heavily, as much as 60%. But her column attack formation once again proved to be highly effective at penetrating the outer perimeter of the enemy point defense. Overall the attacking squadrons had lost a little over 20% of their number. That left almost 250 bombers to run the final gauntlet.

The strike force was coming in at 0.03c, the squadrons stacked up in four columns. The engine burn had left each squadron on a projected intercept course with its target. As she had done at Point Epsilon, Hurley assigned a full squadron to each target...except for her column. Lined up behind the Hawks were six squadrons, all targeting a single enemy vessel. Greta Hurley was going after a Leviathan.

She had no idea how much punishment the massive battleships could take, or even how effective their close-in point defense was. But she knew the fleet had to learn how to destroy the things, and she decided it would start with her bombers.

The squadrons were coming in fast, one ship after another. The light particle accelerators of the enemy vessels raked their formations, taking out ship after ship. The bombers had come straight in, disregarding their own defense and evasive maneuvers to maximize their targeting. All along the vanguard of the First Imperium line, bombers loosed their plasma torpedoes. The weapons were held to the last minute and launched at point blank range. It cost more casualties from point defense, but almost every torpedo they fired found its mark.

Hurley watched the damage reports coming in, silently cheering each kill. Her people were ignoring the Gremlins, targeting the larger Gargoyles instead. They were savaging the enemy, but they were taking losses too. Finally, Hurley turned away from the growing casualty list. There was nothing she could do about it anyway, and there would be time to mourn later. If she made it back.

Her column hadn't fired yet; they were charging right through the front line of the enemy fleet. They took point defense fire from both flanks, and fewer than half her ships reached the Leviathan. Her Hawks were in the forefront, but there were only five left. Every one of them scored a hit.

The hulking battleship shook as the plasma torpedoes slammed into its hull one after another. Hurley's survivors scored at least 20 hits, and the Leviathan was engulfed in a cloud of superheated plasma. The space around the ship was ablaze with multi-gigaton explosions – it had managed to eject its anti-matter missiles just before the attack. Hurley swore under her breath…if they gotten there a few minutes sooner they'd have caught the thing fully armed.

She leaned back in her couch. The job was done - now it was time to get out. Her people had to make it back through the enemy forward line and somehow get back to Saratoga before she transited. The fortress squadrons were heading for the fleet too. Getting back had always been a longshot, but it was a better bet to try to make the fleet than the launch bays at Sandoval. The orbital fortresses were doomed.

She felt the couch expand around her and the familiar injections. The ship would be thrusting at 120% of capacity, a risky move, but necessary if they were going to have any chance at all of getting back in time. The massive pressure of almost 35g of thrust slammed into her, and she drifted off almost immediately. As she felt herself beginning to float away she heard a voice… Scarlett, she thought…talking about the enemy vessel…explosions…minimal power. She wondered dreamily, did we kill the Leviathan? And then she was lost in gauzy hallucinations.

Death was coming at the orbital fortresses. The first line point defense had savaged the enemy volley, and now the shotguns were raking the remaining missiles, killing dozens. But enough were going to get through…and some of them were antimatter warheads. It wouldn't take many to vaporize Sandoval's last line of defense.

The forts had lashed out themselves, sending their own barrage at the enemy fleet. A lot of their missiles were getting through the First Imperium defenses, but most of them were targeting the screen of Gremlins deployed in front of the heavier units. They were taking out ships, but they weren't doing enough to wear down the fighting power of the enemy armada. The Leviathans and most of the Gargoyles had pulled back out of range after they fired. The forts were stuck where they were.

Still, they fought on. They'd done almost all they could... almost. But their bombers were still out there, on their way back after the attack run. The fortresses were doomed, and everyone knew that. None of the Sandoval squadrons were coming back to their launch platforms. The motherships of First Fleet offered them a place to land, if they could make it in time. There were plenty of open bays on the ships; casualties had been high among the fleet's bombers. But the bombers had a long way to go, and not much time. The longer the battle at Sandoval lasted, the better chance they had. By holding out longer, the fortress crews could buy the time their squadrons needed to survive. Harmon and the fleet would stay as long as they could, but if the enemy advanced on them in force, they would transit out. That had been the battle plan all along. The forts were expendable; the bombers were expendable; First Fleet was not.

Harmon had ordered the fortress crews to evacuate before the missiles impacted. The escape pods could get them down to the surface, where they could take refuge with Cain's army. The non-essential personnel had already fled the station, but the point defense crews had remained at their posts. Technically in violation of Harmon's orders, they grimly manned the defensive batteries, gunning down the incoming missiles. The more they could shoot down, the longer the battle would go on. Every missile they took out bought time for the bomber crews to reach the fleet.

"Ok, everyone to the escape pods. Now!" Major Wes Hampton spoke loudly and clearly into the com. They'd pushed things as far as they could, and there was nothing to be gained by keeping his people at their posts. The commander of Fortress 2 was determined to get as many of his people as possible off the station. They had three minutes, maybe four. After that there'd be nothing left of the fortress except a rapidly expanding plasma.

Hampton was standing near the hatch waving his arm.

"Now, people. Move your asses!" His weapons crews were hesitating, trying to program one more round of shots at the wall of incoming missiles. But they'd accomplished what they'd intended, buying time for the bombers. They couldn't do much more, and certainly nothing important enough to be worth their lives.

It was a skeleton crew still on the fortress, and now they began running toward the pods. Hampton had the controls in his hand...the pods were launching in two minutes, no matter what. Anyone still standing around the station after that was SOL. They had to be at least 20 klicks away before the detonations started or they'd all be incinerated in the lifeboats.

"Let's go! Now!" Hampton watched his people moving toward the pods, and he had a moment of pride. There was no panic, no stampede...just an orderly evacuation. He glanced at his chronometer. One minute, fifteen seconds until launch. They were making good time. He wasn't sure it would be good enough to get everybody off, but he figured it was possible. He was going on the last boat, but maybe, he thought...just maybe there's a chance. Some of his people, at least, would get off. He gave himself a 50/50 chance which, he figured, was a lot better than none.

Sandoval was surrounded by nuclear fire. The enemy missiles were detonating all around the fortresses, turning them into heaps of molten slag. Cain watched silently on the bank of monitors, steadily losing images as each of the observation satellites was taken out. It looked like most of the fortress crews managed to eject, but it was hard to get reliable data through the erupting maelstrom. He wouldn't know how many had made it out until they landed, but his people were already tracking the pods. The fortress crews had put up one hell of a fight, and Cain was going to make damned sure that any of them who made it to the surface were picked up and got shelter and medical care.

The fight in space had gone fairly well, Cain thought. Better, at least, than he'd expected. The First Imperium had always enjoyed a vast technology advantage, but their tactics had been weak and unimaginative. Now they were studying the humans and, Cain thought somberly, they were learning quickly. Their screening tactics were becoming more effective, and most of their battle line had come through with only moderate losses. They were still strong enough to invade the planet, that much was certain. Cain smiled grimly. That's just what he wanted. Now it was his turn.

"Captain Carter, I want all units on alert and ready for enemy action in 30 minutes." Cain's voice was slow and deliberative. "Personal confirmations required from all commanders at brigade level and above. No exceptions." He knew his officers thought his precautions were over the top, but he didn't give a shit. He had no idea what the enemy would throw at his people or what weapons they possessed that they hadn't used yet. It didn't matter. Cain wasn't taking any unnecessary chances, and he wasn't about to take losses he couldn't afford because he'd lost focus. He'd been careless once before…never again.

"Yes, sir." Carter snapped the response crisply. The young officer was intimidated by Cain's intensity, but he was also dazzled by him, ready to follow 1st Army's CO anywhere. He hunched over his workstation, transmitting Cain's order over the command line.

Cain leaned back and took a deep breath. The biggest battle of his career was about to begin…and the most important. The fate of the human race potentially hinged on what happened here. It was a pressure few people could handle well, but Cain was the perfect man for the job. He was determined to win, to take his vengeance on the enemy. That was his driving force… his anger, his hatred. He was glad to have those motivations… he wasn't all that sure how he felt about the human race anyway.

He stared straight ahead, his mind drifting back over the years to battles far away and desperate struggles he'd faced. All of that had been part of what brought him here to this place, made him ready to face this enemy. Now it was time. "Well, Darius," he muttered softly to himself. "This is for you, my friend."

Chapter 10

Bridge – AS Hornet
Omega 6 System
Seven Transits from Newton

"Passive scanners on full. Battery power only." Hornet had just transited into the system, and she was running silent, he reactor shut down completely. Jacobs was going to squeeze everything he could from the batteries before risking a reactor startup. That meant no wasted power. Hornet's bridge was dim and cold, and the air was stale.

"Preliminary data indicate no contacts, captain." Ensign Carp rubbed his hands together. His survival suit was a near perfect insulator, and with the vents closed it kept his body warm, despite the near-freezing temperatures. His hands were another matter. It was too hard to manage his workstation in gloves, and his were laying on the side of the panel.

Hornet was deep into uncharted space, and it was starting to wear on the crew. They were in an exposed position, behind enemy lines, cut off from the rest of the fleet, from all of human civilization save the survivors on Adelaide. Assuming anyone was still alive on that isolated colony. To Carp it felt strange, eerie in a way he couldn't entirely describe...sort of like swimming in very deep water. You could drown in 3 meters, but it was a different feeling when there was nothing but seemingly bottomless depths beneath you.

They were very alone, far beyond the possibility of contact with any other human being, but they were pressing on. They had already done their part for the war effort. Strategically, the destruction of the two antimatter transports was worth a hundred ships the size of Hornet.

Carp's thoughts drifted back to that day. Hornet had put a plasma torpedo in each, breaching the containment and causing the antimatter to annihilate. He'd never imagined an explosion that released so much energy, over 800 petatons from each ship. That number was almost meaningless to the human mind, the kind of thing that was usually used to describe astronomical events.

Hornet had fired from extreme range, but the ship was still bathed with a massive blast of gamma rays, and they'd virtually exhausted their meager medical supplies treating the resulting radiation sickness. The space where the ships had been was now a dangerous hotspot and would be for some time.

Carp couldn't imagine the value of the destroyed antimatter, or the damage it would do to the enemy war effort. The elation from the victory had carried the crew's spirits for a long while, but now the relentless emptiness of uncharted space was draining their morale again. Jacobs had proven to be an extraordinary captain. No one else, Carp thought, could have kept this crew functioning at top efficiency so long.

He saw data streaming down his screen, and he focused on it for a few seconds. "No sign of any enemy activity, captain. All scans complete." He paused, reading more of the information scrolling in front of him. "There appear to be four planets, sir, including two in the habitable zone."

Jacobs looked over at his gifted young officer, impressed, as always, by the poise the rookie ensign displayed. "Very well." He could see his breath; it was really starting to get cold on the bridge. He was going to have to risk some energy output soon anyway. Hornet was out of almost everything…food, drinkable water, reaction mass. They were going to have to investigate those two planets and hope that one of them had what they needed.

It was a longshot. Finding a world in the liquid water zone was one thing; locating one with pre-existing flora and fauna edible for humans was quite another. And it wasn't as simple as landing and looking around for something that looked good to eat. New worlds were extremely dangerous. The ship's equipment could heavily modify an alien organic substance, increasing its suitability for human consumption. But a single alien pathogen could kill everyone on Hornet almost immediately. A seemingly safe foodstuff could cause massive genetic damage. The risks were enormous. The scouting service was trained to investigate new planets, not the navy. But Jacobs had to do something; he had to take some risks. Hornet could make it another system or two, but then they'd die anyway, from lack of food and water or when the reactor went cold permanently from lack of fuel.

"Ensign Carp, instruct engineering to prepare to start the reactor at 25%." Jacobs was going to check out the planets, but he was going to put out as little power as possible while doing it. "Plot a course for the innermost of the two potentially habitable worlds, maximum thrust of 1.5g." At less than 2g of thrust, Hornet's baffles would reduce the scanner image put out by its engines. It wouldn't make it impossible for an enemy to detect them, but it would help.

"Yes, sir." Carp relayed the order to engineering, listening to the response on his earpiece. "Captain, engineering reports they can restart the reactor at any time on your command."

"Instruct them to start the reactor and then to initiate thrust plan as soon as power is available." Jacobs leaned back in his chair and looked straight ahead. "Let's see what these two planets have for us.

Cooper Brown walked slowly down the slimy stone floor of the tunnel, trying not to wince at the putrid stench. Conditions in the shelters had steadily worsened, and they had become disease and crime ridden cesspools. The miserable inhabitants huddled against the walls, waiting for Brown's people to bring in their miserly daily rations from the heavily guarded food storage facilities. You had to eat your ration right away; otherwise, when the militia left, someone would steal it. You'd be lucky if they didn't kill you while they were doing it.

Brown had struggled with how to handle the violence problem. He didn't have enough troops to garrison the living areas around the clock, especially not while rebuilding at least some of the planet's defenses. Adelaide had no functioning government now, no courts, no due process, no jails. He was the sole authority, the military commander of a world under martial law. A world with almost no power, not enough food, and no medicine. He hated the responsibility, but there was no other alternative.

He turned the corner, and a pile of garbage came flying from a small crowd. He ducked quickly – combat reflexes were good for a lot of things - and the projectile slammed into the wall behind him, making a splat sound as it did. His escort snapped into action rushing toward the crowd with rifles drawn.

"Halt!" Brown reacted quickly, calling his troops back to their places. He had no idea what would happen if his armed troops charged a group of angry civilians, and he didn't want to find out. "As you were." He was a little concerned that his troops were so ready to charge their friends and neighbors.

He understood the anger, and he really couldn't fault the people for hating him. He'd done all he could to try and ease the suffering, but after a long enough time, all people know is their misery. Brown had gone to boot camp at sixteen, and he'd spent his entire adult life in the Marine Corps and as the commander of Adelaide's militia. War was all he knew, and now he was faced with managing a civilian population under the worst possible circumstances. He had no idea what to do.

There wasn't much to be done about the shortages. They were producing as much food as they could and working around the clock to get additional facilities up and running. He couldn't risk trying to farm on the surface; there was too much danger of detection. Besides, nothing much would grow in the poor Adelaide soil anyway, at least not without fertilizers and equipment he didn't have. All they could efficiently produce in the underground caves was a variety of algae and fungi, not terribly appetizing, but edible and nutritious enough to sustain life.

They were out of medicine too, and routine infectious diseases had become virulent plagues. The tiny medical staff had finally managed to produce some crude antibiotics, and they used them to get the worst of the outbreaks under control. But the health of the colonists was still poor.

He'd been hesitant to crack down hard on the crime. He was uncomfortable with the role of judge, jury, and executioner, and he realized that most of the violence was the inevitable result of people reaching the breaking point. But enough was enough. Now he was going to send the troops in to root out the criminals and the gangs. There would be only one punishment. He didn't have time, manpower, or space to hold captives. Without courts, without proper investigation, he knew there was a risk of executing some innocents along with the guilty, but he didn't see any other way. The last threads of civilization were breaking down in the shelters, and in another few weeks he'd lose all control. He had to do something.

He wondered if they would hate him more or less after the crackdown. He wasn't sure he cared anymore. Brown had gone from the most popular individual on the planet to the most reviled. He was surprised at how quickly that had happened. Intellectually, he understood that suffering people would lash out at any visible target, that they would focus their rage on any authority figure. But comprehending something and accepting it are different things, and the hostility had really bothered him at first. It felt as if his friends and neighbors had turned against him, when his only crime had been to struggle for their survival. He hadn't slept more than a few hours here and there in over a year, and he'd devoted everything he had to the struggle to keep the survivors on Adelaide alive. His reward was their hatred, their bitterness.

He was numb now. He didn't really care what they thought; he was going to do his best to keep them alive anyway. He'd maintained the loyalty of the militia at least, and that was all that was important. If he lost that he was done…and so was the last chance of survival for the people of Adelaide. Without Brown, the militia would probably split into factions, and the colony's tenuous grip on civilization would be lost, consumed by infighting. Or worse, they would get careless and end up drawing the attention of First Imperium forces passing through the system.

He'd done some things he wasn't proud of to maintain his

grip on the militia. The families of his troops were moved to the best locations, and they received preferential rations. He couldn't think of any alternative, but he hated it nevertheless. This is how it starts, he thought. He imagined the way the Alliance was governed; his mind drifted back to the filthy slums of Greater-Miami, were he'd spent the first 16 years of his life in squalor and miser, while those born into the Political Class lived in luxury. Is this really that different, he wondered?

Yes, he told himself…it is different. This is temporary, born of necessity. But he was still uncomfortable, and he couldn't help but imagine some grasping politician or general saying the same thing a century or two past on Earth. All his actions were based on the hope that eventually a relief expedition would reach Adelaide. But what if that didn't happen? What if things stayed as they were for decades, a century? Wouldn't the descendants of his militia and their families become a new privileged class, ruling over a new breed of Cogs? What if he were killed, and his successor craved power?

There was an unspoken creed among most of the Alliance colonists, a belief that what had happened on Earth could not occur out in space. The culture was too different, the colonists were a different breed, the new worlds didn't suffer from the shortages and pollution that plagued the home world…the reasons offered were many and varied. But Brown was seeing firsthand just how quickly things could veer out of control. That confidence, the cocky optimism most of the colonists had about the future, was gone.

More than anything, he just wanted to go back to the Corps. They had a war to fight, and that was something he understood a lot better than trying to manage a crowd of terrified civilians. He'd retired because he decided he'd had enough of fighting, but now he had come to realize that men rarely chose their conflicts, and those struggles followed them to whatever places they sought refuge. His retirement, his new home, had turned into a nightmare. War had followed him, and he felt in his gut that it always would. Peace was a fantasy, an elusive dream, always out of reach.

Chapter 11

Northern Continent
Planet Sandoval
Delta Leonis System
"The Line"

The missiles streaked through the predawn sky, hundreds of them. They were precisely targeted, and as they sliced their way through the atmosphere, they vectored off in different directions, small phalanxes of death approaching dozens of locations across the planet.

After the orbital fortresses were destroyed, the First Imperium fleet moved into position around the planet. In their underground bunkers, Cain's people waited for an assault they thought would come immediately, but the enemy ships remained quietly in orbit and on station around Sandoval. For six days they scanned the planet, but they launched no attack. Until now.

The First Imperium forces had not used nuclear weapons on the ground in any of the prior engagements. They were fighting over worlds they considered part of the Imperium, and their ancient doctrine dictated conventional warfare. Now the Regent had overruled that policy and, for the first time in the war, a target world would receive a nuclear bombardment.

In his underground headquarters bunker, Erik Cain watched the missiles move across his screen. As soon as he saw the initial scanning report he knew in his gut the enemy had shed its prohibition and was using nuclear missiles. He had point defense emplacements in well-protected locations all over the planet, but he held them in check. They were there to shoot down enemy landers, not missiles. Cain had his army deep in reinforced defenses all over Sandoval and, as far as he was concerned, the enemy could do whatever they wanted to the surface. He'd fight them in a verdant paradise or a radioactive hell. He didn't care.

"Code Orange confirmed, general." Carter was a little rattled, but he held himself together. "Verified nuclear warheads, sir." Facing the enemy's first nuclear bombardment, Cain's command staff was sitting silently, nervously watching the incoming wave of atomic devastation.

Cain sat calmly in his chair, unsurprised, a barely perceptible smile on his face. He'd been ready for this, and he was thrilled to see the First Imperium deploying nuclear weapons. He'd been under orders to refrain from going nuclear himself…unless the enemy did first. General Holm didn't want to push the enemy to escalate, but Cain had always believed it would be a net benefit to his forces. He'd argued vociferously, and unsuccessfully, for the go ahead to use his nukes. Now his hands were untied, and he could respond in kind. The enemy would find a warm reception when they finally started landing ground forces, Cain promised himself that much.

"It looks like all major cities and settlements have been targeted, sir." Carter took a deep breath, working hard to remain calm. It wasn't easy to be on the receiving end of a massive nuclear attack…even when you were deep underground in a hardened bunker. "All power stations, transit hubs, and militia facilities as well."

Cain was impassive. That was all standard for a comprehensive planetary bombardment. But none of his strength was deployed in any of those locations. The enemy was wasting all that firepower. Cain was here for one reason only - to beat the First Imperium. He was likely to give Sandoval back to its citizens in considerably rougher shape than he'd gotten it, but he wasn't concerned about that. Such were the fortunes of war.

"I want full Code Yellow protocols in effect." Code Orange was the Alliance designation for imminent nuclear attack. Code Yellow was the directive for a nuclear offensive. "Place all atomic-equipped artillery units on alert and dispatch special ammunition to all ground formations." Cain's voice was steady and grim, but there was a touch of anticipation too. He couldn't

wait to fight the enemy without restrictions. "All units are autho-
rized to use specials at their discretion. Battalion level controls."

"Yes, sir." Carter let out a deep breath. Things were going
to get hot on the surface…quickly. The Battle of Sandoval was
going to be a vicious fight. Carter felt the tension in his gut, but
also a wave of confidence. The enemy had superior technology
and fearless robot warriors…but 1st Army had Erik Cain. All
things considered, Carter rated it even. "Code Yellow parameters transmitted to all units, general."

Cain leaned back and watched the plots of the enemy attack
unfold on his workstation. Go ahead, he thought, beat up the
landscape and a bunch of abandoned towns I couldn't care less
about. He stared at his screen, eyes narrowed, expression cold,
like chiseled marble. He muttered softly to himself. "I'm going
to use my nukes to better effect, you bastards. Just wait and see."

The missiles swooped down like deadly swarms, the multi-
stage vehicles dividing into dozens of small warheads that rained
down over their targets in preset patterns. Each section was a
100 kiloton atomic bomb, and they exploded simultaneously,
a massive version of the enemy's cluster bomb weapon. The
effect was intense, far more thorough than anything a single,
larger warhead could achieve, and the target areas were utterly
devastated. It was nuclear carpet bombing, and everything
within the weapons' blast zones was obliterated.

The capital city of Dawson erupted into a hellish inferno, a
dozen mushroom clouds billowing above the fiery destruction,
the death agony of a place where 100,000 people had once lived.
The shockwave ripped through the city's structures, flattening
everything manmade, and the firestorms raced out of control,
consuming anything in their wake. The city where people had
lived and worked and spent their lives was gone, replaced by a
scene of hell.

Thirty kilometers south of the capital, the sprawling space-
port was engulfed, its plasti-crete landing platforms blasted into
jagged chunks and its support buildings mangled and twisted
under the intense heat. Parked vehicles and orbital shuttles were

blown around like toys by the shockwaves and consumed utterly by the walls of flame.

All across the northern continent, every key location was targeted. The main mag-train terminal north of the capital, the other population centers, the power plants and mining facilities. Factories and storage facilities were demolished, and militia bases were wiped from the map. Everywhere, nuclear death rained down on all that men had built on Sandoval, leaving nothing but ghostly ruins and blasted landscape.

Throughout the formerly inhabited areas of the planet, great clouds of dirt and debris rose high into the atmosphere, darkening the morning skies and spreading radioactive fallout in the high winds. For kilometers in any direction from the target zones, the radiation spiked well beyond lethal levels for unprotected men…but there was no one there to feel those effects. The surface of Sandoval had been abandoned long before the missiles came.

Isaac Merrick peered through the scope of his command tank, mesmerized by what he saw. To the east, along a line running north to south there was nothing but a row of mushroom clouds billowing upward. Merrick was a career officer, but he'd had served all his life in the terrestrial army. He hadn't seen serious combat until a few years earlier, when his division was sent to Arcadia to suppress the rebellion there. He'd been amazed at the intensity of the fighting, and his troops had paid the price of their inexperience. But this was something different, something he'd never seen before. He gazed out through the darkening morning, and he knew he was looking at total war.

Merrick's people were the only ones close to the surface, but they were in the deserted steppe, buttoned up in their heavy tanks. Every one of his vehicles was hull down and in cover. They'd be perfectly safe, as long as the enemy didn't start targeting them directly…and it was very unlikely the stationary tanks would be detected from orbit.

His crews were all from Earth, and he was worried about their lack of combat experience. There hadn't been any war between the Superpowers on Earth for more than a century, and the terrestrial armies were generally unblooded formations. The enlisted ranks were filled with Cog recruits, and superfluous members of Political families occupied the officers' billets. Some infantry and mechanized formations, at least, had been involved in paramilitary activities, keeping order within the Alliance…but main battle tanks hadn't fired in anger since the Unification Wars ended. Not one of Merrick's crew had ever fired their tank's weapons other than in an exercise.

The entire tank corps was under a communications blackout. The last thing they needed was for the enemy ships to pick up pointless comm chatter and drop a few dozen nukes on their heads. Merrick hoped his people had the discipline to obey that directive. He'd shoot anyone who didn't, but that would be too little, too late if the slip brought nuclear devastation down on them.

Inexperienced they might have been, but the tank corps on Sandoval represented the cream of the Earth-based forces. Merrick was hopeful they would perform well, that their training would be enough to carry them through this ordeal that was coming. One thing he was sure of…they would be veterans after this fight. If any of them survived.

Merrick was nervous too. The fear of battle was there, certainly. He had no idea if they could win this fight and, even if they did, losses were going to be horrific. He'd faced death before, in the fighting on Arcadia, but this was different. His insides felt cold, as if an icy hand gripped his spine. He hadn't faced the First Imperium forces yet, but he'd spoken to officers who had, veteran Marines all, and he'd seen the fear in their jaded eyes.

But there was more than just the fear of death. Merrick was grateful to Cain, to the Marines who'd accepted him. He'd been vilified by his own people, unfairly scapegoated and driven into exile. Yet, he'd found a new home among his former enemies. He was determined to justify the trust they'd placed in him. He was ready to do whatever it took to win this fight.

"All ground to air batteries report 100% ready, sir." Carter's voice was sharp and clear. Now that the battle had begun, his edginess faded, pushed into the back of his mind. He was totally focused on the fight unfolding on his display. "All units waiting for the order to fire, general."

The enemy landing craft were coming down in a widely dispersed pattern. Cain was annoyed, but not surprised. He'd hoped they'd land in a dense pattern, making themselves easy targets for his nukes. But having gone nuclear themselves, the First Imperium forces had adopted a formation designed to counter a retaliatory strike.

Cain stared ahead, glancing occasionally at the monitors displaying the status of the invasion force. He'd already waited longer than anyone had expected. The landers were well within range of his surface-to-air rockets. "Batteries 19 through 36… commence firing."

Carter hesitated, just for an instant. He'd expected Cain to order all units to fire. "Batteries 19 through 36, commence firing. I repeat, batteries 19 through 36, commence firing. All other units stand by."

Cain sat quietly, almost unmoving. He was revising his strategy, holding back half his defensive firepower. His original plan was to take out as much of the first wave as possible and to let the enemy land and throw themselves at his defenses. But the battle had gone nuclear, and that changed everything. The enemy was coming down in a dispersed pattern, and their formation would be spread out. Cain was going to attack.

"Get General Warren on the line." Cain spoke deliberatively, his voice utterly without emotion. "He is to put 7th Brigade on alert. They are to report to the surface to support the Tank Corps." Kyle Warren's II Corps was made up mostly of new units rushed through training, with only a leavening of seasoned troops. But 7th Brigade was a veteran formation, organized from retired Marines returning to the colors.

"Yes, sir." Carter had a surprised look on his face, but he spun around and executed Cain's order.

"Major Sawyer, I want a barrage laid down along these coordinates." Cain was looking down at his 'pad, transmitting the data to Sawyer's console. Dave Sawyer had served under Cain since he was a sergeant on Carson's World, during the legendary battle on the Lysandra Plateau. He was one of those extra-tough Marines, reluctant to accept a commission, preferring to remain close to the ranks. Sawyer had gone to Columbia with Jax, in support of the rebel forces there, and, when he returned, Cain flat out ordered him to accept his promotion. Now he'd tapped the wily old veteran as his senior aide.

"Yes, sir." Sawyer's reply was crisp and immediate. Cain had moved Sawyer right from sergeant to captain in the reorganizations after the rebellions...and again to major just before the forces began massing on Sandoval. He was still a little uncomfortable as an officer, but he was getting used to it. "Specials, sir?"

Cain suppressed a smile. Sawyer added "sir" after virtually every sentence when speaking to him. It was the ones like Sawyer, the grizzled old "tough as nails" veterans, who surprised him most with the strange deference they gave him. Respect for a superior officer was one thing, but this was something else. Cain didn't really understand it, but he'd used it to his advantage on many occasions.

"Yes, major. Specials." Cain was running his finger along the 'pad, sending another file to Sawyer. "I want a rolling barrage, moving from east to west, half a klick every five minutes." He glanced up, trying to gauge if Sawyer understood what he was saying. "I want you to supervise this personally, major. We're going to split the enemy and drive the western half of their force farther west...right into the attack of the Tank Corps." He paused then added, "Do you follow, Dave?"

"Yes, sir." Sawyer was nodding as he spoke. "Understood, sir."

"I want to wreak havoc through their positions for the first few minutes, then I want those two flanks kept apart." Cain was looking right at Sawyer, stressing his point. "Be careful we don't end up bombing our own tanks. I want you to stay on top of the bombardment, major, and make sure it stays pinpointed.

I'm depending on you. I know I can count on you." Cain sometimes hated himself for the shameless manipulation, but he was
only telling the truth. Sawyer was one of the best Marines he
had, and he *was* counting on him.

"Yes, sir." Sawyer straightened in his chair. "Understood."

Cain leaned back and rubbed his chin. Ok, you bastards, he
thought…let's see how you like this."

The great plain 100 kilometers north of Dawson was covered with hundreds of landing sleds. In the distance there were
plumes of smoke rising from the ground, dozens of them, the
results of 1st Army's ground to air fire. Cain's batteries had taken
out over a hundred of the enemy landers, destroying over 2,000
battle robots before they touched ground. The batteries had
fired relentlessly, recklessly even…giving up their locations by
staying in place far too long. Fewer than half of them were left
now; the rest were radioactive waste, destroyed by enemy missiles fired from orbit.

Even with the losses, over 10,000 enemy bots had successfully landed in the first wave. They were scattered, spread out
to minimize susceptibility to a nuclear attack, and they moved to
secure the landing zone for the heavier ships, the ones bringing
down the Reapers.

There were no defending forces facing them. The artificial
intelligences directing the First Imperium army had expected
resistance. Their scanning results had confirmed that most of
the formerly populated areas were directly south of the landing zone. Those centers of habitation had been destroyed by
nuclear bombardment, but they were still the likeliest area for
the enemy defense to coalesce, so that was the intended objec-
tive of the pending attack. Half of the first wave was forming
up, preparing to advance in that direction. Then the warning
came. Enemy fire incoming, presumption…nuclear-armed.

The battlebots reacted quickly, spreading into extended
order and going prone. The first shell landed almost dead center in the landing zone. A 50-kiloton round, it erupted into a
200-meter fireball. The shockwave blasted outward, destroying

everything in its path. Rocks, dirt, debris all flew out in every direction from ground zero…and the melted and mangled bodies of the battle robots too, at least those caught in the primary kill zone. More than 50 were destroyed utterly, mostly those within 500 meters of the impact site. Outside the primary destruction zone, bots were knocked down and hit by flying detritus. Most were only lightly damaged, but some stayed down, either destroyed or mangled beyond operability.

The warheads kept coming, spreading atomic fire throughout the landing zone. The First Imperium AIs had always assumed the enemy possessed ground-based nuclear weapons, though they had refrained from using them until this point. Clearly, they were retaliating for the orbital bombardment. The AIs calculated, trying to determine if the escalation they had seemingly provoked was in their favor…or it if had been a mistake. The AIs reviewed every decision, every enemy move. This adversary was disturbingly clever and adept at war, but the AIs were learning…even from their mistakes.

The incoming fire developed into a pattern, with warheads landing on a long line running north to south, effectively splitting the LZ into two halves. Clearly the enemy was planning something, but the AIs were confused. Their analysis of the bombardment pattern suggested an imminent enemy attack, yet this did not match their expectations. Scanning results had determined that the enemy had heavily fortified the planet and that they were deployed in deep underground positions. This was consistent with a defensive strategy…which should have resulted in a bombardment dispersed throughout the LZ to maximize casualties inflicted. This had not happened – the bombardment was focused, targeted. The AIs were uncertain…they hesitated. This enemy continued to confound predictability.

"General Merrick, you may attack." Cain's voice was distant and muffled on the comlink, but the intensity was unmistakable. "Good luck, Isaac."

"Thank you, sir." Merrick had already given his orders. All his units had been on alert, waiting for the go ahead, and now he'd gotten it from Cain. He leaned down and switched over to the corps-wide com. "All units, execute Plan Alpha."

All along the steppe, the massive main battle tanks roared to life, slowly emerging from their dug in positions. They were launching a flank attack against disordered infantry, a tank commander's dream. Of course, these infantry were advanced battle robots…an enemy far deadlier than anything the Scott tanks had been designed to face.

The tanks rumbled across the open steppe, heading east, toward the enemy landing zone. Armored Marines emerged from their underground bunkers and took positions in support of the advancing tanks. The Marines were veterans, but fighting alongside heavy tanks was new to them, and their coordination was a little rough.

Merrick's tank was in the third wave, but his screen displayed the view from Colonel Wing's position in the front line. The steppe rolled by as the tanks raced toward the enemy position. Wing's tank moved up over a small rise, and suddenly Merrick could see the battlefield. The eastern horizon was totally obscured, blocked by at least 20 billowing mushroom clouds. The plain west of the nuclear maelstrom was covered with landing craft and thousands of First Imperium battle robots.

"General Merrick…Colonel Wing here." Wing was reporting what Merrick could already see through the relayed transmission. "Enemy spotted. We will be in firing range in three minutes. Request permission to attack."

"You may attack, colonel." Merrick felt a rush of excitement. Fear, yes, but also exhilaration. He didn't fully understand his feelings, but for the first time he was going into battle believing in a cause. He'd gone to Arcadia when he'd been ordered to, and he'd tried his best to win the war. But his heart was never in crushing rebel colonists. Against this alien menace, however, Isaac Merrick was ready to give his all, to commit everything to the fight.

The first wave of Merrick's corps, a full brigade of tanks, swarmed over the steppe to the edge of the great plain. Almost as one, the line fired, the main guns launching hyper-velocity projectiles into the enemy flank. The ground battle had begun.

"Get this thing moving. We're the point tank now." Lieutenant Carl Weld turned to face Sergeant Law. The driver was already responding, moving 2nd Platoon's command tank forward. All four of 1st Platoon's tanks had been hit; now his people were heading forward to plug the gap. Weld was scared and uncomfortable, his dark green fatigues soaked in sweat. This was the first combat he'd ever seen, and it was one hell of a baptism of fire.

The Scott tanks were huge, and they made an intense racket when they rumbled along at full speed. Even with his helmet on, Weld could barely hear the chatter on the com. He was trying to keep close tabs on the platoon. He knew his crews were wavering…the sight of the Reapers was enough to chill anyone to the bone. But he knew they had to win this battle. Part of his motivation was the urgency of the fight; if the enemy got past Sandoval they'd run rampant through the Alliance, through all human-occupied space. But it was more than that. General Cain had made it clear that no one was leaving Sandoval until the enemy was defeated. Weld had only seen 1st Army's CO once, when he'd addressed the Tank Corps shortly after they arrived. He'd never been so afraid of another human being in his life. Cain's intensity was like nothing he'd ever seen before. People used phrases like "fight to the death" all the time, but he didn't have a doubt that Erik Cain meant exactly what he said.

Colonel Wing's brigade was spearheading the attack. They'd crashed into the disordered enemy formations, pushing them between the wall of advancing tanks and the nuclear barrage that was steadily moving west. They were focusing on the newly-landed Reapers, leaving the standard battle robots to their attached Marines units. The attack was hugely successful at first, and dozens of Reapers were destroyed in just a few minutes. But the enemy line was solidifying and turning to face the surprise attack. The tanks were still taking out Reapers, but they were paying for it now.

Weld stared at the small screen in front of him. He moved

his hands over the compact 'pad, transmitting coordinates to his other three tanks. "OK, 2nd Platoon. We've got half a dozen Reapers at these coordinates...let's take them down. Fire at will." He flipped off the com and turned to his gunner. "Fire."

The tank shook as Private Young let loose a hypervelocity round. The projectile streaked across the sky, leaving a fiery trail in its wake. A hundred meters short of the enemy position it split into 20 sections, each one capable of causing catastrophic damage, even to a Reaper. The shot went wide, barely clipping one of the massive enemy robots. Weld couldn't tell if the thing was damaged or not, but it looked like 3 or 4 of the standard bots had taken hits and were down.

He heard the grating sound of the automatic reloader. The Scotts had an impressive rate of fire...at least 3 a minute, 4 for a really good crew. "Let's go, private. You need to land those shots on target. Those things are gonna shoot back, you know, and they're going to be a hell of a lot more accurate." Weld was sorry he'd said that the second it left his lips. His people were already hanging on by a thread...scaring them more wasn't going to help. "Let's get going, Sergeant Law. I want you advancing after every shot...zigzag pattern. If you see any cover, make for it." He didn't have any more combat experience than his crew, but he knew the worst thing they could do was stop moving for too long. The First Imperium targeting was spot on...if his tanks stayed in one firing position they wouldn't last a minute.

He felt the jarring again...another round being fired. This one was right on target. One of the Reapers took at least three fragments, and the thing was torn apart. He couldn't tell who cheered first, but in a few seconds the whole crew was at it. He let them go...it was morale as much as technology or numbers that would win or lose this battle. But the fighting wasn't going to stop so his people could celebrate a kill. "Let's keep moving," he reminded them.

Weld's tank headed for a small dip in the ground...a good spot to grab some temporary cover. Off to the left, one of his other tanks took a hit right between the turret and the main body. It moved forward, slowing to a crawl and erupted in flames. It was about 200 meters away and over a small ridge, so Weld couldn't see if anyone got out...but he doubted it.

"Keep moving 2nd Platoon." He didn't want to give them too much time to think. "Maintain fire." He heard the sounds of rocks and debris smacking against the hull...a near miss chewing up the ground right behind the tank. Weld took a deep breath and tried not to piss himself. Fuck, he thought, barely keeping panic at bay...none of us are getting out of here.

"Let's go Marines. Fan out between the tanks...none of these fuckers get into the gaps! You understand me?" Sergeant Eliot Storm was jogging alongside one of the hulking monsters. He was glad to have the tanks here, but he was having a hard time effectively working alongside them. He knew infantry's purpose in supporting tanks was to protect the flanks, but none of his people had ever served in that role. The Marines were a mobile force, light infantry wielding massive firepower because of their armor. They were organized and equipped for rapid movement from planet to planet. The Corps had a few light armored vehicles, but transporting main battle tanks around occupied space just wasn't feasible. Not under normal conditions. Combined arms combat was new to the Corps, and it was going to take some time to achieve proficiency at it. Time Storm and his Marines didn't have.

Storm had been in command of the platoon for all of 30 minutes, ever since the lieutenant went down. He wasn't dead – at least he hadn't been half an hour before – but he was badly shot up. They'd left him about two klicks back. Storm hoped he'd been evac'd since then, but he really didn't know. If not, the suit's trauma system could probably keep him alive...for a while at least.

"We're focusing on the battlebots, not the Reapers...don't you grunts forget that." The tanks were much better equipped than the Marines to take out the First Imperium's heavy units, but ignoring the Reapers and trusting to these army pukes to take them out was tough. The big robots were a much worse threat, and the Marines who'd fought against the First Imperium before were used to concentrating on them first.

Storm didn't have anything against the tank crews, but he knew they were virgins who'd been running bloodless exercises their entire careers. He tried to give them the benefit of the doubt, but he just didn't trust them to stand…and if they broke and routed, the Marines supporting them would be screwed.

Storm crouched down behind the crest of a small hill. He had a line of sight to half a dozen bots, and he opened fire immediately, raking their position. At least ten of his Marines were doing the same, and all the enemy robots went down, ripped to shreds by the fire. The new heavy rounds made a huge difference. Storm had fought on Cornwall, where they'd been armed with the old, lighter projectiles, and he'd been amazed at the effectiveness of the new ordnance. There was a price to pay, of course, and the new clips only carried 100 rounds where the old ones had 500. He glanced down at his monitors…ammo wasn't a problem yet, but it was going to be soon.

"Let's go…the tanks are moving out again." Not that there were many of them left. His platoon was supporting a tank company. They'd started with 14 of the heavy vehicles, but they'd lost 8. Two of those were damaged, and they'd pulled back on their own power, but the others had either been destroyed or badly hit and abandoned.

Storm jumped up over the crest and scrambled down the hillside. Shit, he thought, it's really exposed on this side. There was a small gully at the bottom that might give a little protection, but that was it. "Platoon, advance by leapfrogs, odds first, evens covering fire." He started down the hillside. "Odds…now!" Along the crest of the rise, half the platoon opened up, doing their best to cover the advancing forces. The enemy bots were also in cover, formed up in a hasty trench they'd dug about a klick to the west. It was the tanks' job to penetrate that position, but unless reserves came up quickly, the offensive was going to grind to a halt.

"Evens, advance. Odds, fire!" Storm dove headfirst into the gully and popped up, firing prone. The shots weren't very effective…the enemy's cover was strong. It took a direct hit in the open to take out a bot; in cover it was almost hopeless with small arms. "I want the heavies set up in this gully." He glanced back, checking on the progress of the evens. "The SAWs better be firing in three zero seconds or those bots will be the least of your problems."

Storm sounded like a stereotypical old sergeant – and he looked like one too - with a bald head and a huge, crooked scar along the left side of his face. But he was actually an oddball character in the Marines. He'd been born the son of Cogs like most in the Corps, but his father had been the servant of a well-placed political family. Among the perks of a lifetime of loyal service was a decent education for Eliot and his two sisters. The largess of his father's sponsor didn't extend, however, to pulling strings to get the boy out of trouble, and the Marines seemed like a better alternative than the lunar mines.

"And I want those HVMs firing in one minute. One moth-erfucking minute, boys and girls." The hypervelocity missile launchers took longer to set up, but they were probably the most effective weapon the Marines had against the First Imperium bots.

His people were faced off against the enemy position. The firefight was intense, but both sides had some cover, and the losses, while not exactly light, weren't immediately crippling. Storm felt that same cold feeling inside, the insidious fear of an enemy that felt no anxiety or pain or doubt. He was control-ling it…it got easier with time…but he was worried about his Marines. Most of them were veterans, but only a few had faced the First Imperium before. He'd seen even hardened Marine veterans break and run from the bots, something he'd never experienced before.

"Hold your positions and keep up that fire." This was as far as they could go. The ground between his people and the enemy position was dead flat and totally open. If his people came out of the gully, there wouldn't be any of them left in 30 seconds. It would be suicide. If they were going to break through here, the tanks were going to have to do it…though it looked pretty suicidal for them too. At least it did to Storm.

"Sergeant Storm…Lieutenant Weld here." The comlink crackled a little. The army units didn't link perfectly with the Marine equipment. Weld sounded grim, his voice uneven, tenuous. "My orders are to attack and break through that trench line. Be ready to follow us once we're up there." Weld didn't sound all that convinced.

"Understood, lieutenant." Storm shook his head, but he felt a growing respect for Weld and his troopers, far more than he did for most of the army personnel. If that kid goes in, he thought, he's going to get his ass handed to him…but if he makes it back, I'll never call him an army puke again.

"Issue the recall." Cain's voice was cool, unemotional. "There's not sufficient additional gain to justify more losses." He'd just sent 4,000 tank crew and 1,800 Marines to attack on a hellish battlefield, surrounded by nuclear bombardment. Less than 2/3 of them were coming back, but they'd inflicted heavy casualties on the enemy and utterly disordered the right flank of the landing zone. It was a success, but one paid for with buckets of blood, and the mood in 1st Army HQ was a somber one. They'd all expected a tough battle, but they were beginning to understand the hellish death struggle Cain was planning to fight.

"Yes, general." Captain Carter felt a chill listening to Cain's passionless tone. To an impartial observer, it didn't seem like the general was at all concerned with how many men and women he lost. Carter knew better…anyone familiar with Cain knew better…but it was still hard to reconcile with the cold, analytical voice issuing from the commander in chief.

Cain had been there before. When the battle was on, the icy calculus of war prevailed for him. There was always time later for the guilt and recriminations, but they had no place on the field. While this fight was on, Erik Cain cared about one thing and one thing only. Victory.

Chapter 12

Western Alliance Intelligence Directorate HQ
Wash-Balt Metroplex, Earth

"I am hopeful things will proceed perfectly for us. If Admiral Garret and the forces of the Grand Pact are able to defeat the enemy forces along the Line, conditions will be ripe for Plan C." He smiled nervously; for all his planning and scheming, Stark was worried about the war. "The Powers will be in utter disarray...that will be our time." He paused, and the smile slipped off his face. "However..." He spoke slowly, tenuously. "...it may be prudent to prepare a contingency plan in the event the military is unable to withstand the assault of the First Imperium." Stark's plans would be of little account if humanity was destroyed or enslaved by the enemy.

Rafael Samuels sat at the polished wood table across from Stark. What they were discussing was classified at the highest levels, kept secret from even the rest of the Directorate. Stark's plan was beyond ambitious...it was the most audacious thing Samuels had ever imagined. And, he thought, Stark might just pull it off. If the Line held, that is. If the First Imperium broke through the military's defenses, all bets were off. Stark would have to launch the plan early, and use it against the invaders instead of his intended targets. Ironically, Stark was depending on his arch-enemies to clear the way for his plans.

"I agree, Gavin. I am not at all confident that Admiral Garret and his cabal will be able to withstand the attacks now underway." Samuels was fidgeting in his chair. He was uncomfortable with his position, and regretful about the choices he'd made. Though he'd never consciously chosen to betray the Corps, he'd set himself on that course years before, and now he was stuck with the results. He'd slid gradually into treachery, trying first only to secure the Commandant's rank he felt was his due. But he'd long since gone too far to turn back. He'd become the Corps' greatest traitor, and he was reviled by every Marine. He was bitter about how things had played out, and he knew Stark had lured him into what he had done. But however Samuels felt, the head of Alliance Intelligence was his last ally. His die was cast…he'd thrown in with Stark for good, and now he had to live with it. His only other option was to sacrifice himself and accept the punishment the Corps would impose…and he lacked the moral courage to go down that road.

"It will mean an early activation. We will not have the same force concentration we will have if we stay on the original schedule." Stark looked frustrated and angry. "And it will greatly imperil the ultimate success of the original plan." He'd been working on Plan C for years, and he hated the idea of sacrificing it. He wouldn't do it just to save Marines and support the forces in the field, but if the enemy broke through the Line, he knew he'd have no choice. If humanity fell, he'd die with everyone else, and his plans would be moot. "Begin working on a contingency plan to activate if our hand is forced. We should be ready, just in case." His voice was grudging, angry.

"I will begin work immediately, Gavin." Samuels spoke as passionlessly as he could manage, but inside he felt a spark of excitement. If Stark was forced to activate Plan C, Samuels would probably lead the forces against the enemy. It would likely mean the end of Stark's bid for power, but Samuels was beginning to think it would be an opportunity for himself. Perhaps it was his road to redemption. If he came to the rescue after Garret's forces and the Marines failed to stop the enemy… maybe, just maybe his treachery would be forgotten. He would rally the shattered remnants of the Corps, and Holm and Cain and the rest of his enemies would be disgraced…or, better yet, killed on the field.

Stark nodded but didn't say anything. Samuels had become familiar enough with Stark to know he'd been dismissed. "If you'll excuse me, Gavin, I'll see to that contingency plan." Samuels rose slowly from the chair, breathing heavily by the time he'd gotten his great bulk fully vertical.

My God, Stark thought…he looks like he's about to drop dead. Samuels had always been a large man, so strong his boot camp class had called him the Bull. But now he was grossly over-weight and out of shape. That could be useful, Stark mused… when Samuels had finally outlived his usefulness. No one would question a sudden heart attack…

"Maximum security on this, Rafael." Stark's voice deepened. "I'm serious. No leaks. None." Every warm blooded creature felt an unnatural chill when Gavin Stark used that tone. "If I decide we need to activate early, we'll deal with the specifics then. For now, I just want a plan drawn up." Stark had risen, and he walked around the table. He held his hand out to Samuels.

"Of course, Gavin." Samuels smiled at the Alliance's top spy. Maybe, he thought, defeating the First Imperium will give me a chance to get rid of Stark once and for all…then my life will be mine again. He extended his own hand, grasping Stark's firmly. "You can count on me."

Li An sat quietly on a nearly priceless silk couch, a glass of bourbon lying untouched on the table in front of her. She nor-mally enjoyed quiet time in her office, long after business hours had passed. There was always activity at C1 headquarters, of course, but her people knew better than to disturb her at this hour unless it was urgent.

Lately, though, the peace she had customarily enjoyed dur-ing her meditative periods had eluded her. She was concerned about the war, of course, though the role of the intelligence agencies against the First Imperium was extremely limited. She was keeping an eye on the other Powers, watching for signs of treachery, but everyone seemed committed to the Grand Pact. It's amazing, she thought, what fear could accomplish. That was something she already knew, of course, something she'd used herself many times…but she'd never seen it on this scale. Even the Central Committee was on the verge of panic, a bunch of old men who suddenly realized that their privileged lifestyle and jealously guarded power – not to mention their precious hides

- would be wiped away in a wave of blood and fire if the First Imperium reached Earth. Li An had sat quietly at Committee meetings, listening with disgust as they dithered pointlessly.

She was continually repulsed at the base cowardice of those who casually ruled the masses. They could demand sacrifice and herculean feats of courage from their minions and soldiers and impose draconian punishments on those who disobeyed, but when they were threatened themselves they descended into a pit of fear. She was just as ready to send people to their deaths and rule with an iron fist, but no one had ever called Li An a coward.

C1's ancient head was the only one of them who had kept her wits. She knew the combined forces might fail, that the vastly superior legions of the First Imperium might indeed overrun the Line and continue their march of destruction...that even her beloved Hong Kong could lie in ashes, a silent graveyard for all time. But there was nothing she could do to influence this war, and she wasn't one to wallow in pointless fear if there was nothing to be gained. If extinction was mankind's fate, then so be it...if not, she would be ready for what followed this conflict.

Li An was able to coolly and logically analyze a situation, and make decisions based on the facts. Indeed, she'd exerted considerable pressure to insure that Admiral Garret was appointed supreme commander of the Grand Pact. There had been a lot of nationalistic bullshit flying around, each Power arguing to place its own officers in the highest positions. But Li An was no fool, and there was no question that Augustus Garret was the most ingenious naval commander alive...perhaps the finest who had ever lived. And Generals Holm and Cain were the dominant tacticians of ground combat. She knew that only too well, from bitter experience. The Alliance's team of brilliant commanders had ruined all her carefully laid plans...and cost the CAC the Third Frontier War, turning imminent victory into ignominious defeat. It had been almost ten years, but it still stung. She was glad to have Garret on her side, at least for now. If and when the First Imperium was defeated, the Powers would return to their old disputes...of that she had no doubt. Then her problem would once again be countering – or eliminating -

the Alliance's brilliant military leaders.

But it wasn't the war or the First Imperium that was causing her anxiety. It was Gavin Stark. He was up to something… something big. She was sure of it. But she'd been confounded in her every effort to discover what he was planning. He'd clamped down an iron wall of security around his activities, and the intensity of his secrecy only increased her concern. Whatever he was doing, it was serious.

She tried to attack the problem herself, but she knew almost nothing. Stark was spending a lot of time in the western region of the North American section of the Alliance. He'd purchased some type of horse farm under the preposterous cover that he'd taken to riding for relaxation. Li An had tangled with Gavin Stark for years, and she had a pretty good idea of his likes and dislikes. The notion that he'd choose to spend his leisure hours out in the middle of nowhere riding horses was absurd. Stark was a creature of Washbalt, and his every waking hour was spent chasing power. She'd never known the man to relax in any conventional sense…other than a few hours here and there in the company of his many mistresses.

She detested Stark, but she wouldn't let herself underestimate him. The Alliance spymaster was occasionally undone by his outsized ambition, but there was no doubt he was a genius, capable of almost anything. Only a fool would disregard Stark's ambitions or his competence. Li An was many things, but certainly not a fool.

She'd spent her evenings recently considering the problem… and largely coming up blank. But now she had an idea. It was a longshot, she knew that, but it was the best thing she could devise. She reached over and flipped the switch on the comlink. "Jung, I need you to access the special archives." Kan Jung was her junior assistant, usually the one on duty at this hour. "Get me everything we have on General Rafael Samuels."

Roderick Vance looked out over the red sands and enjoyed the quiet. He knew it wouldn't last. It never did. Many people thought the Martian landscape was ugly…forbidding and harsh.

But to him it was uniquely beautiful, a strangely alien landscape that men had converted into a new home, indeed, one they were still adapting. When Vance's grandfather arrived on Mars, the surface was deadly, the sparse atmospheric pressure, low temperatures, and massive cosmic radiation offering a fatal trio to anyone foolish enough to go outside without adequate protection.

A century of terraforming had changed all of that. The Martians, as the transplanted Terrans proudly called themselves, still lived in sealed domes and underground cities, but now they could venture to the surface with a simple breather and a heavy coat. The atmosphere still wasn't dense enough to sustain life, but it was far thicker than it had been, and the temperatures had risen dramatically. Mars was still as cold as Earth's polar regions, but that was a considerable improvement from what the initial settlers had faced. The developing atmosphere and the induced magnetic field had already cut the radiation at the surface to tolerable levels. Prolonged exposure still wasn't healthy, not really, but it was easily controllable with proper treatment.

Vance had no children, and he was far from sure he ever would, but he had half a dozen nieces and nephews. They would probably live to see a Mars where people walked freely on the surface, on a planet with new seas and rain and temperatures above freezing. If they survived. That was what this war was about.

Vance was a true patriot, proud of the Martian Confederation and all it had achieved. It was a government that actually worked, presiding over a society that was, on the whole, happy and prosperous. The Confederation had, admittedly, enjoyed considerable advantages over the Superpowers on Earth. Where the older Powers had ancient ghettoes and crumbling infrastructure, the cities of Mars were new and modern, purpose-built for the needs of a modern society. Earth's ancient social problems and racial and nationalistic hatreds were largely absent, as well, and the Confederation took great pains to insure these problems were not imported.

The original settlers had come to Mars at a time when the

nations of Earth were gripped in the throes of total war. Hundreds of millions of people were bombed into oblivion, and billions more died in the aftermath of battle…from starvation, exposure, disease. The Martian colonists – refugees, really - resolved to form a new society, a new type of government, one that safeguarded a society that looked forward, to advancement, to the future. And they had done it.

Vance knew there was an ugly side to the Confederation's government too. It was an exclusionary society, allowing only the best and brightest to immigrate. The original settlers had been scientists, engineers, scholars. They were ambitious, energetic, and driven to build something better than the squalor and corruption endemic on Earth. Mars didn't want the seething masses of terrestrial poor, so long downtrodden and uneducated. The Confederation sought only those who could make it stronger, wealthier, more prosperous. Immigrants had to prove they could contribute to the society or they were turned away.

The Martian government adopted the trappings of democracy, just as the Alliance did on Earth, but it was really an oligarchy, predominantly ruled by the descendants of the original families. Without the legacy problems of the nations of Earth – poverty, pollution, economic chaos – the Confederation grew rapidly in wealth and power. The culture of Mars was focused on improvement, advancement, success. Insuring greater prosperity for each new generation was almost a religion, deeply ingrained in the mindset of the people and relentlessly promoted by the government through education and the media.

The Confederation celebrated the ideals of personal freedom too, but there as well, the reality differed somewhat from the image. The Martians enjoyed unrestricted speech and the right to live their lives largely as they pleased. Taxation was low and opportunities abundant, and most Martians considered themselves extremely fortunate to be citizens of the Confederation. But much of the freedom was illusory, superficial, and the government managed the lives of its citizens…not as overtly as the Powers on Earth did, certainly, but significantly, nevertheless.

Genetics were controlled, with approval required for any

prospective pairing. There were no restrictions or meaningful discrimination based on living arrangements or sexual practices, but reproduction was subject to considerable regulation. The next generation of Martians was considered a national asset, one that had to be protected, and unsuitable genetic matches were forbidden. The government lacked the will to enforce these dictates with harsh punishments, but nevertheless, most of the people voluntarily complied. The mantra of improving the Confederation, even the race, was nearly universal. The Martians had only to look at the seething, sweltering cities of nearby Earth to appreciate what they had.

Vance wondered, sometimes, if the Confederation could withstand the pressures of time. What would happen in five generations? Ten? Would an underclass develop, sowing the seeds of poverty and decay? Would future citizens rebel against being told who they could and could not choose as reproductive partners? Would the ruling families lose the spirit of the founders, becoming, in time, as dissolute and drunk on power as the upper classes on Earth? Vance didn't know, and in his more contemplative moments, he pondered his deep concerns and doubts for the future.

But there were more pressing issues at present. The future of Mars, the chance for its still embryonic society to develop for good or for ill, was tied to the fate of all mankind. The war against the First Imperium was a fight for survival, one that had to be won.

Vance had, more than anyone else, been responsible for forging the Grand Pact, and he was pleased with the results. The nations of Earth were truly cooperating, in a way they never had. Fear had gripped the elite classes, and their own rivalries and arguments fell away…at least while the threat from outside faced them all.

Now, Vance focused on insuring the fighting forces on the front lines got the reinforcements and supplies they needed. His operatives infiltrated factories, shipyards, spaceports, doing whatever was necessary to keep the production going. When necessary, his agents had assassinated corrupt managers and manipulated assignments to insure the most capable candidates were placed in charge. All the Powers were mired down in patronage and entrenched seniority-based systems, and Vance wasn't about to let foolishness like that impede production. If a Senator's nephew couldn't handle managing a munitions plant, he could easily be found in a hotel room, dead from a drug overdose. Nothing could be allowed to detract from the war effort.

He was keeping an eye on the other intelligence agencies too. He had no doubt that the Powers were still maneuvering for position, seeking to come out of the current conflict with an edge…a strong negotiating position at least, and possibly an advantage in the next war. Vance was darkly amused to watch fear and greed struggle against each other among Earth's competing Superpowers.

He'd spent very little time on Mars since the crisis began. He'd only been back a week, and he was leaving again in a few days. He'd vindicated the resources put into the development of the Torch transports. The superfast ships had proven themselves invaluable, though he was more or less constantly bruised and sore from the enormous pressures endured at 40g+ acceleration.

He leaned back and panned his eyes again over the hilly landscape. He was going to Epsilon Eridani IV to check on Friederich Hofstader and make sure the German scientist had everything he needed. The brilliant physicist had proven himself an able manager as well. He'd worked nothing less than wonders since Vance's Marines had put him in undisputed control over the research facility, but the war effort demanded even more. If there was anything Hofstader needed, anything at all, Vance would see that he got it.

Then he was going to Armstrong to meet with Admiral Garret. The enemy had attacked Sandoval, but so far not Garrison or Samvar. Vance expected them to eventually hit all three worlds, but if they wanted to make Sandoval the primary target, Vance was happy with that. Cain was in command on Sandoval, and Vance didn't think there was another officer in any of the Powers more suited to this fight than Erik Daniel Cain.

Chapter 13

Marin Highlands
Northern Continent
Planet Sandoval
Delta Leonis System
"The Line"

"Incoming!"

The warning came first from his AI and then, a second later, from half a dozen Marines in the HQ group. Kyle Warren reacted on instinct, diving forward and landing unceremoniously in a deep muddy puddle as the enemy cluster bombs dropped all around his position. The bombardment was short...there wasn't a major concentration of troops anywhere near Warren, and the enemy didn't know they'd inadvertently targeted the commander of II Corps.

The First Imperium forces were far more advanced technologically than the humans, but their tactics were cruder and less developed. That didn't exactly even the score, but it gave the defenders a chance at least. The invaders certainly hadn't seemed to master the concept of targeting command groups and high-ranking officers. But that, too, was even between the two sides, since the humans still hadn't figured out how the First Imperium command structure even functioned.

Warren pulled himself out of the mud, an effort made much easier by the massive strength amplification provided by his armor. He suit was covered head to toe in the slimy near-black mud common to the Sandoval highlands...quite an undignified appearance for a general commanding almost 40,000 troops, he thought with mild amusement.

II Corps was holding the line south of the primary enemy

LZ. Cain's nuclear bombardment and Merrick's counterattack had hit the First Imperium forces hard, and it took them almost a week to get organized and bring additional units down to the surface. Cain had continued to mass his remaining point defense batteries against the enemy landing craft, ignoring the largely ineffectual follow-up nuclear strikes launched from the orbiting fleet. The surface of Sandoval had gone from paradise to blasted hell, but 1st Army remained safe in its hardened fortifications. Now the ground to air defenses were mostly gone, relentlessly targeted by orbital counter-battery attacks and wiped out.

General Merrick had performed well, driving his unblooded troops hard into the maelstrom of battle. He'd lost almost a third of his tanks, but the rest had successfully disengaged and pulled back to their fortified positions along the enemy's flank. Some of his units had frozen, and a few had broken, but overall they'd performed better than he'd expected. Better than anyone had expected.

There were a few genuine heroes too, including a lieutenant who ended up commanding his entire company, and led it right through a fortified enemy position. After he took that, he turned and drove north, rolling up the enemy line for 5 klicks. He'd lost heavily...by the time his attack petered out, his own tank was the only one from his original platoon still moving, and the entire company fielded only three. Lieutenant Weld was now Captain Weld, and Merrick moved him to permanent command of a full-strength company, one that had broken and fled, with orders to whip it into shape.

Warren had heard a few other things, too, but they were just rumors...the kind that tend to run rampant in an army. Still, he wondered if there was any truth to them...if Merrick had actually shot the officers who'd panicked in the face of the enemy. In the more colorful tellings, the general pulled the trigger himself, but most versions had a firing squad doing the deed. The Marines had been almost universally skeptical of this terrestrial army officer from a political family, but the Battle of the LZ, as it had come to be called, changed that doubt to respect...and a little fear as well. Now he was Merrick the Killer, the protégé of Erik Cain, who shot down any of his troops who failed him.

Warren laughed to himself. He was more familiar with Merrick than anyone on Sandoval, and he knew the Earth officer was a fair and honorable man, far more so than most of those he'd met. Warren had formed that favorable opinion as an enemy, fighting against Merrick's forces on Arcadia during the rebellions. He didn't doubt Merrick had executed some soldiers after the battle, but if that was the case, he was sure they were guilty of gross cowardice or desertion, not simply officers who had been unable to prevent their troops from breaking and fleeing during the fight. Merrick didn't have veteran Marines under him; he had regular army troops who'd never been in battle before. Warren wasn't going to second guess what Merrick thought was necessary to keep his troops in the line.

Cain had thrown the army back on the defensive after the LZ attack, and Warren's people were manning a largely subterranean network of bunkers and fortifications ten klicks south of the enemy LZ. Kyle's corps had pulled the assignment to hold the entire defensive perimeter, allowing Cain to keep a large part of the army in reserve. His position was strong…there was no doubt about that. But his corps consisted mostly of new recruits, rushed through the normal six year Marine training program in less than 18 months. He did have some veteran cadres to stiffen his newbs, at least, and Cain had assigned one of Commander Farooq's Janissary contingents to support him as a mobile reserve.

The Janissaries were elite troops, no question, on a par with any veteran Marine unit in 1st Army. The two forces had fought each other for over a century, and each had won the other's grudging respect. Now they'd begun to earn mutual admiration as allies. Old hatreds still lingered, but they were gradually falling away, and 1st Army was starting to become a cohesive force instead of a multinational hodgepodge. That process had started with Erik Cain, who vowed never to let his old prejudices interfere with his battlefield judgment again. That had happened on Farpoint, and it had cost General Jax his life…at least that's how Cain saw it. Never again, he swore, and he had been true to his oath.

The enemy offensive had started gradually, mostly small probing attacks all along the line. Warren kept most of his forces in their bunkers, rotating units out to man the trenches. This battle had already gone nuclear and done it in a big way. He wasn't about to mass his troops and serve the enemy a nice juicy target.

Now the attacks, while still localized and sporadic, were getting heavy. He'd been compelled to bring more troops to the surface to beat back the enemy assaults. There had been a few nuclear exchanges, but he'd managed to avoid taking heavy losses from the strikes. It was a chess game of sorts. If the enemy massed its troops for an attack, he'd hit the formation with a nuclear bombardment; if he strengthened his line to receive an assault, the First Imperium forces would blast a hole in the defenses with their own nukes.

His scouting reports showed the enemy forming up in front of his center, with dozens of successive skirmish lines, widely spaced. It was a buildup of force, but it was dispersed enough to minimize vulnerability to battlefield nukes. Warren sighed as he looked at the display. They're learning, he thought somberly.

"Colonel Jarvis, put your brigade on alert immediately." Warren was going on instinct, but he was convinced the enemy was getting ready to launch an all-out assault. They couldn't mass tightly, so they were spread out and deep. It was a guess, but he was sure he was right…he was sure because it's what he would have done.

"Yes, general." Jarvis sounded a little surprised, but his response was sharp and crisp. Antoine Jarvis was a veteran who'd fought through the entire Third Frontier War. He hadn't been in General Holm's I Corps on Carson's World during the final campaign, like most of the other old veterans in 1st Army, but he'd been in his share of other hotspots. His Marines were mostly raw, however, fresh from the truncated training program on Armstrong. Warren's entire corps was green, in fact, except 7th Brigade…and they'd been detached to support General Merrick's tanks. He had the unit of Janissaries, of course, but he had to keep at least one dependable formation in reserve.

"Antoine, I know your people are wet behind the ears." Warren decided he might as well address what they were both thinking. "I'm counting on you to be five places at once. We're asking a lot of your newbs, but we need the best you can get out of them."

"Understood, sir." Jarvis' voice was decisive. "I'll make sure they do their duty." There was a brief silence. "Whatever it takes."

"Third wave…attack!" Merrick wiped the sweat from his forehead. The command tank was hot, and the air was stale. They'd been operating on recycled atmosphere for 30 hours, trying to keep out the radiation. The enemy had blasted the steppe with atomic shells for two days, trying to wipe out his force. The bombardment had been largely ineffective – Merrick had pulled his tanks back after their offensive, into dispersed, fortified positions. The nukes took out a few tanks here and there, but Merrick's corps was still combat effective when the First Imperium forces swarmed onto the steppe.

"Acknowledged, sir." It was Major Tomkins…Colonel Graves had been killed a few hours before…one of the unlucky nuclear bombardment victims. "Commencing attack."

Merrick leaned back in the cramped chair. What a place for a corps HQ, he thought with grim amusement. He'd considered positioning himself in one of the bunkers, but he decided he needed to be mobile, to be in the line with his troops. He'd stayed back in the third wave, however, despite the urge to move to the front line. The commander of 1st Army had expressly forbidden him to go farther forward. Erik Cain had spent much of his career being scolded by his own commanders for taking too many risks, but now he understood what they'd been pounding into his head all those years. He couldn't afford to lose Merrick, and certainly not for no gain, just because the Earth general wanted to salve his conscience by needlessly exposing himself to the enemy.

"Fuck!" Merrick recoiled from the plasti-steel support. That was the fourth time he'd slammed his head into it. Or was it the fifth? He wasn't used to such cramped quarters, and it was working his last nerve. Merrick had come from a powerful political family, and his army service had been exclusively as a senior officer. He'd been in a tank a couple times before Sandoval, but never for more than a few minutes. He didn't think he'd have any desire to return once he got out of this one, either. It was ripe in the tank, almost enough to make his eyes tear…and he knew he'd contributed to that as much as any of the others. He had a new respect for tank crews. The infantry tended to envy the armor, but Merrick decided he'd rather be in the mud with the ground pounders any day.

The comlink buzzed, and he flipped the switch. "Merrick here."

"Captain Weld reporting, sir." Weld was in the first wave, which had been overrun. "I've got 31 tanks, sir. Enemy forces penetrating our line at all points." He paused, and Merrick could hear him coughing, trying to clear his dry throat. "I think I'm in command, sir. I can't find a superior officer."

"You are in command, captain," Merrick snapped, "regardless of who you find. The first wave is now your responsibility. Try to pull back and join the second wave." Weld's force had suffered 85% casualties since the enemy landed on Sandoval. Merrick couldn't ask any more of them. The second wave wasn't doing nearly as well, but they still were hanging on… mostly.

"Sir…" Weld paused, uncertain if he should continue.

"What is it, captain?" Merrick's voice was sharp, impatient. "Speak!"

"Request permission to advance, sir. I believe we can penetrate to the enemy's rear and then turn about and attack."

Merrick hesitated. God, he thought, this kid's got balls. Weld's suggestion would have been extraordinary among the Marines, but from a junior officer in a terrestrial army unit it was unprecedented. "Captain, you don't have the strength…you'd be crushed."

"Respectfully, sir, we're going to catch hell trying to fall back to the second line. We've got Reaper swarms around us on all sides...between us and the fallback position." Weld's voice was getting stronger, more determined. "At least moving forward we might be able to do something other than getting shot to pieces." Another brief pause then: "And we'll surprise them."

Well, Merrick thought, it looks like we've got one of the first heroes of the Sandoval campaign. "Very well, captain." Weld was right, at least mathematically. The first wave was a spent force...they weren't going to help much holding the line...if they even made it back. But as a loose cannon deep behind the enemy advance? Maybe they could do something. Still, it was hard for him to send such a small force off by itself. If things went wrong, not one of Weld's people would make it back. He hesitated, but finally he finished what he was going to say. "Advance to the enemy rear and then act at your own discretion."

"Yes, sir!"

"And Weld?"

"Sir?"

"Good luck."

"Thank you, sir."

"You're doing what?" Storm was stunned.

"I'm taking the tanks through the rest of the enemy formation and attacking from the rear." Weld sounded calm, matter-of-fact. He was resigned to what he was doing, and he'd shoved the doubts and fear aside. "You need to get your people out of here. Try to get back to the second line."

Storm couldn't believe what he was hearing. It was insane. He'd had the same doubts about the terrestrial army units that all the Marines had, but Weld kept surprising the hell out of him. He'd been fighting alongside the army officer's tanks since the battle started, and he wasn't about to abandon him now. Marines retreating while the army advanced? Not on Storm's watch.

"Negative. You can't move forward with no support...you'll

get swarmed by the bots." Storm's voice was rock solid. "If you're moving up, we're coming with you." Storm commanded all the Marines supporting Weld's tanks. After the initial attack, General Cain had given him a battlefield promotion to captain and put him in charge of the battalion. It didn't look much like a battalion anymore...casualties were well over 50%. But Storm had kept them in the field fighting, despite a couple moments when it looked like they were ready to break.

"We don't need support. You have to fall back." Weld was determined to take his forces in, but he didn't want to commit the Marines along with his own people. "The tanks can get through – your Marines will be too exposed"

"Shove it, Carl. We're coming." Storm allowed himself a brief smile. One thing was certain...the next time he heard any of his Marines talking down the army forces they were going to have words.

There was no point in arguing with him, Weld thought... these Marines are the most pigheaded grunts I've ever seen. He sighed hard. "Alright, but stay close to the tanks...and be ready to move. We're slicing through and not stopping for anything."

"We're with you." Storm took a deep breath, allowing the oxygen rich mixture in his suit to clear his head. He was uncomfortable...he'd been in his armor more than a week without a break. The suit could recycle just about everything, but after a while it got pretty nasty inside. This wasn't the longest Storm had been in armor, but it was getting close. "Just give the word when you're ready."

"Moving out in one minute." Weld replied crisply. "Good luck, Eliot...and thanks."

"I can't let you get all the glory, can I?" Storm smiled again. Somewhere along the line he'd started to really liked Weld. How, he wondered, is this guy not in the Corps? "We'll be ready." He flipped his com to the battalion-wide circuit. "Attention 11th Battalion, this is Captain Storm..."

"They did what?" Cain's voice was stunned, but behind the surprise was understanding...and admiration.

"Sir, a detachment of General Merrick's tanks have sliced through the enemy force advancing on the Tewksbury Steppe. They've turned about and attacked from the rear." Carter paused, staring down at the incoming data. "It was Captain Weld, sir, leading the remnants of Merrick's first wave." Carter was silent for a few seconds, still reading. Suddenly, he looked up and snapped around to face Cain. "General, Captain Storm's battalion is with them. They're reporting losses over 75%."

And they're still attacking, Cain thought. That was extraordinary in any battle, but against the First Imperium it was unprecedented. Amid the shock and excitement in the command center, a tiny smile crept across Cain's lips. His officers were finally learning how to lead their units...and keep them in the line against the enemy robots. Morale would still be a problem, but Cain knew they'd turned the corner. The fear of the mysterious, of the cold and relentless new enemy was slowly giving way, overcome by the fighting spirit of the Marines and their allies. It would start slowly, with scattered units like this. But Cain was sure of it...mankind was learning to fight the First Imperium.

"I want a full report." He returned Carter's stare. "Get me Merrick now."

"Yes, sir." Carter whipped around and worked his controls rapidly. "Sir, I have General Merrick on your line."

"Isaac, what's up with the officer of yours?"

"I assume you mean Weld, sir?" Merrick phrased his response as a question, but he answered it immediately. "They were overrun...it was problematic for them to retreat, so Captain Weld requested permission to advance to the enemy's rear." Merrick's voice was a bit tentative. He wasn't sure Cain would approve...but that was only because he hadn't known 1st Army's commander as long as some of the others.

"Brilliant. Great work, general." He was skimming the reports coming across his screen as he spoke. "It looks like they're raising hell back there."

"Yes, they've disrupted the entire enemy attack." Merrick's voice was halting, tentative. "But the losses..."

"Don't worry about the losses, Isaac. Not now." Cain's voice softened. He was trying to help Merrick, show him the way to keep himself going as a commander in a battle everyone knew was going to be a bloodbath. "We're going to take heavy losses here…you and I both know that." He paused, then he added sadly, "There's time later…there's always time later to mourn the dead."

"Yes, sir." His voice was a confused mass of emotion. Exhaustion, gratitude for Cain's words, shock at how coldly detached 1st Army's commander could be.

Erik Cain was an enigma, even to those who knew him best. His small circle of friends and loved ones had seen the way he tortured himself, tormented by guilt for the Marines he'd lost, the ones he'd sent to their deaths, the ones he felt he'd failed. But that was after the battle…always after. When the fight was raging, he turned it off completely. If men and women needed to die for the combat to be won, Cain coolly sent them to their deaths. He would punish himself later, but on the field of battle, victory was all that mattered to him.

There was a long pause. Cain could hear the distant sounds of battle from Merrick's end, but neither man spoke. Finally, Merrick broke the silence. "It looks like the enemy is pausing, sir. They're very disordered, but there are still a lot of them." Merrick took a breath, holding it briefly before exhaling. "My corps is really shot up, and we're low on ammo." He hesitated again. "And if any of Weld's and Storm's people are left, they're still stuck behind enemy lines. What do you want me to do, sir?"

"I want you to attack, general. My orders are attack across the line. We're not abandoning heroes."

Major Hal "Iron Hand" Desmond banked his fighter bomber around the rocky hillside. He was flying fast and low, far too low according to all his training. But Desmond had thrown away the book. Against the First Imperium, the book would get you killed.

The Marines usually went to war without significant air-power. Transporting planes, and the vast tail of support services it took to keep them armed and flying, simply wasn't feasible…not across the vastness of interplanetary space. Major forces had a few support squadrons, but nothing more. But the transport resources marshalled to fortify the Line were unprecedented. Cain's First Army had fifteen squadrons of fighter-bombers, the largest concentration of air units to go to battle since the Unification Wars over a century before.

It would have been a commander's dream in any of the battles the Marines had fought over the past century…but the First Imperium's anti-aircraft capability was enormously effective. They didn't appear to utilize aircraft themselves; they just shot down anything that dared fly near them. The casualty rate on sorties had been off the charts. Cain had been conservative in deploying his air assets, and he'd still lost half of them already.

"Alright, 'Stalkers, stay tight with me…and for fuck's sake, keep low." Desmond was one of a few pilots starting to develop effective tactics for dealing with the enemy. He'd had some success, but his style of flying required extremely skilled pilots. His Deathstalkers were one of the best squadrons, and he'd been training them for months. His per-sortie loss rate over five missions had been 30%, less than half the average for 1st Army's air corps.

"I'm with you, major." Lieutenant Franz was tucked in just behind Desmond's plane. Franz was probably the best pilot in the squadron after Desmond. She was young – there were definitely more experienced flyers in the Deathstalkers – but she was a natural.

"I'm here major." Captain Renner was Desmond's exec. General Cain had ordered the best on this mission and, by God, that's what Desmond was giving him.

"One minute to target." The last 30 seconds were going to be the toughest. It wasn't easy to fly through the rocky hills at high speed, but at least the terrain gave cover against the enemy's defenses. In a few seconds, the three planes would come out over the open steppe…and they'd be targeted by every First Imperium unit within 20 klicks.

Desmond rubbed his hand along his right leg three times. It was an affectation, a habit he'd had going back nearly as long as he could remember. His rational mind thought superstitions were foolish, but that didn't stop him from having a few of his own. Most of the pilots did. And if they didn't, they usually picked up a couple after facing the First Imperium.

The sleek F-2000s ripped through the dense lower atmosphere, flying out over the steppe, only a few meters above the tanks and Marines fighting below. The hypersonic aircraft cleared the friendly lines in just a few seconds. Now there were enemies below…hundreds of the battle robots…no, thousands…and the hulking Reapers, turning to bring their anti-aircraft defenses to bear.

"Evasive maneuver Beta." Desmond was counting softly to himself. "Execute." The three planes banked hard, spreading out as they abruptly changed direction. Desmond wanted a random pattern…it was the best way to confound the ground defenses.

The air filled with missiles and anti-aircraft drones, but this low to the ground they'd have a hard time targeting the three fighters. The enemy canister was the real danger this low… and the Reapers were already beginning to fire. The name was an informal one, borrowed from Earth history to designate the small, multi-projectile coilguns the larger enemy robots used as an anti-aircraft defense.

"Maneuver Theta….execute." Desmond banked his plane again, pushing his craft to full throttle. The cockpit shook wildly, and he gasped, trying unsuccessfully to force a breath into his screaming lungs. The gee forces were almost unbearable, but they only lasted a short while. Desmond had developed the maneuvers to escape the enemy fire, not to make his pilots comfortable.

"Arm PBS system." The plasma bombardment system was an enormously effective new weapon. Indeed, it was the only thing that made air attacks worthwhile despite the enormous casualties.

"PBS armed, sir." Franz's reply was sharp, immediate.

"Armed, maj…"

Renner's response was cut short. Desmond's eyes shot down

to his display. His exec's icon on the plot screen was flashing red. "Fuck," Desmond muttered under his breath. He couldn't tell if Renner had managed to eject, but he knew the answer in his gut. It was almost impossible to bail at this altitude. His exec would have been lucky if he even realized he was hit before his plane slammed into the ground at 1,800 meters per second.

Desmond forced his head back to the mission. He could see the target area on the plotting screen. There they were…a small group of Marines and tanks, virtually surrounded by the enemy. "Let's fuck these bastards up…break!"

Storm could hear the cheering on the comlink. He was going to tell them to shut up, but he realized he was doing it too. The planes were coming in quick, so fast he couldn't focus on them…they were more of a blur. They were low, really low. He didn't think he'd ever seen a plane flying so close to the ground.

There were two of them…one streaking across the enemy line to the east, the other to the west. "Battalion…hit the deck. Visors off." Storm knew what was coming. It's just what they needed, but they were close. They were awfully goddamned close.

He dove to the ground, sliding a few meters in the soft, slippery clay. His visor was blacked out, and he watched the attack unfold on his monitor. "Everyone down," he repeated.

The planes flew across the enemy positions, dropping their payloads. All along the lines of Reapers and battle robots, the small PBS packages dropped…and almost immediately they erupted into enormous clouds, emitting searing white light. Inside the expanding, superheated plasmas, the enemy robots, even the fearsome Reapers, were blown to bits, melted, vaporized. The planes barely kept ahead of the small bits of hell they dropped, and then they whipped around, flying southwest, back to their base. To the front and rear of Storm's position, the enemy forces were virtually annihilated…dozens of bots just gone, consumed by the fury of the plasmas.

Storm's monitors told him how close his people had come to joining the enemy in death. The outside temperature was over 2,000 degrees…nearly the maximum his armor could withstand. He rose slowly, carefully reactivating his visor and glancing around at the nightmarish aftermath of the air attack. He had just about given up hope, but now his people – the few that were left – had a respite. Maybe they'd get back, after all.

The enemy forces to the east were badly disordered, and they began to fall back toward the landing zone, abandoning the attack. The surviving units to the west were caught between Weld's and Storm's remaining troops and Merrick's main body.

"Captain Storm?" It was Weld, on the comlink.

"Yes, captain?" Storm had almost forgotten the tanks for an instant. He was glad to hear from Weld…at least he'd made it. He didn't know the melting point of the tanks' armor, but he suspected it had been a close call. He tried not to think about how uncomfortable it was inside those vehicles.

"I just got a communication from General Merrick." He paused, taking a labored breath. "We are to attack to the west. Immediately."

Chapter 14

Critical Care Unit 3
Armstrong Joint Services Medical Center
Armstrong - Gamma Pavonis III

He could see something. It was far away, a fuzzy light…distant, very distant. No, it was close, moving closer. And brighter. There was sound too. Was there sound before? He didn't know. He couldn't remember.

"Admiral?" The words were soft, close. "Admiral Compton? Can you hear me, sir?"

The words were clearer; he could understand. Someone was calling him. The light was closer too, and shaper. It was over his head, on a field of white…the ceiling. It was the light on the ceiling. Where was he?

"Admiral Compton, squeeze my hand if you can hear me…"

He was confused. It was coming back, slowly, partially. Then he remembered. Pain! He was hit, he could feel his body pierced in a dozen places, the strength leaving him…the searing agony as he fell to the cold deck. He was dying…yes, now he remembered. But the pain was gone…and the sound and the burning, smoky smell too. He was somewhere else, someplace clean, someplace warm. There was pressure on his arm…someone was touching him.

"Admiral Compton?"

His eyes focused. He saw a head leaning over him. A woman. She was dressed all in white. "Yes…that's me." He croaked out a reply. His throat was raw, dry…the words scratched their way out slowly, painfully.

The white-clad figure smiled. "Welcome back, admiral. You are on Armstrong, in the hospital. You were wounded at Point

Epsilon. Do you remember?" She spoke slowly, clearly.

It was coming back. He'd been on the flag bridge. The battle...the enemy missile barrage. They were hit. "The fleet?" He swallowed hard, forcing the words from his parched mouth.

"The fleet successfully transited out, Terry." Another voice, deep, authoritative, but there was concern there too. "Your people performed brilliantly."

He tried to turn his head, tried to find the new voice. The room spun wildly...he was falling, spinning. His guts wretched, but there was nothing to come up.

"Don't try to move, admiral." The first voice again, gentle, calming. He could feel warmth, pressure...hands on his arms, touching him, holding him lightly. "Your body needs a few minutes to adapt. You have been unconscious for over two months."

Compton lay still, listening. He understood the words, and the memories were coming back...the battle, the impact, the ship rolling and shaking. The ship! Elizabeth! "Bunker Hill? Elizabeth?" His voice was still weak, barely audible.

"Bunker Hill made it out, Terry. Captain Arlington worked wonders...and she got out of there too." The man's voice again. He was closer now, leaning in. The face was familiar...

"Augustus..." Compton's eyes moved slowly, finding Garret's. "...it's you. I guess I made it myself too." He closed his eyes and took a deep breath. He was exhausted; even speaking was an effort. "Barely, it looks like."

"Barely is right, my old friend." Garret's voice relaxed... he was relieved to see Compton really coming out of his coma. "Captain Arlington's people got you in medical stasis just in time." Garret looked down at his oldest friend and smiled. "She's on the way here, by the way. I didn't want to take her off Bunker Hill until the ship was safely berthed at Wolf 359." He paused and let out a small laugh. "I'm afraid your flagship is a little worse for wear. She's going to be laid up for quite a while." Another laugh. "Just like you."

"She's coming here?" Compton exhaled. He was exhausted, but there was much he wanted to know, needed to know.

"I presume you are referring to our good Captain Arlington." Garret's smile widened. "Yes. She should be here sometime next week. I'm afraid I'm going to have to deprive you of the good captain's services. I've got a star in my desk for her, and this time I'm going to order her to accept it." He paused, looking down at Compton. "Her conspicuous skill and coolness under fire have become far too obvious to ignore. I'm giving her one of the task forces in 1st Fleet under Admiral Harmon." He gave Compton a sly look. "I'm sure you will miss having her on your flagship, but I daresay you may be able to find some advantage in that." Garret knew very well how Compton felt about his now former flag captain. He'd been completely prepared to look the other way on any relationship that developed, but Compton was too much a creature of duty to let his personal feelings get in the way of his job.

"We'll see." Compton was a little uncomfortable with the topic. Changing the subject: "How about Max Harmon?"

"Garret smiled. He wasn't going to push, not now. Later maybe, when Compton was stronger and they had a good bottle of Cognac to make the talk flow a little freer. He owed his friend one on matters of the heart. Compton had tried to save Garret from a tragic mistake once. It was a lifetime ago and, when Garret didn't listen, Compton nursed him through the heartbreak. It was time to repay the debt, and Garret had no intention of letting his friend make the same mistakes he had. Of course, that assumed any of it was relevant. They had to survive the war first.

"Max is fine. Your whole staff is billeted on Armstrong. God knows, I could use them elsewhere, but I want your team ready to go as soon as you're out of here."

"And when is that going to be?" Compton had a disgusted look on his face. "I can't even move my head."

"It will be faster than you think, Admiral Compton." Compton could see a hazy image in the doorway, at the edge of his peripheral vision. "I will have you out of here in six weeks…a month if you follow my instructions to the letter."

Compton tried to turn to face the new visitor, but the room

started spinning again almost immediately. "Can I get that in writing?" He let his head fall back onto the pillow and took a deep breath, fighting the urge to retch.

The newcomer walked across the room and stood next to Compton's bed. "I assure you, admiral…you will be back to duty in 4-6 weeks. Normally, I'd insist on a longer therapy period, but I understand the exigencies of the situation. We are a military hospital, after all." He was looking at the bank of monitors on the wall behind Compton. "Allow me to introduce myself. I am Dr. Thomas Lazenby. I'm the acting chief of staff of the hospital." Sarah Linden was the normal CO of Armstrong Medical, but she was heading up the field hospitals on Sandoval. Lazenby was her exec and filling in while she was absent.

Compton managed to focus. Lazenby was tall, well over two meters, and he was clad in a spotless white uniform. He had a medical insignia on one collar and a colonel's eagle on the other. Compton tried to guess his age, but with rejuv treatments it was hard to tell. He decided to go with a well-preserved sixty, thought he figured anything from forty to eighty was possible.

"I'd introduce myself, though I suspect you already know a fair amount about me." Compton's throat was dry, his voice scratchy."

"Indeed I do, admiral…though who doesn't know about Fleet Admiral Terrance Compton?" Lazenby had a flamboyant, almost theatrical personality. He tended to make overstated, sweeping gestures when he spoke. "And for now, I'm going to insist this reunion be cut short. You have been in a medically-induced coma for a considerable period, and I'm afraid it is going to take a few days for your strength to come back."

Compton glanced over at Garret then back to Lazenby. "I just need to catch up on the military situation. That shouldn't ta…"

"And you will be able to do that very soon." Lazenby's manner changed, and his voice became firm, commanding. "But now you are going to rest."

Compton looked back at Garret. "Augustus…"

"Don't look at me, my friend. I'm with your doctor here

100%." Garret smiled. "Get some rest. I'll fill you in later."

Compton looked as if he was going to argue, but he just sighed and let his head slip back onto the pillow. He was asleep in a few seconds.

Garret turned and walked out into the corridor, his grin slowly slipping away. Other than Compton's recovery, there wasn't much to smile about.

"Admiral Garret, it is good to see you again." Vance extended a hand as he climbed out of the shuttle and saw the admiral standing alongside the docking bay. He was genuinely pleased to see Garret, but the admiral's presence in the bay could mean only one thing. Bad news.

"And to see you, Roderick." Garret smiled weakly...clearly he had something on his mind. "And it's Augustus...we've discussed that before, have we not?" Garret's tenuous smile briefly widened. "I know it's a mouthful. A bit of a family curse, I'm afraid. Oldest boy in every generation as long as anyone can remember. No one's sure why."

Vance returned the smile. He'd always been a bit of a misanthrope, and he'd tended to keep his interpersonal relationships businesslike. But he had to admit to himself that he genuinely liked some of his Alliance colleagues. Garret, certainly, and Compton as well. And, of course, Erik Cain. Vance considered Cain a bit of a kindred spirit. The Marine general didn't seem particularly fond of most people either. Like Vance, he'd give his all for the cause, and he'd do anything for the men and women serving under him. But his true inner circle, his real friends...they were a very small group.

"So Augustus..." Vance pulled his arm back after shaking hands with Garret. "...why don't you tell me?"

"That obvious, is it?"

Vance smiled. "Well, I know I'm good company, but I suspect you could have waited until I got to your office...unless there was something important. And since I can hardly remember the last time I heard good news, I assume it's bad."

"Good guess." Garret paused, but only for a second. "The

enemy hit Garrison. We just got word yesterday." Garret's expression was serious, all traces of his earlier smile gone. "The naval battle's still going on." His eyes met Vance's. "It's not going well."

"Admiral Hausser is in command at Garrison?" It sounded like a question, but Vance knew he was correct.

"Yes." Garret's face was non-descript, as if he was trying to decide what he thought of Hausser. "He's a good officer, by all accounts." His face showed his doubt. "But he's never faced the First Imperium before." Garret's expression morphed into a frown. "I'd have rather put Erica West in command, but we've only got one Alliance task force there, and the CEL sent damned near their whole fleet." He looked at Vance, a wry smile back on his lips. "This diplomacy may be the death of me. I can't wait to ditch this supreme commander nonsense." He turned and took a step. "Come on...let's head back to my office while we talk."

Vance returned the grin, turning to walk alongside Garret. "I understand your frustrations, admir...Augustus, but I must thank you for your considerations toward inter-power relations. I assure you, it was not easy to assemble the Grand Pact, and anything we can do to keep things running smoothly is helpful in maintaining it. And you were the only choice for the top command that made any sense."

Garret nodded. "Our good friend Erik Cain would call me a damned fool for such considerations."

Vance had to stifle a small laugh. "Erik is an extraordinary Marine...and quite a character. But he's certainly no diplomat... and he'd be the last one to claim otherwise."

The HQ building was only a few steps from Vance's ship... Garret had directed the shuttle to the priority landing pad. They covered the distance quickly, and in just a minute or two they were walking into a large conference room...the same place they'd had their strategy sessions during the initial stages of the First Imperium invasion. This time, the massive chamber was almost empty, the prior cast now scattered, on assignments or in the hospital...or dead. There was a lone figure sitting quietly, reading data from a small 'pad.

"Elias…always a pleasure to see you." Vance spoke first as he walked into the room. He tended to be formal in his demeanor, using titles and surnames far more frequently than first names…even with close associates. But his Alliance friends were looser and more relaxed in their conduct, especially when it was just the senior personnel present. Vance made an effort to conform…to "loosen up" as Garret had so delicately put it. He was getting used to it, but it wasn't always easy. He'd been raised in a very strict household; he'd called his father, "sir" until the day the old man died.

"Roderick." Elias smiled and nodded a greeting. "I hope your trip wasn't too uncomfortable. Those ships of yours are a technological marvel, but they're hard on the body. My aging one, at least."

"And mine." Roderick smiled, walking to one of the chairs. "They've come in handy, but I'm afraid I've been bruised from head to toe since this whole thing began." He pulled out a chair and sat down. Garret was doing the same at the head of the table.

"We've got some updates from Garrison, gentlemen." Holm's eyes were moving from his 'pad first to Garret then to Vance. They could tell from his tone the news wasn't good. "I'm afraid Admiral Hausser has been badly defeated and, it appears, killed in action. Fourth Fleet is attempting to withdraw to Moonstone, but it appears a significant number of units are deep in-system, cut off from the warp gate. "The Konig Friederich has been destroyed."

Garret looked out impassively. The CEL flagship, he thought…and their top admiral. The pain in this conflict was rapidly spreading beyond just the Alliance forces. "What else do we know?"

Holm's eyes flicked down to the 'pad again. "Admiral Yoshiru has taken command, but it appears Mikasa is with the trapped fleet units. We don't have any data on who is commanding the withdrawing vessels or how many ships are trapped with Admiral Yoshiru."

Vance sat quietly, listening to the unfolding disaster, but saying nothing. This was the province of the military, and two of the most gifted warriors in history were sitting in the room with him.

"Do we have any confirmations on fleet units that have transited?" Garret was starting to get very worried about losses. Fourth Fleet had 7 capital ships. It looked like they were going to lose at least two, and maybe more. They couldn't afford that kind of attrition.

"Negative." Holm was still glancing down. The stream of information coming through on his 'pad was continuing, but it was frustratingly incomplete. "I'm not sure anything has transited yet."

Garret stared across the table, his mind lost, wondering how bad the losses were going to be. Finally, he glanced at Vance and back at Holm. "Well, I guess it's General Gilson's show on Garrison now."

Holm nodded silently.

Chapter 15

Hobson's Ridge
Planet Garrison
Alpha Corvi III
"The Line"

"We've got Reapers breaking through in sector 9." Captain John Horace shouted into the com. He was trying to stay in control, but his lines were caving in all around him. He could feel the fear, the panic starting to build, but he pushed back hard against it. "We can't hold them. Half the battalion is down, and the rest are falling back." There were too many of them…and the Reapers were just too damned hard to bring down.

"Hold your position, Horace." It was Major Timmons. Horace's mind raced – what happened to the colonel? "I've got three companies of panzergrenadiers on their way to reinforce you." There was a pause, only a few seconds, and then, "ETA ten minutes."

Horace took a deep breath. Ten minutes, he thought…it might as well be a year. "Ok, 7th battalion, we've got friendlies inbound. We need to hold for ten minutes." He was struggling to sound calm. He was as scared shitless by these things as anybody in the battalion, but his troops were hanging on by a thread, and the last thing they needed was him sounding anything less than 100% in control. "Everybody grab the best cover you can, and fire everything you've got."

Horace had commanded the battalion for 20 minutes, the fourth officer to hold the posting since morning. Major Klein was dead…he wasn't sure about Pinter and Vine…they may have made it to a field hospital. Whether they were alive or dead, they were out of action, and that left 7th battalion in the hands of its junior captain.

Horace clicked a reload into his mag-rifle and made his was forward. The battalion was going to need every bit of firepower they could scrape up if they were going to hold out. The enemy fire was thick as he made his way to the front. He crouched down, staying low as he moved slowly toward the line. The battalion was pinned down behind a small lip at the top of the ridge. They'd had a better position 300 meters farther forward, but they hadn't managed to hold it. The enemy hit them in force, and they had to fall back. That's where Captain Pinter got hit…and Vine a few minutes later.

There were dead Marines everywhere. There were a lot of wounded, too, but most of them were still in the firing line. His people were clinging to the tiny ridge, firing their weapons with grim resolve. They'd beaten back the first two enemy assaults against the new position, but now the Reapers were coming.

He crouched behind the lip, bringing his rifle to bear. It was nearly impossible to take out a Reaper with a mag-rifle…it took a SAW at least, and usually more. But there were regular bots advancing too, and a perfect shot could hurt one of them.

"Captain Horace, I've got air support approaching your sector, inbound and hot. ETA one minute." It was Major Timmons again, and he cut the line before Horace could acknowledge. It was starting to look like Timmons had inherited the brigade and, if that was the case, he had more problems to deal with than just 7th Battalion.

Horace was grateful for the air; he knew resources were stretched thin right now. He looked out over the field and exhaled hard. Maybe we can hold out after all. He checked his scanners, and he saw the approaching aircraft already. It looked like two fighter-bombers coming in from the west, parallel to the enemy line. The humans had air superiority of a sort, but it was only because the First Imperium forces didn't seem to field aircraft. They could shoot them down, though, and their accuracy made running ground support missions the closest thing to suicide this side of putting your head in a noose. Still, the flyers were ready to go in wherever they were needed. General Gilson would run out of planes and pilots eventually, but Horace was glad she still had at least two to spare.

The planes dove madly for the enemy position, and the Reapers redirected their fire, filling the sky with hypersonic projectiles. One of the planes was hit almost immediately. It lost a wing and cartwheeled for a few seconds before crashing into the ground behind enemy lines. Horace closed his eyes for a few seconds, not wanting to look at the rising plume of smoke and flame.

The second craft veered off wildly, dodging the heaviest fire as it angled down to launch its attack. Damn, that's one hell of a pilot, Horace thought. He had nothing but respect and admiration for the crews of those planes. That flyer was playing Russian Roulette with four barrels loaded, just to take the pressure off his people. Horace watched the bomber level off about 500 meters from the ground and loose its payload. The plasma bombardment system was one of the most effective new weapons to reach the front lines from Colonel Sparks' labs, and it made the bombing runs worth the risk at almost any casualty rate.

Horace stared at the field in front of him as the massive clouds of superheated plasma erupted all along the edge of the enemy's advance. His visor darkened automatically to save his eyes from the blinding white light, but he couldn't stop watching. The enemy bots caught within the expanding plasmas were destroyed, vaporized or blown to bits. Even the Reapers were consumed in the maelstrom, falling prone as their hulking bodies melted and disappeared.

The plane arced up, climbing rapidly, trying to escape. The pilot was obviously a veteran, and he almost made it…but the fire from the enemy second line was too heavy, and a stream of hypervelocity rounds shredded the tail of his aircraft. The stricken bomber tumbled end over end and plummeted to the ground. Horace was watching on his scanner, and he felt a sick feeling in his gut. They were suffering thousands of casualties on Garrison, but the thought of that courageous pilot dying was particularly hard for him to take. He was watching on his scanner, and he saw that the pilot managed to eject. Maybe he'll make it, Horace thought, grasping. He tried to draw comfort from that faint hope, but he could see the escape pod coming down in the middle of the enemy position.

"Attention all personnel." He was speaking on the battalion-wide com. "This is Captain Horace. Those pilots just went in there to buy us a respite, and now we're going to pay them back." He was breathing heavily, deeply inhaling the oxygen-rich mixture his suit circulated. "We're taking back the forward position before the enemy reorganizes. The battalion will advance on my mark." He flipped off the com. "Jonesy, give me a stim." He was feeling growing fatigue, and he needed to be 100% right now.

"Yes, captain." The AI obeyed immediately, and Horace felt a prick in his arm, followed by a feeling of new strength spreading through his body. The heaviness in his limbs was relieved, and the dull headache was pushed back.

He flipped the com back on and gripped his mag rifle. "7th Battalion...attack!" He leapt over the small lip and ran toward the heavier rock outcropping ahead. It was a better position, one he was determined to hold this time, especially once he was reinforced. He focused on his stride - running in armor required some concentration, at least if you didn't want to end up taking high leaps and getting blown to bits by enemy fire. He'd covered half the distance before he glanced at his display to see who was following. He sighed and almost stopped right where he was, but he kept his head and ran the rest of the way to the ridge.

"Let's go 7th Battalion. Move your asses!" He was pissed, and it came through in his tone. The battalion was all strung out from the forward ridge back to the original position. Half his people had hesitated and moved grudgingly, late. All along the line, platoon sergeants and junior officers were haranguing them onward. Horace knew the battalion was almost spent, but he'd never seen a veteran Marine formation attack so raggedly. These things are really getting into their heads, he thought grimly. "At least none of them broke," he muttered to himself. "Yet."

Heinrich Shultz moved swiftly over the blasted terrain. The fighting had been heavy, and the ground was torn to shreds. There were huge craters all around, half-filled from the high water table. A heavy tactical nuke had hit a klick north, and all the trees and vegetation were gone, blasted away by the shockwave.

The Marines had been in a vicious fight here, and there were bodies everywhere. Shultz could only take a wild guess, but he figured 7th Battalion had lost half its strength. His Panzergrenadiers were here to reinforce the Marines. The enemy was attacking hard, but the position was vital, and his orders were to hold at all costs. If the First Imperium forces broke through here it would compromise the lines to the north and south. The human forces would have to pull back at least 20 klicks, and the whole defense of the Gregor Valley would be in jeopardy.

Shultz had a rump battalion, 3 companies of Panzergrenadiers. The Central European League's armored infantry didn't have much experience fighting either alongside or against the Alliance Marines, but the two formations had a strong respect for each other. The CEL had spent most of the last century waging its own private war with the French-dominated Europa Federalis, and Shultz's troops were veterans of those battles. But his people knew the history of the Alliance Marines, and they greatly respected their new allies.

The League division landed just before the enemy fleet arrived and blockaded the planet, and they were assigned as a general reserve. Generalmajor Baer had been upset at being positioned to the rear, but his complaints quickly became superfluous. The enemy hit the Alliance lines hard, and the reserves were already being committed. His troops started moving to the front lines almost immediately.

Shultz could see the Marines on his display. They were moving forward. Attacking! He smiled. The Marines were living up to their reputation, and Shultz was damned if the panzergrenadiers would do less. "3rd battalion...forward at the double. Advance and support the Marine units at the ridge."

The CEL troops swarmed up and over the secondary posi-

tion, the one the Marines had just left. The steel gray armor of
the panzergrenadiers was a bit sleeker than the Alliance suits,
and they moved quickly across the broken ground.

"Captain Horace, do you read me?" Shultz was trying to
reach the Marine commander. The com systems had been
synced to facilitate communication between the multinational
forces.

"Horace here." His voice was distracted, tense. He was in
the middle of a firefight.

"Captain Shultz here. I've got three companies of panzergrenadiers. Where do you need us?"

Horace paused. He didn't think "everywhere" would be a
productive answer. "Move onto the left and take over that section of the line. I'll pull my people right." There was a short
pause. "And thanks, captain. You got here just in time."

Catherine Gilson paced around her headquarters. Her boots
clicked loudly on the metal floor, and the sound reverberated
off the low ceiling. She wore a set of gray fatigues in the HQ,
her combat suit hanging on a rack against the wall. The armor
was already scarred and blackened. Gilson had been up to the
surface half a dozen times, checking on her positions. The
Corps didn't breed commanders who were comfortable leading
from behind, and Gilson was no exception.

Gilson sat out the rebellions, and she'd been the commander
of the training program until General Holm tapped her to take
charge on Garrison. It had been close to ten years since she'd
had a field command, and she was hesitant to jump into such a
massive role. But she understood the importance of holding the
Line, and when Holm asked her to take charge on Garrison, she
reluctantly agreed.

Most of her Marines were raw and unblooded. Worse,
they'd been hurried through a drastically truncated training program, one she had grave doubts about despite the fact that she'd
run it. The First Imperium invasion had forced the issue and
compelled the Corps to rush recruits into the field. Most of the
veteran formations were in General Cain's First Army. She'd

been a bit envious at first, but from the reports she'd seen, Cain had it even worse than she did. As bad as things were on Garrison, it looked like the enemy was making its biggest push on Sandoval. Cain had his hands full, even with most of the Marine veterans under his command.

The forces on Garrison were more multinational than those on Sandoval, and she faced a hard time molding the many different detachments in her 2nd Army into a cohesive force. Cain's army wasn't homogenous either, but it was more so than Gilson's. Cain had Commander Farooq's Janissaries, which could have been a trouble spot. Erik Cain was nobody's idea of a diplomat, and he'd fought against the Janissaries his entire career. But the Caliphate officer and his troops had won Cain's grudging respect in the closing stages of the Battle of Farpoint, and he and Farooq made their peace long before enemy forces arrived at Sandoval. Cain's other foreign units were from the PRC and the Martian Confederation, both historical Alliance allies.

Gilson had a CEL division as well as forces from the Russian-Indian Confederation and, most problematic of all, the Central Asian Combine. The Chinese-dominated CAC was another Alliance enemy, and there was every bit as much enmity as there was with the Caliphate.

The CEL division was a crack formation by anyone's standards, and she was grateful to have them. She had one experienced brigade of Marines too, and a few hundred Russian commandos. The rest of 2nd Army was made up of new recruits and reserve formations.

The Grand Pact was working, at least to an extent. The Powers were united against the threat, but they were also scared and looking to protect their own possessions. The Line was intended as a bulwark to defend all human-occupied space, but there was no guarantee the enemy wouldn't find a different series of warp gates leading to another populated world. The Powers had committed troops to the combined forces, but they'd all held back some of the best formations to defend their own planets if the First Imperium opened another front somewhere. That meant there were a lot of second line units fighting in the battles on the Line.

"I need a report from the center." She snapped out her orders abruptly. Gilson had a reputation of being an aggressive and impatient commander. It was richly deserved. "Get me Major Timmons."

"Major Timmons is not responding. I have Captain Horace, general." Kevin Morton was young for a major. He'd earned his chops in the fighting on Carson's World at the end of the Third Frontier War, and he'd been on Gilson's staff ever since.

"Captain Horace, report." Gilson tended to a bit abrupt with her people, but they loved her anyway. The tale of how she was wounded on Carson's World and walked out of the hospital to get back to the front had attained legendary status among the rank and file. It had become one of those stories where more people claimed to be there than were actually present. Gilson had, in fact, demanded to be released once her wounds were dressed, but she hadn't had to argue too much. Sarah Linden and her people were swamped with casualties and low on supplies. Sarah had been thrilled to get rid of a difficult patient who could walk out on her own steam.

"Yes, general." Horace sounded harried and a little distracted at first, but he focused quickly. When the army commander was on the com, everything else seemed less urgent. "We've retaken our original position. The air attack hit the enemy hard and opened the door." His throat was dry, and his voice hoarse. "The panzergrenadiers took position on our left, and I was able to create a reserve from the troops they relieved. We're in reasonably good shape, general, but it's not going to last." Horace had been trying to hide his fear, but it was starting to show anyway. "We have a column of Reapers forming up…at least a hundred. I don't know how we're going to hold them back. And there are more units moving up…I don't have complete data yet. I've launched drones, but they've all been shot down."

Horace hadn't said it, but Gilson knew his heavy weapons had to be low on ammunition. His people had been in serious combat for hours…they had to be exhausted. She was determined to hold in the center, but now she thought, will I just be throwing troops away? The entire line would be exposed if the enemy managed a breakthrough anywhere. She hated to give ground, but realism won battles, not empty bluster.

"Major Morton…" She hesitated, as if she was having trouble forcing out the words. "…the entire line will withdraw to the secondary position." She'd just ordered 20,000 troops to retreat over 10 kilometers. Morton didn't turn to see, but he'd have bet her expression would have curdled milk. "Immediately, major."

Chapter 16

Bridge – AS Hornet
Sigma 4 System
Nine Transits from Newton

"Oh my God." Jacobs was speaking to himself, softly under his breath. The bridge was silent…not a sound except the beeping of the alarm. Jacobs and his four bridge officers were transfixed, staring in shock at the main display. The data was clear… Ensign Carp had checked it twice, but it was still hard to accept.

"Cut the reactor. Now!" Jacobs' eyes didn't deviate from the main screen as he fired out the command. "Full silent running protocols." The reactor had barely been operating, producing just enough energy to power Hornet's basic systems. But Jacobs wanted it stone cold. Immediately.

The data on the screen was divided into sections, lines of text scrolling alongside several diagrams. The picture they told was a nightmare unleashed. There were fleets, presumably First Imperium armadas, everywhere in the system. Two groups of ships were inbound from the Zeta 2 warp gate, and another was on a course that would take it just past Hornet and on to the Omicron 3 system…the one from which Jacob's ship had just transited. And around the system's fourth planet, dozens of ships orbited, both individually and clustered around six colossal space stations.

The orbital installations were like nothing Jacobs had ever seen. Unfathomably massive, they were ten or twenty times the size of the Alliance facilities at Earth. He could only imagine the power of those fortresses, the massive arrays of weaponry protecting this previously unknown planet. Jacobs took in a deep breath, holding it for a few seconds. His heart raced, and his stomach was clenched. A cold feeling took him, chilling his soul. There was one terrifying, inescapable conclusion. Hornet had found a world of the First Imperium.

"Ensign Carp, I want a course projection for that approaching force." The flotilla heading toward the warp gate was thrusting hard, executing a vector change. Jacobs figured they intended to transit, but he wanted to know how close they were going to come.

Carp leaned over his workstation for a few seconds. "I had to make some estimates, sir, but I'm projecting the likeliest course." The main screen showed a new plot, with a line connecting the First Imperium task force with the warp gate. The line was curved at the start, showing the course change in progress, before continuing straight to the Omicron 3 gate. "If this projection is correct, the closest vessel in the enemy force will pass within 2,374,500 kilometers of Hornet." He'd turned to face Jacobs, and his voice was soft...an instinctive reaction to the silent running. It was pointless - the enemy couldn't detect sound through space. Carp could have blown a trumpet and it wouldn't have mattered. But the reaction was a subconscious one...and very common among spacers in the attack ships. "Of course, I had to estimate the enemy's velocity, so we have to allow a margin of plus or minus 1,000,000 kilometers to be safe."

Jacobs could feel the headache forming, like a black cloud seeping into his temples. This was going to be close...2.3 million was bad enough, and they ran a big risk of detection even running silent. But if the enemy came within 1.3 million, they'd be almost certain to scan Hornet. Jacobs couldn't imagine his ship surviving that by more than a few minutes.

But what to do? He didn't dare fire the engines...the enemy would find his tiny ship in seconds at this range. His mind raced. "Think man, think," he whispered to himself. Finally, he lifted his head. "Lieutenant Mink, prepare to engage the positioning thrusters. I want a plan to maximize our distance from the projected enemy course."

"Sir?" Mink looked confused. "Without the reactor power,

we've only got the compressed gas jets. We're not going to get far on those, sir."

"I'm aware of that, lieutenant. But we need every kilometer we can get. We're at a relatively low velocity. Even a moderate nudge will change our vector measurably." Like all spaceships, Hornet was equipped with a number of positioning thrusters located at various places on the hull. The main engines were in the rear, so when the crew wanted to conduct a burn to change their vector or velocity, they used the smaller jets to spin the ship around, positioning the engines to provide thrust along the desired angle. The jets were powered by the main reactor, but they had secondary systems utilizing compressed gas. Mostly used for docking maneuvers, the gas jets were virtually undetectable, and they would allow Hornet to exert a small amount of thrust without meaningfully increasing the chance of detection.

"Yes, sir." She worked the controls for a few seconds. "Thrust pattern calculated, captain. We can run the compressed air system for approximately 87 seconds before exhausting the gas reserves.

Jacobs sat silently for half a minute, a minute, longer. Every eye on the bridge was on him when he finally spoke. "Divert 50% of life support reserves to the jets and recalculate."

Mink sat unmoving, staring across the cramped bridge at Jacobs. Carp and the others were doing the same.

"Now, lieutenant," Jacobs scolded. He wasn't too harsh with her...he understood the implications of what he was ordering. Diverting half of Hornet's breathing air to the jets would allow the ship to exert more thrust, but it would leave her with the bare minimum necessary to maintain the delicate equilibrium that sustained the lives of her crew. If they ran out of power, even for a short while...or if the support system took any damage, they'd suffocate...all of them. "Do it. Immediately." His voice was soft, but he'd repeated himself three times. Mink turned slowly and looked down at her workstation.

"Diverting ship's air to positing thrusters, captain." She paused, counting softly as she calculated the effect. "Estimated thrust duration now 5 minutes, 42 seconds."

Jacobs leaned back in his chair, his eyes fixed directly ahead. He was staring at the screen, but he was seeing nothing. He was deep in thought, considering his plans, trying to look ahead. No room for mistakes here, he thought...none at all. "Lieutenant Mink, execute thrust plan."

Jacobs braced for the pressure his body had come to expect from engine burns, but it didn't come. The gas jets put out minimal thrust compared to the main engines...the crew could just barely feel it, though the small change from zero gravity to about 0.33g was more noticeable when he moved.

"Positioning jets engaged, captain."

Jacobs sat quietly. Hopefully, this will be enough, he thought.

"I don't think they scanned us, captain." Mink's voice was soft, her speech slow and tentative. Everyone on Hornet had been sitting on a knife's edge, waiting to see if they'd gotten far enough to avoid detection. The enemy fleet had already passed by the closest point, and they were on their way to the warp gate. They were still in potential detection range, but the fact that they were on their original course was a good sign.

"They have no reason to deploy active scanners, lieutenant." Jacobs spoke loudly, trying to shake the crew from the pointless whispering. He understood the impulse, but it got annoying after a while. It wasn't like the enemy could hear even the loudest scream across 2,000,000 kilometers of vacuum that did not transmit sound waves. "We're not supposed to be here."

Jacobs had been on edge himself. He'd thought he and his crew were on a streak of good luck. They'd been low on supplies and reaction mass, but they found both on the first planet they explored. He'd been cautious when they discovered the native foodstuffs, and his tiny science team repeatedly tested the fruits and vegetables they harvested there. They found nothing harmful and, in the month since, none of the crew had shown any ill-effects. That didn't mean there were none, but Jacobs figured so far, so good. If some miracle ever brought Hornet back home, he figured they'd all be quarantined for a long time...and poked and prodded by half the Alliance's medical personnel.

But that was tomorrow's problem. Today's was staying alive in the middle of what appeared to be a massive enemy base.

The military significance of this discovery was enormous. So far, the First Imperium had been some mysterious enemy, appearing from the unexplored depths of space. Now Jacobs and his people knew where the enemy forces were coming from, or at least where some of them were. He had to get this information back to HQ. But how?

"Ensign Carp, I want you to collect every scrap of data you can without violating silent running protocols." That restricted the young officer to passive scans only, and it forbade him from launching Hornet's two remaining probes. It was like working with one hand tied behind his back, and Jacobs knew it. But anything else risked detection…and that would mean death for all of them.

"Yes, sir." He turned and started to scan the incoming readings. "It looks like at least 120 ships in the system, sir. I have identified what appear to be nine large battleships, much larger than any vessels we have yet encountered." The Leviathans were new to Hornet's crew…these were the first ones they'd seen. He projected a mockup of the larger ship on the main display.

Every eye on the bridge focused on the massive vessel on the screen. "That must be twice the size of a Yorktown class battleship." It was Mink who spoke, but everyone was thinking it.

"Actually, it is just over 2.5 times the tonnage of a Yorktown." Carp had run the calculations. The data was rough – they were still too far out to get a good scan. But it painted a pretty clear picture.

"Ensign Carp, how close will our present course bring us to the fourth planet?" Jacobs was trying to take everyone's attention off the nightmare ship, but he was also trying to plan ahead. He had no idea what to do next.

"A little over 6 million kilometers, sir." He paused, looking across the tiny bridge. "What are your orders, sir?"

Jacobs sat quietly, thinking. "We're going to do a fly by on that planet and get all the readings we can." He paused again, and added, "And then we're going to get out of this system somehow and get back to Alliance space with the data."

Chapter 17

Marin Highlands
Northern Continent
Planet Sandoval
Delta Leonis System
"The Line"

"I want those fucking things up and firing in one minute. Do you motherfucking understand me?" Warren was pissed, really pissed. He was normally laid back and circumspect in his speech, but when he got upset enough the curses flowed. He knew most of his troops were green, but they really had their heads up their asses right now, and he wasn't going to put up with it.

"But sir, conditions are very difficult up here. You don't understand what we are dealing wi…"

"Silence, Captain Jones." Warren's voice was cold as death. "You are fired. Report to headquarters at once. And if you're not here in ten minutes I will consider you a deserter and send the special action teams after you. Do you understand me?"

Warren didn't wait for the flummoxed Jones to reply. He cut the line and commed Lieutenant Mackey, Jones' number two. "Lieutenant, Captain Jones has been relieved. Effective immediately, you are in command. You have two minutes to get the HVM batteries deployed and firing. Two fucking minutes. Am I clear?"

"Yes, sir!" Mackey snapped back his response. He knew better than to argue, but he wasn't sure how he was going to manage it either. The troops were too raw; they didn't have the training and experience. His detachment was on rough ground and under heavy fire. Enough, he thought, you've already wasted

15 seconds. "Sergeant Vick, get those things up and firing." Mackey scrambled up over the rocky ground to get a closer look.

"Yes, Lieutenant Mackey." Vick was the best Mackey had, but it didn't look like his group would be firing in time. The others were in worse shape.

Warren's entire corps was taking hard punishment. He couldn't mass his forces anywhere...every time he did the enemy hit them with a nuclear strike. The enemy faced the same problem, but they were less sensitive to losses...and they didn't have the same morale problems. Human troops, even Marines, can only sit under threat of nuclear bombardment for so long before their fighting spirit erodes. The two sides had faced each other for several days, but finally the First Imperium forces formed up in a deep series of extended lines and began throwing themselves at Warren's defenses. Their tactics were crude, but their enormous firepower and total lack of fear made them hard to resist.

Merrick's tank corps had fought a titanic battle to the north and west, and the ferocity and the duration of that engagement had bought Warren time, delaying the enemy assault on his positions. Merrick's people got the best of the fight, defeating the enemy and driving them back with heavy casualties. But the tank corps was worn down to a nub, barely 120 of its original 600 armored vehicles still fully-functional and in the field. They'd launched a major attack then fought a desperate defensive battle. They were exhausted and low on supplies and ammunition. The enemy set up a defensive perimeter at the edge of the steppe and focused their attention south, toward Warren's II Corps.

Merrick wanted to attack...to slice through to the enemy flank and relieve the pressure on Warren. But it just wasn't possible, at least not until he'd been able to refit and rearm. Even then, he wasn't sure his troops would obey an attack order. The terrestrial army forces had exceeded everyone's expectation, but they were done...a spent force. The enemy hadn't mastered the concept of morale yet...if they had, they'd have hit Merrick again before his troops had a chance to rest and dig in.

The attacks against II Corps had been going on for three

days now, wave after wave of enemy bots and Reapers throwing themselves against the network of interlocked bunkers and entrenchments along Warren's line. Cain's insistence on constructing massive fortifications was paying off, and II Corps was inflicting enormous casualties on the enemy forces. But the orbiting fleet just kept sending down reinforcements...it seemed there was no end to the battle robots on those ships, the deadly legions waiting to land and attack Cain's dwindling army.

Warren flipped the com to Mackey's line. "Status report, lieutenant." He was cheating the harried young officer...it had only been a minute and forty seconds.

"HVMs deployed and commencing fire, General Warren." Mackey's voice was shaky, but he managed to get it out clearly. It was a bit of an exaggeration...if would be another half minute before anything fired...but it was close enough. What was the corps commander doing, he wondered, riding him, a lowly lieutenant? Warren was micromanaging like crazy, skipping multiple layers of the chain of command, directly supervising the troops anywhere he considered a critical spot.

"Good job, lieutenant." Warren was surprised. He made a note to himself. He was going to move this kid up...and give him his captain's bars. If he lived through the next couple days. "I want maximum fire. The enemy's moving against your section of line. Deploy your SAWs on the slope below the HVMs and get them engaged, ASAP. Make sure your fire is disciplined... missiles target the Reapers, autocannons the bots." Warren was speaking rapidly, and he forced himself to slow down. He didn't want to overload the young officer. "I've got ammo resupply en route, so don't worry about reloads. Just keep up the intensity."

"Understood, sir."

"Warren out." Kyle looked down at the tactical table. It was essentially a large 'pad displaying a real time plot of the battle raging on the surface. The enemy just kept pounding, one line after another charging across the hilly ground. His green troops weren't going to hold much longer; he needed to do something.

He knew as well as Mackey did that he'd been micromanaging, involving himself in minutia far below a corps commander's usual level. But he needed to make every strongpoint as tough as he could. He wished he could direct the positioning of every autocannon and deploy every squad. Cain was counting on him to hold out, and he wasn't about to fail that trust.

Warren put his hand to his head, adjusting the earpiece of his com. "Commander Jaffer?" Barir Jaffer commanded a tac-force of Janissaries attached to Warren's corps. With 7th Brigade detached to support Merrick's tanks, Jaffer's troops were Warren's largest veteran formation.

"Yes, General Warren?" There was a slightly odd cadence to Jaffer's speech, his AI translating his Arabic to English and transmitting. Warren's system could just as easily done the translations, but these types of things flowed uphill, from lower ranks to higher.

"I need you to deploy your troops." Warren was staring at the tactical map as he spoke. "Use the tunnels and get your people along the enemy's left flank, starting about a quarter klick out from our main position. If we don't take some pressure off the line, we're not going to have a line much longer."

"Yes, general." Warren had originally expected resentment from the Caliphate officers, but Jaffer was nothing but respectful and polite. "I will have them in position directly, sir."

"Very well, commander. Advise me when you are in place." Warren had thought of the Janissaries as enemies for so long, it felt surreal fighting alongside them. The Janissary officers had adjusted well to being under his command, at least on the surface. He wondered how well he would follow the orders of some Caliphate general. Then he wondered how Cain would manage in that situation, and he couldn't help but allow himself an amused grin.

"Colonel Linden, this is triage. We've got more wounded coming. ETA 15 minutes." Lieutenant Ploor's voice was hoarse, her mouth dry. She tried to clear her throat, but it didn't do much good. She'd been commanding the main triage station for thirty hours, and she needed another stim. Actually, she needed a good night's sleep, but it didn't look like that was in the cards.

The wounded kept coming and, as long as they did, she was staying right where she was.

Sarah started to sigh, but she caught herself and suppressed it. Her people were as worn down as she was. They didn't need to see or hear it in her. "Very well, lieutenant." Things were starting to get crowded in the hospital…and the aid stations were even worse. "Critical cases only. Stabilize the rest and put them in holding." There was a long pause. "And Allison…" Sarah's voice softened considerably. "…start taking out the hopeless cases. We need to focus on the ones we can save."

Sarah hated that part of her job. She was driven, and loath to admit she couldn't save them all. But she was a veteran too, and she understood reality. At least there weren't too many hopeless ones. For the most part, if they got to her hospital alive, her people could save them. At least until she started to run out of supplies and med units. Then, she knew from bitter experience, the definition of hopeless would begin to expand.

Merrick's wounded were still pouring in days after the fighting in the north had exhausted itself. Most of them were pretty bad, and even worse for the fact that many had lain for several days, wounded inside their crippled tanks. Armor crews were usually wounded superficially, or they were critically injured. The light wounds were treated in the field at the aid stations. The ones that got to Sarah were usually burned beyond recognition or torn to shreds by heavy weapons fire. They didn't have the trauma control systems the powered infantry did, so their condition tended to deteriorate as they lay waiting for transit to the hospital.

The wounded were mostly green troops, fighting their first battles on Sandoval. She could tell the difference as they came in. They were terrified, some of them panicked and screaming as they lay on the stretchers waiting. Her team was struggling to keep them calm and reassure them. The veteran Marines in her other battles had been more stoic. Experienced fighters, they knew if they were in real trouble or not, and most of them lay quietly until the surgeons treated them. They were scared too, of course, and in pain, but the veterans knew the Corps' medical service was the best anywhere, and they trusted Sarah and her crew to pull them through.

There were veterans in 1st Army too, she knew that. But Erik was keeping most of them in reserve. Other commanders would have committed them by now, fed them into the line to stiffen the raw troops. But Sarah knew Erik wouldn't…not until he was ready. He'd keep sacrificing the rookies, letting the enemy throw themselves at his prepared positions. He had a plan for the elite forces. She didn't know what it was, but she was sure he had one, and she knew he would follow it relentlessly, no matter how many casualties flowed into her hospital.

She loved Erik, but for all their years together, she knew she didn't understand him completely. There was always a part of him that remained an enigma. An outsider could judge him a cold-blooded monster, a relentless warmongering leader who didn't care how much his men and women bled to win his glory. But that wasn't him; he was nothing like that. No one who knew him would give that thought credence, least of all her. She'd shared his suffering, his nightmares. She'd held his sweatsoaked body in the middle of the night, when the ghosts tormented him and sleep wouldn't come. She'd never known anyone who agonized more over the suffering of the troops than he did. Or cared less for the glory his battles accrued to his name.

But on the field he was a different man. He would coolly, relentlessly do what he felt was necessary to win the fight. Nothing would deter him, not losses, not fear, not doubt. Victory was all that mattered, and he expected everyone under his command to show the same level of commitment. Most generals in his shoes on Sandoval would look to hold out, to defend as long as possible. But she knew better. She knew he wasn't trying to hold out against the First Imperium forces…he was planning to destroy them. This was going to be a fight to the death. Only one side would leave Sandoval.

That meant her people were going to be getting even busier. She took a breath and stepped back into her makeshift OR. She didn't have any more time to waste on introspection. The wounded would keep coming; she was sure of that.

Majdi Yusef peered around the jagged rock formation. His heavy tac-group was on the extreme right flank of the enemy advance. Half the men were still underground, climbing slowly to the surface through the small access portal. His orders were clear. Set up a firing position and hit the advancing First Imperium forces hard on the flank. His small force wasn't enough to seriously hurt the enemy, but he knew there were groups like his deploying in multiple locations. The entire tac-force was going in. In another few minutes, the First Imperium would meet the Janissaries once again, and Yusef was determined that his team would do their part. They had not been with the forces under Commander Farooq on Farpoint, but those brothers had covered themselves in glory, and Yusef was anxious to follow down that honorable path.

"Pashia, lead your team to the top of that far ridge...coordinates 357x96...and deploy your weapons." Caliphate support weapons tended to be light, with high rates of fire. They were very effective against the Alliance forces and their other traditional enemies, but fighting the First Imperium required heavy, harder-hitting ordnance. Yusef's men had been reequipped with the Alliance's new HVMs and Martian Confederation heavy SAWs. The foreign weapons were a little unfamiliar, but his troops were veterans, and he was sure they could adapt. Using Alliance-manufactured equipment felt a little strange. His men had been on the receiving end of those weapons far too often.

The Janissary Corps was named for the ancient slave soldiers of the Ottoman Empire, the finest infantry of their day. The modern Janissaries weren't slaves, at least not technically. But they did commit their lives to the force, beginning in childhood. It was a great honor for a peasant family to have a son accepted into the ranks of the Janissaries. Boys of 5 and 6 years were rigorously tested each year, with only the very best accepted into the training program...and a lifetime of soldiering.

Yusef directed his troops as they emerged from the tunnel. They had moderate cover just behind a crooked ridge, and he intended to make the best of it. The enemy forces were already reacting, detaching units to form a firing line facing his position. "Pashia, commence fire as soon as possible. We have enemy forces moving in our direction. Maintain maximum cover." His people were going to be under fire any second.

His unit was supporting the Marines, trying to take pressure off the Alliance II Corps that was defending the main line. Yusef had hated the Alliance Marines for as long as he had conscious memory. They had killed many of his friends and comrades, and he had fought them on countless worlds. He'd been uncomfortable when he first arrived on Sandoval, but it had been easier than he'd expected to battle alongside the Marines. They'd been enemies, yes, but there had always been respect between them. The Janissaries considered themselves superior to every other formation fielded by the Powers…except the Marines. Even as enemies, they'd had to bestow a grudging acknowledgement of equality on the Alliance Marine Corps.

Yusef looked over to his right. Good, he thought…Pashia's troops are firing. "Officer Sarwar, hurry that deployment. We need your fire. Now." He had three other teams rushing to their designated areas, but only Pashia's and Sarwar's men were in place."

"Yes, Commander Yusef." Sarwar sounded nervous, definitely edgier than usual. Pashia had too. Both men were veterans who had served under Yusef before, and neither had ever faltered. It was unsettling to see them rattled before the fighting had even begun. He'd heard that the First Imperium forces exerted a strange morale effect, even on veteran troops, but he wasn't sure he'd believed it. Not until he saw it himself. Not until now.

"General Warren is requesting reinforcements, sir." Carter turned to face Cain. "He says his situation is urgent." The second he saw the expression on the face of 1st Army's commander, he knew Warren was out of luck.

"Tell General Warren he has to make do with what he has, captain." Cain sat in his chair, his face a mask of granite.

"Yes, sir." Carter paused a second, as if some part of him

expected Cain to change his mind. I Corps was still completely uncommitted. The elite units of the Alliance and Martian armed forces were deployed in their underground bunkers, out of action while II Corps was being slaughtered on the surface.

Cain angled his head, targeting Carter with a stare that chilled the young officer to his core. "Now, captain." He didn't like it any better than Carter did. He'd known Kyle Warren since the Third Frontier War, and he hated leaving him on the line unsupported. But Cain had a plan, and he was going to follow it... whatever the cost.

"Yes, sir." Carter was flustered from Cain's admonition. He couldn't explain the effect the general had on him...on most of the troops on Sandoval. Erik Cain's will was the one force on the planet that could counter the fear of the First Imperium. "Sorry, sir."

"Don't apologize...just do it." Cain took a breath, thinking. "Major Sawyer, I need an update on the status of our air assets."

"We have 39 fighter-bombers capable of immediate flight, sir. Ten of those have minor damage and are still under repair. We have 36 pilots fit for duty." Sawyer had served with Cain longer than Carter, and he seemed to know in advance what the army commander wanted.

Cain frowned and let out a long breath. It wasn't enough. His air had been decimated by the effectiveness of the enemy interdiction. It was no better than murder sending pilots out against these things, he thought. He needed to save some airpower for the final attack...and anything he sent out now was unlikely to return. Finally, he sighed again and looked over at Sawyer. "Commit ten fighters to ground support for II Corps, major."

"Yes, sir." Sawyer turned and began speaking into his com.

"Captain Carter..." Cain turned to face his junior aide again. "...advise General Warren that I've assigned ten fighter-bombers to his control. He may call them in as he sees fit." He paused, only for a second or two. "And tell him that's all he's getting."

"Yes, general." Carter spun around and put his hand to his

earpiece, contacting Warren. He spoke softly, relaying Cain's message.

"And captain…get General Frasier up here now. He's in charge until I get back." Cain rose abruptly and walked toward the locker that held his combat armor. "I'm going to the surface again."

Every head in the command center snapped around. They knew better than to say anything, but the horror in their expressions was clear. It didn't matter…Cain wasn't paying attention to any of them.

Sawyer turned back to his com. "Captain Cole, the general is going to the surface. Have his escort ready." The veteran major knew very well Cain would go up alone…and he wasn't about to allow that, not if he had any say. Cain paused briefly when he heard Sawyer on the com, but he just moved forward again and stepped onto the lift. Sawyer smiled. No one could accuse him of insubordination for doing his job.

Chapter 18

Officer's Housing Block
Armstrong Joint Services Medical Center
Armstrong - Gamma Pavonis III

Alex was on the couch, wearing only her underwear, sitting quietly and thinking. She was drunk, something very unlike her. Alex Linden had lived by her wits since she was an eleven year old orphan, trying to survive in some of the worst slums in the Alliance. She rarely allowed her judgment to become impaired. But the haziness was welcome now. Anything to make the pain go away.

She was troubled, and she didn't know what to do. And not knowing what to do was an alien concept for her, one that tore her apart. She'd pursued her goals ruthlessly, with a razor sharp focus, for 30 years. For all those years, through all the disgusting things she'd done to survive, all the people she'd killed to advance her position, she had believed her hated sister was long-dead. Then she discovered Sarah Linden was alive...not just alive, but prospering. The anger, the bitterness flooded over her, fueling her rage. But she'd been compelled to wait...wait until the time was right for her to take her revenge.

Now that vengeance was almost at hand, and she was plagued with doubts. She'd blamed her sister for so long, hating her for the disaster that had befallen their family. Young Sarah had attracted the unwanted attention of a member of a powerful political family. Her refusal started a sequence of events that led to her being kidnapped and held hostage, ultimately killing her captor and escaping. The repercussions on the family were tragic.

Alex survived after the deaths of their parents, but she'd

been forced to live an endless nightmare alone, making her way in the violent slums however she could. She blamed her sister for her refusal to give in to her admirer's demands. If she'd just spread her legs for the bastard, Alex had always thought, not only would the family have survived, they likely would have enjoyed the perks of a powerful benefactor's sponsorship. Alex had done far worse to survive, and she suspected Sarah had too.

Now that she'd met her sister again, and the two had spent time together, she questioned her hatred. She felt feelings that had long been buried, that she had thought dead and gone. Perhaps she'd made Sarah a scapegoat, she thought, using her anger to manage the pain and fear she'd endured. They were sisters, even though they'd been separated for three decades…the only family either of them had left. Part of her wanted to embrace her sister, to catch up for all the lost years, to be part of a family again.

She'd come to Armstrong to reunite with Sarah and use her to spy on the Marines, preparing for the day when Alliance Intelligence finally did away with the troublesome Corps. When the war against the First Imperium was over, her orders were to kill Erik Cain. Cain, the hated Marine who'd freed Admiral Garret from captivity and rallied the Corps, turning the rebellions into a complete disaster for Gavin Stark and Alliance Intelligence. Cain, the target who would secure her the Number Two position on the Directorate. Then, mission accomplished, it would be time for personal business. She'd have her own vengeance… she'd kill her cursed sister, who'd plunged her into the depths of despair so many years before. Revenge would be sweeter for the wait.

Or so she had thought. But now, confusion swept over her. The years of hate, the hardness, the icy cold calculations…she questioned it all. Maybe she could stay on Armstrong…let go of the hatred, have a sister again. She felt herself split in two… the scheming, manipulative creature who'd clawed herself a heartbeat away from the top intelligence post in the Alliance and the long lost little girl, flashing back to a time ages ago, a time she now imagined she could bring back.

She sat long in the dark, deep in thought, fighting with herself. No, she thought. That time was long gone. That Alex was dead, buried in the crumbling urban wastes 30 years before. Too much had happened. Too much death, too much pain. The road back was illusory…she was what she had become, what she'd made herself into to survive. What Sarah had forced her to become. There was no turning back. It was too late. But still, the doubts lingered, nagging at her in the darkness as sleep eluded her.

Elizabeth Arlington was struggling to hold back a tear. If she let one fall, she knew, more would follow. It was stress…and joy…and the pain of seeing Compton so weak, so hurt. She still remembered the report from the flag bridge, clear in her mind as if it had been yesterday. She'd felt as if her heart had stopped and, for a few terrible moments, she'd been sure Compton was dead. That she'd lost him. That he was gone before she'd even managed to tell him anything.

But she was Bunker Hill's captain, and her ship needed her then. She loved Compton, but her duty had been clear. She trusted her crew to save the admiral, and they hadn't failed her. Now…only now was she able to see him, to prove to herself he really was alive, that he was going to be fine.

"You look better than when I saw you last." Better, of course, was a relative term. Compton was still weak, and he was hooked up to a dozen monitors and medical systems. She was still struggling to keep her emotions in check, but it was easier if she spoke. It was a distraction…and hearing his voice only helped.

"If you have any feelings for me at all, you'll head down to the commissary and sneak me some food…something I don't have to drink." He smiled and gave her a wink, something he hadn't been able to do until that morning. The doctors had repaired the extensive nerve damage, but it was taking some time for his fine facial control to return. It was perfect timing for the recovery…if Terrance Compton was going to wink at someone, it was Elizabeth. "If you get me a roast beef sandwich, I'll give you my stars." Another smile, and even a small laugh. "With spicy mustard."

"What makes you think I want your job?" She returned his smile warmly. "And you, sir, are going to do exactly what the doctors tell you. Do you understand me?" She put her hand gently on his arm. "It's not every day I get to order the fleet admiral around. I've got to enjoy it while I can."

"How is a man supposed to recover slurping swill out of a straw? I need real food." He was grouchy, but only a little. Seeing Elizabeth had greatly improved his mood. Before she arrived he'd spent the morning terrorizing the hospital staff. They were used to difficult patients, of course, but it was particularly tough handling one of such stratospheric rank. It took a courageous orderly to stare down a fleet admiral.

"Stopping whining." She was trying to hold back a chuckle. Seeing Compton well enough to be complaining incessantly was a huge relief. She could feel some of the stress draining away. "You're not the only one who has been in this hospital, Admiral Compton. I happen to know from personal experience that those nutritional shakes aren't that bad."

She dragged a chair closer to the bed and sat down next to him. "You probably know this already, but your whole staff is fine. You were the only one seriously injured. The rest had mostly radiation exposure. None of them even made it to Armstrong; they were all treated in sickbay once we stabilized the ship." She'd launched into the routine update almost involuntarily, deflecting herself from the far more personal conversation lurking just below the surface. She had a lot she wanted to say to Compton, but she stopped short of letting it out. It was new ground for them both, and it was going to take some time. There was still a war on, and personal attractions and feelings didn't seem very important…or even appropriate.

"I'm glad to hear that." He had known about his staff, but he saw no reason to mention that. "At least they're all being fed." He smiled again. He was happy to see her, and just having her in the room improved his mood. But he was relieved she moved the discussion toward business. There was more for them to talk about, he knew that, but now wasn't the time. He was confused and needed time to think. She wouldn't be in his chain of command anymore, and that opened some doors. But now he wasn't sure what to do or say. She'd be in another fleet, probably lightyears away, and he didn't know what the chances were of both – or either – of them surviving this war. The feelings were there, he was sure of that…and he was pretty sure she felt the same thing. But it would have to wait. Duty before love. And victory before everything…especially in this war.

"Augustus is gunning for you, by the way." He smiled again. "He's determined to make you an admiral whether you like it or not."

Chapter 19

Bridge – AS Hornet
Tarsus A System
Two Transits Rimward of Newton

Flip a coin ten times, and get heads each one. What are the odds on the 11th toss? It was an old memory…a lesson in probability someone had taught him as a child. He still found it hard to believe the chance was still 50/50, just as he did then. Intellectually he knew it was true, but having lived through the ten, it was hard to shake the feeling that the odds had to catch up with you.

Jacobs and the rest of Hornet's crew had already made the ten tosses, metaphorically speaking at least. They'd flown past the First Imperium planet, gathering all the data they could and then, through an extraordinary series of wild gambles, they'd slipped past all the enemy fleets and escaped the system. They'd made six more transits since then, all without being detected. No one on Hornet had expected to get this far.

Their success had an odd psychological effect, increasing the tension onboard. They'd considered themselves lost, dead men and women living on borrowed time. Resigned to their fate, they were calm and in control. But now they were starting to think they might actually survive. Hope was a dangerous emotion, and it carried with it all the stress and fear they'd managed to keep bottled up before. Jacobs knew they had another twenty tosses of that coin ahead of them…they weren't even halfway back yet. But even he started to feel a glimmer of hope.

He tried to fight it. He'd made the decisions that got them this far because he'd been unburdened by any expectation of salvation. They were dead anyway, so he could follow his hunches, try the unorthodox strategies that got them so much further than they'd expected. But now prudence crept into his thinking…the feeling that finally they had something to lose, that they had a real chance to get home. His decisions became more difficult, and he second-guessed each one now. Intellectually, he knew getting back was still a massive longshot, but still, there it was, a dim light at the back of his mind. Hope.

"Ensign Carp, I want a projected course for the enemy vessel based on warp gate locations and current heading." Hornet wasn't alone in the system. The First Imperium ship was a Gargoyle, and she was badly damaged, presumably heading back to the enemy base for repairs. She'd been hit pretty hard, but Jacobs wasn't at all sure Hornet could take her, especially as depleted as his own ship was. He'd prefer to avoid a fight if he could. But that meant remaining hidden, and there was no guarantee of that. Either way it was another coin toss.

"Yes, captain." Normally, it would be fairly easy to project a course, but there were two warp gates in this system that ultimately led back to the First Imperium base, and the enemy ship could take either one. She was still making a vector adjustment, and it wasn't yet apparent which way she was going to head. Carp put together a plot that was more than half guesswork and sent it to Jacob's screen.

Hornet was moving along at 0.02c, her reactor shut down, hiding in the vastness of interplanetary space. An hour passed… two. Finally, Carp turned to face Jacobs. "Sir, it appears the enemy is making a course for the Psi 3 warp gate." His original guess had proven accurate. It was a trajectory that would bring the enemy vessel almost directly at Hornet.

Jacobs leaned back in his chair, thinking. He could feel the tension on the bridge, his officers waiting to see what he would do. Part of him wanted to take the enemy vessel on. If he attacked, there was a good chance Hornet would have the element of surprise. If she tried to escape and was detected, that advantage would be lost. But there was no way to know if Hornet could win the battle or how much damage she would take if she did. They just didn't have enough information…they didn't know how badly hurt the enemy ship was.

There it was again, he realized…the hope, clouding his mind, fueling his indecision. He debated himself, silently trying to consider the situation from every point of view. Finally, Jacobs scowled, angry with himself for his prevarication. He let out a deep breath. His jaw was set, his eyes focused like lasers. He'd made a decision.

"Ensign Carp, calculate estimated time until the enemy vessel reaches the minimum projected distance from Hornet." His voice was grim, determined.

"Yes, sir. Calculating now."

Jacobs turned. "Lieutenant Mink, advise engineering I'm going to want a crash start on the reactor…directly to 100%."

Mink hesitated, just for an instant, as she realized what Jacobs planned to do. "Yes, sir."

"And, lieutenant…ask the engineer how long he will need to arm the plasma torpedoes." He paused then added, "And I mean his best possible time."

"Yes, sir." Mink turned slowly back to her console. Her face was a mix of satisfaction and apprehension. She was nervous, but she wanted to take on the enemy too.

"Captain, at present course and speed, the enemy vessel and Hornet will pass approximately 2,107,500 kilometers from each other in 47.35 minutes."

"Very well, ensign." Jacobs felt his heart beating in his ears. The tension was there, the stress of battle and the fear…but the doubt was gone. He was committed. They were going in. "Plot optimal thrust pattern to close that range below 2,000,000 kilometers." That wasn't exactly the kind of point blank, knife-edge range he would like, but he was confident they had a good chance to score hits from there. If he tried to get closer, he'd have to burn the engines sooner and longer. And he wanted to maintain as much surprise as possible. If the enemy ship had functioning particle accelerators, they could easily slice Hornet apart if he gave them time. It wouldn't take more than a couple shots to turn his ship into a lifeless hulk.

"Captain, the engineer reports best recommended time to

start up the reactor is ten minutes." Mink's voice was tentative...she knew what Jacob's response would be.

"Not even close, lieutenant." Jacobs' voice was sharp, not angry, but close to it. "Tell them to try harder."

"Yes, captain." Mink adjusted her com, getting engineering back on the line. She spoke quietly. Jacobs couldn't quite hear what she was saying, but he suspected she was urging them to drastically improve the startup time.

"Plot is complete, captain. We can execute a 3g burn for one minute, forty-three seconds, commencing in approximately 44.5 minutes. That will close us to 1,977,300 kilometers of the enemy, approaching from a vector slightly aft of their current heading." Carp had been staring down at his plotting screen as he spoke, but now he turned to face the captain. "That is assuming they continue thrusting at current levels and vector, of course."

"Very good, ensign." Carp had done a solid job of tactical plotting. Jacobs had roughed out the course in his head, and he didn't expect it to take less than two minutes. The kid managed to shave better than fifteen seconds from that mark. And arrange to approach the enemy from the aft. "Lock into the navcom. We'll modify if the enemy executes any changes."

Jacobs could see Mink out of the corner of his eye. She was looking over, waiting for his attention. "Yes, lieutenant?"

"Engineering says two minutes on the reactor. They can do a crash start in 30 seconds, but the engineer strongly recommends against it."

Jacobs paused for the briefest instant. "Advise engineer to prepare for a 30-second crash start." Another toss of the coin. "We will be executing an engine burn of approximately one minute, forty seconds immediately following reactor restart. Instruct engineering to prepare to arm plasma torpedoes during the burn." His eyes fixed on Mink's. "We will be firing *immediately* after cutting thrust."

"Yes, sir. Understood."

Jacobs leaned back in his chair. Now, he thought, we just have to sit tight for three-quarters of an hour. He knew how

long three-quarters of an hour could be when you were counting the seconds.

Cooper Brown was kneeling in the soft, wet dirt. He'd just
emptied the contents of his stomach onto the ground. Brown
had been a rock solid Marine, and he'd taken all his enemies
could throw at him. But beating up on terrified civilians made
him sick.

His militia had executed a dozen of the worst offenders who
had been preying on the residents of the slumlike tunnels. All
those who died that day were killers themselves, once-civilized
citizens of Adelaide who'd turned into savages, beating and
murdering their fellow refugees for their meager food rations.

It had worked. For a while at least. But eventually a new
crop of criminals rose…and the firing squad was formed up
again. Three times now. Three times his militia had dragged
a group of rogue refugees out of the tunnels and shot them
against a stone wall.

Brown didn't like it, not one bit. Especially the last time,
when two of those shot were boys of fifteen. But he could live
with it. It was rough justice, but it was justice of a sort. One of
those boys had brutally murdered a 123-year old woman for the
scrap of a nutribar she had saved.

Things were quiet for a while after the third round of execu-
tions. Brown had proven he was serious, and order returned to
the shelters, at least for a short time. But the conditions in the
tunnels were deplorable and getting worse…disease-ridden and
infested with Adelaide's native pest, the boreworm. The people
wanted to leave the shelters, to go back to the surface and live
where it was warm and dry and they could see the sun.

But Brown wouldn't allow it. Twice now, since Hornet
departed, huge enemy task forces had moved through the system. The second one found one of the warp gate scanners
Hornet had left behind…and they sent a Gremlin to scan the
planet. The enemy ship discovered the relay satellite that had
been feeding Brown his intel, and they shot it down. Brown
was blind again…he had no idea what was going on, in orbit or

anywhere else in the system.

The Gremlin scanned the surface...Brown was almost certain of that. He kept everyone underground for a month, just to be sure, and even after that, he only allowed small militia patrols to the surface. Two weeks later, it happened. It began with crowds gathering in the common areas of the shelters, grumbling at first, then chanting, shouting. They charged his men, driving them back toward the exits. Brown had forbidden firing on civilians without his direct authorization, so the troopers pulled back when the crowd pelted them with debris.

It started in shelter 3, in a wide corridor near the exit. The crowd charged one of the militia squads and knocked three of the soldiers to the ground. They surged over them, grabbing them, pulling them under the enraged mass, beating them, trying to wrest their rifles away.

It was one shot at first. No one seemed to know if it was a soldier or a civilian trying to get a gun away, but the trooper felt back, his chest a widening circle of red. By all accounts the lieutenant on the scene tried to stop the soldiers, but it was futile. The squad began firing into the crowd, half of them on full auto. It was only a few seconds before the officer regained control, but that was enough. Two dozen civilians were down, and the rest were stampeding wildly, climbing over each other to flee. Dozens more were killed, trampled to death by their terrified neighbors. The toll was 53 and rising, and it was hours before order was restored, before help got through to the wounded.

Brown was furious when he heard, but anger quickly gave way to sorrow. To guilt. He knew there would be more trouble, that the hatred of the people would flare hot now. But he didn't care about that anymore. All he could think about was the horror of an Alliance militia gunning down civilian colonists. He issued the orders he had to, the ones that couldn't wait. Then he walked out of the command post and up to the surface. He needed to be alone.

He spat the last bits of vomit from his mouth and straightened up slowly, wiping his hands on the sides of his pants, trying to get the mud off. Or was it blood he was trying to scrape away? His head arced upwards, staring into the sky. It had been close to a year since Hornet had blasted off on its crazy mission. Brown wondered what fate had befallen the brave little ship. How, he wondered sadly, did Jacobs die? He couldn't imagine his friend was still alive. Enemy ships had been pouring through the system. One of those task forces must have found Hornet…if the ship hadn't already succumbed to some random failure or accident.

"Well, my friend, I hope you died well, a death with some honor and purpose. There is none of that here, only misery and despair. My death will be meaningless, shrouded in shame. And it will be a relief."

"Crash start reactor now!" Jacobs gave the order and sat quietly. He'd have power in 30 seconds…or Hornet would be a rapidly-expanding plasma. He was counting down to himself, imagining that coin spinning in the air, waiting to see if he could pull heads again.

"Reactor at 100%, sir. Engineering reports ready to execute burn on your command." Mink's voice was a little shrill. She was a veteran, but they were all worn down, and the stress was hanging heavy on the bridge.

"Execute burn." That couldn't have been twenty seconds, he thought. They did a great job down there. Why, he wondered, couldn't they just do it in the first place instead of always angling for more time?

He gripped the handrests on his chair, an unnecessary effort at 3g, especially since everyone was strapped in. He could feel the pressure almost immediately. Three gees wasn't fun, but a short burn wasn't going to be too hard on anyone.

"Plasma torpedoes armed and in the tubes, captain." Mink's voice was lower, steadier. She was getting into her battle persona, and her hunter's instincts were taking over. She wanted to nail that ship, possibly even more than Jacobs did.

"Ensign Carp, transfer optimum firing point data to Lieutenant Mink's station." Jacobs knew the rest of this was out of his hands. But he trusted his crew. They'd already been to hell and back, and he believed – truly believed – they'd get through this too.

"Transferred, sir." Carp turned to face Mink's station.

"Receipt confirmed." Mink's tone was distracted now. She was prepping he shot, and all her concentration was focused. "Torpedo launch in 30 seconds."

Jacobs had been in combat many times, but he still got the cold feeling in his stomach. Anticipation, uncertainty, fear.

"Twenty seconds to launch."

Jacobs watched Mink with admiration. Sometimes he forgot just how good she was. He was counting down himself. He was trying to keep it in his head, but his lips were moving silently.

"Ten seconds to…"

"Energy spike in enemy vessel." That was Carp, his voice urgent, but controlled as always.

Jacobs knew immediately. "Fuck," he muttered under his breath. His hands clenched tightly, gripping the handrests, his fingers white. This enemy ship had active weapons.

Carp's faced was buried in his display. "I think it's…"

Hornet shook violently. The bridge wasn't hit, but there were sounds of explosions aft. The ship started to roll, pitching end over end…probably a hull breach spewing atmosphere into space. The damage control system would seal off the compromised section. But Mink's shot! The ship was totally out of the plotted firing window, spinning wildly.

"Ensign Carp, stabilize the ship." Jacobs snapped the order crisply.

"Yes, sir." Carps hands were already dancing across his work station. He was firing the positioning jets, calculating most of it on the fly. The rolling slowed gradually. The ship wasn't exactly stabilized, not yet. But the violent pitching had stopped.

"Lieutenant Mink…"

"On it, captain." He face was buried in the targeting scope.

My God, Jacobs thought, stunned…she's going to eyeball it. Everything depended on this shot. If the enemy got off another blast of its particle accelerator the fight was as good as over. Mink had been technically insubordinate interrupting the captain, but there was a place for everything…and this wasn't the time for formality on the bridge. Jacobs had to trust her… and, to his surprise, he found he did. Everything was against her, but Hornet's captain had complete faith in his tactical officer. He sat quietly in his chair, and a fleeting smile even crossed his lips. He imagined throwing her the coin. It was her toss now.

Hornet bucked twice in rapid succession. "Two torpedoes away." Mink's voice was soft, distant. Every bit of her focus was on the targeting scope. It would take the torpedoes about twenty seconds to reach the target. In half a minute they'd know.

Time seemed to stop on Hornet's bridge. Carp was monitoring the scanners, looking for the energy spike they all knew was coming. They knew the enemy weapons needed to recharge between shots, but they had no hard data on how long. And if that particle accelerator fired again, Hornet would die.

"Torpedo impact in five seconds…four…three…"

Jacobs wiped the sweat from his forehead and took a deep breath.

"Two…one…."

There was a pause after one…an instant that hung frozen in the air, testing the mettle of Hornet's crew.

"Two direct hits, sir!" Mink spun around to face the captain. She tried to jump out of her chair, but the straps held her in place.

"Enemy vessel is rolling captain." Carp now, his face glued to the scanners. "Secondary explosions." A pause…ten seconds, maybe twenty. "Sir, I am not reading any internal energy generation." His voice was becoming more excited. He looked up and turned to face Mink, then the captain. "I think it's dead, sir. I think we did it!"

"Well done, Lieutenant Mink." Jacobs smiled broadly as he looked over at his gleeful officer. "Well done."

Jacobs leaned back again and sighed loudly. Heads again.

Chapter 20

South of the Great Sea
Planet Samvar
Theta 7 System
"The Line"

"Attack!" Force Commander Rafiq Zafar shouted the command into his comlink. His Blue Force was the senior unit in the Janissary corps, the cream of the Caliphate's elite troops. Admission into the Blues required a minimum of ten years' combat service, though many of his troops had twice that. Now they were going to show the First Imperium what the Janissaries could do.

Samvar's system was the third segment of the Line. Sandoval has been hit early and, by all accounts, its defenders faced the largest enemy invasion force. But the First Imperium hit Garrison as well, and finally Samvar. A minor sector capital, Samvar had been heavily fortified and reinforced since the Grand Pact came into being. The Caliphate's CAC allies sent a strong corps to back up the Janissary regiments, and Europa Federalis dispatched two heavy infantry divisions. These regular forces were reinforced by colonial levies, called in from every Caliphate world within five transits.

The fleet had put up a fight, and for a time it looked as though they might hold the system. But the enemy brought up its Leviathans, and the massive dreadnoughts were more than the Pact fleet could handle. The Caliphate battleship Tamerlane was destroyed, along with the CAC's Shanghai. The Europan contingent's Austerlitz and Marshal Lannes were gutted by antimatter explosions and had to be abandoned as the shattered fleet fell back and fled the system.

Having secured the space around the planet, the First Imperium fleet bombarded the surface from space, laying waste to all the populated areas, as they had on the other worlds of the Line. Unlike Garrison and Sandoval, however, Samvar had not been evacuated. Despite Admiral Garret's entreaties, the Caliph would not relent from his decree that the planet's occupants would remain, that they would join the fight to save their world. The nuclear bombardment became a humanitarian catastrophe, with over a million dead in less than two hours. The cities and towns built painstakingly over 80 years of human occupation were consumed by the nuclear fire, the terrified civilians trying, hopelessly, to flee the winged death swooping down on them.

Pasha Murad held the top command on Samvar. A cousin of the Caliph, Murad had long been a senior military officer, but he had spent those years at a desk, not in the field. Garret had originally assigned a senior Janissary officer to the overall command, but the Caliph overruled him and sent Murad instead. Garret was troubled by the choice, but there was little he could do. Samvar was a Caliphate world and, trying desperately to hold the embryonic Pact together, Garret didn't push the issue. There was no delicate way for the Alliance's top military commander to make demands on the absolute monarch of the Caliphate, even if he had been named supreme military commander of the Pact.

Murad had not put significant resources into digging the types of extensive subterranean fortifications Cain and Gilson had. The enemy hadn't used nuclear weapons in any ground engagements to that point, and he decided it was a waste of time to prepare for an attack that was unlikely to occur. Murad was accustomed to a life of extreme decadence, and he was unsuited to the rigors of aggressive field command. While Cain was driving his engineers nearly to the point of madness, Murad was expanding his underground headquarters, outfitting it with priceless furnishings and luxuries imported from his palace on Earth.

Most of his troops were sheltered in shallow trenches when the nuclear attack came. Thousands of soldiers died in those first hours, detected from space and obliterated by targeted bombardments. Soldiers in powered armor were well-equipped to survive on the nuclear battlefield, but no combat suit ever made could save those caught too close to the primary blast zones.

Murad's electronic systems were inadequately shielded as well, and the EMP from the nuclear airbursts wreaked havoc on the targeting systems for the planetary point defense. The First Imperium landing craft came down virtually without loss, and Murad's scattered and shell-shocked defenders were in no condition to interfere.

The surface of Samvar was mostly covered with a giant ocean, a hundred kilometers deep. It was dotted with large islands, jutting plateaus sitting just above shallow veins of volcanic activity. These hot, sulfuric land masses were virtually uninhabitable, and the entire population was located on a single small continent in the southern polar region. Once a warm but pleasant savanna dotted with settlements, it was now a blasted hell, strewn with the melted remains of manmade structures and swept by fallout-laden winds.

The First Imperium army assembled in a single landing zone along the northern coast and formed up to march south, sweeping up the remaining defenders as they did. It was less than 200 kilometers to the opposite coast. The battle for Samvar would be short and sharp.

The surviving defenders clung grimly to their inadequate fortifications, awaiting the onslaught. The front line units had suffered casualties of 5-20% from the bombardments, and they were too disordered to seize the initiative. Many of their supply depots had been above ground, inadequately protected, and their logistics were disrupted. Morale was faltering, even before the enemy forces began their advance. The troops were already shaken, and their lines were fragile, tenuous.

Except for the Janissaries. The Caliphate's elite corps had as much pride as the Alliance Marines, and they were determined to hold at all costs. They'd been badly beaten in the Third Frontier War a decade earlier, largely because their leaders couldn't match Elias Holm and Erik Cain and the rest of the Alliance's high command. They were anxious to show what they could do, to regain the honor and prestige of their regiments.

"High Commander, my forces are advancing as ordered." Zafar's troops were moving against the enemy flank, trying to take the pressure off the colonial levies holding the trenches in the center.

"Very well, commander." Ali Khaled's voice was deep, commanding. He sounded like a man born to power, though he had not been. Khaled had been conscripted into the Janissary Corps at age 6, the same as Zafar. In a highly stratified and rigidly hereditary society, the Janissaries themselves were, like the Marines, almost entirely egalitarian. A peasant boy from the slums of New Cairo could rise to the highest levels of command, as Ali Khaled had done. That power and prestige did not extend beyond the military, however. Service as a Janissary was for life. There was no retirement, no return to Earth to enjoy the rewards of a lifetime of war. Older and infirm Janissaries were moved to training positions or reserve formations, but only with death did they finally leave the corps.

There was no family for the Caliph's elite troops, no home other than the regimental depot. Officers were allowed permanent concubines, but the closest the rank and file came to ongoing relationships were favorites in the regimental brothels. The Marines fought for a future, for colonies they would call home when they mustered out…but the Janissaries existed only to fight. War was their purpose, their reason for being. For them there was nothing else. Now, the First Imperium would feel their sting.

"Your forces are performing well, commander." Zafar's troops were advancing smartly and in good order, and Khaled knew the commander would benefit from his praise. Ali Khaled knew how to encourage his men.

"Thank you, commander." Zafar could hear the sincerity in Khaled's voice, and he waxed with pride. "We should be engaged in less than two minutes."

"Good luck, commander. And keep me well informed."

Khaled had other fronts to worry about too. Pasha Murad had panicked, and he had placed the Janissary High Commander in charge of the overall battle. *He's terrified the Caliph will have his head,* Khaled thought…*if the First Imperium doesn't take it first.* But Khaled's concern was for the troops, and he would do his best, not to save Murad's stinking carcass nor for the rewards that would accompany victory. He would give his all for his men, and he knew in defeat they would all die.

The cowardly and bloated Murad would take most of the credit if he was successful, Khaled knew that, and his didn't care. Not really. There was a time he might have, but he'd become resigned to the way of things. He thought momentarily of the Marines, the enemy he had fought all his life. They were unappreciated and mistreated by their government too, though not as badly as the Janissaries. He wondered, only for a fleeting moment, if they both hadn't both been fighting the wrong enemies all these years. It was a compelling contemplation, but not one he could address now. He had work to do. Perhaps later there would be time to revisit the idea.

Kemal Raschid popped his armor and pried himself out in a far less dignified manner than he typically carried himself. Raschid was an emir, the ruler of three worlds and, in most situations, answerable only to the Caliph. While his position and rank carried with it the military command of his levies, he was not a soldier by trade. He found the armor difficult to use, even with the built-in AI doing most of the work. And getting out was particularly humiliating for a man who prided himself on his dignity and nobility.

Raschid's worlds had been the first in the Caliphate to endure the attack of the First Imperium. The invaders annihilated his tiny spacefleet and occupied his capital of Bokhara, exterminating the population in the process. He escaped, along with 500 of his Spahi petty nobles. The Spahi levies were an anachronism in the ranks of the Caliph's forces. Nobles, albeit lowly ones, they were the social betters of the Janissaries. But in the field, the regulars were vastly superior, and the levied nobles served a supporting role in battle.

The Caliphate drafted peasants too but, unarmored and without significant training, these militias were of limited value, rarely worth transporting from their native worlds to fight else-where. The Spahis were wealthy enough to purchase fighting suits, at least basic ones, and they had the time and resources to obtain at least rudimentary training. They occupied a difficult place in the hierarchy – they had wartime obligations as part of their social pact, but they had enough influence and standing to avoid most of the rigors of military life between combats. Against other second line troops they could sometimes acquit themselves well, but they were typically crushed when facing a first tier opponent like the Alliance Marines. Raschid didn't have much hope for his forces in a battle with the First Imperium, but desperation could be its own source of strength. Perhaps the levies will understand what is at stake…that they fight now for their own worlds and families against an enemy that would exterminate all mankind.

Raschid was the highest ranked colonial noble present, and he commanded not only his own Spahis, but all the noble levies in the army, over 10,000. They'd been deployed to the cen-ter, not because of their ability to hold, but because sitting in a trench was about all Ali Khaled trusted them to do.

Kemal Raschid was the often ignored son of a powerful noble house. No one had expected anything from him except a life of decadence and dissolution. But he'd surprised his critics, becoming one of the most successful colonial lords in the Caliphate's history. Before the First Imperium destroyed his handiwork, he had ruled over a prosperous and growing colony world and was in the process of founding two more. Now, Kemal shocked everyone again. He had no military train-ing at all, but he showed an aptitude even he would never have expected. Though he was certainly an amateur, Kemal Raschid proved to be a formidable soldier.

"Abdul, I want Lord Ghanem's levies to move forward and reinforce the first line." Abdul Nouri was his closest advisor, a longtime retainer of House Raschid, who had accompanied

Kemal into space. "This is the second time I am issuing this order. Advise Lord Ghanem there will not be a third." Raschid's voice was calm, but the menace was there, a coldness that was hard to miss. The Caliphate's military code was clear and harsh. All Raschid required to execute a lesser noble like Ghanem was the inclination to do so.

"Yes, my lord." Abdul's voice was the perfectly evolved combination of familiarity and submission. There was an informality between the two of them, but Abdul never forgot the high rank of his lord. Like the master, the retainer seemed to have an innate ability to function in battle, and the two worked seamlessly together, directing the levy with far greater skill than Khaled could have expected.

"Emir Raschid." It was Khaled. "I need you to reinforce your first line. I do not believe it will hold against the next attack." Khaled had managed to keep the pressure off the center with targeted nuclear strikes, but now the enemy had adopted a deeper, looser order formation that was less vulnerable to weapons of mass destruction.

"Yes, General Khaled. I have already ordered Lord Ghanem's levies to reinforce the line." Raschid used the purely military title when addressing Khaled. The two had a potentially uncomfortable relationship on the battlefield. Khaled effectively commanded the army, though Murad was still the official leader. While Raschid held a military command under Khaled, he was vastly above the Janissary general in the Caliphate's overall hierarchy, a potential source of friction between the two. But Raschid, while haughty and protective of his noble perquisites, was also intelligent and realistic. He knew the Janissary commander had the skill and experience to lead the army, and he and Khaled had managed to work together...far better than either had expected.

"Send another contingent." A slight pause. "The enemy is coming in with Reapers, and we need all the firepower we can get." Khaled fired out the order, but he added the explanation to soften the tone. As long as Raschid followed his military commands, Khaled was willing to respect his social rank.

"Yes, general." Raschid recognized Khaled's efforts toward a good working relationship between them, and he was prepared to meet the Janissary general halfway. "I will send Lord Qadir's levies." He hadn't intended to say any more, but a second later he added, "And I will move forward myself and direct the defense." Raschid wasn't sure where that had come from, but he realized he did, indeed, feel the urge to move forward.

"Very well, Emir Raschid." There was something in Khaled's voice that hadn't been there before…a deeper respect, perhaps. "Good luck to you. And be careful…you are not expendable."

"Thank you, general. I assure you, I have no intention of expending myself." Raschid felt something new…a pride he'd never experienced. He'd been proud of his high birth, and certainly of his achievements on Bokhara, but this was different, deeper, more intense. "We must win this battle, general, and you can be certain I will do my part." He closed the line and turned slowly. "Abdul, order Lord Qadir to move his levies to the front line."

"Yes, my lord."

Raschid walked toward the armor he'd just escaped. "I want full reports on everything relayed to me, Abdul. I am going back to the front myself."

Chapter 21

South of the Marin Highlands
Northern Continent
Planet Sandoval
Delta Leonis System
"The Line"

"Sir, we can't hold here. These kids just can't do it." Jarvis was a veteran, but Warren could hear the frustration in his voice…and the strain. "We need seasoned troops to stiffen the line." Warren's corps had been falling back slowly, moving from one prepared position to the next. But the enemy kept coming…no matter how many the Marines took down, they kept coming.

"Colonel Jarvis, the commanding general will not dispatch any reserves to this position. I have argued for it repeatedly to no avail." Warren was frustrated too. He knew how fragile his line was. His corps had been holding out for days, but barely. Most of his people were Marines in name only…they didn't have the training or experience level that had always been the norm in the Corps. The Marines had held their standards high for a century, through wars and crises, and desperate need. But the First Imperium invasion had brought that to an end. The Corps needed bodies, and it needed them quickly. They got them, but it cost heavily in terms of the battlefield proficiency of the new units. Half the men and women he had in the field would have washed out if they'd had to complete the full training program. Warren didn't even have enough experienced cadres to prop up his green units. There were sergeants running squads who were fighting their first battles.

Kyle Warren was the man for the situation, though. He'd

been number two in the rebel army on Arcadia, a command he later inherited when General Thompson was killed in action. He knew how to handle inexperienced troops and manage their fragile morale…but he'd never faced the First Imperium before. It was hard enough to maintain the fighting spirit of veterans in the face of the relentless attacks of the deadly robot warriors… and all he had was a bunch of half-trained kids.

Cain had sent the fighter-bombers in again, hitting the advancing enemy with PBS runs, buying time for Warren to rally his faltering troops. But the bombers were almost all gone. Sending them against the First Imperium was almost murder, but the pilots still clamored to go. Veterans all, they understood the calculus of this war. In the air, they could help win the victory…and far better to meet death airborne doing their duty than cowering meekly in the hangers, waiting for the army to fall. If 1st Army survived this epic struggle, there were going to be a lot of medals issued to members of the flying corps. Most of those were going to be posthumous.

"Sir, they're going to break. I have whole battalions in complete disarray. Half of them aren't even firing back anymore." Antoine Jarvis was a hardened veteran. There was no exaggeration in his report, no panic dictating what he said…and Warren knew it.

"I know. It's bad over here too." Kyle Warren had always been cool under pressure, and he'd managed to handle every crisis he'd faced. But now he had no idea what to do. He hesitated for an instant, pushing back his own fear, getting hold of the rising panic. "Antoine, we're just going to have to hold them together. I need you in the front lines. Right now." He paused and took a deep breath. "You take the left, I'll move up to your right. It's on us now to hold this thing together."

"Kyle, you can't come up here. This line's gonna go no matter what we do." Jarvis didn't mention he was already in the forward trench. His troops would have run already if he hadn't been there. He'd been ready to shoot the first Marine who ran, and for a few minutes the newbs were more afraid of him than the enemy. But that was wearing off quickly. "Stay back…it's too big a risk for you to move forward."

Warren knew Jarvis was serious. The colonel was a stickler for military formalities…the fact that he'd addressed his commander by his first name only reinforced the intensity of his concern. But Warren knew what he had to do. "You just worry about the left, my friend. I've got the center."

"But, sir…"

"End of discussion, colonel." Warren started moving forward through one of the lateral trenches. The enemy's cluster bombs were starting to land all around the command post. Pretty soon, he thought, it's going to be as hot back here as it is at the front line anyway.

"Yes, sir." Jarvis' voice was sullen but still respectful. He had a bad feeling about things, but Warren had slammed the door shut. And Antoine Jarvis knew how to obey orders.

Cain sat impassively in his chair. His headquarters was in an uproar. The enemy was throwing its forces against II Corps, particularly the center. Warren's people had inflicted heavy casualties, and Cain's targeted nuclear strikes had destroyed thousands of battle robots. But the enemy was *still* landing reinforcements from orbit. Even Cain was becoming uncertain. How many, he thought…how many can they have on that fleet?

He knew his people wanted him to commit I Corps. Warren's troops were green, and they'd already taken a lot of punishment. He knew what they were all thinking. Cain has gone crazy. Cain is unreasonable. He wants the impossible from his troops. He knew everything they were saying. And he didn't care.

This war was different, the enemy unlike any they had ever faced. Feeding in reserves in the face of the advance would buy time. It would slow the retreat. It was what they had done in every battle so far. And each of those engagements had ended the same way…in annihilation, or at least in a frantic withdrawal. This battle had to be different. It had to end in victory.

"I have General Warren again, sir." The stress was clear in Carter's voice. Everyone on Cain's staff was a combat veteran, and they all knew what the troops on the surface were going through.

"Put him through."

Carter turned to his board. "He's on your line, sir."

"Kyle...what's your status?" The question seemed absurdly obvious, but Cain was looking for a level of specificity beyond his staff's cursory analysis. "For real, I mean."

"It's bad, sir." Cain could hear the stress in Warren's voice. "My lines could go at any minute. These kids just don't have the training and experience."

Cain wasn't one to listen to excuses, and he usually figured people could do better than expected if they were pushed. But he knew Kyle Warren, and he trusted him. Warren had served as a junior officer under his command during the Third Frontier War, and the two had reconnected when Cain led the relief force that reinforced Warren's rebel army on Arcadia. If Warren said his people couldn't hold, he was probably right.

"Ok..." Cain was thinking, deciding what he could spare. "...can you stabilize things if I give you two veteran battalions?" He was reluctant to dissipate his reserves...he needed them for his final plan. In truth, II Corps was tactically expendable...just not yet. But Cain couldn't just cut Warren and his people loose, whatever the tactical situation. Whatever opinions were floating around HQ, every Marine lost still cut at Cain deeply.

"It would help, sir, but things are really bad up here." Cain could hear explosions in the background. Warren was close to the action...closer than he should be. "I'm sure two battalions will buy some time, but I don't know how long."

"Ok, I'm sending them now." Cain paused, thinking of the times he'd been in Warren's position. He wanted to jump in his armor and go back up to the surface...get in the line with those Marines. If Warren's people were going to stand at his orders, he wanted to be there to stand with them. But now he needed to be here. The next few days would decide the battle... and determine if the enemy was stopped at Sandoval or if the rest of human-occupied space would become a battlefield. His duty was clear. "Good luck, Kyle." Despite his best effort, Cain couldn't keep the emotion entirely out of his voice. "I have total faith in you."

There was a pause. Finally Warren spoke, his voice soft, strained with emotion. "Thank you, Erik. That means a lot. I'll do my best."

Cain closed the line. Warren would do everything he could, he knew that. He sighed and wondered when in his rise through the ranks sincere good wishes and manipulation had become the same thing.

"Let's go. Keep it moving." Major Calvin Grant stood on a rocky ledge, watching the 5th Battalion file out of the tunnel onto the plain below. It was a narrow accessway, and only two abreast could get through. His people were moving quickly, but Grant wanted more. "Speed it up, people. The war's not going to wait forever." General Cain had personally ordered him to move his battalion to the front. The urgency in the general's voice was clear, and Grant understood the unspoken message. Every minute counted.

His Marines were veterans, and they'd bristled at sitting in their bunkers while the battle raged above. Now they finally had a chance to get at the enemy. Most of his people had fought in the Third Frontier War, and rejoined the colors when General Holm called for veterans to return. They'd mustered on Armstrong and shipped out to Sandoval, but the battalion had not yet faced the First Imperium.

"Captain Quill, your company is on point. Move out." Quill's people were the first out of the bunker, and Grant wasn't going to wait until the whole battalion was formed up.

"Yes, sir." Quill's reply was crisp, eager. Grant knew even seasoned forces had morale problems against the First Imperium, but his Marines sounded as ready as any group of veterans he'd ever heard. He hoped it would last, because he had a funny feeling in his gut. He felt like they were walking into a firestorm.

Quill was just ahead, pushing two of his platoons forward, spread out in a loose skirmish line. There had been heavy nuclear exchanges by both sides, and any dense formation was just an invitation to wipe out the company with a single shot. Quill put the heavy weapons behind the lead groups, close enough to move up quickly in support. The third platoon was in reserve, bringing up the rear. They didn't know what to expect ahead, and Quill wanted the ability to react to any situation. It only took a few minutes for his caution to be rewarded.

"Captain Quill, cease your advance and form up for defense." Major Grant on the com, speaking quickly, nervously. "Immediately."

"Yes, sir." Quill had no idea what was going on. They still had at least five klicks to go to reach the front lines. He switched to the companywide com. "Company A, halt." His eyes were panning the landscape. "Prepare to repel an attack." That was a guess…he didn't have any hostiles on his scanner yet, but Grant didn't halt them for nothing. "Dig in and deploy heavy weapons and SAWs." They weren't going to get dug in very deep, but even some rough foxholes would help.

He trotted forward…he was going to make sure they set up the best fields of fire. "Weapons platoon…advance to the front, and deploy between 1st and 2nd Platoons. I want all weapons in place in three minutes." It wasn't a realistic order, but he wanted them moving as quickly as possible.

"Yes, sir." Lieutenant Harper, commander of the company's reserve heavy weapons. "Moving forward now." Quill figured that was exaggeration, but he knew Harper was a good officer and that he'd get things in place as quickly as possible. He wanted as much firepower in the line as possible. Battles were usually won by the side that maneuvered better and held back the most reserves, but fighting the First Imperium was different, more about bringing maximum fire to bear. It was the only way to even have a chance to destroy enough of the battle robots. And without the HVMs and SAWs, it was almost impossible to take out the Reapers.

Quill reached his forward line a minute later. The SAWs were in place and ready to fire, but the HVM teams were still deploying their heavier pieces. There was one just to the left of where he stood. The crew had chosen a good position, but Quill liked a spot a few meters south. He thought the line of sight would be better, and there was a small bulge in the ground...not much, but any bit of cover was helpful.

He walked over, waving his arms...pointing to where he wanted the launcher deployed. The crew understood immediately, and they picked up the partially deployed weapon and carried it over. Quill followed and crouched down, helping to level the launcher.

Quill looked up from the HVM emplacement and his face turned white. "Major Grant, are you seeing this?" Though they were talking on the com, the two were barely fifty meters apart, both standing along the front edge of the deployment area.

Grant's reply was slow in coming, and the battalion commander's voice was shaky when it finally did. "I see it, captain." Grant swallowed hard and let out a deep breath. "I see it."

They were figures in powered armor...Marine armor. Hundreds of them...thousands. And they were running toward his people. Fleeing.

Grant's mind couldn't absorb it at first. He'd never seen Marine units broken and routing. Until now.

"Fuck..." Hal Desmond muttered under his breath as he skimmed low over the battlefield at 1,700 mps. Below him as far he could see, there were troops fleeing. II Corps was broken, at least its center was, and whole units had abandoned their positions across five kilometers of the line and fled for their lives.

Colonel Desmond was quickly claiming a place as the most successful ground support pilot in 1st Army. The way casualties were mounting among the flyers, it wouldn't be long before he was the *only* pilot flying. Barely 10% of the army's airpower was still effective; the rest had been blown away by the enemy's precision anti-aircraft fire. The air wings had been virtually wiped out, but things on the ground looked pretty damned bad too, and Desmond was going to keep going up as long as they had a plane he could get in the air.

Flying low was the key to a successful bombing run against the First Imperium forces, but it took a hell of a pilot to handle a plane at hypersonic speeds less than 100 meters from the ground. "Iron Hand" Desmond was a smoking hot fighter jock…and then some.

"Control, this is Colonel Desmond." He spoke softly and with effort into the com. At the gee forces he was pulling, that was all he could manage. "The whole center is pulling back in extreme disorder." That was a generous characterization…the center was routing. "There's a concentration of Reapers I'm heading for." He paused, panning his head as much as he could manage in the cockpit. "The pursuing enemy forces are bunching, especially to the south. Suggest targeted nuclear strikes to try to break up the pursuit."

"Acknowledged, colonel. We are forwarding your suggestion to army HQ." The voice on the com was shaky. The air corps had been so badly battered, even the control center staff was at the breaking point. "Good luck, Iron Hand."

Desmond pushed down on the throttle. He was already well above maximum safe velocity for this altitude, but he wanted more speed. He needed it if he was going to outfly these God-forsaken robots and their anti-air defenses. He'd taken up a double load of PBS modules – a massive violation of regulations - and his plane was handling like a pig because of it. He had the reactor at 115% already, which meant he was running a good 10% chance of turning into a miniature sun before he even got to the drop point.

He arced around at a tight angle and felt the blood draining from his head. He was maxed out on stims and antipressure meds, but he still had to fight to keep from blacking out. A second of unconsciousness would be fatal. His altitude was 100 meters, moving now at 3,700 meters per second. There was no margin for error.

He was coming in parallel to the enemy front line. He swooped down even lower, his plane streaking along barely 40 meters over the ground. He zigzagged wildly as he came in, then flew straight through the heart of the enemy formations. He dropped the first batch of PBS modules, leaving a trail of billowing hellfire behind him, consuming anything in its path.

Bots, Reapers, heavy weapons…they were all vaporized by the superheated clouds of plasma.

Normally, he'd already be arcing up, climbing away, trying to escape the defensive fire. But he had a second payload, and he intended to deliver it. He swung around and targeted another cluster of Reapers. The anti-aircraft fire was intense. He zigzagged wildly, but this time he was hit. A hypersonic particle ripped away a section of his wing. The plane lurched wildly, but he managed to keep it in the air. He pulled the release and dropped the second load, then he pulled back on the throttle and climbed as quickly as his damaged plane could go.

The plasma erupted below him…it wasn't the targeted drop he'd wanted, but it still caught dozens of enemy bots in its deadly clouds. He tried to fly in an irregular pattern, but he didn't have the control anymore. The plane was blasting almost straight up, and half a dozen Reapers targeted it, tearing it to shreds with hypersonic fire.

Desmond waited until the last second, and he pulled the latch, engaging his escape pod. The small capsule fired out of the cockpit, throwing Desmond clear of his disintegrating aircraft. He had figured he was dead, but now there was a spark of hope in the back of his mind…a flickering light that grew dimmer as he looked at the positional scanner. He was coming right down in the middle of the enemy army…and dead center in the target area for the nuclear strike he'd called in.

"Goddamn it, hold your places. Maintain fire." Kyle Warren was losing control of his forces. It had started with 15th Battalion. They just broke and fled from their trenches. Some of their officers tried in vain to rally the shattered unit, but there was no holding them back. Then it started to spread, from one green unit to another. Now, half of II Corps was in full-scale rout, and the whole center was caving in.

Warren stood there, dead center behind the crumbling front line, shouting into his com, trying to reach someone…anyone… in command of the broken units. But most of the officers were dead. Warren hated to admit it, but a few of the unit commanders had joined their men and women, throwing down their weapons and fleeing along with everyone else.

"Rally on me." Warren's plea took on a note of desperation. A few of the routers responded, but most just kept running, though it did them little good. The enemy was raking the fleeing forces with hypervelocity rounds and bombarding them with cluster bombs. They were taking heavier losses than they had in the trenches. But panic knows no reason.

Warren gathered up every man and woman he could find, mostly his staff and about 50 of the routers who'd heeded his rally call. "Forward...we have to hold the line. We have reinforcements coming." Warren knew Cain had sent reserves. He just had to hang on for a few more minutes. He pulled out his mag-rifle and heard the click as the autoloader slammed a clip in place. "Follow me! We need to hold for ten minutes. Just ten minutes." It was a battlecry...and a plea. He didn't know how they were going to do it, but he couldn't let the line cave in...not when help was a few minutes away. If the enemy broke through it would compromise the rest of the position...and the units still holding would be flanked and destroyed.

Warren ran forward, up over a small ridge toward the trench line the routers had just abandoned. He'd known what was waiting from his scanner, but actually seeing it was another thing entirely. There were hundreds of Reapers, advancing in extended order, at least 50 ranks deep. He couldn't even see the end of the column, though his scanners confirmed it was almost 5 klicks from front to back.

He almost stopped. He felt weakness in his legs, looseness in his stomach. He was scared...more afraid then he'd ever been in his life. Kyle Warren stood, for a brief second, on the precipice...then he shouted into the com and ran forward to the trenchline.

"To the trenches! We're going to hold this line!" His hoarse screams tore at his raw throat. He raised his arm, rotating it like a windmill. He'd lost some of his people. The sight of the enemy had been too much for them, and they froze...or turned and ran after the routing troops. But half had stayed with him, and they were already leaning forward, pouring fire into the advancing enemy forces.

"Man the heavy weapons." They were facing Reapers, and Warren realized small arms weren't going to do the job. The broken units had left behind their SAWs and HVMs. "Team up in twos and get some of these weapons firing. Now!" He turned and moved to the right, powering his way through the waist-deep mud and water in the partially-collapsed trench. There was a heavy autocannon a few meters away, and it looked like it was set up and ready to go.

The fire coming in was thick, and Warren bent over, making sure to stay below the front lip of the trench. A few of his people were less careful, and he heard their cries on the com line when they were hit. He dove the last two meters, splashing muddy water all around as his hands gripped the 500kg weapon.

A few of his people had other weapons firing – at least one other autocannon and two HVMs. A couple enemy bots went down, but Warren's people were just too few, their fire too light. They weren't making a difference, not enough of one. The enemy was coming…they'd be in the trench in a few seconds.

He grabbed the autocannon, pulling hard and ripping it from its stand. It was a massive weapon, designed for a two-man crew, but Kyle Warren held it like a rifle and stood up, firing out at the advancing enemy. He was strong enough in his armor to hold the thing, but the kick almost knocked him over. He dug his back foot deep into the mud, finally reaching solid ground, and he sprayed the oncoming battle robots with hypersonic death. They went down under his unrelenting fire. Two, five, ten…maybe a dozen. His shooting was deadly accurate, and for an instant…an ephemeral, passing second…it seemed that he might hold his tiny section of trench.

The first shot hit him in the shoulder. He felt the pain, but only for an instant. The trauma control system flooded his bloodstream with painkillers and stimulants. He managed to hang onto the autocannon, barely. He kept firing, but only for a few seconds more. The second hit took his arm off clean. It was a heavy round from one of the Reapers, and the force of it knocked him off his feet.

There was still no pain...he had the drugs to thank for that. But he could taste the blood in his mouth. He tried to get up, and he made it to his hands and knees. He paused there a few seconds, trying to force himself to his feet. He raised his head, just in time to see a battle robot standing on the edge of the trench leveling its rifle.

The shot took him in the chest, and he fell back into the mud. He lay there, almost buried in the muck, feeling the blood pumping from his body, the slickness inside his suit. It couldn't have been more than a few seconds, but time lost its meaning. He was adrift, not sure where he was, his mind floating, vague images moving in and out of his fading consciousness. Fleeting thoughts...Cain...the battle...failure...defeat.

The trauma control system tried to save him...futile attempts to close the wound, treat the blood loss. But the damage was just too extensive. He took a last breath and his watery eyes looked up through his visor, one last glimpse at the sky. Then he was gone. Kyle Warren - general, revolutionary hero, Marine – was dead.

"Match up those lines! Get those HVMs deployed. Now!" Major Grant was running forward as he fired out commands. He flipped his com to the command line. "Terrell, your people need to form up on our flank. I've got my line refused on the right, but you need to cover the left or they're going to sweep around us."

There were two battalions in the center of the battlefield, just over 1,000 seasoned Marines in total. Two full brigades of routers had streamed by, the dour veterans watching in stunned silence. Now the full center of the First Imperium army was bearing down, a maelstrom of death following just minutes behind the flight of the broken formations. The attackers had been savaged by plasma bombardments and a barrage of tactical nukes, but they still outnumbered the grim defenders at least 10-1.

"We're on the way, Cal." Major Terrell Carson commanded

6th Battalion. His Marines were already marching toward Grant's 5th Battalion, trying to close the gap between the two units before the attack came in. The two forces originally intended to march forward and reinforce the front line…but that line no longer existed, and now the two lone battalions were virtually all that stood in the path of the enemy.

Carson and Grant were both majors, but Grant had seniority, and with it the overall field command. "When you get in place, refuse your left." Grant was watching his own Marines deploy on his scanner as he spoke. "We can't even come close to covering this frontage. We've got to form a square." A square was an ancient formation, not something Marines did on the modern battlefield. But the only chance to hold off the First Imperium forces was to hose them down with heavy fire…and if the Marines gave the enemy a flank, the whole thing would be over in a few minutes.

"Got it, Cal." Carson didn't question Grant's directive. He knew the chain of command, and now wasn't the time for the two of them to argue. Besides, Grant had been on the scene and had more time to evaluate the situation…and he was a rock solid officer Carson trusted completely. "I'll make the hinge on that refusal closer to the center. We'll need enough force to cover the rear if it comes to that."

"Perfect." Grant's voice was getting edgier. "You really need to get here APAP. They're going to hit us any minute."

"Hang on, Cal. We're on the way." He flipped the com to his own battalion line. "Let's step it up, 5th Battalion. The 6th is catching hell. Doubletime…move it!"

The air was thick with foreboding, the mood stark. Carter wanted to double over and retch, but he summoned the strength to stand firm. He'd never seen Cain like this, and it was an experience he knew he would never forget. No matter how hard he tried. He didn't dare speak…not a word.

Erik Daniel Cain, full general and the commander of 1st Army walked into the chamber. It was a cave, really, a manmade one. Carved out of the solid base rock to hold fighter bombers, it was empty now. All the planes that had been based here were gone, shot down over the battlefield. Most of the pilots who'd flown missions from here were dead as well, though a couple had managed to eject and get back…two, maybe three of them.

Cain was wearing fatigues, but for once they were neatly pressed and spotless. Four polished platinum stars gleamed on each shoulder, and an officer's cap covered his wavy brown hair. Along the walls of the room were Marines, a hundred on each side, and they snapped to attention as one when Cain entered, the clicking from the heels of their boots echoing off the high stone ceiling.

"Major Sawyer, bring in the prisoners." Cain spoke matter-of-factly, but his voice was cold, like the depths of space. His eyes blazed like frozen fire.

"Yes, sir." Sawyer turned abruptly and walked toward a closed hatch. "Lieutenant Sand, have the prisoners brought in."

Sand acknowledged and opened the hatch, relaying the command for the captives to be marched in. A ragged line of Marines stepped forward. No…no longer Marines. Cain's decree had stripped them already of that distinction. They were prisoners, deserters, cowards. Thus had Cain proclaimed them and, therefore, thus they were. Their names would be expunged from all records. To the Corps, they will never have existed.

They stumbled forward slowly, broken men and women, their feet shuffling, scraping on the rough stone floor. Their misery was palpable, and they moved with hunched shoulders, gradually herded into line by alert-looking Marines carrying assault rifles. At least a dozen of them were wounded, and they hobbled in as well as they could manage. They'd been dragged from Sarah's hospital by Cain's order and against her angry objections. She'd protested, and his response had included the harshest words he'd ever spoken to her. She'd loved him for years, but now she didn't recognize him, the man he had become, and the darkness she saw in his eyes chilled her blood.

Sawyer snapped a series of orders, and the guards moved up and took positions around the prisoners. There was a loud clang as the armored hatch slammed shut, leaving 140 men and women standing raggedly, pathetically…awaiting Cain's judgment.

He paused, but only for a moment. He walked forward, climbing up on a small platform that had been assembled about 10 meters from the line of prisoners. He stood at attention, or close to it, and looked out over the miserable captives. He was the embodiment of judgment, of vengeance. These former Marines, these cowards…they were responsible for Kyle Warren's death.

Another friend lost…another great Marine dead. Warren had served the Corps and the cause of liberty all his life – on the battlefields of the Third Frontier War, on Arcadia during the rebellions. And here, when all was lost, standing with his last breath between the First Imperium and their victory over humankind. He was gone now like so many others, dead because these cowards had broken and run in the face of the enemy. Now they were going to pay the price. Cain had initially wanted to punish the entire division, but he knew that wasn't possible. He still needed those troops, though he no longer considered any of them Marines. These 140 were the ones who broke first, the ones who started the rout. They would carry the guilt for all who had failed in their duty.

"You are here, all of you, because you are guilty of cowardice in the face of the enemy." He owed them no preamble, no ceremony, and they weren't going to get any from him. He would accord them no hint of respect, no pity. "Of desertion in the face of the enemy." He stared straight ahead as he spoke, and there wasn't a sign of emotion in his expression. "Of gross dereliction of duty that resulted in the death of your commanding officer and hundreds of your comrades."

The prisoners stood in place. A few tried to meet Cain's stare, but most of them looked down, eyes focused miserably on the floor. Some were crying; two or three lost the strength in their legs and fell to their knees.

Cain knew what he was going to do. Carter and Sawyer knew as well, and they realized they couldn't stop him. No one could. Jax might have, but Jax was gone. Holm could have ordered Cain not to proceed, but he was on Armstrong, unreachable through the enemy blockade. Erik Daniel Cain was the final arbiter of all things on Sandoval.

"There can be only one punishment for your actions." He didn't move his head; he wouldn't dignify any of those standing before him with so much as a glance. "You are hereby sentenced to die by firing squad, punishment to be carried out immediately." He turned and nodded to Major Sawyer before he snapped around and stepped off the platform.

"Major Sawyer, carry out the sentence at once." In his voice there had been no trace of pity or mercy…perhaps not even humanity.

"Attack force Alpha…this is General Erik Cain." Cain's voice was deep, his iron determination clear in every word. His words were relayed to every man and woman now formed up in the tunnels and sally ports of the great underground defense system. "We are about to launch the attack that will determine the outcome of the battle for Sandoval. You have been held in reserve, and I know many of you have ached to get into the fight. Now is your time."

Cain was addressing the entire attack force…1st Division, Commander Farooq's Janissaries, the Martian Marines. Elite troops all, they'd bristled at being held back for so long. Now Cain's words filled them with fire, and they longed to get at the enemy, to avenge their comrades already slain in this and the other combats of the war.

"This battle may well determine the outcome of the war… even the fate of mankind." His voice was rising in volume, its energy building. "I know you all understand what is at stake. You are veterans of past battles, all of you, warriors who have bled on the battlefield before. Some of us have fought against each other, but that was then. Now we are all brothers and sisters, comrades in arms…united against a new and terrible enemy."

Cain paused. He was standing in one of the access tunnels, ready to step out onto the surface. He knew it wasn't the wise thing to do, but was going to lead this attack himself…and no one was going to stop him. The men and women of the special action teams were lined up behind him, the reformed elite of the Marine Corps, veterans of fifteen or twenty years in the line…ready to follow Cain to hell if he commanded it.

"We march now to the relief of heroes, the men and women of the 5th and 6th battalions, comrades of ours who held back the enemy when the rest of the line collapsed and defeat loomed over us like a shadow. We march now to erase the stain on our honor, the shame of our units that covered themselves with disgrace. We march now to victory, to at last drive the First Imperium from one of our worlds. We march now to insure that the Line will hold!"

Cain felt the words stick in his throat when he spoke of the units that had fled. Those most responsible had paid the ultimate price…and the troops still on the surface didn't doubt Cain's promise that every one of them would face the executioner if they ran again. He'd gone up himself to supervise the return to the fight of the broken units. He shamed them…and he threatened them with such cold resolve not one of them doubted he would sacrifice them all if he had to. He spared no tool, no trick, no manipulation. The army needed those men and women in the line, and Cain's combination of threats and encouragement got them there. They were still scared of the enemy, but they were terrified of Erik Cain. Every one of the broken units reformed and advanced to stabilize the line where the heroic 5th and 6th battalions had grimly stood against the entire First Imperium army.

"Follow me now." His voice had reached a thundering crescendo. "Forward to battle…to vengeance…to victory!"

"All battalions commanders, form up now!" General James Prescott stood on the edge of a jagged finger of rock, just east of the First Imperium LZ. "We're moving out in two minutes."

Prescott had led his second division through the kilometers-long tunnel Cain's engineers had dug under the rugged highlands. The strategy was unorthodox…and very risky. His people were hitting the enemy landing zone while Cain and the rest of I Corps attacked from dozens of hidden strongpoints and bunkers across the battlefield. The two parts of I Corps were kilometers apart, well out of mutual support range. And Cain's forces would be scattered throughout the enemy army, with no real battle lines. It would be a massive brawl...a fight to the death. And Prescott's division would take the landing zone, 20 klicks to the rear, and cut off the enemy retreat. At least that was the plan.

Prescott had his own regiment of Canadians in the lead, with the rest of the division formed up behind in a column of battalions. The division had mostly veteran troops, and the newbs he did have had been fed into experienced units. "Second Division, move out." He flipped to the regimental com. "Let's go 4th Regiment." His Canadians included a large contingent of the veterans who'd served under him during the massive battle on Carson's World ten years before. Some had mustered out during the rebellions, choosing to fight alongside the rebels on the largely Canadian-settled world of Victoria...Prescott included. But the survivors had mostly returned to the colors with their former colonel. Despite his command of the entire division, Prescott chose to lead his own regiment personally.

They were moving smartly, not quite a jog, but more than a march. It took about fifteen minutes for the leading units to clear the rocky spur and get a clear view of the landing zone. There was a perimeter defense all around the LZ. It was narrow, but strongly fortified...bristling with heavy weapons.

"General Prescott, thirty seconds to bombardment. Need final authorization." The voice from the command post was sharp, precise.

Prescott looked out at the enemy defensive line. His people were six kilometers out. It wouldn't take them long to cover that distance. "Authorization code Sigma 9." He answered almost immediately. It was time.

"All units...visors off now." His own helmet darkened, as the visor turned black, blocking any light from outside. He looked at the plotting map projected just in front of his eyes, confirming the incoming ordnance. "Impact in fifteen seconds." He was listening in on the division-wide com. He could hear the unit commanders down the chain of command, prepping their Marines.

"Ten seconds." Prescott knelt down himself, ready to lean forward and shield himself from the detonations.

"We attack one minute after impact." He addressed the entire division. He wanted everyone ready to go. "Repeat, one minute after impact."

"Three...two...one..."

Prescott pushed himself forward, shielding his visor and the equipment on the front of his armor. He was outside the serious damage zone, but he wasn't taking any chances. He wasn't looking ahead, not with his eyes, at least. Six kilometers away, 16 tactical nuclear weapons detonated all along the enemy defensive perimeter. The fireballs engulfed the heavy weapon emplacements, and the expanding shockwave slammed into the nearby enemy bots with deadly effect. Deeper in the LZ, First Imperium reserve units began to move toward the threatened perimeter, reacting almost immediately, trying to plug the gap blasted open by the nuclear attack.

The warning light in Prescott's helmet went off and he activated his visor and looked around the edge of the rocky spur. He paused, transfixed by the site ahead of him...sixteen billowing mushroom clouds silhouetted against the setting sun. Rushing ahead toward nuclear hell, he thought...what an odd life I've chosen. But he was too much of a veteran to be distracted for more than an instant. "Now, 2nd Division...attack!"

He moved forward, knowing his Canadians were on his heels. "Attack!"

"Attack!" Cain's order was raw, primal. The Marines of 1st Division were veterans, survivors of combat against the First Imperium, stone cold killers ready to take their vengeance. Cain was their leader, their hero. They heard his battlecry not with their ears, but with their hearts, with their guts.

First Division was scattered all across the battlefield, coming out of three dozen hidden sally points. Cain had gambled that his strategy was too unorthodox for the First Imperium to comprehend. He had no battle line, no protected flanks, no clear line of retreat. It was going to be a knife fight, brutal, close in, to the death. The best of the Marine Corps was here, and they were focused as one. They knew what was at stake. They would win this fight here and now…or none of them would return.

Cain had 200 members of the special action teams at his back, and now they moved out, targeting the closest enemy forces. This was a search and destroy mission. They weren't after territory, they had no objectives…they were here to exterminate the First Imperium warriors.

His force fanned out, moving for whatever bits of cover they could find. They were close to the enemy – very close – and Cain had equipped all the teams with heavy weapons. There were 30 snipers, armed with the new heavy marksman's rifle… another development from Colonel Spark's magic weapons factory. The projectile was hypersonic and explosive…allegedly, a single perfect shot would take down even a Reaper. That remained to be seen, however. Cain's two and a half dozen sharpshooters were giving the thing its first field test.

"Alright people…let's go get us some enemy scalps!" He could hear the cheers on the comlink as he surged forward, leaping over a small mound and heading toward an outcropping that looked like a vantage point with decent cover.

The final round had begun.

Chapter 22

Conference Room 2
Combined Powers Research Facility
Carson's World – Epsilon Eridani IV

"Research on the enemy debris recovered from numerous sites strongly supports the conclusion." Henry Borden stood in front of the massive presentation screen. "I reiterate my hypothesis. To date, we have faced no organic beings in this war, neither in space nor on the ground." He paused, adding emphasis to the point. "The forces of the First Imperium appear to be entirely robotic, up to and including overall theater command functions."

It was the kind of statement that would typically generate gasps of surprise, but everyone in the room had already come to suspect this fact, or something very similar to it. "Thank you, Dr. Borden. Your data has been enormously helpful. I think we all agree that your hypothesis is correct, but we must be as certain as possible before we relay this information to Admiral Garret." Friederich Hofstader sat at the head of the table, looking out at the assembled experts. When he had first returned to Carson's World, he'd been uncomfortable with the administrative burden of running the place. Over time, he learned to adapt, and now he could tolerate it…he even enjoyed it sometimes. "Dr. Travers, would you care to present your findings next."

Travers stood up slowly, mostly to give Borden a chance to get back to his seat. "Thank you, Frie…Dr. Hofstader." The two had been friends for some time and, since the German scientist had returned and taken over control of the research facility, that relationship had only become closer. Travers was one of humanity's foremost xenobiologists…and one of Roderick

Vance's spies as well. Hofstader was aware of that, but as far as Travers knew, no one else on the staff was.

Travers pressed a button on his controller. The main presentation screen displayed a diagram of a large and very complex organic molecule. "We have found fossilized traces of this substance in multiple locations on Epsilon Eridani IV." He turned and looked over at those assembled. "As most of you will recall, I put forth an immediate – and admittedly premature – suggestion that this molecule served a similar purpose to our own DNA and that it was, in fact, biological material from the builders of this place."

He paused, remembering his excitement when he first discovered the molecule. He hadn't been ridiculed – he was far too accomplished in his field for that – but his suggestion had been largely ignored. "At the time, my belief was little more than a hunch, based solely on my determination that this substance could indeed perform a function similar to that of DNA." He pressed the button again. The diagram shrank and slid to the left half of the screen. A similar image appeared on the right side.

"But now we have discovered traces of this substance as well." Everyone was staring at the screen. The new diagram looked superficially like the original one, but close inspection showed some differences. "My team has just completed a round of intensive analysis, and we have determined that this molecule would be capable of performing a messenger function with the first one…in essence, it appears to be the RNA equivalent to our alternative DNA. I now feel comfortable in asserting that these molecules are, in fact, genetic remains of the organic creatures responsible for the construction of this antimatter production facility."

This was fresh news. Travers hadn't even had time to discuss it with Hofstader before the meeting. "Obviously, we have much to discuss regarding this discovery and the potential impact on future research, but for now, Dr. Travers, would you attempt to briefly address the aspects you consider most relevant to the war effort?" Hofstader was trying to keep the meeting focused.

Clearly the discovery of alien DNA was a historic watershed. But first they had to do their part to make sure mankind survived to research it further.

"Yes, of course." Travers nodded toward Hofstader. "First, and please excuse me for the highly speculative nature of this observation, it appears the enemy is not enormously unlike us in basic body chemistry. The molecules themselves are different, but the uses appear to be quite similar. This similarity in body chemistry, combined with the roughly human shapes of the enemy robots, we can hypothesize that we are dealing with a species moderately comparable to our own, at least physically."

Hofstader nodded for Travers to continue. Ok, he thought, so we're probably not fighting hordes of intelligent insects or sentient algaes...we figured that already.

"Second, these molecules do not appear to be entirely natural." He pressed the button again, and a number of arrows appeared on the image. "It looks like there were some changes made, probably deliberately. We have experimented with similar modifications to our own DNA, for example in efforts to remove genetic defects or eradicate harmful recessives. However, our attempts have always been frustrated by the need to make the desired change simultaneously throughout the body, so that the new version entirely replaces the old." Travers tried to remain calm, but his excitement was nearly uncontainable. He was calmly presenting one of the greatest discoveries in history. He wanted to lock himself in his lab and throw away the key. The data he was discussing could advance the state of bioscience millennia in just a few years.

"What do you consider the primary implications of this, Dr. Travers?" Hofstader again, trying to keep things moving. "With regard to the war effort, of course."

"Well, it certainly points to a technology far in advance of our own, though that seems like a highly redundant conclusion at this point." Travers turned from the screen to glance back at the table. "But it also suggests that the original naturally-occurring version of this substance may have been much closer to our own DNA, suggesting even greater potential similarities between humanity and the alien species.

Travers cleared his throat and walked back toward the table. "Third, I believe we can provide some support for Dr. Borden's theory that we have not, in any of the conflicts that have been fought, faced these organic beings. While we have found fossilized remains of both of these molecules at multiple locations on Epsilon Eridani IV, we have been unable to discover even a fragment in the debris from the war zone." He took a quick breath. "If any of the beings we are hypothesizing had been on any of those ships or had touched any of the equipment we have studied, it is virtually inconceivable for us not to find a single trace." He paused.

"Please continue, doctor." Hofstader knew where Travers was going, but he wanted it to be clear to everyone.

"My only conclusion is that members of the species who founded the First Imperium were physically on this planet at one time, very long ago…" He paused again, but continued when Hofstader nodded. "…but that none of them has ever set foot on the spaceships we are fighting. Or at least the ones from which we have examined wreckage."

Hofstader paused for a few seconds, allowing Traver's statements to sink in. He nodded. "Thank you, Dr. Travers. Your insights are fascinating." He turned his head. "Dr. Wessen, if you are ready, I think it would be an appropriate time to hear your data."

Wessen was short and stocky, an odd looking fellow with long, greasy brown hair. He stood up slowly, as if the effort was considerable. His rumpled gray jumpsuit was dingy and stained. His appearance was underwhelming, but Wessen was the Alliance's top expert in computers and artificial intelligences. He'd designed most of the major AIs in use by both the Marines and the navy.

"Thank you, Dr. Hofstader." He turned toward the table. He wasn't looking at anyone in particular, just glancing in the general direction. "I have reviewed the data on the enemy's tactics, and I am quite convinced that the First Imperium forces are entirely directed by artificial intelligences. This is only a guess based on my analysis, however I strongly believe it to be true. The enemy – whether directed organically or electronically – seems to display a relatively poor aptitude for war. This is apparent from a cursory review of their tactics. If the technology and weaponry had been equal in this fight, our military would almost certainly have won the war very quickly."

He cleared his throat and continued, "What is less apparent, without detailed study, are the patterns with which they have responded to situations where knowledge and skill were lacking. A human being, placed in the role of a general with inadequate training and experience, might react in a variety of ways. But I have detected certain patterns in the enemy's actions that strongly suggest the types of decisions an artificial intelligence would make. There is a certain type of logic being employed by the enemy that is highly consistent with artificially-programmed thought."

Wessen thought for a few seconds, considering how to proceed. "Imagine a computer playing chess. It would be impossible for any of us to defeat the machine. The game has a finite number of moves, and even a child's computer can analyze all possible combinations, and select those that are optimal. Warfare, conversely, is full of variables, many based on the emotions of the participants. Morale is crucial, for example, but so are a nearly unlimited number of other factors. Troops may fight better, for example, alongside those they have served with for many years. A normally cowardly soldier may stand firm to defend a wounded comrade. Considerations of this sort are the most difficult to program into an AI. It is possible that with more research we may be able to develop a significant ability to predict the enemy's actions."

Wessen paused, taking a deep breath before he continued. "I am also prepared to offer a more specific, multi-layer hypothesis. It is my belief that the enemy forces are directed at the top by an artificial intelligence that was programmed by organic beings… a first generation AI, if you will." Wessen's voice was high-pitched and nasal, but his comment caught everyone's attention.

"Below our AI general, for lack of a better designation,

we would have a layer of AIs programmed directly by the top level intelligence…and below these, more junior computers, themselves created by other, mid-level thinking machines." He looked around the table, and he could see none of them had anticipated where his argument was leading.

"If I am correct, we will be able to analyze the enemy in ways that offer profound advantages to the military." He paused, thinking about how to explain. "You are all familiar with the concept of replicative decay. No copy made of anything is a perfect replica; there will always be some deviation, even if only at the atomic level. Therefore, if we make a copy of a copy, the similarity to the original will gradually decrease. Thus, the first copy is a 99.9% accurate facsimile, the second is 99.8%, and so on. There is some level of degradation at each level."

Hofstader looked at him and nodded for him to continue. It looked like the German scientist knew where he was going, though most of the faces staring at him still looked uncertain. "There is a similar concept in high-level programming." He paused and took a breath. "I can design an AI. At our current level of proficiency, I can create a system that simulates emotion…even one that comes close to some definitions of experiencing true feelings. But similar to the general inability to make a perfect copy, I can never achieve an exact imitation of organic sentience. I can come close, and with greater technology and proficiency, even closer, but if the theory holds, my simulation will never be a perfect match."

Wessen rubbed his hand over his forehead, wiping away the beads of sweat that had accumulated there. "Now, let's assume that my AI designs another. That second generation system will never precisely match the level of sentience of the AI that created it…and so on, exactly like replicative decay."

He reached down to the table and grabbed a glass of water from the table. "So, if you will bear with me, the First Imperium command structure could consist entirely of computers, each layer at least somewhat less sentient than the one immediately above it." He put the glass to his lips and took a short drink. "Let's assume that our supreme commander is a highly sophisticated AI, one that may or may not be under the control of organic beings. Considering the enemy level of technology, there is little doubt they could create an AI of staggering sophistication. Indeed, such a system could very well feel emotions, at least based on most common definitions of the concept. It could become angry, even obsessed, but it would still be less sentient that its creators. Its actions would be more predictable, even if marginally so."

He set the glass on the table. "By extension, any systems it created lower in the command structure would be less sentient than the master system…and so on down the line. This would mean that the lower level of command, the more predictable… the more 'machine-like,' for lack of a better term, we can expect them to behave."

Hofstader stood up slowly. "Thank you, Dr. Wessen. I believe you have offered us a theory that will be of great interest to the military. It would be very helpful if you can organize a presentation to be included in the dispatch to Admiral Garret."

"Certainly, Dr. Hofstader. I believe I can have that ready in a day, perhaps two."

Hofstader nodded silently. Yes, he thought, Admiral Garret will want to hear this immediately.

Chapter 23

Battlezone Alpha-Omega
Northern Continent
Planet Sandoval
Delta Leonis System
"The Line"

Linus Wagner could feel the sweat streaming down his back. His suit was climate-controlled, of course, but there was only so much even nuclear-powered air-conditioning could do. The fight was raging out on the ridge, and he could feel the tension – the fear – in every sinew of his body. It was sweating out of every pore, as if his body could expel his stress like some toxin. The Martian general had been in action non-stop for almost 48 hours and, despite the stims, he could feel the burning fatigue in his arms and legs. He doubted he could even lift his rifle if it wasn't for his powered armor.

Wagner had never seen a battle like this...or a commander like Erik Cain. He'd met Cain on Phobos during the Alliance rebellions. Roderick Vance and Cain were working together on something secretive, and Wagner was there for security. He'd liked Cain immediately, but he didn't get a true feeling for the man's relentless intensity until he'd fought with him on Farpoint. They'd lost that fight, but they did better than anyone expected, forcing the enemy to commit reserves and supplies, and delaying their advance to the Line for almost a year.

First Army's general in chief had ordered all senior officers to the surface to command their units personally in this final stage of the battle. Never one to lead from behind, Cain set the example himself. Somewhere out on this nightmarish battlefield was the commander in chief, rifle in hand, fighting the enemy alongside his Marines. It defied every convention of warfare for a general lightyears away from his replacement to be up in the front line, but Wagner understood it. In a war against an enemy so powerful, so relentless that even veteran units wavered at their approach, what could inspire the ranks more than to see their generals in the line with them?

He was prone in a small dip in the ground, meager cover, but better than nothing. He was with a Martian platoon that was in the middle of a nasty firefight with a cluster of enemy battlebots. Both sides had gone to ground, and the combat had stalemated.

It was strange for a general to be up in the line, hooked up with a single platoon, but across the entire battlefield, the army was deployed in small, scattered units engaging their counterparts. Cain had loosed over 15,000 veteran troops on the surface, their only orders to find First Imperium units and destroy them.

Wagner hesitated, watching the action. By God, he thought, Cain was right again. The First Imperium forces had taken cover, but their deployments were sloppy, sub-optimal. Enemy ground tactics had always been mediocre, but Cain's seemingly crazy plan had them even more uncertain and disordered. Their deployments failed to maximize their overwhelming firepower and left their flanks vulnerable to attack.

The Marines, on the other hand, were masters of small unit tactics. Wagner was about to order the lieutenant in command to move on the enemy position, when he saw one of the squads begin to advance to the flank. They moved swiftly, alternating, with one team providing cover while the other moved forward.

Wagner remained silent, crouched behind his tiny patch of cover, watching. The platoon had no idea their general was standing behind them, observing their maneuvers – and Wagner didn't see any reason to put them on the spot. He just stayed quiet and observed.

A second squad was on the move now, advancing in the same manner. The first group was in a small gully, off to the side of the enemy front. They had partial cover, and they were out of the primary firing arc of the enemy formation. Wagner knew he was watching a textbook example of a small unit attack, one conducted against the most fearsome enemy man had ever faced. His pride waxed strongly, watching these men and women he'd trained for so long. The Alliance Marines were a celebrated formation that had fought far more battles than their Martian counterparts and sometimes allies. But his Blackhats were holding their own with Cain's veteran leathernecks.

He glanced down at his display, IDing the unit he was watching. It was 2nd Platoon, B Company, 1st Battalion, Lieutenant Wren commanding. Wren's service record scrolled slowly down the display. He hadn't seen a lot of action, but he was a promising young officer. He'll be a captain before this battle is over, Wagner thought…if he survives.

Wren's first squad had almost worked around the enemy flank. Another few seconds and they'd be firing from an enfilade position, raking the First Imperium line. Wagner nodded approvingly to himself. Wren was executing the attack well. His advancing units had decent cover, and a clear path to a great firing position. If the enemy tried to hit his weak spot – the hinge between his two attacking squads and the two covering ones – both wings would catch the advancing force in a crossfire. If they stayed where they were, the enfilade fire would hit them hard.

They should pull back now, Wagner thought. If he was the enemy commander, he would acknowledge he'd been finessed out of a poorly chosen position, and he'd drop back 500 meters and find a better chunk of ground…and protect his flanks next time. But the enemy stayed in place, focusing mostly on the covering force, but beginning to send some fire in the direction of the attacking squads. But, by the time they reacted, the lead teams were in place and deploying their SAWs. A few seconds later, the enemy position was taking heavy flank fire from two autocannons, and losses started to mount.

Wagner knew what would happen next, and he watched with growing respect for Lieutenant Wren and his platoon. They had just sent a team out to move around the other flank when

Wagner's com crackled to life.

"General Wagner, Major Kluck here. We've got a major force of Reapers moving on our position." Kluck sounded sharp, but worried too. The heavy enemy units were a bitch, well-armed and almost invulnerable to small arms attacks. "We need more heavy weapons, sir." Kluck's battalion heavy weapons had been detached to deal with another crisis, and that left him in rough shape against a Reaper attack.

"I'll get you what I can, major." Wagner climbed to his feet, still crouching low to stay in cover. "And I'm coming over there myself." He took one last look at Wren's people and skittered down the slope toward Kluck's position.

Cain was firing on full auto, and he picked off two of the smaller battlebots. He had to rely on the heavy-weapon armed teams to hit the Reapers…his assault rifle wasn't strong enough to take one of those monsters down. He saw the ammo warning light flash, and he felt the brief delay in his fire as the system fed a new clip into his rifle. He was used to having 500 shots a load, and he was burning through the new, larger rounds way too quickly. He switched to semi-auto, three round bursts. Ok, you dumb jarhead, he thought, time to actually aim.

Cain hadn't been this thick in the fight for a long time. He thought about General Holm and how horrified the Commandant would be to see his protégé in the front line fighting like a private. But Cain knew what he was doing. He needed to be where he was…it was the only way he could bring himself to ask such sacrifice from his people. The only way he could live with himself.

He felt his heart pounding…in his chest, his head, his ears… like a drum beating the call of battle. He was tense, edgy… scared. He hadn't been sure he cared enough to be afraid anymore, and he was glad to see he was. The fear made him feel alive, like something more than a ruthless automaton sending his people to their deaths. He remembered what he felt like on his first mission, as a green private dropping onto an enemy held world. That was a good squad, he thought with a smile, though his grin quickly faded. Everyone in that unit was dead now… all but Cain. He wondered, would he have been happier to stay a simple soldier…remain in the enlisted ranks? He'd be a very senior NCO now, probably a regimental sergeant major. He'd have responsibilities, no doubt. But not the crushing pressure of the top command. Not the blood of thousands on his hands.

He shook out of his daydreams, scolding himself for wasting time on such nonsense. He was what he was, and his responsibilities were his and his alone. Someone had to be here, and shirking his obligations, refusing to accept the mantle of command, would have been the worst sort of cowardice. Sergeant Major Cain would have been a failure, he told himself, a man who chose to hide from the true call of his duty.

His forces were heading south, slowly pulling back to the original defensive line, still anchored by the battered 5th and 6th battalions. That position had seemed about to fall again, but Cain's attacks all across the field had disoriented the First Imperium forces and taken the pressure off Colonel Grant's savaged battalions and the reformed but shaky units of II Corps.

The enemy units between Cain's attack force and the line to the south were caught between two fields of fire, and they went down in huge numbers. But the Marines were losing heavily as well…too heavily. It was a battle of attrition, and the First Imperium was winning. Their forces would fight to the last bot…no fear, no fatigue, no doubt. The final one left standing would fight with the focus and relentlessness it had when it first exited the landing craft. Cain's veterans were the best warriors Earth and its progeny had to offer…but they were still human. They wouldn't run, not the veterans, at least…Cain had faith in that. They were prepared to die here if duty demanded it. But they were exhausted and disordered. Their effectiveness was slipping. They were going to come close, but they were going to lose…or at least it looked that way. But Cain's mind was still focused, and inside his visor his face bore an unseen grin. Things were going exactly as he'd planned.

Commander Farooq's Janissaries were pulling back toward

the main line, retreating by halves. They'd popped a line of smoke to the north, covering their pullback. The dense radio-active steam seemed to work as well at confounding the First Imperium's targeting as it ever had against their old human adversaries. Farooq never understood why the Alliance hadn't copied the system.

The cover was welcome. Farooq only had about half his men left, and they still had two klicks to go before they linked up with the defensive line. And those two kilometers were swarming with enemy forces, cut off and soon to be trapped between the Janissaries and the main line. All across the battlefield, disordered groups of First Imperium bots were sandwiched between the dug in remnants of II Corps and Cain's attack forces.

"Green teams, cover the approaches from the north. Red teams, engage encircled enemy forces." Farooq had never fought a battle like this before. At first he'd thought Cain was crazy, that his bizarre plan would get their forces sliced up and destroyed. But the First Imperium units had failed to react to the lightning assaults. They seemed confounded and unable to understand what Cain was doing. The departure from battlefield orthodoxy confused them…and the Marines and Janissaries slaughtered thousands of them.

"Reds, advance to the south by leapfrogs – 100 meter intervals every minute. Red 1s first." Farooq was directing 2,800 Janissaries scattered over six kilometers of front. He allowed himself a moment of pride as he watched his units execute perfectly while facing enemy forces to their front and rear. He'd come to respect the Marines even more than he had when they'd been his enemy, the one adversary that could take on his people and win. Now he smiled as he saw his own troops behaving as the veterans they were. We may not be enemies anymore, he thought, but we're damned sure not going to let the Marines show us up.

He thought of Cain, of Darius Jax, whom he'd known for all too brief a time on Farpoint. Kyle Warren, dead now too. James Teller, General Holm. He'd fought these men and their comrades his whole life. Now he hoped he would never meet them again except as friends, as brothers in arms. He hoped that with all his heart, but he had his doubts. If mankind won this war, if they survived and drove away the First Imperium, would the political masters change? Would they learn anything? He doubted it. One day, and sooner than most would expect, he and others like him would be ordered to battle their old allies. What would happen then? He didn't know…and he didn't have time to think about it now. But if he got off Sandoval he would. He would think about it very seriously.

Farooq watched his troopers advancing south, moving well but paying for every meter. When they reached the battle line to the south, his people would have pinched out the pocket of First Imperium units, and cleared a section of the field. He had another motivation as well. Commander Jaffer's force had been detached earlier in the battle. They'd stood their ground during the routs, and they'd paid the price for their courage. Barely 1 in 3 was left standing, and Farooq was determined to link up with them as soon as possible.

His tactical alarm sounded, and he glanced at the plot on his visor display. The enemy pressure from the north was slackening. The enemy was moving forces away, marching them up north. Why, Farooq wondered, would they be doing that? All of the attacking forces were driving south. What was going on in the north?

Jarvis peered out over the lip of the trench, watching the maelstrom to the north. Even his tactical display was a jumbled mess, with friendly and enemy forces intermingled throughout the combat zone. I Corps had finally attacked, emerging from the hidden tunnels running under the battlefield. The most veteran troops in the army were now fighting a confused melee across 300 square klicks of ground.

He wasn't sure how it was going, but it was damned sure taking pressure off his people, at least for a while. Jarvis had been there when Kyle Warren was killed trying to rally II Corps' routing units. He blamed himself for Warren's death…a good portion of those routers were his own people. If he'd only managed to keep them in the line a little longer. Somehow.

Jarvis commanded II Corps now. He understood why Cain put him in charge, but still, the battlefield promotion to brigadier felt somehow…wrong. Standing so soon in Warren's shoes only inflamed his guilt. But there was no time for such nonsense now, he thought. He'd only let Warren down again if he didn't take care of the corps…and he wasn't about to fail Cain either. The rallied II Corps wasn't exactly a solid formation, but they'd held their place since returning to the line. Cain had handled the situation speedily and ruthlessly…and stopped the morale failure cold. He'd given Jarvis clear instructions…easy to understand, though perhaps harder to follow. In no uncertain terms: he was to shoot anyone who ran.

He hadn't been tested on that. Yet. He was grateful, and he knew it would tear him apart to shoot his own people. But he'd do it. He'd do it because he'd been ordered to…but also because he began to understand Cain's motivations. The Corps was more than a group of men and women with deadly weapons. It was an idea…more than that, an ideal. The Marines were brothers and sisters. They may face more powerful enemies; they may march off to hopeless battles. But wherever they went, they knew their fellow Marines were at their side… that they had their backs. If their comrades couldn't depend on them to stand shoulder to shoulder through the fires of hell, they weren't Marines. Not to Erik Cain.

The great crime committed by the routers wasn't being scared. Every human being on Sandoval was afraid, even the grittiest veteran in the ranks. But the broken units let their fear overwhelm their duty to their comrades. They turned their backs on their fellow Marines, many of whom died because of it. These recruits didn't yet understand what it was to be a Marine. Fate had denied them the chance to learn it in training or in battles fighting alongside experienced cadres. They should never have been part of the Corps, not without more training. Now they would learn the hard way exactly what that meant. What the Corps expected of every Marine.

Jarvis forced his mind back to the tactical situation. I Corps was driving the disordered enemy forces south, against the anvil of II Corps and the 5th and 6th battalions. "All units…General Cain and I Corps are driving the enemy to the slaughter. And that's us. All units on full alert. If you have a shot, take 'em down. And watch your transponders…I don't want anyone taking out friendlies."

"Move it!" Prescott's voice was demanding, and the urgency was front and center. "Get those damned things in place."

His forces had stormed through the gap Cain's nuclear strike opened in the enemy's perimeter. The nukes saved thousands of his people…if they'd had to assault that line unsoftened it would have been an abattoir. But the opening was a short one. First Imperium forces positioned farther back reacted almost immediately. There was no hesitation, no morale degradation from the nuclear attack, no hesitation to advance into the maelstrom…none of the emotional effects a human enemy would have experienced. By the time Prescott's troops got to the LZ, the bots had set up a new line. It wasn't anything like the fortified position the nukes had taken out, but any First Imperium line was serious business. Taking the landing zone had been expensive, but his people had done it. He doubted they could hold it…but they didn't have to. Not if the engineers could finish in time.

They were working as quickly as they could, burying the massive devices across the field. It was a tough job without heavy construction equipment, but the engineers were Marines, not building contractors. They knew what they had to do. It wasn't too hard to dig a hole in an engineer's suit, but it still took time. And with the enemy preparing to launch a counterattack, Prescott would be happy to finish the job and get the hell out. He would put up a defense if he had to, but he'd much rather retreat, just like Cain had told him to do.

"Status report, Major Tomlinson." Prescott's voice clearly telegraphed his impatience.

"Twenty minutes, sir." Tomlinson was out of breath. He sounded harried, distracted.

"No good, major." Prescott's answer was almost an involuntary response. "I need time to pull back the division."

"There's no way we can finish faster." Tomlinson's voice was sincere. Prescott knew the engineer was giving him a straight answer. "Start pulling back now, sir. We will finish up and follow."

"Out of the question, major. If the enemy counterattacks, your people will be slaughtered"

"It's gonna take a lot longer to pull the division back. My engineers can take off and run the minute we're done. We can cover the distance in ten minutes." Tomlinson was still breathing hard – he was clearly working while he was talking.

Prescott frowned. He hated leaving the engineers unprotected. But Tomlinson was right. A division couldn't withdraw as quickly as a small team. He paused, frozen by momentary indecision. Finally: "OK, major. But I want your word that your people are out of here in 20 minutes. That's two zero minutes…not 21 not 20 minutes and 30 seconds. Do we understand each other?"

"Yes, sir." Tomlinson sounded relieved. "You have my word. We'll be on our way in 20 minutes or less."

"That's good news, major." Prescott had a grim smile on his face. "'Cause I'm staying until your people bug out." He cut the line before Tomlinson could protest, and he commed his exec. "Colonel Jung, I want you to start pulling the division back…"

Erin McDaniels had been waiting for the word. Cain had forbidden her to attack until he gave the go ahead. Her people had been in an underground bunker since the enemy arrived on Sandoval, and not one of them had seen battle yet. She'd expected to be the centerpiece of the defense, and instead she was the last reserve unit committed.

She had the HQ feed running through the sophisticated com system of her Obliterator suit, and her AI was feeding her reports as they came in. The AI's vocal system had been upgraded during the last maintenance session. The cold, mechanical tones were gone, replaced by a calmly professional female voice. It was a welcome change, though the softer tones were marginally incongruous with the horrific casualty reports it recited. The troops on the surface were catching hell, with losses of at least 30% in most units…and over 60% in the hardest hit.

Twice, McDaniels had almost disobeyed and ordered her people to move to the surface and attack. But she hadn't. She was a veteran, and a Marine with grit in her soul…but she didn't have the guts to disregard Erik Cain's orders. Instead, she stood on alert and listened to the reports coming in from the surface…more of her comrades and allies killed in the desperate fighting her people were sitting out.

Finally: "McDaniels…Cain here."

She felt a rush of adrenalin…as strong as a heavy stim dose. "Yes, sir…McDaniels here."

"You may attack, colonel." Cain's voice was resolute as always, but she could hear the fatigue in it too.

"Yes, sir. I will attack at once."

"And colonel?" Cain's voice again, this time a bit more of the fatigue evident. "I want an all-out attack. Let them have it."

"Yes, sir!"

Merrick's tanks were a spent force. They'd been the first people heavily engaged, and they'd taken losses no one ever expected them to withstand. They were low on ammo and spare parts, and most of the surviving tanks had at least some damage. The support and repair vehicles were almost all gone, and it was hard to distribute the few supplies Merrick still had. The tank corps had done its part, and it was in no condition to return to the fight.

But Cain had given the all-out attack order to every unit on the field, and Isaac Merrick had no intention of sitting still while the rest of the army fought the final battle. The next 72 hours would decide the fate of Sandoval, of the Line. A few days that would determine whether mankind had what it took to stop the First Imperium. If the survival of Merrick's people was going to be decided, they were going to be there, in the thick of the fight.

"All tank units, prepare to advance in five minutes." His order was sharp, his voice almost hostile, seething with his anger and hatred for the enemy. He could almost hear the groans inside the cramped cockpits of his surviving tanks. Let them grumble, he thought, as long as they obey. He wasn't entirely sure how many of them would.

He flipped his com to the Marine line. "Captain Storm, are your people still combat-capable?"

"We're Marines, sir." As far as Storm was concerned, he'd given Merrick all the answer his question required.

Merrick was confused, but only for a few seconds. He was getting used to the Marines by now. "Captain Weld's tanks will be advancing to hit the enemy flank. Form up your battalion and provide close support."

"Yes, sir."

"And, Storm…this is the final battle…so give it everything you've got, ok? It wasn't a very eloquent battle cry, but Merrick knew it was all the Marine needed.

"Always, sir." Storm's voice was sharp and crisp, as usual. "We're Marines, sir."

Merrick knew that was the only response he'd get. It was all he wanted.

Sarah Linden was exhausted…fatigued like nothing she had ever experienced. She was a beautiful woman, but now her normally sparkling eyes were lifeless, sunken deeply in her gaunt face. Her reddish blonde hair, normally soft and silky, was pinned up haphazardly, dirty and crusted with dried clumps of blood.

She'd lost count of the casualties. The AI had the running total, she realized that…but she didn't want to know. It wouldn't do any good, and she wasn't sure she could bear to hear it.

She hadn't slept in days, maybe even a week. She'd lost touch with that too. The stims were great for a while, but sooner or later they caught up with you. They still kept you awake, but things became blurrier, out of focus. Some people hallucinated, others eventually became catatonic. Everyone reacted differently.

Sarah got the shakes, which was far from the worst side effect of a stim overdose, but a major problem for a surgeon in any event. She needed to get a few hours of real sleep soon. But how could I, she thought...with hundreds of wounded stacked up...and dozens dying before a doctor can get to them?

"Colonel Linden?" Lieutenant Ploor, sounding very worried.

Sarah had come to dread the sound of the young officer's voice. It wasn't fair, she thought...Ploor had proven to be one of the true heroes in the hospital. She was the one person on the staff who'd probably gotten less sleep than Sarah. "Yes, lieutenant?"

"We just got a new batch of wounded..."

Sarah didn't interrupt, but she thought to herself, I hope she has more to say than that. They were getting new loads of wounded every few minutes. No reason to interrupt her to tell her what she already knew.

"It's Commander Farooq, colonel. And he's in bad shape. Very bad."

Shit, she thought. "Get him up here right now." Sarah looked up from the patient on her table locking her eyes on one of the junior surgeons. "Simon, finish here for me," she shouted across the room. Back to the com: "Now, Clarissa! Get moving."

"Yes, colonel. We're on the way."

Sarah felt the despair bubbling up. She was strong, and she'd been through some of the worst battles men had ever fought. But everyone had a limit. She felt adrift on a sea of blood, and she didn't think she could take much more. She still couldn't get the image of Kyle Warren out of her mind. His Marines had carried him back, hoping for some miracle. She'd been waiting when they told her he was coming, but she could tell with one look he was gone. He'd been dead at least half an hour, and he was completely bled out. There had been nothing for her to do, and she had to tell the Marines who'd carried him to the hospital. They were tough veterans, but every one of them wept.

Now the Janissaries' top commander was on his way to her

table. What did that mean to his troops in the field? She knew Erik was depending on the Janissaries. He'd built a good relationship with Farooq, possibly even a friendship. Would he be able to work as well with Farooq's exec?

Erik...where was he? Was he hurt? Was he dead? Fatigue non-stop work had taken her mind off her worry...for a short time. Things had been strained between them recently, but now all she could think about was her desperate fear. Erik acted like he was immortal...but she knew he wasn't. Jax had died. Kyle Warren had died. Will Thompson on Arcadia and Lucius Anton on Columbia. She knew Erik Cain could join that list any time. She was suddenly aware that if Erik was dead on the field somewhere, their last words would have been cross ones. She had to fight the urge to run out of the hospital, to find him and take back the things she had said.

"Colonel, we have Commander Farooq prepped for you." Lieutenant Ploor stood next to the portable med unit, looking over at her.

She submerged her personal thoughts once again, though it was getting more and more difficult. "Ok, lieutenant...you stay and assist." She walked toward the unit. "Let's get started." She was scanning the extent of his wounds, her face hardening as she did. "We don't have any time to waste."

"Here they come." Prescott stood behind the rocky spur... back where his attack on the LZ had begun. His head was bent back, staring up into the sky. The division had taken heavy losses, at least 25%, and the Canadian regiment that stayed behind with him and the engineers had casualties over 40%. He'd hoped to withdraw completely before the enemy counterattacked, but the engineers were still working, and he'd had to fight a delaying action with his Canadian veterans. They'd suffered most of their losses holding the LZ for an extra twenty minutes...and in the subsequent withdrawal under fire. But they eventually managed to break off, and now they were back at the original jumping off point.

"Yes, sir." Major Dillon stood just behind Prescott. "It

looks like at least 50 landing craft." The First Imperium landers were mostly heavy transports, much larger than the Marines' Gordons.

Prescott nodded silently, though the gesture was unnoticeable in armor. There was an amazed grin on his face, hidden inside his helmet. Son of a bitch, he thought, shaking his head...Cain was right again.

"Major, confirm all units are deployed behind the cover of the ridgeline." Prescott had the entire division pulled back behind the rocky spine, sheltered from the landing zone. He'd given the order twice and checked on it three times, but he wanted to be sure. Anybody caught out in the open was going to end up a stain.

"All units report they are in place and under cover."

The response was fast. Too fast, Prescott thought. Then he realized Dillon had already confirmed unit statuses before being ordered to. "Very well, major. It should be showtime any minute."

"Yes, sir." Dillon paused an instant and then added, "You should take heavier cover, sir."

Prescott hesitated a few seconds, taking one last look out over the landing zone. "You're right, major. Let's go."

The two armored officers jogged down the steep path, moving further behind the rocky hill between them and the LZ. They reached the end of the small trail, near one of the access points where the division had emerged from the tunnels. Prescott went prone, motioning for Dillon to do the same.

Over the LZ, squadrons of First Imperium shuttles fired their landing jets, stabilizing themselves 500 meters from the ground and preparing for a final descent. The AI in Cain's headquarters was monitoring the approach, and at 500 meters it triggered the buried atomic mines.

All across the LZ, twenty large nuclear devices detonated... not tactical warheads, but giant 100 megaton city-killers. Billowing plumes rose rapidly from the surface, engulfing the descending landing craft. Shuttles were thrown about, some colliding, others plummeting to the ground with major systems knocked out by the shockwaves. The entire landing zone was consumed by nuclear fire, sweeping away the enemy bots and gouging deep craters in the tortured landscape.

Prescott's people were close…too close but for the line of rocky hills that gave them cover. An unarmored man would have received a lethal radiation dosage in seconds, but everyone in 2nd Division was suited up and well-protected from the blast effects that reached them. It was a hellish nightmare all around Prescott's dug-in troops. The temperature rose, nearly to the maximum the osmium-iridium alloy in their suits could withstand. Their life support systems were taxed to the limit, barely maintaining survivable conditions. It got hot inside the suits, but still within bearable levels. Shattered chunks of rock flew around, broken loose by the massive shockwaves and propelled through the air by the vortex of winds.

Prescott was hunched over, shielding himself as much as possible from the hell surrounding him. But he was laughing. It started as a grin and, as he continued to think of the trap they'd set, he began to chuckle. The blasts had taken out thousands of the enemy, on the ground and in the landing craft. The LZ was clear. The entire counterattack force – and all the reinforcements sent down from orbit – were gone, wiped off the face of Sandoval by atomic fire.

They may be thousands of years ahead of us, Prescott thought, but they're naïve as hell when it comes to war…and they're no match for Erik Cain.

The Obliterators were an awesome sight, stomping across the battlefield, spreading destruction through the ranks of the First Imperium forces. The enemy still had its technological edge – and a Reaper was still more powerful than an Obliterator – but now it was a match of training and skill. The First Imperium forces were confused, and the intelligences directing them hesitated, uncertain. The situation on the field didn't match any logical pattern of strategy or warfare. They didn't know what to do.

The human forces sliced into them, launching hundreds of

well-executed small unit assaults across the field. The enemy bots were isolated into scattered surrounded groups and destroyed in detail. On the flank, Merrick's shattered tank corps roared to life and, contrary to everyone's expectations of their capabilities, launched a savage attack, ripping right through the center of the enemy concentrations.

"Keep your formations tight, people." McDaniels' Obliterators were positioned at 100 meters intervals, each supported by a Marine squad. They were hunting the Reapers, leaving the rest of the enemy combatants to their conventionally armored comrades.

McDaniels swung around as she fired her dual launchers and loosed two HVMs at an isolated Reaper. She crouched low, taking cover behind a large rock outcropping, just as a cluster of enemy bots returned the fire. She loved the Obliterator suit. Her only complaint was its size. It was hard to find cover for a hulking four-meter osmium-iridium gorilla. The multi-layer armor could absorb a lot of damage, and it could turn away even a hyper-velocity round, but it was always better to avoid getting hit rather than counting on your protection to save you.

She watched the scanner, waiting for the AI's damage assessment. The Obliterator suits had small drones, nanobots really, that it could launch, giving it a field of vision even when the suit itself was hunkered down under cover. The drones could collect data to evaluate damage, among other uses. The assessment was good news. The Reaper was down, probably not entirely out of action, but in bad shape nevertheless.

"Pull back." It was Sergeant Walton, the leader of her attached squad. "We've got bogies advancing on the left."

McDaniels redirected her monitors over to the left. There were standard battle bots approaching, at least twenty. She waited…another few seconds, and the advancing enemy would be partially in the open. There was another chunk of rock about 40 meters away where she could take cover…and between the two she'd have a great shot at the attacking bots.

She turned and started to run toward the other outcropping, angling her upper body and unloading with the two heavy autocannons attached to her arms. They fired 1,200 rounds a minute at a velocity of 4,800 meters per second. Her AI-assisted targeting gave her pinpoint accuracy, and the entire area around the enemy bots was hosed down with devastating fire.

Three of the bots went down almost immediately, the massive projectiles from McDaniels' cannons tearing them to pieces. The rest scattered, trying to duck into cover and return fire. Her AI tracked them, calculating the most exposed targets in real time and highlighting them on her tactical screen. Another four bots went down – she didn't know if they were all destroyed, but they were hit hard enough that none got back up…and that was good enough for her at the moment.

There was a loud whooshing sound, followed by a sharp click – her suit reloading the cannons. She sprayed the enemy position one last time before diving behind her new cover. She could hear the impacts on the other side of the rock, the return fire from the bots, perfectly targeted but just a second too late.

Her heart was pounding, and she was sweaty and uncomfortable. She would have given half her pension to get her arm around and wipe the grime off the back of her neck. But she was excited too, almost giddy to be hunting the enemy down. For the first time in the war, she felt like they had the upper hand. The First Imperium forces were confused, disordered, uncertain…and her people were focused like predators howling at the scent of blood. Finally, she thought…finally we have them on the run. At least on Sandoval.

She glanced down at her display. The line of Obliterators was advancing across the entire field. They were taking losses, but they were giving out fivefold. That was another new feeling for this war; up until now they'd felt like targets. Now they were changing that dynamic.

Her people were large blue ovals on the display, and the enemy Reapers were red versions of the same symbol. Now she noticed something else moving slowly onto the plot, a gray triangle…no two…three. All off to the left flank of her line. "Identify gray triangles." She hadn't spoken much to the AI. Simulated or not, she missed the camaraderie she'd had with

Mystic, and the clinical coldness of the new unit made her uncomfortable.

"Gray triangles represent M-275A main battle tanks, class designation "Scott.""

"Yes!" she shouted, glad the outgoing com was off once she realized how exuberant her outburst had been. Merrick's tanks, she thought, still excited. We've sliced straight through the enemy position, and now we're linking up with the tank corps.

She flipped on the unit-wide com. "Let's go people." Her voice was loud and confident. "We're linking up with the tanks. We've got these bastards on the run...let's finish 'em off now!" She started moving around the outcropping, getting ready to lunge forward to the next position. "And watch out for the friendlies!"

James Teller made his way slowly up the embankment. He was staggering a little, but not from any wound. The entire army had been fighting nonstop for days and days, a brutal slugging match. Teller couldn't remember ever feeling fatigue like this before. He knew the stims were the only thing keeping him from falling over, but even they were losing their effect. He'd taken a shot less than half an hour before. It perked him up, but now it was already wearing off. He knew he couldn't take much more of the stuff...he was already feeling like shit and pissing blood, which his suit helpfully advised him was interfering with the efficient recycling of his bodily wastes.

All across the field the 1st Army's personnel had fought as small units...companies, platoons, squads...hundreds of savage little combats. In the radioactive craters and shattered ruins of cities and towns, the humans had the advantage, their experience at war and small unit training making the difference. For the first time, Cain's forces were inflicting more casualties than they took.

Teller cleared the top of the ridge and looked out over the field. It was all over but the mopping up. The First Imperium army was gone, destroyed. Not broken...wiped out. Other than the scattered units being tracked down and exterminated, there wasn't a functioning enemy robot on Sandoval. That hadn't come without a price. They wouldn't know the casualty totals for some time. No one knew how many of the missing were out there alive, with damaged suits, dropped out of the net. But it was a good bet that 1ˢᵗ Army lost half its number…and possibly more than that.

He turned and walked toward the makeshift command post. There were armored figures moving in every direction, and tables set up with workstations. He saw a lone figure, standing near the edge of the ridge, calmly looking out over the same scene he'd just surveyed. His armor was dented in several places, and scorch marks marred its torso. One of the arms had a bulge of stringy foam, the self-expanding material the Mark VIII armor used to seal breaches. The spongy gray material was tinted pink…the occupant of the armor had been wounded, and his blood had mingled with the sealant.

"Hello, general." Teller walked up from behind, and he stood erect and offered the best salute he could manage in his armor. Saluting on the battlefield wasn't normal practice, but Teller figured 1ˢᵗ Army's now-victorious commander deserved one.

Cain turned slowly, stiffly. He was definitely hurting, though Teller thought it couldn't be too serious if he was standing here so casually…without a crowd of aides begging him to go to the hospital.

"James…" Cain's voice was hoarse, his speech slow, almost sad. "I'm glad to see you made it through this one in better shape than your last." Teller had been grievously wounded in the fighting on Cornwall. Sarah's people had put him back together, but it had been a close thing.

"Not a scratch." Teller laughed softly. "Go figure."

Cain turned to directly face Teller. "Seriously, James…your people fought like heroes. You should be very proud." Cain glanced down at his arm. "I'd shake your hand, but I'm afraid my arm's seen better days." He let out a short laugh. "It's always more trouble than it's worth in armor anyway. You've got one coming to you, though. A handshake…and a chestful of medals too."

"More fruit salad for my dress blues?" Teller's tone was somber. "I'll take a pass, if it's all the same, sir. After a while it starts to feel like all these men and women get torn to shreds so we can pin decorations on each other." He paused. "Sorry, sir. I don't mean to be ungrateful...it just doesn't feel right."

"No apologies necessary, my friend. I feel the same way." Cain turned back and looked over the field again as he spoke. "But all bets are off...they're probably going to give me some too. And when they do I'll be thinking of Kyle Warren. I coaxed him back into active duty, you know. I pulled his away from a good life on Arcadia so he could die on this miserable rock. But when they come at me with those medals, I have to be graceful and accept them...and you are damned well going to do the same."

Teller paused, standing next to Cain, looking out over the plains below. "Kyle's death wasn't your fault, sir. And it's not your fault he was here." Teller's voice was gentle, even wistful. "I didn't get to know him too well. We'd met a few times on Carson's World years back...and then not until we mustered in here. But a Marine like Kyle Warren doesn't sit out a battle like this. He knew damned well what was at stake, and he came here just like the rest of us...like you and me, sir...ready to give whatever it took to win this fight. That's what we are, Erik. That's what makes us tick. It almost killed me not to be on Farpoint...and I was still eating through a tube when you guys fought that battle. You do Kyle a disservice taking the blame. He'd have been here no matter what."

Cain turned again and looked over at Teller. "Well who knew? A philosopher Marine." Cain's voice was mocking, but gently so. He knew Teller was right. "Thanks, James. I know all that's true, but it's still good to hear someone else say it."

Teller was silent for a few seconds. There wasn't much else to say about Kyle Warren, so he changed the subject. "Are you worried they have even more bots up in that fleet, sir? Their LZ is toast, but there's a whole planet they can land on." Teller's voice became softer, a little tentative. "The army is ecstatic, but I don't think they can take on a fresh force. They're spent, Erik…all of them. If that fleet lands another 10,000 bots, we're screwed."

"Well, I *was* concerned about it." Cain smiled. Teller couldn't see it, of course, but he could hear the lighter tone in the CO's voice. "But now we're picking up multiple transmissions. The fleet's here."

Teller stood still, in shocked silence. The fleet. They'd have one hell of a fight up there…he was sure of that. But he doubted the enemy would launch a new ground assault while they were facing a battle in space. They'd get some time at least. And if Garret's people could prevail, Teller thought, maybe it was really possible…maybe the Line would actually hold.

Cain turned slowly, looking back over his shoulder. "If you can manage things here for a few, I'm going to head to the hospital. I need to check on the wounded." He took a few steps and stopped, turning back again. "And I said some things to Sarah I wish I could take back. I've been hurting lately, in more ways than one, but that's no excuse to take it out on her." He turned again and started walking, adding softly, "And now it's time for me to apologize."

Chapter 24

AS Lexington, Flag Bridge
Approaching Planet Sandoval
Delta Leonis System
"The Line"

Augustus Garret pulled himself upright in his command chair. His acceleration couch had just retracted, and the stimulant was bringing him out of the dreamy state caused by the rigors of deceleration. His ships had been thrusting hard, reducing velocity as they approached the enemy forces deployed around Sandoval. He didn't want to zip past the stationary First Imperium fleet. It wasn't any hit and run raid this time. Combined Fleet was here for a fight to the death.

The enemy had expended all of their antimatter weapons during the initial fighting in the system; Garret was fairly certain of that. He didn't know if they'd been resupplied, and he guessed it was 50/50 they had. He'd sent Admiral Vargus' attack ships in first to find out…87 suicide boats, all blasting at 0.04c. He figured the enemy would have to launch whatever ordnance they had or risk taking plasma torpedo hits with antimatter weapons still in the racks. It was an inelegant way to force the enemy's hand, but it was all Garret had. It was likely to be expensive too. He knew most of those boats weren't going to make it back, and he didn't want to think of how many of the 6,500 crew manning them would die in the next 30 minutes.

The main body was two light minutes back, still outside maximum missile range. If he'd timed everything right, he'd launch Greta Hurley's bombers almost immediately after the suicide boats made their run, and then the rest of the fleet would move into range and launch its missile salvoes.

The fleet was blasting out announcements of its arrival to the planet, too. Garret had no idea if any of the signals would penetrate the enemy's jamming screen and reach Cain's troops, but he had to try. They'd been cut off and on their own for months, and they deserved to know the fleet had returned.

Garret wasn't even sure that Cain or any of his people were still alive. The fleet around Sandoval was by far the largest concentration of First Imperium power he'd seen, and he couldn't even begin to estimate how many thousands of battle robots those ships carried. Cain's army was a powerful fighting force, the largest mankind had ever deployed off of Earth. But 1st Army had a lot of green troops, Marines who hadn't even finished the normal training program. Throwing them against the First Imperium was something Holm knew he'd always regret, but there had been no choice. There just weren't enough veterans left. Too many of them lay dead on the battlefields of the Third Frontier War and the rebellions…and the Rim worlds where the First Imperium initially struck.

"Sir, Admiral Vargus' boats are making their run." Max Harmon was Terrence Compton's senior staff officer. Normally, Garret would never poach another admiral's people, but Compton was still laid up on Armstrong, and Garret figured Harmon wouldn't want to miss the battle. His mother led one of the task forces, and Max deserved to be there too. He'd give him back once Compton was on his feet again. Probably.

"Very well, Max. Keep me posted." Garret found he tended to use Harmon's first name, or he simply avoided using a name at all in responding to his new aide. Harmon had deserved the promotion to captain, and Garret had given it without hesitation. But Lexington already had a captain, so Harmon was typically given a courtesy promotion to commodore when addressed onboard. Garret thought the whole thing was a little silly, but even the navy's top officer had to respect its traditions, ancient and inexplicable though they may be. Once these things were ingrained in the culture they were hard to change. Captain Muldoon would likely be offended if Garret started calling Harmon captain. She'd never say anything, of course, but he was sure it would bother her. Garret was always amazed at the amount of superficial silliness that accrued to the job of killing one's enemies. But he didn't care enough to try to change it.

"Sir, Admiral Vargus' boats are entering missile detonation range." The First Imperium fleet had launched a large volley at the attack ships. None of the ordnance showed the higher acceleration rates of the antimatter missiles, but that wasn't conclusive. Now they would see. In a few minutes, Garret would know if Vargus' people were flushing out the antimatter weapons…or if he'd simply wasted their lives.

Wolverine zipped straight through the barrage, her shotguns firing wildly, tearing apart missile after missile. She didn't have a scratch yet, but that wasn't something Desmond Vargus could say about the rest of his force. The Delta-Z transmissions were pouring in far too quickly. He wanted to ignore them, but he felt the least he could do for his people was listen to the reports of their deaths.

"Still no antimatter detonations detected, sir." Lieutenant Lane's report was businesslike, matter-of-fact. Lane was a veteran of the attack ships, and she was used to running gauntlets. The suicide boats didn't take a lot of punishment, and a near miss by a large nuke could vaporize one of them in an instant. Experienced crews tended to become fatalistic, shoving aside insecurities, developing a bravado to cover the fear.

"Keep reporting to fleetcom in real time, lieutenant. Confirm that all ships are reporting as ordered." There was no way of knowing when a missile would get close enough to take out a given ship, so Vargus had his entire task force sending reports back to the fleet every two minutes.

"Yes, sir." Lane had just confirmed the transmissions, but she leaned over and rechecked them all. "All vessels sending full scanning reports every 120 seconds, as ordered, sir."

"Very well." Vargus leaned back in the command chair. There was nothing else for him to do right now but wait. The captain's station was an odd place for him to be – fast attack ships weren't designed to support an admiral's flag. It was rare for anything more than a squadron to be commanded from a suicide boat…usually more than 3 or 4 ships would be part of a force with larger vessels as well. But this was a special situation. Garret had to know if he was facing antimatter ordnance, and only a major attack force would compel the enemy to launch their heavy weapons. The boats were relying on maneuverability for their survival, and a cruiser or other heavy ship would only slow the armada down.

Vargus was the right choice for the mission. Though he'd been an admiral running cruiser squadrons for four or five years, he'd come up through the attack ship service. The suicide boats didn't always get the respect they deserved from the brass, but that wasn't the case under Augustus Garret. The fleet admiral's first command had been a fast attack ship, and he was very aware of what well-led vessels could do. And he knew any boats he sent in under Desmond Vargus would be superbly led.

"Sir, we have cleared the missile detonation zone." Lane was reading from her screen as she spoke. "Projecting particle accelerator range in 15 minutes."

Ok, Vargus thought. We're through…and not one antimatter warhead. They didn't make it unscathed, not by any definition. His own mental count had 21 ships destroyed…and at least another 20 that had taken serious hits. Any of those with damage affecting their engines had almost no shot of getting back. Not that anyone's chances were all that great. And the particle accelerators were probably going to exact a greater toll than the missiles.

"Send this to Admiral Garret." Vargus looked across the cramped bridge. His view of his tactical officer was partially obscured – the designers of the Snow Leopard class attack ships hadn't been particularly concerned with comfort or aesthetics; that much was obvious. They were damned good boats in battle, but they were a chaotic jumble of support structures and low-hanging conduits inside. "Admiral, we have passed through the enemy missile barrage. As per the real time data we have transmitted, it appears highly unlikely that the enemy is armed with antimatter warheads. We are about to enter energy weapons range. Will report before we launch our attack run. We'll try to soften them up for you, sir."

Lane worked her board for a few seconds. "Message transmitted, sir."

"Ok, we don't have anything to do for the next few minutes, so let's have all ships doublecheck their plasma torpedoes. I don't know how many of us are going to make it past the particle accelerator fire, but everyone who does better damned well paint those targets and land two solid hits. Or I'll have their asses."

"Yes sir...ordering all ships to conduct weapons diagnostic."

Vargus sighed. He knew the energy weapons fire was going to be bad. The enemy's particle accelerators had twice the range of the fleet's lasers. That meant his ships would be in the kill zone for twice as long. And they didn't have anything to fire back. The tiny laser batteries on the boats were no better than flashlights against a First Imperium hull. The plasma torpedoes were the real punch, but they had to get close first...and that meant silently taking all the enemy could dish out.

Garret sat stonefaced as he listened to Vargus' transmission. It was all extraneous, really. The data had been transmitted multiple times already. To everyone else on Lexington's flag bridge, it seemed like Vargus was just being meticulous. But Garret understood. It was a goodbye. Desmond Vargus was almost as old a spacehound as Garret, and he was under no illusions about his chances of making it back from this one. No more than Garret was.

The flag bridge was silent, everyone waiting for Garret to speak. But he just sat silently, an emotionless, almost blank look on his face. He and Vargus hadn't served much together, but he'd known the man for almost 40 years. He knew the attack ships would suffer terrible losses, and he'd been reluctant to send them in. But he *had* to know if the enemy fleet was armed with antimatter weapons. Combined Fleet had 21 capital ships and almost 300 cruisers, destroyers, and other vessels, by far the largest force mankind had ever put into space. Assembling this much power in one place was a massive gamble – if the fleet was lost, the war was as good as over. Garret was willing to take the risk for a straight-up fight, but he wasn't prepared to throw humanity's strongest concentration of military power into the teeth of hellish antimatter attack.

Garret had needed someone he trusted, someone he could count on…someone with enough experience in the suicide boats to give them a chance to make it back. That was Vargus. The only man more qualified for the job was Terrence Compton…and he was still in the hospital, barely able to stand without help. He wondered, would you really have sent Terry? Compton was his best friend, his only real friend. Probably not, he thought. Compton was a fleet admiral, and the second highest officer in the Alliance navy. He'd probably have been Garret's exec. Still, he was grateful that circumstance had relieved him of that choice.

Finally he turned and spoke softly. "Commodore Harmon…" He frowned slightly. Stupid tradition, he thought. "…Fleetwide order. All bomber crews to their craft. We will be launching in 15 minutes." Greta Hurley was another one… down in Lexington's launch bay she was Commodore Hurley, but once her bomber blasted into space he could call her captain again.

"Yes sir." Harmon turned toward his com. "Attention all fleet units. All bomber squadrons are to be placed on alert. Projected launch in fifteen minutes…that's one five minutes."

"And get me Greta Hurley."

"Yes, sir," Harmon snapped out crisply. A brief pause. "I have Commodore Hurley, sir."

Garret looked like he tasted something bad. We don't even have commodores anymore, he thought. "Greta, I just wanted to wish you and your people luck." He hesitated, taking a quick breath. "I don't suppose there's anything I need to tell you. Except there is no one I trust more to lead this attack." A brief pause. "No one."

"Thank you, sir." Hurley's voice was usually deadpan, but a little emotion crept in. She wasn't one to be worked up by speeches and empty praise. But Augustus Garret didn't give unwarranted tribute. She had tremendous respect for the fleet admiral, and his confidence in her stiffened her morale. "We'll get the job done, sir."

"I know you will." She was about to lead the largest strike force ever launched – over 600 bombers. Hurley had considerable experience fighting the First Imperium, but most of her crews were going against the enemy for the first time. Garret and she both knew how much pressure that put on her. The attack was critically important, and the admiral was confident she'd do whatever was necessary. "Now, Commodore Hurley… go make those bastards pay."

Squadron Captain Vernon was focusing on the tactical display, trying to concentrate on the attack run…and not the particle beam that sliced Wolverine in half a few minutes earlier. Vernon doubted Admiral Vargus and his crew even had the time to react. One instant they were alive…the next they were dead. And Alex Vernon found himself in command of the task force. What was left of it, anyway.

He had 36 ships still able to attack. That was less than half, considerably less. But it was still a lot of firepower…and he wasn't going to see it wasted. In all probability, they were paying with their lives for these shots. By God, he thought, we're going to make them count.

The bombers were moving up right behind his people, running the gantlet of the enemy point defense, just as his force had braved the missile and energy weapons fire. The bomber wings would hit the enemy right after the attack ships, a one-two punch designed to inflict maximum damage before any of the stricken vessels would withdraw or conduct meaningful damage control.

"Lieutenant Yantz, put me on forcewide com." Yes, they were going to repay the enemy in full…and it was time to make sure the rest of the taskforce felt the same way.

It only took a few seconds for the tactical officer to set up the link. "You are on the line now, sir."

"Attention Task Force Gamma." He tried to sound commanding, impervious to fear and grief…which he most certainly was not. He felt like a poor substitute for Desmond Vargus, but he knew his duty. "We all knew this was a tough mission, but now we're finally getting a chance to hurt these bastards. This battle is going to decide if the Line holds…and probably if mankind survives this onslaught. We are fighting for our friends and comrades, our families, wherever they may be. We are here with our brothers and sister in arms, and our allies, old and new. Every blow struck in this battle could be the one that tips the scale. Every attack ship landing a torpedo hit – or missing one - could be the margin of victory or defeat. No one is unimportant…we need everyone in this fight. Each of us must now give our all. I'm expecting every ship to land two solid hits." He paused briefly and added, "Now let's pay these bastards back for everyone we've lost today. Time to avenge the admiral!"

He didn't have two-way sound, so he couldn't hear the cheering on every ship of the task force. His people – though they'd only been his for a few minutes – were ready. It was time.

"Woooo…" Hurley wasn't sure who it was at first; then she decided it was Commander Farrelly. "They're so busy fighting off the attack ships, we're getting a free ride!"

That wasn't true, Hurley thought, not entirely. There was still plenty of defensive fire to go around. She'd lost about thirty bombers, but that was a lot less than she'd expected. They were still too far out to get accurate scanner reports, but whatever was going on up there, the enemy's defense network were definitely sub-par.

"Let's stay cool, people." Hurley didn't want to clamp down too hard on anything that pumped up morale…but she wasn't going to let her people get sloppy either. They had a long way to go. "Let's check and recheck those weapons systems. Anybody who misses is going to have to answer to me when we get back."

She looked down at the tactical screen. She couldn't even get her whole force to display. Fifty squadrons. Every one of them under her command. It was hard to wrap her mind around it all.

And she had Martian and PRC bombers too. Different training, different systems. Now she had to forge it all into a single potent weapon. She knew Admiral Garret was counting on her, and she wasn't going to fail him.

"Scarlett, report on squadron formations." Hurley still wasn't comfortable with the AI, but she knew there was no way she could keep track of the massive force under her command without it.

"All squadron deployments consistent with battle plan, captain." Here we go, she thought. Her strategy was daring… some would say crazy. She'd been stunned when Garret rubber-stamped it, relying entirely on her opinion she could pull it off. The strikeforce had only six targets, with 8 squadrons assigned to each. Hurley was going after the Leviathans, the enemy's massive battleships. There were ten of them in the Delta Leonis system, and if Greta Hurley had her way there would be only four left for Garret's capital ships to face.

Her forces had gutted one of the monsters in the First Battle of Sandoval. Now she was back to finish the job…and this time she wasn't even going to leave burned out hulks. She was going to vaporize the things. She flipped on the main com. "Strikeforce, arm plasma torpedoes."

She leaned back in her seat as Lieutenant Potter went through the arming procedure for the command bomber. Half the officers in the strikeforce begged her to keep her craft back, but Greta Hurley had always piloted the lead ship, and that wasn't going to change now.

"Execute attack plan Zeta. All ships begin final approach." One after another, the bombers executed short burns, changing their vectors and forming themselves from deep columns into lines approaching the target vessels. They would launch their torpedoes in six second intervals, targeting the entire length of the huge enemy ships from two sides.

"OK, Lieutenant Potter. The strikeforce is on its own. Now let's make sure we drop our bird right down their throats."

"Yes, captain." She worked the controls at her station. "Targeting info on your station now." Potter didn't need to be told.

She knew Hurley was going to take the shot herself.

The bombers were coming in close, well beyond maximum firing range. These shots were going to be point blank. It was costing more casualties, but the enemy fleet was still disrupted from the attack of the suicide boats…and Hurley wanted these torpedoes on the mark.

"Scanners report considerable damage to target, captain." Potter was staring at the screen, feeding Hurley updates. "It appears the vessel suffered at least two direct hits from the fast attack ships." The damage was significant, but the Leviathan was enormous. It was going to take a lot more to knock it out.

Hurley was focused on the targeting display. "Scarlett, countdown to firing position."

The AI responded to Hurley's order. "Optimum firing point in twelve seconds…eleven…ten."

Hurley's face was pressed against the scope. She was going to target these shots herself.

"Seven…six…five…"

The Leviathan was thrusting, trying to escape the approach vectors of the incoming bombers. But there were over 70 incoming, and they were zipping in from every direction. Hurley had allowed for every possibility. There was no escaping her squadrons.

"Three…two…one…"

Hurley held her fire, continuing the countdown under her breath. The target was moving, and her instincts told her to wait an extra beat. "Minus 1, minus 2…" She pulled the trigger, and the bomber shook from the force of expelling the torpedo.

"Thrust plan Sigma-2." She leaned back in her chair as the AI fired the engines. The thrust was a little under 3g, perfectly bearable without engaging the acceleration couch. Once the rest of her people had finished their attack runs they'd button up and blast full out for the fleet.

"Direct hit, captain." The excitement in Potter's voice was clear. Their bomber, at least, had hit the bullseye.

The AI was filtering scanning results and reporting in real time. It was hit after hit. Her people were raking the enemy battleships, savaging the behemoths with searing plasma. She kept her cool…until the Leviathan she'd targeted erupted into a massive fireball. Then Greta Hurley lost her control and let out a howling battle cry.

"Take that, you pieces of shit!"

Chapter 25

"The Valley of Death"
Planet Garrison
Alpha Corvi III
"The Line"

"It's fine. My medsystem stopped the bleeding, and the nanos patched my suit." Heinrich Shultz spoke loudly, trying to compensate with volume for the weakness he felt. "I will not leave my troopers. Not now."

Horace opened his mouth then closed it without speaking. He'd been trying to get Shultz to go to the field hospital, but he realized it was futile. He knew he wouldn't leave the field now either…and the CEL captain was every bit the fighter he was.

Their two units had fallen back, first from Hobson's Ridge to the Jackson River line…and from there through the ruins of Garrison City and its satellite settlements. The towns had been nuked hard, and only a few remnants of superhardened buildings had been left standing. They weren't standing anymore.

At every point the forces of the Pact fought the enemy grimly, extracting a price for each kilometer, forcing the enemy to twice land reinforcements. But they still fell back. They were inflicting heavy casualties, but they were losing the battle.

Horace ordered his AI to give him another stim. The enemy would attack soon, and he needed to be 100%…especially with Shultz no better than walking wounded. The German officer could push himself as hard as he wanted, but eventually his body was going to give out. Horace knew he had to shoulder most of the load now.

"Alright…stay." Horace was doing the best he could. "But sit for a few…rest. Don't be in such a hurry to tear those wounds open." He turned and glanced down the hill where their interspersed units were positioning what was left of the heavy weapons. "I can supervise the deployment. You save your strength for the fight."

Shultz was going to argue, but when he turned to face Horace he could feel the ground coming up at him. He froze, and the vertigo started to fade. The suit had pumped its entire supply of blood substitute into him, but he was still woozy. Maybe a few minutes of rest will help, he thought, frustrated with his own weakness. "Ok, but just for a few minutes." He looked over at the Alliance officer. "But you don't need to nursemaid me. Get down there and make sure those weapons are well-sited. We don't have long."

Horace smiled inside his armor and turned to head down the hill. "I'll keep you posted." He started to trot down the rugged slope.

"And John?"

Horace stopped and turned back to face Shultz. It was entirely unnecessary gesture – their suits were sealed, and their discussion was on the com. Horace heard Shultz through the speaker in his helmet, not from the direction of the CEL captain. But still, he paused and turned toward his companion. "Yes, Heinrich?"

"Thank you." His voice was soft, the exhaustion obvious.

The two officers had known each other for less than five days, but a real kinship had evolved during that time. They had developed an almost-immediate trust for each other, and their units had fought superbly together.

"Just get some rest." Horace had grown to respect his CEL counterpart enormously. "I'm going to need your ass spitting fire when those Reapers hit us again." He grinned to himself and trotted down the hill, wondering with amusement how literally the AI translated his English into German.

Cate Gilson was a trim, erudite woman, the epitome of the cool, intelligent professional. She could have passed for a professor at any university in the Alliance. But Gilson wasn't a teacher; she was a Marine, and on the battlefield she shed that refined veneer, and the curses flowed like water from a hose. There wasn't a career sergeant in the Corps with a fouler mouth than General Catherine Gilson in the middle of a desperate battle.

"Morton, tell that fucking lazy piece of shit I'm sick and tired of his motherfucking excuses." She wasn't shouting, not exactly, but she was getting her point across.

"Yes, general." Kevin Morton was used to the boss' tirades. He'd seen her withering invective reduce 20-year veterans to sobbing wrecks, but he was as close to immune to it as a Marine could get. He loved Gilson and would follow her anywhere, but he'd never met anyone who drove people harder or demanded greater perfection. Of course, he hadn't served under Erik Cain. He had heard the stories, though. He knew some of Cain's people, and they'd compared notes in a couple of well-lubricated get-togethers before they all shipped out from Armstrong. The results were inconclusive – the title of hardest SOB commander in the Corps was still up for grabs.

"I want those goddamned heavy weapons teams over here NOW!" She was pissed, no question...and with good reason. Colonel Lin's heavy brigade had been making shitty time, and her people needed those autocannons and rocket batteries. It didn't help that Lin was a CAC officer. Gilson had been fighting against the Central Asian Combine her entire career. She didn't like Lin, and she didn't trust him. But she didn't have any choice but to depend on him...and it wasn't improving her mood at all.

"I'm on it, general." Morton was a calmer sort than Gilson, which is probably why they worked together so well. He also knew how important it was to keep the Pact functioning and all the human forces working together. He'd even had a personal message from General Holm before they left for Garrison. The Commandant had asked him to try to keep Gilson as diplomatic as possible. He'd found the easiest way to do that was to interpose himself between the general and the targets of her anger. He was going to ride Colonel Lin hard for sure. Gilson wasn't wrong; the CAC officer was a political crony and not a real soldier. He'd been dragging his feet all morning, probably scared shitless to actually go into battle. Still, he was going to edit Gilson's remarks a bit. He knew she wanted him to give it to Lin loud and dirty, but he'd tone things down enough to avoid an international incident. He just hoped Lin listened this time… because if he didn't move his ass Gilson was going to handle it personally. If she didn't just find the SOB and shoot him herself.

"We're out of ammo, sarge." Corporal Jahn leaned over the heavy autocannon, staring into the empty magazine as though his gaze could somehow fill it with fresh rounds. There were empty ammunition crates everywhere. The fighting had been hot all day.

"We're out too, sarge." Corporal Carslon, 200 meters to the south.

"We're down to 12,000 rounds, sergeant."

"Just under 10k here."

"Supply dump's got plenty of CAC shit, boys and girls, but none of ours." Sergeant Hull's voice was deep and gravelly. "So get your rifles out, Marines. And when you're out of ammo for those, get your blades out. We fight with what we got." Hull had no idea how long it would take to get more ordnance up to his people. Every time they'd tried to set up a decent ammo dump on the surface, the enemy took it out with a nuke or a cluster bomb barrage. The CAC troops had gotten to the party late, and they still had plenty of ammo. His Marines were armed with Alliance equipment, though, and the CAC rounds wouldn't fit. What a clusterfuck, he thought, gripping his rifle firmly. The enemy would be coming soon. His Marines had kept them back with their withering fire, but as his teams ran out of ammo, it opened the door for an enemy attack to breach the line. If they got through here, they'd flank the units on either side…the whole battle line could be compromised. "Not on my watch," Hull muttered softly to himself. "The captain'll get supplies through."

"CHQ…Captain John Horace, provisionally commanding 11th Brigade." No one knew what had happened to Major Timmons. He was probably dead somewhere on the field, kilometers behind enemy lines. His transponder signal was out, which meant his armor was in bad shape, wherever it was. Horace kept telling himself Timmons was probably at one of the field hospitals, but he didn't really believe it. "I have units all across the line low on ammo or completely out. We need resupply ASAP."

"Negative, captain."

Shit, Horace thought…that's Major Morton on the line. He knew he wouldn't get General Gilson's top aide unless things were about to get worse.

Morton's voice was grim. "We had a cave in on the main access tunnel to the primary underground supply dump. Enemy nuke went off target, hit the mountain. Dumb luck for them." Morton exhaled hard. "We're working on it."

"Sir, if we don't get resupply now, the enemy's gonna rip through my lines like crap through a goose." He tried to suck the words back in, but it was too late. "Excuse me, sir. Sorry for the language." Morton was a superior officer, and Horace was a "by the book" kind of Marine…except when the world was falling apart around him. "It really is that desperate, sir."

"Don't worry about language, captain." Morton knew what the Marines and their allies were going through on the surface, and it was tearing at him. "John, if I had anything to give you right now except the rounds in my sidearm, I'd bring it to you myself." He wiped his face and stared at the pool of sweat in his palm. Disasters were coming in from every direction, and Gilson was still on the surface. He knew the troops needed her there, but that left him in charge of everything else. "You're just going to have to improvise, captain. I've got everybody who isn't on the surface fighting down in that tunnel digging out your supplies."

"I hope they dig fast, sir. I've got Marines out here with nothing but their blades." The molecular blades were a potent weapon, one that might even cut through a First Imperium battle bot…assuming anyone could get close enough to one and still be alive.

"You've got CAC heavies moving up to support you too, captain." That was an exaggeration. Morton still hadn't managed to get Colonel Lin moving. He hoped Lin picked things up before Gilson asked again, because otherwise there was going to be a shitstorm…and Lin would be buried under it. "So hang on there…however you do it. Redistribute some ammo…move some people around. Whatever."

"Yes, sir." Horace wasn't satisfied, but he knew there was nothing Morton could do. "Horace out." He turned and looked at his display. They were coming, and there were Reapers there too. He flipped on the unitwide com. "Alright boys and girls, here's how we're gonna do this…"

Gilson pulled herself slowly to her feet. That was close, she thought. Too close. Her AI reported her armor was fully operational, but she could tell by the pain in her arm she hadn't escaped unscathed. Those cluster bombs are a nasty fucking weapon, she thought angrily.

"General!"

She could see them running up the hillside, and the panicked shouts bombarded her com. "I'm alright," she snapped. "It's just a fucking scratch. Get back to work."

She straightened up, fighting the dizziness that almost took her. It was more than a scratch, and she knew it. Her arm hurt like hell, even with a heavy dose of painkillers injected by her suit. She glanced at the monitors. Fuck, she thought…the bone is shattered. She didn't relish the thought of regenerating that arm for the third time, but she put it out of her mind. It certainly wasn't going to keep her out of the fight.

She waved her other arm toward the cluster of officers hesitating on the hillside. "I said get back to work. I'm fine." She hated being doted on…and they all had better things to do than stand there and stare at her. The lines were caving in, and she couldn't even get ammo to her forces on the front lines. What the hell did she care about a shot up arm? Chance are they'd all be dead in another week anyway.

She stood still, looking out over the rugged terrain to the north. She couldn't see much of the front line from here, but she knew it was just over the line of hills in front of her. There was a lull right now, with both sides dug in facing each other, but she didn't expect it to last much longer. Her forces were close to breaking. They'd fought brilliantly, valiantly. But it just wasn't enough. If she had time to regroup, to resupply…then maybe. But the enemy didn't need that break. They fought without distraction, without fatigue. They didn't feel pain from their wounds. No fears crawled from the psyche and gripped their spines. They just kept coming. She couldn't imagine the current stalemate would last much longer. The enemy would not stay in their trenches much longer.

Time. If only she had more time. But the clock was ticking away the final minutes. This is it, she thought…35 years in the Corps. Three and a half decades since that first drop, a milk run with no casualties. She'd been in much worse places since then, and she'd risen to levels she couldn't have imagined. "So," she whispered softly, "this is how it ends. In defeat."

Her morale wavered, just for a second. Fuck this, she thought…if you're going to die, you're going to go down alongside what is left of your Marines. She pulled her rifle around, not an easy task with one arm. She heard the loud click as her suit slid a clip in place. "Alright, you fuckers, let's do this." She started down the hillside, heading toward the front lines.

"General Gilson!" It was Morton, and the usually unflappable officer was clearly excited. "We have dropships inbound, general."

Gilson stopped where she was and sighed. Things were bad enough already; the lines were on the verge of caving all across the front…and now the enemy is bringing down even more forces? Maybe that's why they've paused – they're waiting for reinforcements. Didn't these shitheads ever run out of these godforsaken robots? She was so lost in gloom she almost missed the next thing out of Morton's mouth.

"They're not First Imperium craft." His voice was excited, giddy. "They're ours, general. They're ours!"

Chapter 26

Bridge – AS Hornet
Beta 93A System
Warp Gate to Delta Leonis System

"Warp gate insertion calculations complete, sir." Ensign Carp's voice was raw, hoarse. He'd been a brick, rock solid through Hornet's unprecedented run. Jacobs was going to get him his lieutenancy at the very least, but he really wanted to jump the gifted officer right to lieutenant commander if he could convince Garret to approve it. The young ensign had earned it, every bit of it. But even the seemingly tireless Carp was starting to wear down.

Jacobs had stopped trying to calculate the odds at least five systems back. They'd hidden on half a dozen occasions, waiting for First Imperium forces to pass by, but they'd remained undiscovered every time. Hornet had travelled all the way to a First Imperium world and made it back. Or almost back...all the Alliance worlds they'd passed so far had been lifeless ruins, a grim trail of destruction left by the invading enemy. For all they knew the First Imperium had ravaged human-occupied space, leaving nothing to come back to except desolate, depopulated worlds.

Jacobs wondered about Adelaide, about Cooper Brown. Hornet had come back through Adelaide's system, but Jacobs hadn't dared to stop at the planet. Hornet had been a forlorn hope when it left that world, a tiny ship caught behind the lines with little to lose by its daring. But now she and her crew were vitally important, their intel precious. As far as Jacobs knew, they were the only humans in the universe who had the location of a First Imperium base. His duty had become clear. If he could get that information back to Admiral Garret, that was the priority. More important than survivors on a distant colony. More important than anything else. But he felt bad not even stopping to see if Cooper Brown and his people were still alive. It's not like there was anything we could do to help them, he told himself. Still, it nagged at him.

"OK, ensign. Let's start the sequence." They had to execute another burn…another risk of being detected. How many times can we push our luck, he thought, before we get burned? As far as their scanners could tell, the system was empty; they hadn't picked up a single signal. Jacobs knew that meant almost nothing. There were a myriad of ways the enemy could hide, just as Hornet had. But there was no choice…this was the only way back home.

Jacobs was proud of his ship…and his crew. Hornet had been through hell and back, but the old girl was holding together like a champ. They'd had a few malfunctions along the way but, miraculously, no serious breakdowns. In Jacob's estimation, it was nothing short of a miracle.

"Sequence underway, captain. Engine burn in 15 seconds."

Carp sounds tired, Jacobs thought…but how could he not be? Everyone on Hornet was exhausted, their nerves stretched to the breaking point. "Very well, ensign." The burn was a small one, the minimum required to change Hornet's vector to a course that would lead through the gate. Just four minutes, at less than 3g.

Jacobs felt the vibrations of the engines as they fired. The pressure from the acceleration pushed against him. He forced a deep breath – 3g wasn't a lot for veteran spacers, but they'd spent a lot of time at zero gee, and the difference was stark.

Jacobs wondered what they would find on the other side of the warp gate. They'd passed nothing but lifeless, devastated worlds so far, but now they were transiting into Sandoval's system. The planet was a large and successful colony, the gateway to the worlds on the Rim. Jacobs wasn't sure of the population, but his AI helpfully provided the figure. What are we going to find there, he thought…will we finally be home, or will Sandoval be a graveyard too, one with a million and a half headstones?

"Disengaging engines now, sir."

Jacobs shook out of his daydreaming. The four minutes had passed in an instant. He was relieved to feel the pressure vanish and weightlessness return. "Very well, Ensign Carp. Time to transit?"

"We will enter the warp gate in one minute, forty five seconds, sir."

"Very well." Jacobs leaned back in his chair. He was one of those who felt little or no effect when passing through a warp gate, but he knew most of his crew would feel something. Most would be only moderately affected, but for some the transit would be unpleasant. No one had been able to determine why there was such a disparity in descriptions of the warp gate experience. Most research was currently focused on studying differing genetic patterns but, the truth was, no one had any real idea.

Hornet passed slowly into the blackness of the warp gate. Slow was a relative term, of course. By most conventional reckoning, an object moving at 1,800 kilometers per second was not slow. But for a spaceship it was a crawl. Jacobs didn't want to zip too deeply into Sandoval's system until he had an idea what was waiting. If the colony was still there, they'd pick up heavy civilian chatter almost immediately. Then they could all relax, at least a little. He wasn't sure he remembered what that felt like.

The trip through the warp gate was short, some still-uncalculated fraction of a second, but to the Hornet's crew it was instantaneous. The gate was deep, inky black on the entry side, a rotating disk in space that lacked detectable substance but blocked light nevertheless. It would begin to dimly glow around the edges, Jacobs knew, from the energy generated by Hornet's passage. But no one on the ship would see that…they would be 13 lightyears away by then.

"Entering Delta Leonis system, captain. Engaging long range scan…" Carp stopped abruptly. He sat at his station frozen, his eyes glued to his screen, hands frantically working the controls.

"What is it?" Jacobs' head snapped around. He could feel

the tightness in his stomach. Anything that unnerved Carp required his immediate attention. "Report, ensign."

"Sir…" Carp's response was slow at first, but he recovered his focus quickly. "We are receiving multiple signals. But it doesn't appear to be commercial." He looked over at Jacobs. "Captain, it's definitely military traffic. I'm picking up First Imperium signals *and* Alliance protocols." He looked back at the screen. "I'm getting massive energy readings too, sir. Nuclear explosions, engine outputs…almost more than we can track." He paused, but only for an instant. "Captain, it looks like we've transited into the middle of a battle." Another brief hesitation. "A big one, sir."

Jacobs blinked his eyes, trying to absorb what he was being told. He sat rigidly upright, almost like a statue. For an instant he was silent, and when he spoke, he uttered just one word. "Battlestations."

Chapter 27

AS Lexington, Flag Bridge
Approaching Planet Sandoval
Delta Leonis System
"The Line"

Garret's eyes burned. The smoke on Lexington's bridge was acrid. He wasn't sure what it was from, but it was hanging thick in the air. There was light debris scattered around, but the flag bridge was well-protected, and everything was still functioning. Other areas of the ship were definitely harder hit. Combined Fleet's flagship had taken a pounding, but she was still in the fight.

Most of the fleet was battered, but the First Imperium forces had taken it hard too. Hurley's wings had savaged their targets. Four of the Leviathans had been destroyed outright, reduced to plasmas and scattered fields of debris. The other two she'd targeted were gutted...one was still firing a few light particle accelerators; the other seemed completely dead. But there were four more in action, and the Combined Fleet finally got to see what a First Imperium Leviathan could do. It wasn't pretty.

Garret sent his missiles in on the heels of the bombers. The enemy fleet had taken three successive blows – attack ships, bombers, missiles – and ship after ship went down. First a group of Gargoyles...then another Leviathan. But now the enemy was shooting back, and Combined Fleet's own losses mounted.

The PRC's Shogun was the first capital ship to go, closely followed by Blenheim...both victims of the enemy missile barrage. Then the particle accelerators opened up, long before Garret's own lasers were in range. Sword of Mars, the largest ship built by man, was next. She wasn't destroyed, but her reactors were down and 90% of her crew was dead. The last Garret heard before her com went out, a lieutenant was in command, and he was trying to get her pulled out of range on emergency power.

Garret knew the range and effectiveness of the enemy's energy weapons, and he'd prepared his own response. Every remaining fast attack ship in the fleet had been loaded up with x-ray laser buoys, and the suicide boats zipped forward as the enemy savaged the fleet's battle line. They dropped their deadly cargoes along both sides of the occupied enemy fleet and bugged out, losing only two ships in the process.

Now Augustus Garret sat in his command chair, a feral expression on his face. His fingers played over a large red button, one recently installed on his workstation. There was a clear plastic lid covering the button, but Garret had already pried it open. His staff was busy, chattering loudly with the various task forces of the fleet, directing over 70,000 naval personnel in the biggest space battle in human history. But the commander-in-chief − fleet admiral and supreme military leader of the Grand Pact - sat quietly. He glanced down at the glowing red control under his finger. This was something he was going to do himself.

He didn't say anything, didn't check his displays, didn't even take a breath. He just calmly pressed his finger down. The signal would take 20 seconds to reach its destination, and another 20 would pass before the scanner confirmed the results. Five million kilometers from Lexington's flag bridge, 600 atomic bombs detonated. They weren't missiles or mines, but they were deadly nevertheless. Each one was a power source, pouring its energy into one fleeting x-ray laser blast.

The signal reached each buoy at a slightly different time, but in less than 3/1000ths of a second, 600 deadly lances of x-ray energy shot toward the First Imperium fleet. The blasts were invisible to the eye, and each one lasted a small fraction of a second. But when they struck the enemy vessels, they tore through their dark matter infused hulls and inflicted enormous damage. The buoys were positioned on both sides of the enemy fleet, and the First Imperium ships were caught in a deadly crossfire.

The chatter on Lexington's flag bridge rose in pitch. The enemy fire was suddenly disrupted, its intensity significantly lessened. Then the damage assessments started coming in, ship after ship torn apart by the focused nuclear energy. Another few minutes and the ships of Combined Fleet would open up with their own lasers. The human vessels were moving in slowly, and the First Imperium ships were almost stationary. This was the final stage of the battle, a close in knife fight, both sides standing toe to toe. A fight to the death.

Garret was ready. "Commodore Harmon…now, if you please."

Harmon flipped a few switches and looked back at Garret. "You are on fleetwide com, sir."

"Attention Combined Fleet." Garret's voice was strong, soaring. He was by no means certain his people would win this fight, but he was relieved to finally stand and have it out with the invaders. No more fencing with the enemy, no more hit and run. Victory or death. And that's how he wanted it. "We have waited for this moment for a long time. Our worlds, our comrades, have been attacked without provocation. The blood of uncounted thousands is on the hands of the enemy. Now it is time to pay them back measure for measure."

He paused, taking a deep breath. Every eye on Lexington's flag bridge was on him, just as every ear in the fleet listened for his words. "You have fought brilliantly, valiantly. You have made me proud. All of you…my Alliance brethren and valued allies, new and old. You have stood up to the enemy, matched their technology with your courage and steadfastness. Now we stand, for the first time on the verge of defeating a major First Imperium fleet. You have given much, but now I must ask more of you. Stand with me now. We will not stop while any enemy vessel remains in this system. Now, my friends, my allies, my comrades…fight with me now!"

On every ship of the fleet, in damaged hanger bays and smoke-filled bridges, in cramped maintenance tubes and frantically-manned weapons stations, a great cheer rose. Garret's people were ready to finish the job.

"C'mon, crew chief. I need these reloads finished now." Greta Hurley was standing next to her bomber, looking down at the bald, sweating head of her maintenance team. "We need to launch again ASAP."

"Cap…Commodore, we're moving as quickly as we can. The birds are refueled, but there's no way we're getting another load of torpedoes in place in less than an hour."

Hurley opened her mouth to argue, but she closed it again. Flight Sergeant Jones was the best. He'd been keeping her craft flying since before the war, and she knew he always gave his best. "How about rocket packs?"

Jones looked up at her, thinking for an instant. "They're quicker, no question. But will they hurt those things?" He motioned to the right with his thumb, a pointless gesture…and in nearly the opposite direction of the enemy fleet, but she knew what he meant.

"I don't know, flight sergeant." She sighed, wondering herself. The rocket packs were outdated…the weapons of choice for bombers before the development of the miniaturized plasma torpedo. They weren't as strong as the torpedoes, that much was certain. But with the right targeting, she thought, who knows? "They're what we can get loaded in time. Do it."

"Yes, commodore." He pulled himself to his feet and walked behind the bomber, shouting instructions to a cluster of technicians standing there.

Hurley didn't know how effective this strike would be, but she was determined to do it. Garret had been skeptical, telling her that her people had done their part. But Hurley knew this battle was going to be close…and the fleet needed every edge. Besides, Garret, of all people, should know a mission like this could work. She'd been a junior officer flying one of the birds when the fleet admiral used his fighter-bombers for a close-in attack at the Battle of Gliese 250. It was an unorthodox and risky strategy…and a huge success. Granted, she thought, those ships were fresh, not the shot up remnants of a just-completed attack. Her crews were exhausted, and they'd just lost over 30%

of their number. But Hurley didn't care. She was determined.

She pulled out her remote com, her connection to Scarlett. The AI was monitoring preparations on the other capital ships. Her strikeforce was a large multinational conglomeration, based on sixteen different vessels. There had been 21 capital ships, but three had been blown to bits and the other two were gutted, landing bays destroyed and damage control crews desperately trying to save them.

"Scarlett, advise all wings we will be launching in fifteen minutes." She turned and shouted back over her shoulder. "Ten minutes, crew chief. That's all you've got."

"Many of the motherships are running behind in rearming the bombers." Scarlett's information would be accurate, Hurley knew that much. "I currently project you will have approximately 40% of squadrons available in your designated time frame. It is likely that a second wave can launch approximately 20 minutes after the first."

"Damn," Hurley huffed under her breath. She commanded a huge force with four different nationalities. There was just no way to run it as tightly as she wanted. Well, she thought, 40% will have to do. It was still over 150 bombers, and she knew she could do a lot of damage with that.

"Fifteen minutes, Scarlett." She started walking toward her ship. She was going to preflight it herself. "I want all available squadrons launched in fifteen minutes."

Gwen Beacham was strapped firmly into her command chair. The ship was at zero gravity and running on batteries. She still wasn't used to the idea of commanding 18 cruisers... though only 12 of them were still in action. Eleven if you didn't count Marlborough, though Beacham expected the reactor to be back online any minute. She missed John Paul Jones, but her old command was still at Wolf 359, waiting its turn for repairs at the massive orbital shipyards. Her new flagship was a more appropriate place to fly an admiral's flag anyway. The third ship of the King George class, she was the state of the art in Alliance heavy cruiser design.

Garret had bumped Beacham to admiral right after the battle at Point Epsilon, and he transferred her to First Fleet to run one of his cruiser squadrons. It was an abrupt change – Beacham had expected years of service as a captain before getting a shot at her star. But Combined Fleet was low on senior officers, so she ended up wearing two hats…commanding the fleet and skippering Marlborough. She was grateful for the extra job. Running the ship was more familiar. It made the transition easier for her.

The battlelines had been pounding each other, sitting at a dead stop and blasting away. At close range, the advantage of the enemy particle accelerators was less severe, and the laser cannons of the battlewagons were at least reasonably effective against the enemy armor. The fight was a close run thing, and she knew either side could still prevail.

Beacham's cruisers had driven through the enemy line, going after ships with major breaches and finishing them off with targeted fire. Many of the First Imperium vessels had been badly damaged by the x-ray lasers, and the cruisers closed to point blank range and completed the work begun by the buoys. First Imperium ships were dangerous until they were completely dead, and Beacham knew her targets would fight back ferociously.

"Captain, we've got a Gargoyle closing on us." Lieutenant Commander Furth snapped out the warning. "It's targeting us."

Beacham felt her insides clench. She needed the reactor back online immediately. They were sitting ducks like this. She flipped the com. "Engineering, I need the reactor. Now."

"Negative, admiral." It was Commander Powell, the chief engineer. "If I restart now it'll just scrag immediately. Or it will blow." He took a quick breath. "I need eight minutes, admiral. Maybe ten."

"I don't think we've got it, commander." Powell was one of the best. There was no reason to argue. He'd get the reactor started as soon as possible without her riding him. "It's urgent. Begin the startup the second you can. Even if it's risky. Understood, commander?"

"Yes, admiral." His voice was distracted; he was working as he spoke. "Understood."

"Commander Furth, I want life support and maintenance systems on minimal. Divert all available power to damage control systems." It was all she could do. She didn't have weapons or maneuver capability right now.

"Yes, admiral." Furth turned toward his workstation and paused. "Admiral Beacham, we're getting massive energy readings from the enemy vessel." A brief silence while he continued scanning the incoming data. "It just lost thrust...another energy spike, internal explosions." Furth's head snapped around. "Admiral Beacham! Someone just planted two plasma torpedoes in the guts of that thing."

Beacham stared back wordlessly. None of her cruisers were in position to fire...and they weren't armed with plasma torpedoes anyway. Who was firing on that Gargoyle?

"Admiral, it looks like the Gargoyle's dead. I'm not getting any readings of energy generation."

"Scan the area. Are you picking up any friendlies?" Beacham didn't have a clue. She *knew for a fact* there were no Combined Fleet ships over there!

Furth started to reply, but the main com crackled to life before he got any words out. "Alliance cruiser Marlborough... this is AS Hornet. Are we glad to see you!"

Hurley's bombers zipped around the wounded behemoth, stinging it with short-ranged high velocity rockets. The tiny sprint missiles didn't have much penetrating power, but they packed a nice punch with 3-kiloton nuclear warheads. They had a hard time getting through the First Imperium armor, but the Leviathan they were attacking had already been hit hard. There were three large gashes in its hull, including one almost half a kilometer in length. Despite the heavy damage, the thing was still firing, ripping into Garret's flagship with heavy particle accelerators.

Her squadrons didn't have much velocity, and they were able to maneuver with precision, changing vectors abruptly and operating much closer than normal to the wounded enemy vessel. The Leviathan's point defense was badly damaged, and

Hurley's people flew almost with impunity.

"OK, lieutenant, here we go again." Hurley turned the flying over to Potter. She was focused on the targeting scope. "We've got one last shot."

The bombers had been blasting the hull of the enemy battleship, picking away at it bit by bit. But Hurley intended to fire a rocket through one of the breaches to detonate inside the vessel. It was a hard shot, but she was determined to make it. The gashes were long, but the largest was only about three meters wide…barely twice the size of the rockets. She'd missed three times, and the bombers carried four rounds. This was it.

"Get me close, lieutenant." Potter was a strong pilot, but getting in too tight was dangerous. A hit, or a minor malfunction, could cause the bomber to career into the target vessel. But Greta Hurley was determined, and now she had Potter's blood up too.

"Yes, captain." Her voice was distracted, distant. There was nothing on Emma Potter's mind but the bomber she was flying. She angled the sleek little craft and tapped on the throttle. She was burning the engines hard, but just for a second or two each time. It was an uncomfortable ride. The 6g pulses of thrust felt like getting hit in the chest with a bat. But she was swinging around, bringing the bomber directly at the ragged gash in the Leviathan's side. "You'll only have a second, admiral." Her voice was hoarse, strained with tension. "Then I'll have to spin around and execute a burn. Otherwise we'll crash into the hull."

Hurley didn't answer. Her face was pressed against the scope. The targeting computer was feeding her data through her earpiece, but she was doing this with her gut.

"Now, admiral. You've got three seconds."

Hurley nudged the stick, massaging the targeting angle. Three seconds, she thought, three seconds. She could feel the sweat beading on her forehead, droplets sliding down the side of her neck. She knew she was running out of time. Take the shot, she thought….take the bloody shot.

Her fingers tightened, pulling the trigger than launched the tiny sprint missile. She felt a giant fist slam into her as Potter spun the bomber and blasted away at 10g. She was pushed back into her chair, gasping for breath. It wasn't just the pressure... there was another pain there as well, something new. She'd cracked a rib...at least that's what it felt like. It wasn't important now, so she gritted her teeth and ignored the pain. A few seconds later, Potter killed the thrust and she could breathe again.

"Scarlett...damage assessment." Every word hurt, like a burning knife slicing through her chest.

"Direct hit, admiral. Your rocket detonated inside the enemy vessel. Still scanning for specific effects, but the damage appears to be catastrophic. Remaining craft in the squadron are launching at the now-expanded breach. Projecting multiple additional hits."

Hurley leaned back, eyes tearing from the pain as she tried to catch her breath. She was dirty, hurt, and sore, but she'd never felt better in her life.

"Lieutenant, take us home."

Augustus Garret stood on Lexington's battered flag bridge. He had no idea how many hits the ship had taken, but there was damage everywhere. The air was thick with smoke, though it was less caustic than before, and the smell was one of burnt circuitry instead of chemicals. There was a collapsed girder lying on the deck, and a dusty layer of grit covered the workstations and survival suits of his staff.

There had been casualties on Lexington, he was sure of that, but his staff had escaped all but minor injuries. He knew the flagship was in rough shape, but all its systems seemed to be functioning. Both reactors were operating, one at full, the other at half power. There was a lot of damage in the landing bays, but Captain Stone and his people had managed to get Hurley and all of her survivors landed.

There were vessels of the Pact everywhere in the system. Some were lightly hit, but most had taken considerable damage. A number were drifting, waiting for propulsion systems to come back online. More than a few were fighting to get internal fires under control and restart vital systems. The already lengthy list of destroyed vessels was likely to grow, and Garret had given strict orders to abandon any ship that was beyond saving. He didn't like the thought of losing more ships, but he was adamant that no more of his people be needlessly added to the roster of those killed in action.

In all of the vast, mostly empty space that made up the Delta Leonis system, there was not a live First Alliance vessel remaining. There were dead hulks and massive fields of floating debris…enough to keep Hofstader and Sparks and the rest of their whitecoats busy for years. But there wasn't a functioning enemy ship anywhere.

Augustus Garret and the Combined Fleet of the Grand Pact had swept the system clean, and the last forty or so enemy vessels had retreated through the warp gate. It was the first time a First Imperium force of that size had run, and Garret figured it was a turning point of some kind. He wasn't sure what it meant long term, and he certainly didn't fool himself into thinking the war was over. But it had been a good few days for the cause. The cost had been high, as it usually was, but at least those who died gave their lives for a victory, one that saved countless human lives on the planets beyond Sandoval. Garret's people weren't running, they weren't pulling back. Here they stood in possession of the battleground, and their pride swelled, momentarily overcoming the crushing exhaustion.

Garret's own elation was on hold, however. He stood behind Max Harmon, staring down as his chief of staff worked the com circuits. Lexington's communications were functional, but they were far from 100%. "It's ready, sir. We're transmitting to the surface."

"Garret to 1st Army HQ." He nodded his thanks for Harmon. His legs were a little weak, and there was a tightness in his gut. "This is Combined Fleet Command to General Cain. Please respond." Where they in time to save Cain and his people? How bad would things be down there? Combined Fleet didn't have much in the way of land forces, and Garret wasn't sure how much he could do if the First Imperium forces had Cain's army on the run. Or worse.

The flag bridge was silent, everyone waiting, wondering... praying that 1ˢᵗ Army was still holding out. All through the vicious battle in space the worry had been there. Had the enemy wiped out Cain and his forces?

Garret knew the delay in orbital communications was short, less than a third of a second. But he could have sworn he'd been waiting for hours, listening to nothing but staticky silence. His stomach was churning, and he could feel the tightness in his chest.

"Combined Fleet, 1ˢᵗ Army HQ here." The voice was immediately familiar. Lexington's flag bridge erupted into wild cheers. "Cain here, admiral." A short pause, then: "What took you so long, sir? We could use a ride. It's getting pretty boring down here."

Chapter 28

Upper Atmosphere
Planet Garrison
Alpha Corvi III
"The Line"

"Attack force Alpha, three minutes to landing." John Marek's voice was like a knife slicing through the clouds. His force was small, but it was fresh and well-equipped. And Marek figured General Gilson needed everything she could get right about now.

Marek had disobeyed orders by coming to Garrison... sort of. His plan bordered on insane, and Admiral Garret had rejected it. But Marek's troops were from Columbia, veterans of the bloody rebellion there. And John Marek was the president of that world and the commander of its small army. He was a Marine too, as he would be until he died, but he was inactive and therefore not subject to the chain of command. At least that was his interpretation. With Garrison only two transits from Columbia, he was also doing his duty to defend his adopted homeworld. If Garrison fell and 2nd Army was destroyed, he'd have very little chance of holding Columbia alone.

The Alpha Corvi system was occupied by a First Imperium fleet, and the defenders on Garrison were completely cut off. The Grand Pact fleet assigned to defend the system had been badly defeated in the initial battle, and there wasn't enough strength to even consider a return engagement...especially not with the resources diverted for the relief of Sandoval. But Marek's plan didn't require a fleet. The layout of the Alpha Corvi system allowed a ship to trace a straight course from the warp gate to the planet Garrison.

Marek's ships had come in silent, engines shut down, energy emissions at a minimum. It was a gamble...a big one. If the unarmed transports had been detected they'd have been destroyed in an instant. They had no escort – no force of warships Marek could have mustered would have meant anything in a fight against the First Imperium fleet. He was counting on stealth, and a careful use of the gravity of Garrison's two large moons to position his fleet into planetary orbit with a minimum of energy output.

He'd intended to use whatever ships he could scrape up, but Roderick Vance had intervened and provided six modern troop transports, packed with the newest ECM and stealth equipment. Marek had no idea how Vance found out about his plan, but he was grateful. The Martian equipment vastly increased his chances of getting through.

The launch had gone off perfectly, the sleek 10-man Confederation landers gliding down to the surface carrying his 2,800 troops...and the skeleton crews of the transports. For the ships themselves, it was a suicide mission. Detected as they braked to enter orbit, they had barely enough time to launch the landers before they were blown to plasma. But they'd gotten everyone off, and the expedition didn't suffer a casualty until the first of the landers was shot down.

The enemy was taken entirely by surprise. The plan was beyond unorthodox...it was crazy. The intelligences directing the First Imperium expeditionary force were bewildered, and they hesitated...just as Marek had hoped. Only three landers were intercepted. The rest of the force made it safely to the ground.

The choice of landing zone was a surprise as well. The new arrivals didn't land in an area already controlled by their forces. Marek set down 40 kilometers behind the enemy position and over 80 klicks from Gilson's front line. He wasn't there to feed a small reserve into the existing army – he was there to attack the First Imperium from behind. To relieve the pressure on Gilson and hopefully allow her to go on the offensive. It was risky to open a second line with less than 3,000 troops, but Marek was willing to gamble. He knew victory against this enemy required taking chances. They'd already defied the odds just reaching the planet. Now they were going to show these robots how to wage war.

"Who the hell are they?" Gilson stared at the monitor, a confused scowl on her face, trying to understand what was happening. She'd been surprised when her scanners detected the incoming landings…and stunned when the craft were ID'd as Martian Ares II landers. There hadn't been a signal from the fleet, not the slightest indication that they'd returned to the system. Yet friendly troops had apparently landed. At least she presumed they were friendly – they were definitely launching attacks against the enemy. Even more inexplicable, they'd come down on the opposite side of the First Imperium army, almost 100 klicks from her positions. Their attacks were falling on the lightly defended enemy rear areas.

"Impossible to tell, general." Kevin Morton was as mystified as his boss. He stared down at his workstation, feeling he must have missed something. But there was nothing…nothing but what they already knew. The landing craft were definitely Martian Confederation design, but there were no identification beacons at all. And definitely no indication of any kind of battle going on in space. "I have no idea who they are or how they got here. We can't reach them on the com…the jamming's too heavy and we don't have a satellite to bounce off."

Gilson stared at her own screen for a minute, though her eyes weren't seeing anything. She wondered, could this force have run the enemy blockade? Was that even possible? If they had, who were they? Any force sent by Garret or Holm would have normal identification transponders. She paused a moment longer, than scowled and looked up, a determined expression on her face. "It doesn't matter who they are. The enemy of my enemy is my friend. And this friend is wreaking havoc in the enemy rear areas."

"Yes, general, but…"

"No buts, Kevin. That force is too small to hold out for

long. They're benefiting from surprise right now, but that won't last. The enemy will eventually redeploy enough strength to crush them." She paused again, but only for a few seconds. "Unless they've got something else to worry about."

Morton stared back quietly, a concerned expression on his face. The battle had been raging for weeks, but things had slowed the last few days, the two sides settling into fortified lines. To Morton's thinking, that was a good thing. The army had put up a great fight, but he and Gilson both knew they'd eventually lose the war of attrition. He figured anything that slowed the pace of events was in their favor. If they could hold out longer, maybe the fleet would return. Maybe they'd be reinforced.

Gilson's mind worked differently. She wasn't interested in buying useless time – she was looking for a way to win, even a longshot. She wanted victory, and if she couldn't have it then death was the alternative...and if they were all to die choking on the bitter taste of defeat, what did it matter when?

Morton knew what Gilson was going to say, and he dreaded it. The battle on Garrison had been brutally waged, and the exhausted human forces needed time to rest and recover. Now he knew that lull was over...he could hear the words in his head before Gilson spoke them, and his shoulders slumped forward in resignation.

"Major Morton..." Her voice was strong, determined, defiant. "...it is time to end this. My orders to all units...attack!"

The intelligences directing the First Imperium army were stunned by Marek's attack, and they reacted sluggishly to the new threat. The enemy actions were unorthodox, inexplicable. The new force was small, grossly inadequate to launch a major offensive...yet that is precisely what they had done.

The new attackers had used their surprise to great effect, slicing deep into the support areas, isolating and annihilating the token forces left to garrison the First Imperium rear. Now the new forces were threatening the primary supply areas. They had become more than an annoyance...the menace to the supply depots threatened the entire army. The commanding intelligences finally responded, recognizing the grave threat to their logistics.

Units were directed north, sent against the new attackers. Reaper squadrons were repositioned, pulled out of the stationary lines to the south and sent north. All along the First Imperium line, combat units were withdrawn from the existing but static battle line and sent to defend the support areas.

Then it happened. Suddenly, unexpectedly, the forces in the south launched their own attack, cutting through the weakened and disrupted First Imperium lines. The intelligences hesitated again. This enemy defied all attempts at understanding; their actions were unpredictable, illogical. Some units were ordered to return to the old line, to face the enemy in the south. Others were sent northward.

These actions were too late. In the north, the enemy was overrunning the supply areas, destroying the army's stockpiled ordnance. In the south the formerly beaten enemy units had abandoned their entrenchments, and they were slicing through the disordered First Imperium lines. Chaos spread throughout the battlefield. The intelligences studied the map, trying to develop a new strategy, but the situation was fluid, and their orders were too late. Their forces fought without fear, of course, but they failed to stop the enemy assaults.

None of this made sense. The battle had been won. The intelligences had analyzed everything, and they had determined that victory was assured. Now their plans were unraveling. They reviewed the incoming data and considered every option. They sent out orders, moving units from location to location, plugging breaches in the line. But none of it seemed to work. Slowly, reluctantly, they began to reach a stunning conclusion. They were losing the battle.

"I want that supply dump blown." Marek could tell he was almost screaming, but he didn't care. His forces had sliced deep into the First Imperium positions, and now they had reached the main supply areas. "Now, captain!"

"Yes, sir." Josh Davies stood on the edge of the depot, his

right foot perched on the twisted remains of an enemy battle robot. "We'll have the charges in place in two minutes, general."

"Make it 90 seconds, Captain Davies. We've got Reapers inbound."

"Yes, sir. We'll try." Davies tension level rose. He hadn't padded that 2 minute estimate, and he didn't think they could make 90 seconds. He wasn't even sure about the two minutes.

"Don't try. Do." Marek flipped the com to another line, cutting Davies off before he could respond. "Colonel Powell, how is your line holding?" The enemy counterattacks had intensified. Marek's people had gotten lucky at first, and they'd sliced through the weak security units posted in the enemy's rear. But now they were under increasingly heavy pressure, from Reapers as well as standard bots.

"We're hanging on, sir." Powell's voice was labored, strained. "We beat back the normal robots, but they started hitting us with the big ones, the Reapers. We managed to push them back again, but if they throw many more at us I doubt we can hold."

"Are you injured, colonel?" He could hear it in Powell's voice.

Powell took a deep, difficult breath. "I got clipped, sir, but I'm OK. It's nothing." The sound of his breathing suggested it was considerably more than nothing.

Marek's face twisted into a frown. In his Marine armor he'd have gotten an alert immediately if one of his senior officers was hit. He'd have medical data in real time fed directly into his own information system. But his troops wore outdated Mark V armor, surplus material from before the Third Frontier War. Few colonies fielded any powered infantry in their militias and defense forces, and none – not even one as prosperous as Columbia – could afford state of the art Marine gear.

"Don't bullshit me, colonel." The Mark V armor didn't have anything nearly as effective as the newest trauma control systems. "You sound like crap. Put Major Jindal in command and get back to the aid station. I want you at least partially patched up before you come back up."

"But sir, I'm reall…"

"No arguments, colonel. That's an order." He snapped off the com. He knew Bill Powell, and the big ox would argue all day if he allowed it. He worked his way through his key commands, reviewing status reports and issuing orders. The enemy pressure was ramping up everywhere. His surprise advantage was gone. Whatever else he was going to accomplish, it had to be now.

"Captain Davies, what's the status over there?" Marek wasn't sure if he'd given the beleaguered engineer the full 90 seconds or not, and he didn't care.

"We just finished, sir." Davies coughed loudly, clearing his throat. "The unit's pulling back now. We can detonate in about a minute, sir."

"Do it." Marek's response was immediate. "As soon as you have everyone out of the blast radius, blow the damned thing." His forces were still too far from Gilson's to communicate through the heavy enemy jamming, but he couldn't think of anything more useful to her than blowing the supplies.

"Yes, sir."

Marek glanced down at his display. It was a lot harder to read than the visor projection systems the Marines had, but it still gave him a decent plot of the overall battlefield. His section, at least. His impromptu invasion force wasn't plugged into the Marine network, so his system couldn't draw on any of their surveillance. Normally, a Marine general's tracking system could pull data from any assets on the field – satellites, drones, visors of any of the troops in the line. Anything that wasn't being actively jammed fed data to the commanding officers. But Marek had to make do with what he had.

He was focused on his plotting screen when he heard the blast. It was nearly deafening, even with his armor sealed. He turned and looked at the hillside, watching a huge plume of smoke and fire rising high into the atmosphere, expanding, taking on the familiar mushroom shape. His first thought was for his troopers...that Davies had gotten his people far enough back. That concern was quickly resolved when the engineer captain checked in a few seconds later.

His second thought was more satisfying, and he felt his face twist into a bloodthirsty scowl. "Let's see how you fight without ammunition, you bastards."

The intelligences directing the fleet in the Alpha Corvi system checked and rechecked their calculations. Their conclusions seemed illogical, but they were accurate nonetheless. The ground forces were in disarray, most of their supplies destroyed. The projections were clear. They were going to be defeated.

The fleet lacked adequate supplies and reinforcements to change that outcome. All excess units and supply had been diverted to the primary attack force in Delta Leonis. The conclusion was inescapable. The ground battle would soon be lost, and there was nothing that could be done to prevent that.

The intelligences considered the next action for the fleet. There was no enemy force in the system at present, no threat to the warships themselves. But this enemy was unpredictable… that had been demonstrated multiple times now. Perhaps there was a large battlefleet lurking just behind the warp gate. Perhaps there was some sort of trap in the works. There was no way to know.

The fleet was expendable, of course, but only if there was prospect of compensating gain. Here, there was none. The planet could not be occupied without more ground forces. A nuclear bombardment would be unlikely to eradicate the enemy presence…and the fleet was low on heavy nuclear warheads anyway. Risking the loss of so many fleet units for no apparent gain was illogical.

The intelligences conferred and considered, carefully reviewing all of the data. At last they issued orders to the ships of the fleet. For the first time in the war a First Imperium battlefleet fired its thrusters…and retreated.

Chapter 29

Theta 7 System
Orbiting Planet Samvar
"The Line"

The admiral's conference room on Bunker Hill was gleaming, every surface new. The crews at the Wolf 359 shipyards had worked around the clock for eight months, and Terrance Compton's flagship was as good as new. The admiral wasn't sure he'd characterize himself quite the same way, but the staff at Armstrong Medical had pronounced him fully healed several months before Bunker Hill returned to the line.

He'd missed out on the action at Sandoval and Garrison, but he was ready when the call came to drive the enemy from Samvar's system. It hadn't taken much of a fight – the First Imperium fleet withdrew after a perfunctory missile exchange. The Samvar force had been the smallest of the three invasion fleets, and with the defeats at Sandoval and Garrison, the enemy decided not to fight it out over Samvar.

Compton sighed softly, still not sure he truly believed it. The First Imperium forces had been turned back at all three Line worlds. The heart of human space was safe…for now. Compton knew that situation was profoundly temporary, as did Garret and Holm and Cain. None of them could imagine the enemy wouldn't be back, and they knew it would be worse the second time. The First Imperium had underestimated humanity, but no one could even guess at how massive an entity it was or what gargantuan forces it could muster given time. There was joy over the victories, but it was sharply tempered by the high cost and the realization that all victory had bought was a respite.

The hatch slid open, and Augustus Garret walked in. He

moved slowly, his shoulders hunched forward. "It's good to have you back, old friend." Garret's tone was casual, but there was real feeling behind it. He'd carried an enormous load as supreme commander, and Terrence Compton was like a brother, possibly the only person he could truly share his burden with.

"It's good to be back, Augustus." My God, Compton thought...he looks exhausted...he looks old. Garret's face was lined with deep crevices that hadn't been there a few years earlier, and his formerly salt and pepper hair had turned almost entirely gray. Augustus Garret had shouldered more responsibility than any man in human history. Nothing less than the fate of mankind had hinged on his military ability. "Or should I call you Supreme Commander?" Compton gave his friend a wry smile.

Garret frowned. "Don't you dare." He plopped down hard into one of the chairs. "I can't wait to give this godforsaken job back."

"We're lucky you had it, my friend. Can you imagine if we'd been under the orders of some CAC political lapdog?" Compton's face was sour, like he'd tasted something bad.

"Why Admiral Compton, you are speaking of our allies." Garret smiled. He didn't look like he had a full laugh in him, but he was definitely amused.

"I'm fine with the real soldiers." Compton grinned himself. "It's the political appointees I can't abide. Somehow we managed to escape that in the Alliance."

Garret grinned again, darkly this time. "I wouldn't say we've escaped it." Garret and the military had been through more than one run in with Alliance Intelligence and their political masters. He could see Compton about to respond, but he beat him to it. "I know. Whatever problems we've had, at least we can depend on each other."

They were interrupted by the door sliding open again. Six Marines walked in, clad in five neatly pressed and one slightly disheveled set of fatigues. Elias Holm led the group and he paused and looked toward Compton and Garret. "Augustus, Terrance...it's good to see you both again." Garret's companions nodded.

"And you, Elias. It's always a pleasure to have our Marine friends onboard." Garret paused, his eyes fixed on Cain. He spoke more slowly, and his voice became somber. "I'm sorry about Kyle Warren. I'm afraid I didn't know him very well, but he died a hero."

There was an uncomfortable pause. It was the right thing for Garret to say, but they'd all been through so much blood, so much death…the aura of heroism was getting thin with them all, and with Cain especially. Warren was a hero, Cain thought, but he was also just as dead as any of the cowards executed in the hanger. Did it matter? Was one better off than the other?

"Thank you, admiral." Cain broke the silence. "It means a lot for you to say that." Cain wasn't sure what he believed about heroes, but he knew Garret meant well.

"For the love of God, Erik…don't admiral me and I won't general you. Ok? We've all got more shiny junk on our uniforms than we can handle. No ship crew or fresh-faced corporals to impress here."

Cain smiled. "You've got a deal, adm…Augustus." He walked slowly toward the table, his arm bound tightly to his chest by an expertly wrapped sling. Sarah had worked on his arm herself. That is, after he told her he was wounded, which wasn't until well after the battle was over. She scolded him and threatened to amputate the thing and regenerate it if he didn't follow her instructions to the letter. The arm was a mess, but she managed to repair everything.

Compton noticed Isaac Merrick standing in the rear of the group, wearing a crisp new set of Marine fatigues, a single platinum star on each collar. "So they finally taught you the secret handshake, Isaac?"

Merrick tried to suppress a laugh. "Yes, it was General Holm's doing." He glanced over at Erik. "Though I think General Cain had something to do with it." Isaac Merrick was the first outsider admitted to the Marine Corps in over a century. A younger Cain would have thought the idea outrageous, but now that circumstance had forced thousands of half-trained, substandard recruits into the field units, he couldn't abide shutting out a true hero…and a faithful friend. Holm had agreed completely, signing the commission the day Cain brought it to him.

The shortest of the figures fidgeted uncomfortably. An old Marine, gone for a time but now back home again, John Marek remained silent. Unlike the others present, he hadn't met the Alliance's two top admirals before. He stood respectfully and listened to the exchanges.

Holm noticed Marek's discomfort. He turned to the new Marine general then back toward Garret and Compton. "I don't think you've ever met John Marek. He was one of ours back on Carson's World. As you know, he came to help out on Garrison. He resigned the presidency of Columbia to stay with us."

Garret nodded at Marek. "Welcome, John. Your compatriots have been telling me the same thing for years…once a Marine, always a Marine. I see they really meant it."

Marek nodded. "Yes, sir. I guess that's true. This is where I belong…and I can't leave now, not while this war is still going on." He panned his head around the room, an uncomfortable look on his face. "And none of us thinks it's over, right?" No one responded right away, but their expressions suggested that none of them disagreed either.

Catherine Gilson broke the silence, glancing over at Marek with a smile. Her arm was wrapped from wrist to shoulder in a light gray cast. "Well…I, for one, am glad the siren call of the Corps reached out to General Marek and brought him back. His destruction of the enemy supply depots won the battle for us. Not just on the planet, but also in space. I'm a ground pounder myself, but I'd speculate the fleet didn't need another major battle right now. Not when the enemy was willing to pick up and leave."

Garret laughed. "Your speculation is extraordinarily astute, Cate." He glanced at Marek. "So General Marek has my profound thanks as well. Columbia will just have to find another politician. Great generals are harder to find."

Marek look embarrassed, and he just nodded gratefully. "Thank you all. But I was just doing my duty…to Columbia as well as the Corps."

"Please, sit down. You all must be tired." Garret motioned to the chairs along one side of the table. His eyes focused on James Teller. "You seem to have made it through this fight in one piece, James."

Teller grinned. "Yes. I've always felt getting missed was a Marine's greatest skill. Not sure what I was thinking on Cornwall. But not a scratch this time." Teller had been grievously wounded while commanding the Alliance forces on Cornwall. He'd been in the hospital over a year, and missed the campaign on Farpoint entirely. He moved forward, pulling out a chair and sitting between Cain and Gilson.

The door slid open again. A naval officer walked in. Tall and thin, he was wearing a spotless new dress uniform with a single star on the collar. He stepped into the room and hesitated, looking over at Garret.

"Ah…Admiral Jacobs. Come in, please." Garret motioned to the chair next to him. "Have a seat." He looked out over the table. "I'd like you all to meet one of the true heroes of the war…Admiral William Jacobs."

Jacobs was immediately uncomfortable. Fleet Admiral Garret was the greatest naval officer in history as far as he was concerned, and it was very strange to sit quietly while the navy's commander-in-chief heaped praise on him. He was still getting over the shock of Garret promoting him to admiral on the spot. Hornet had done her part, there was no doubt there. But Jacobs tended to credit luck for that more than his own skill.

"Admiral Jacobs accomplished as much to defeat the enemy with only a fast attack ship as anyone else with a division of capital ships." Garret glanced around the room as he spoke. "He destroyed an enemy convoy of antimatter that was bound for the front…which is why we didn't face any in the final battles. He scouted deep into enemy-held space and located a major base, the probable starting point for the invasion. After all this, on the way back, Hornet transits into the middle of the battle… and destroys a Gargoyle, probably saving a heavy cruiser in the process." He turned back to Jacobs. "Well done, admiral."

"Thank you, sir." Jacob's throat had gone dry, and he barely managed to croak out the words. "You are far too kind."

"Nonsense, admiral." Garret leaned back in his chair. "It is hardly possible to overstate your achievements. I'm proud to have you as one of my command officers."

"Thank you again, sir." It was all Jacobs could manage. The whole thing was a bit too much for him.

The hatch slid open again, and a tall, distinguished looking man entered. His blue and gold silk uniform was far more colorful and exotic than those of the Alliance Marines and navy. Ali Khaled was the commander of the Caliphate's Janissary corps and, until recently, the hated enemy of the Marines.

"Lord Khaled, please have a seat." Garret stood, and the rest of those present followed his lead. "I am very pleased you could attend."

"Thank you, Supreme Commander." Khaled's voice was deep and commanding. He had no AI translating for him, and he spoke almost accentless English. He sounded like one born to high position, though everyone present knew he'd been the whelp of a New Cairo housekeeper. "It is my great pleasure." He turned and looked over at the Marines. "With your permission, I would like to speak with General Cain before we begin."

Garret motioned toward Cain. "Certainly, Lord Khaled."

"General Cain, I wish to extend my heartfelt thanks to you. It is my understanding that Commander Farooq received extraordinary care from your...consort, Colonel Linden." He'd struggled for the word. Male-female social dynamics were considerably different in the Caliphate, and translations were sometimes difficult. Janissaries didn't marry, though the officers were allowed to keep regular concubines. Khaled knew the comparable Alliance relationship was considerably different, but since Marines tended not to marry either before they retired, he knew wife wasn't the proper designation.

Cain had to suppress a laugh. He wondered how Sarah would react to being called his consort. But he managed to stifle the amusement. Khaled was making a serious effort to be gracious, and Cain wasn't going to quibble over cultural vagaries, no matter how humorous they might be. "Thank you, Lord Khaled. I will relay your kind words to Sarah." He paused, then added, "And your great concern for your officer is honorable indeed. Commander Farooq is a great warrior and a highly skilled leader. It was my honor to have him under my command."

Cain had to hold back another grin. It was widely believed in the Corps that he was incapable of diplomacy. But Cain knew when it was necessary, and he was perfectly capable of matching any Caliphate commanders' charm and grace. Besides, despite his deep-seeded prejudices, Cain had come to truly respect the Janissaries. They had served faithfully alongside his men and women, and they'd shown no friction or discontent. Whatever negative feelings they harbored, they buried them and focused on duty. Cain knew that couldn't have been any easier for them than it was for him. He and his Marines had killed thousands of their brethren, just as the Janissaries had done to them.

Khaled smiled. "Thank you, General Cain. You are most gracious." The Janissary commander sat slowly, skillfully arranging the billowing fabric of his dress uniform as he did.

Garret stood up slowly and looked out over those assembled. "Now that the immediate enemy threat has receded, I wanted to discuss with our next steps." He took a breath and scanned the faces at the table. "I don't think any of us believes we have seen the last of the First Imperium."

There was a combination of grunting and headshaking in response. They all knew the war was far from over. The battles on the Line had been so savage, no one had really had the time or focus to look ahead. Until now.

Cain stood up slowly, nodded as Garret motioned for him to speak. He knew everyone expected him to be the first to say it, and he didn't want to disappoint. "It is my opinion, sir, that we should attack…and that we should do so as soon as reasonably possible. We now have a roadmap back to a major enemy base. We must try to bring the war to the enemy, to visit destruction on their worlds. To bring them the pain they have brought to our people. We must pursue them, to hell's heart if need be, and end this war on our terms." He looked around the table. Most of those present were aggressive commanders, not terribly different from himself. He knew he wouldn't be the only one who felt the way he did. But from the expressions he could read, it looked like they were all of one mind.

Garret nodded. "I agree, Erik." He took another breath, deeper this time. "I see no gain in waiting for a new invasion, one which will undoubtedly be vastly more powerful than the last. The enemy failed to break us, and I suspect they are surprised by that result. They underestimated us. They will not do it again."

Khaled stood next. "I am in complete agreement." He spoke slowly, deliberately. "The blood of our dead must be avenged. Honor demands it. We must attack."

Garret could feel the spirit in the room. They all wanted to take the war to the enemy, and despite the losses, the suffering, the crushing fatigue, not one of them wanted to hold back. It was a grim determination; no one thought such an attack would be easy. Indeed, the odds were still sharply against them in this war, whether they marched out to force the issue or waited or an overwhelming second invasion.

"We all know that this is not a decision that I can make, that we can make. I suspect our political leaders will have differing opinions. The civilians will want to pull our forces back and surround our worlds. They will want to hide behind defenses and feel superficially secure. They will fear an audacious plan. They will resist."

Garret could see Cain starting to fidget. God only knew what he had to say about how to handle the politicians. They would be there for hours discussing it, he knew that much. But Garret had other business first. He held his hand up, signaling for Cain to wait. He pressed a small button on the table, and a group of attendants walked into the room carrying silver trays. They walked around the table, placing a flute of champagne in front of each officer present.

"We have much to discuss, my friends, and tremendous planning ahead of us, but first, let us take a moment to celebrate our achievements...and pay our respects to those we have lost."

Garret stood, followed immediately by everyone else. He took his glass in his hand. Garret had arranged for two glasses to be placed in front of Ali Khaled, one champagne and one non-alcoholic cider. He knew the Janissaries weren't allowed to drink, but he wasn't sure how rigidly that was observed. Khaled noted the courtesy, and he flashed Garret an appreciative glance…then he took the champagne into his hand.

Garret held his glass in front of him. "First, let us toast our brothers and sisters lost in these battles, our comrades who gave their last full measure to our cause. To the fallen."

"To the fallen." The chorus echoed in the room as the glasses were raised to lips all around the table.

"And now to all those who fought and will fight again. Those who struggled and bled and battled with all their strength. To the forces of the Grand Pact. To victory." The volume of Garret's voice was rising steadily. "They did their duty. The line held."

Crimson Worlds Series

Marines (Crimson Worlds I)

The Cost of Victory (Crimson Worlds II)

A Little Rebellion (Crimson Worlds III)

The First Imperium (Crimson Worlds IV)

The Line Must Hold (Crimson Worlds V)

To Hell's Heart (Crimson Worlds VI)
(September 2013)

Also By Jay Allan

The Dragon's Banner

www.crimsonworlds.com

Made in the USA
San Bernardino, CA
23 April 2014